Okechukwu Nzelu is a writer and teac... Manchester in 1988, read English at Girton Coll... and completed the Teach First programme. His w... published in *Agenda*, *PN Review*, *E-magazine* and *The L...* and his radio play, *Me and Alan*, was broadcast on Roundh... Radio in 2013. His essay 'Troubles with God' was published in the anthology *Safe: On Black British Men Reclaiming Space* (Trapeze, 2019). In 2015 he was the recipient of a New Writing North Award for *The Private Joys of Nnenna Maloney*, which is his debut novel.

Find him on Twitter: @Nzeluwrites

'A magnificent novel, full of wit, warmth and tenderness; Nzelu shows us that fully becoming who we are is a lifelong journey and that identity, of the self, of family and of a community, is infinitely complex' Andrew McMillan

'Okechukwu writes with confidence, wit and humour. Unforgettable characters and a voice that stays with you even after the final page. Edifying and hilarious, *The Private of Joys of Nnenna Maloney* is a beautiful debut that you won't want to put down' Derek Owusu, writer, poet and podcaster

'Okechukwu Nzelu has effortlessly captured the tricky nuance of life, love, race, sexuality and familial relationships ... I haven't been able to put it down' Candice Carty-Williams, author of *Queenie*

'Nzelu writes with a witty confidence rarely seen in debut fiction. Smart, serious and entertaining, I expect this book to have wide appeal and for this writer to go far' Bernardine Evaristo, author of Booker-winning novel *Girl, Woman, Other*

'[An] effervescent depiction of race and sexuality in 21st-century Britain. Nzelu is a delightfully generous writer and treats the conflicts of his characters with equal sympathy but he ... which the most ... sexuality and race to "other" even their closest friends. He's also very funny ... zesty social comedy that skewers religious, racial and sexual prejudice with a light touch' *Metro*

'Witty narrative ... [a] well-written tale' *Financial Times*

'This debut is the big-hearted story of a half-Nigerian teenager growing up in Manchester, desperate to find out the truth about her Igbo heritage' *iNews*

'[A] tender, funny debut ... Nzelu writes with compelling honesty, but he's also gifted with a warm sense of humour' *Daily Mail*

'A vivid picture of people seeking security and identity in the maze of modern-day England. This is fiction as sculpture: skilfully paring down a scene to reveal the shape of the pain hidden within. Jonathan's search for validation, and Nnenna's drive to create an identity for herself, are moving and relatable stories, intimately told' *Guardian*

'A promising debut novel about race, class, family, belief and sexuality' *Attitude*

'Figuring out who you truly are is the central theme of this open-hearted debut ... a quietly complex plot comes together and a lyrical epilogue takes over' *Irish Times*

'One of my earliest pieces for the *Church Times* was about Chimamanda Ngozi Adichie's debut novel *Purple Hibiscus*, and I remember feeling reluctant to use the word "masterpiece" of that book, which indeed it was. Okechukwu Nzelu is another new Nigerian writer to celebrate: *The Private Joys of Nnenna Maloney* has the same clear, well-written prose and natural dialogue, the same important human issues deftly touched on, the clashes between generations, and, crucially, how skin-colour can warp, but also illuminate, a human life' *Church Times*

The Private Joys of NNENNA MALONEY

OKECHUKWU NZELU

dialogue
books

DIALOGUE BOOKS

First published in Great Britain in 2019 by Dialogue Books

This paperback edition published in 2020

10 9 8 7 6 5 4 3 2 1

A CIP catalogue record for this book
is available from the British Library.

Hardback ISBN 978-0-349-70103-5

Typeset in Berling by M Rules
Printed and bound in Great Britain by Clays Ltd, Elcograf S.p.A.

Papers used by Dialogue Books are from well-managed forests and other responsible sources.

Dialogue Books
An imprint of
Little, Brown Book Group
Carmelite House
50 Victoria Embankment
London EC4Y 0DZ

An Hachette UK Company
www.hachette.co.uk

www.littlebrown.co.uk

Here it is: the Heart ...

'The Soldier', Gerard Manley Hopkins

1992

'We *can't* use that quote, Joel,' said Maurice, trying not to lose his temper. He took a deep breath and wondered if he could eat a ginger snap without anyone noticing.

Maurice Nyemaka had finally given in and agreed to host a meeting for their newly formed (but already turbulent) evangelical group in his flat, which was a fifteen-minute cycle from the centre of Cambridge. It was 1992 – two years since he had graduated from university – and he saw fewer and fewer familiar faces with every passing day. When Maurice first joined the group, he had thought it might be a good way to meet new people. The only drawback, he realised, was that he did not like the new people he had met.

This was the third day of the third meeting, and it was threatening dangerously to spill over into a fourth. He welcomed the Bible study group into his poky flat, which he had refused to clean beforehand in case it made them feel like they were welcome to stay beyond the parameters of the study group – parameters which he had now decided were strictly, even ascetically, ecclesiastical. He distributed own-brand digestives and thin squash. He hid the good biscuits under the sink.

'Why can't we use it?' said Joel. 'I think it's beautiful.'

'Yes,' said Maurice, 'but—'

'But what?'

Joel Eberhardt, whose voice had begun to take on a somewhat confrontational tone, was a Cambridge Economics graduate who was rumoured to have turned down a six-figure starting salary to care for his ailing mother. Both salary and sciatica remained unverified, but he cultivated a trying air of martyrdom which had made more than one person at St Jude's think about breaking him on the wheel. And he chewed his biscuits with his mouth open.

'Listen,' he said, generously.

> *'For he is hated by the hypocrite and miser.*
> *For the former is afraid of detection.*
> *For the latter refuses the charge.*
> *For he camels his back to bear the first notion of business.*
> *For he is good to think on, if a man would express him-*
> *   self neatly.*
> *For he made a great figure in Egypt for his signal services . . .*

'Can't you see how beautiful it is?' he said.

'Well,' said Maurice, trying to be reasonable, 'it's very beautiful, but that isn't from the Bible, is it? It's from *Jubilate Agno* by Christopher Smart.' (Why did people always assume he didn't read? Was it because he was an engineer? Or because he was Nigerian? Or both?) 'It's a nice poem, Joel, but he's talking about his cat.'

'And what's wrong with that?' Joel huffed.

'Well, there's nothing *wrong* with it, but this is supposed to be an extension of the Bible study group. The whole point of this was to get to know the Bible better by sharing it with others. To explore how we can spread the Good News in a real-world setting.'

This setting was to be Bertie's, a small, independent café on Huntingdon Road, the route northwards out of the city. It was noticeably more popular with the locals than with your average Cambridge student, liable to blanch at the prospect of a fifteen-minute walk in a city where everything was a stone's throw away. For Maurice and the young men who accompanied him in baggy T-shirts and contrite expressions, the café was ideal because the clientele mostly consisted of working professionals who were usually too busy to respond to their evangelism with lengthy arguments about the Big Bang and natural selection, which academics brandished with such glee. These people were much easier: they simply frowned, accepted the postcards with Biblical extracts written on them ('For God so loved the world that he gave his only son' said the picture of King's College Chapel; 'in all your ways acknowledge him, and he will make your paths straight' said the River Cam) and went back to their godless lives, perhaps somewhat inspired, perhaps not. While lawyers and estate agents and consultants spread thick-cut marmalade on their toast, Maurice and his friends spread the Word of God.

Maurice, however, thought they might be laying it on a bit thick.

Maurice came from a devout family: prayers at home each morning before school and two church services on Sundays. There was nothing in the Bible Maurice hadn't already seen and heard many times. But surely even English people – even fair-weather, sit-at-the-back *English Anglicans* – should have found it easy to pick a few quotations? Surely everyone knew the kind of thing that was called for: 'God is love', 'I am the way, the truth, and the life', 'No one comes to the Father except through *blah blah blah*'.

But when, one Sunday morning in their meeting after the service, Maurice had first suggested these words, Joel had spoken up and complained in his plaintive, weedy voice: these quotations had been *done to death*; the public was *hungry* for something *fresher*; Maurice's selections from the Book of Jeremiah simply weren't *current*. To Maurice's horror, the idea of a public starved of fresh Biblical exegesis caught the imagination of the study group like a Pentecostal fire. They raised their eyes heavenward and dreamed about atheists walking aimlessly around the city, crying out for obscure passages from Deuteronomy and Habakkuk. Maurice tried to point out that the Bible had been around for thousands of years – that the God of Abraham and of Isaac was not in the habit of leaking anything 'never-before-seen' – that the Word of God was old, and that it was the evangelist's job to make His message *seem* new. In Maurice's view, their job was almost like that of a magician, or a messiah: to reveal the wondrous in the ordinary; to spin gold out of flax; even, he ventured, to turn *water into wine*.

But nobody listened. Joel talked on; eyes sparkled, murmurs of assent spread through the room; and Maurice was overruled by a crushing margin.

But not today. Not today.

'Besides, Joel, it isn't very punchy. We want something that gets people's attention right away, something that delivers God's message with a bit more ... *oomph*. We almost want slogans, really. Sound bites, if you like.'

The other members of the group appeared much more susceptible to logic when faced with the looming possibility of public humiliation (and, worse, poetry), and they nodded and hummed their assent to Maurice's sensible words. Joel huffed and munched on a digestive with a long-suffering expression on his face.

'Well then,' said Jonathan Tucker, a Maths graduate whose strategy in meetings consisted of staying silent for the first twenty minutes, then calmly and evenly saying something deeply stupid. 'If we're after something attention-grabbing, why don't we go with something a bit more *Sturm und Drang*? A little fire and brimstone never hurt anyone. What about ...' he feigned uncertainty. 'What about ... oh, I don't know ... Leviticus 18:22?'

Maurice quoted without hesitation: '"You shall not lie with a male as with a woman; it is an abomination"?'

'Yes.'

Maurice sighed. He liked Jonathan. Truth be told, he was the most earnest one of the group; more so even than Maurice, perhaps, who was passionate but unsure. Jonathan's fervour was different: it burned off him constantly, like sulphur, and there were days when you could smell it on him from across the room. To Jonathan, they weren't merely students of the Bible, or Christians, or even evangelicals. They were the latest in a long line of prophets, like Jeremiah, called to teach the way of the Lord to an uninterested world. Unfortunately, Maurice often got the sense that Jonathan actually liked the world to be as uninterested as possible.

He spoke gently.

'We're going to cafés, Jonathan. *Cafés*. And I'm not being funny, but at the end of the day, we *are* in Cambridge.'

'What are you saying?'

'I'm saying I think we have to be realistic about the kind of people we're likely to come across.'

'*I* think we ought to lay our beliefs on the line. "You shall not lie with a male as with a woman,"' he said again, for emphasis. 'Call me old-fashioned, but our beliefs—'

'They're not all of our beliefs. I mean, they're mine – sort of – maybe. But—'

'I agree with Maurice,' said Alastair, a calm and muscular carpenter, who had come to the meetings with the hope of lying with Jonathan as he had never lain with anyone else. He found Jonathan's broodiness irresistible, and Jonathan's oddly tight button-down shirts (no tie; top button done up) transported Alastair's mind to somewhere south of Eden. That Jonathan was a raging homophobe was apparently no concern of his.

'Besides,' said Joel, still smarting, 'shouldn't we open with something slightly less confrontational? And everyone likes ca—'

'Absolutely,' said Alastair. 'And I'm with Maurice about the likely audience thing, too. We can believe what we believe, but aren't we here to spread the *Good* News? If someone's sitting there enjoying a latte, you can't just march up to them and tell them they're going to burn in hell for being a woofter.'

'Not everyone who likes frothy coffee is *gay*, Alastair,' said Jonathan, glancing nervously at his latte. He put on a gruff voice that made Alastair cross his legs, hum and fold his hands in his lap. Jonathan, conspicuous for bringing the newly fashionable takeaway cups of café latte to every meeting, huffed again.

'What are you looking at?' he said.

'You've got foam on your lip,' breathed Alastair, gesturing oh-so-delicately at Jonathan's mouth. Jonathan blushed and quickly wiped it away.

'Right,' said Maurice, firmly. 'So, we aren't going to use Leviticus 18:22. And we can't use the poem, I'm afraid. No, Joel – don't look at me like that. We can't, I'm sorry. So. Let's keep thinking.'

They went back to work, flicking through passages familiar and unfamiliar; Joel glancing resentfully at Jonathan, Alastair glancing longingly at Jonathan, Maurice pretending to read but too resentful and frustrated at all the glancing to see any of the words.

Eventually, Alastair spoke up, his finger on a verse in his Bible. He was excited but cautious, like an archaeologist unearthing a delicate find that still might crumble before it saw the light.

'I think … I think I've found something,' he said.

'What have you got, Alastair?' said Maurice, hardly daring to hope. He was almost coming round to the idea of Christopher Smart, when Alastair began to read from his Bible, a much older translation.

He had been reading Job. Of course. How had Maurice forgotten Job, to whom God had spoken directly in his suffering?

'Canst thou lift up thy voice to the clouds
that abundance of waters may cover thee?

Who hath put wisdom in the inward parts
or who hath given understanding to the heart?'

What could be better? Job was the one whom God, on a whim, had stripped bare of all his luck, of all the contentment that supposedly makes belief *easy*. Job was the one God had made naked before him. And in return, God had bared himself to the man, as much as he was ever going to bare himself to anyone. He had answered Job with typical indirectness: not with answers, but more questions.

Maurice was relieved. Finally, they had found a new way to deliver the old message. It felt precisely right. (For comic relief, Joel had wanted to include the verse in which God told Job to 'Gird up thy loins now like a man: I will demand of thee, and declare thou unto me', but the others decided against this, unsure if most people would appreciate the humour, and afraid that it might send the wrong message about what they were trying to achieve.)

Maurice beamed at Alastair and shook his hand.

'You think it'll work?' said Alastair.

'I think it will,' said Maurice.

In those days, Joanie was an ordinary girl, minding her own ordinary business, figuring out her ordinary undergraduate life at Cambridge and glumly revising an uninspiring translation of an Ancient Greek account of the Peloponnesian War.

In fact, Joanie Maloney (Joan, to her supervisors and lecturers) was looking forward to graduating next year, and ready to start again in the Real World. Most people would say that she was too young to need a fresh start, but Joanie Maloney wasn't most people: she had been moved ahead one year at school, successfully applied to Cambridge a year early, and was having a thoroughly miserable time.

Having succeeded at school almost entirely as a result of incessant parental pressure and total lack of a social life, she had opted for a change of pace when she got to university. She put in only a nominal amount of effort at Cambridge and focused her energies on the things that would carry her far in her post-university life: enlarging her already-impressive collection of linen scarves; being seen wearing oversized sunglasses in attractive locations; and perpetrating a series of extravagant romantic mistakes with men her mother would hate.

To wit: second year, Michaelmas Term, Roderick Cleaves (alias 'Hotrod', 'Cleavage', 'Smelly Roderick'), the beagle-loving Classicist who didn't own a toothbrush and who dumped her *via his best friend* after three weeks of pretending not to see her in the faculty library. Years later he was the head of an internet security firm.

To wit: Cliff Harper, the mathematician she slept with after a starchy formal dinner. They both had trapped wind and Cliff (ever the generous lover) gave her two STIs.

Rebelling turned out to be a little trickier than she'd realised. Too late, Joanie began to see that frequent trips to the pharmacist and an inability to cross her legs were not conducive to the hours of serious study that her contemporaries seemed to be putting in. Not for the last time, it occurred to her that she wasn't a serious enough person.

And, worse than the itching, there was the shame. She couldn't work through it. She couldn't think through it. In the years that followed, she would eventually come to appreciate the irony of the situation (her conjugation with Cliff had made her forget her verb tables) and chuckle about it – but she wasn't laughing now. She was one of the first women ever to be admitted to her college, and she had the feeling she was supposed to fly the flag for academic women everywhere; instead she was failing. Miserably. And *publicly*: only this afternoon, she had been asked to leave a seminar, after half an hour of mumbled incorrect answers. The professor had calmly, but very audibly, explained to her that she had misread the reading list, that she had read the wrong texts, that she was unlikely to benefit from the seminar or, by implication, the university. And she was starting to think that he was right.

So, when four Christians walked into a certain café on Huntingdon Road, Joanie was already at her lowest ebb, wondering where it had all gone wrong.

When the men walked in, they fanned out immediately, apart from Alastair, who tried (unsuccessfully) to stay inconspicuously close to Jonathan. Joanie had seen them before, but she had never been this close, and she watched them now with a keen but wary fascination.

It wasn't Maurice but Jonathan who first caught her eye, as he nervously tried to pretend he was an ordinary patron of the café. He had a theory that it put people at ease to see them ordering coffees, cakes and biscuits as though they had no agenda and their evangelism was entirely spontaneous. The others in the group disagreed: they all said it made them look and feel as if the agendas which they certainly *did* have were somehow unsavoury, as if they needed to be hidden. And it was true that, nine times out of ten, when Jonathan approached a stranger over biscotti and began steering the conversation, inexorably, towards a certain passage in Leviticus, people tended to feel not only bored and confused, but also that they had been cruelly deceived by this nervous-looking man who only a moment ago had been contentedly sipping his frothy coffee and minding his own sodding business.

It was Jonathan's discontent that Joanie noticed. Although she didn't know about Alastair's passing comment regarding the relationship between homosexuality and frothy coffee, she could see that Jonathan was deeply uncomfortable. It hung off him like a heavy coat in summer.

From her seat in the corner, Joanie watched him sip from the huge, unwieldy bowl of a cup. She watched him gingerly turn it around in its saucer as though it were a new and hostile territory whose perimeters he must examine. She watched him sniff suspiciously at the cinnamon shaker before guiltily tipping some over his drink. She watched him paw fastidiously at his upper lip, wiping away a phantom foam moustache every few minutes.

It was like a pantomime, each expression magnified to the point of parody. He looked around feverishly as though he were being secretly filmed – as though the whole thing were a honeytrap, and a net might descend on him at any moment, hoisting him up, red-handed, for all the respectable, heteronormative coffee-drinkers to see.

As soon as he finished his latte (his face said), he would hunt down the nancy responsible for this unmanly act of deliciousness and give them a piece of his mind.

As soon as he finished his latte.

Joanie didn't know whether to laugh or cry. Men! They put so much time and energy into this kind of performance, but then they did everything they could to make the effort seem natural and easy. They were like swans above water, or Michael Flatley above the waist.

It seemed to her that men – most men, certainly not the man at the table next to Jonathan's, who had quite happily asked for a shot of caramel on top of his coffee and could they give him a napkin and did they have some sprinkles behind the counter? – it seemed as if most men spent their entire lives guarding and grooming their masculinity, the way a princess in a fairy tale might brush her hair a thousand times before bed. What kind of life was that, to be constantly guarding something so fragile? How could you live life while you were hunched over a chrysalis? She could never do that, she mused, as she took another swig of her mint tea. She wanted to stand up! She wanted to walk around . . .

She wanted to duck under the table and hide.

Three students came in with the lunchtime rush, the ends of their college scarves flying heroically in the wind. She only knew the first two men by sight, but the third was unmistakable.

It was none other than Cliff Harper: he of the trapped wind. He of the gonorrhoea – he of the chlamydia – he of the allergy to latex. And polyisoprene. And hands.

From her vantage point in the corner, Joanie scowled silently. The men and their scarves loitered smugly by the door, chuckling to themselves about something, she couldn't hear what. They were probably laughing at Maths, she thought. Or telling each other riddles in Elvish.

Once again, Joanie found herself wondering why she had ever got involved with a man who could process neither carbohydrates nor social cues. Was she being punished? Was there no other café in the city? The mere memory of that benighted evening was bad enough, but now he and his friends and their scarves were here, in her café, waiting for a free seat. It was only a matter of time before one of them spotted her.

Why were they even *here*? She couldn't leave without bumping into Cliff, but if she stayed she would be thrown mercilessly to the Christians . . . What to do?

She didn't have time to make up her mind. Before she could move, a man was walking purposefully towards her. Not a mathematician, though . . . Even without the cross around his neck, she would have known he was one of them. Even before she read the back of the postcard, she could tell what was on it, from the way he gave it to her. As though he were handing it to her in spite of some unspoken protest.

'Excuse me – can I give you this?'

On one side, there was a faded photograph of King's College Chapel taken from the rear, the River Cam running calmly behind it and a swallow, frozen in flight, a single sign of summer and happier times to come. On the back was a quote in polite, careful handwriting:

Canst thou bind the sweet influences of the
Pleiades, or loose the bands of Orion?

'Excuse me?' he repeated.

'I said, I've seen this,' said Joanie.

'Yes, it's from the Bible,' he said.

'Yes, I know. That's where I've seen it,' she said.

Bible-bashers. They always assumed that because she didn't carry visible evidence of a belief in God, she must be stupid or depraved. One fortnight, last summer, she had read Genesis, Leviticus, Deuteronomy, and Job. Her mother had accused her of trying to avoid tidying her room; but it was really nothing quite so wilful. It was more like scepticism, with a dash of curiosity. She'd seen God written about, heard Him spoken about and spoken for; she had heard Him praised, scorned, rejected, interrogated ... but she'd never seen Him for herself. That summer, in very small, densely printed text, she had wanted simply to see God. And she had seen Him, the way He usually is seen: through slightly narrowed eyes.

While she was thinking this – it all passed in a few seconds – the man's handsomeness crept up on her, like a sly salesman. He was tall, had perfectly smooth skin, and the build of a swimmer. True, he had a certain severity in the natural set of his features which made him seem rather forbidding at first. But when Joanie told him that she had read the quotation before, he smiled so warmly that something made her want to talk to him more; to explore him.

And he, her: the smell of her hair; the dents in her fingers from writing essays, which he hadn't had to do since school; her soft, full lips when she spoke . . .

Out of the corner of her eye, Joanie saw Cliff and his friends resign themselves to sitting down, reluctantly, on the same table as the man with the phantom latte-moustache. This was an interesting development, she realised. She decided that, since Cliff was squarely in her line of sight, she might as well enjoy herself.

'I've read this before,' she said, quickly, afraid that the handsome man might take the postcard back and move on to someone else. But he seemed more interested in her than before.

'Are you already a churchgoer?' he said. It was an oddly specific question. *He had done this before.* If he had asked her whether she was a Christian, she could have said 'no', daring him to ask the source of her mysterious Biblical knowledge. She could have relished the secret of her literary curiosity like a hidden superpower; instead he had asked her whether she went to church. He had raised the bar and dared her to leap it.

'No,' she said.

'Lapsed?'

'I wasn't raised as a Christian or anything.'

Maurice cocked his head and smiled.

'I'm rather curious, I suppose,' she said.

'Yes . . . Yes, you are.'

Presumptuous. But with such a lovely smile, perhaps his presumption was correct.

And how much had Cliff seen? Joanie's eyes flicked involuntarily back to him. He was still there, still chuckling with his friends. But whereas before they had been ignoring the man at the table, now they were laughing at him. At first, she couldn't quite hear what was being said, but then she heard the word 'woofter' and she knew something was wrong.

Maurice followed her eyes to where Jonathan sat. He was besieged by mathematicians. Maurice could see that trouble was brewing, but ... Well, Jonathan had probably earned it.

'"You shall not lie with a male"?' drawled an incredulous, militantly atheist and now very loud Cliff. The words themselves were barely audible above the nasal whine of his boarding-school vowels. 'Why are you telling me *that*?'

'It's the Word of God,' said Jonathan, flicking at his upper lip again, suddenly conscious of the fact that the cinnamon from his coffee might be sitting, accusatorially, beneath his nose, mixed with the foam. And that the mixture was *brown*.

'Yes,' said Cliff, 'but didn't He say anything else? Do you people have to keep banging the bum-drum?'

'I just think that—'

'And why do you keep fussing with your upper lip? Have you got some kind of twitch? Are you a pervert?'

'I am *not* a pervert—'

'Bloody Christians!' drawled Cliff's friend, Artie, in a confident, plush tenor. Artie knew the story of Cliff and Joanie: how Joanie had tricked Cliff into bed before ravishing him for hours, draining him of at least two bodily fluids and giving him three STIs. How he loathed her. How he *hated* her. How he wanted to tie her to his bedpost with one of her stupid linen scarves and ... and ...

Cliff nodded sharply. He had noticed Maurice when they came in – had noticed him talking to Joanie now, and the way she looked at him – and was eyeballing the two of them as he spoke. 'Why do you always have to make everything about sex? And *bumming*! Perverts, the lot of you! Bloody put me off my hash browns.'

'How come?' asked the other friend. 'Fancy a sausage, now, do you?'

'Shut up, Beefy,' said the first friend to the second.

'Oh, come on, Artie, you know you like it up the arse of a Tuesday afternoon. Cheer up! Maybe Latte Boy can sort you out. Just give him a minute to wipe off his last poo-moustache.'

Jonathan, mortified, was powerless as the three of them descended into guffaws, nudging each other and grinning and saying some very unkind things about 'hot milk'. He desperately wanted to wipe his mouth and walk away, but if they saw him leave it would be tantamount to an admission of guilt. He was trapped.

'Shouldn't you do something?' said Joanie. She wasn't particularly fond of either Christians or mathematicians, but she was inclined to think that at least most of the Christians had *met* a few women before deciding they were worthless.

'I think he needs to learn,' said Maurice.

'Learn what?'

At exactly that moment, Joanie saw another of the Christians, a tall man with large arms and a determined expression, step into the fray. It was the man from the next table, the one who'd asked for sprinkles.

'I think you ought to leave him alone,' said Alastair.

'Who are you?' said Cliff, hurling the challenge at him. 'His *boy*friend?'

Having made a dramatic entrance, Alastair paused to review the situation into which he had entered, and to consider his options:

- He could pretend to be Jonathan's boyfriend. But that was probably a dead end, as Jonathan would never corroborate the story.
- He could suggest that he would *like* to be Jonathan's boyfriend, thus shifting the focus from Cliff and hopefully giving Jonathan time to regroup ... but that, too, was problematic on many levels.

- He could opt to ignore Cliff's question, and defend Jonathan dispassionately, on moral grounds. This was probably the most pragmatic course of action but defending Jonathan Tucker on moral grounds was a task, he knew, of Herculean proportions.
- Still . . .

Alastair folded his considerable arms across his chest. 'Yes.'

Jonathan, down but not quite out, hung his mouth open in horror as Alastair took the situation into his own rough, muscular hands.

'And I don't like the way you're talking to him,' said Alastair.

'Oh,' said Beefy. 'We know what *you* like.'

Beefy looked at Alastair.

Alastair looked at Beefy.

Now it was personal. Now it wasn't only about Jonathan, who, in this moment, was just a stuck-up closet-case with a peachy arse. Now it was about Alastair standing his ground.

Joanie's heart went out to him, the brave man who'd asked for sprinkles. She wanted to shame Cliff, to stand up and denounce him as the wilful disseminator of lies and venereal diseases that she knew him to be.

Alastair planted his feet and placed his hand firmly on the back of Jonathan's chair.

'You *like* him, don't you?' sneered Cliff. He had the air of a little boy who'd found a newt in the school pond and brought it into the playground to dangle in front of the girls. It wasn't his own disgust he was interested in: he wanted Alastair's. He wanted to shame him publicly for wanting this man.

But Alastair would not be shamed.

It was like the showdown-scene in a Western: time stood still, all eyes turned to the two men and a wave of anticipation rolled out across the room. A woman froze while feeding the soup of the day to her infant son and, perhaps sensing the onset of a rather fruity monologue, she covered his ears. A newly trained barista hovered close by, holding a ginseng-and-vanilla infusion that quivered noisily in its saucer. Joel sat back smugly in his seat, thinking that none of this would have happened if they'd used that poem about the cat.

(Meanwhile, in the corner: Joanie and Maurice, trapped; innocent by disassociation; God and desire naked before them.)

'He's all right,' said Alastair.

'"He's all right"?' asked Cliff, sarcastically gesturing towards Jonathan with both hands.

'What does that mean?' Beefy snorted, but Alastair was still trying to decide and Jonathan was looking at Alastair desperately – *what?!* – when Alastair kissed him.

It was only for a moment, but for Jonathan it was long enough for everything about him, everything he had built up, to unravel. He had never kissed anyone before, never even dared to admit to himself that he'd wanted to, or to admit that he'd wanted to kiss Alastair since the first time they'd met in the Bible study group when Alastair had walked in and seated himself, casually, heavily, next to him, and smiled. He'd used every ounce of his strength to suppress it and, in a moment, his strength was entirely laid waste.

Jonathan knew what Alastair was like; he could tell Alastair only wanted to sleep with him, and he was well aware that this might be a pretext. But in the long moment of being kissed for the first time, it didn't matter to him. It was like a summons, as though he was being called upon to act. Was this the call? Did the prophet Jeremiah feel his whole body seize up and relax when God called him? Did Jonah? Did they fear that the voice calling to them in the darkness was an evil spirit, leading them to harm? Or worse, that it might really be Him after all, a God as irresistible as love?

Distantly, he heard Cliff speak. 'Come on,' he said, 'we're going to choir practice.' It was with the discomfort of someone who has found more than he set out to find that Cliff stood up.

'What?' said Art.

'Let's go! Before the whole bloody gay mafia gets here.' After a moment, Beefy followed with Art in tow, frowning at the anti-climax. Cliff scowled at Joanie before he left.

Time unfroze. The lady with the soup of the day allowed herself to exhale. Her baby son clapped uproariously, the vanilla-ginseng infusion landed safely on the table and Alastair handed Jonathan a napkin.

'What the hell is wrong with you?' said Jonathan, shaking his head.

'The same thing that's wrong with you, I suppose,' said Alastair. Jonathan looked at him so hungrily it made him start.

'Would you like to have coffee?' said Maurice.

'Somewhere else?' asked Joanie.

'Yes.'

'Yes.'

PART I

2009

Chapter 1

Iron sharpens iron; and one person
sharpens another.

Proverbs 27:17

'An *outdoor wedding*,' said Joanie in the car to her daughter, Nnenna, as she drove down the tiny country lanes through Cheshire. Her tone was somewhere between plaintive and incredulous, as though being asked to attend the wedding of an old (and annoyingly successful) friend was bad enough, but being asked to attend a wedding *outside* was a bridge too far.

'What's wrong with that?' said Nnenna, from deep within a book. It was a copy of *Their Eyes Were Watching God*, given to her by her Aunty Mary a few weeks ago. She was halfway through and not paying much attention to her mother.

'Nothing, I suppose. I never quite feel ready for spring, that's all.'

'What do you mean?' Nnenna said, distantly. 'Mum, you look gorgeous.' Joanie glanced at Nnenna and smiled at this typically generous comment that had flown somewhat wide. It wasn't (or wasn't *just*) that she didn't feel she looked the part; it was spring itself. You waited and waited for it for such a long time ... and then, there the blossoms were, laughing to you from the trees and you were standing under them, without any similar transformation of your own. The same old Joanie.

They were on their way to the wedding of one of Joanie's classmates from university, Ophelia Frall.

'Ophelia!' Nnenna had scoffed at this choice of name, despite Joanie observing that it was nearly forty years too late for anything to be done about it. 'Of course she'd have to be called Ophelia,' Nnenna had said, rolling her eyes. As far as she was concerned, it was yet another confirmation of the sort of people with whom her mother had consorted at Cambridge. Unfortunately, the names of Joanie's other friends (Cressida Featherstone and Juliet Morley-Hinchfield) did little to challenge Nnenna's opinion.

'Don't be mean, Nnenna. Ophelia and I have been friends for a very long time.'

Nnenna put her book aside, frowning. 'But you never see her. You never mention her.'

'Well ... we're very different people. And sometimes, when you go through certain things, it changes some of your relationships. It doesn't mean that you hate the person or ... Sometimes you just need some space.'

Nnenna wasn't sure she understood this idea, but she heard the note of finality in her mother's voice and let it go. Ophelia, an eminent journalist at a worthy broadsheet in London, was getting married to Hugh Todd, an equally eminent but staggeringly unworthy investment banker from Cardiff. Hugh had solemnly undertaken to pay for the entire wedding himself, and just as solemnly undertaken to resent every penny he spent.

The couple had met years after graduating from Cambridge, at a drinking society reunion dinner where the men had all dressed up in women's clothes. It had soon become apparent that Hugh and Ophelia were wearing the same dress. Hugh had walked over boldly and introduced himself; 'and the rest', Ophelia had smiled at the engagement party, 'is history'.

'History,' however, covers a multitude of sins. Like many men, Hugh had ensured that history took his favoured course by careful, military-style planning: upon discovering that his office was across the road from hers, he had watched Ophelia from afar for a week or two, culminating in a choice sighting of her in a sleek, dark blue dress.

That dress worked its magic on Hugh and, within the hour, he'd asked Juliet, Ophelia's flatmate at the time, to find out where she'd got it, buy him the same one, and convince Ophelia to wear hers to the party. Ophelia, completely unaware at the time, had slipped duly into her blue dress, and dully into Hugh's arms, where she remained for the better part of the evening. A few months later, he proposed; she accepted.

That was history.

Ophelia was very careful to whom she told this story: Joanie was not the only person to notice that it had the propensity to cast Hugh in a rather nefarious, stalkerish light. But Joanie saw what the story was told for, what it implied about Ophelia: that she, unlike Joanie, was the type of woman whom men – albeit investment bankers – pursued relentlessly. Ophelia, unlike Joanie, was the type of woman for whom a man with far more hair than was natural at that age set aside his bespoke tailored suit and squeezed himself into a size 16 dress from Marks and Spencer. Joanie drew some consolation from the sure knowledge that Hugh had not done anything so carefully since.

The ceremony itself took place in an old, ruined monastery in deepest Cheshire: the roof had vanished centuries ago (along with about a quarter of the walls), but on a beautiful spring day like this one, it was perfect.

Nnenna had only ever heard her mother speak about Ophelia as the brilliant Economics student who breezed her way through three years of cripplingly difficult exams. But it was Ophelia's ability to keep smiling through the entire ninety-minute service that astounded Nnenna. Smiling constantly is no mean feat under ordinary circumstances, and Ophelia had gone to great lengths to ensure that these circumstances were anything but ordinary. A team of photographers had been employed to circulate like butterflies in a Disney film. No matter how stealthily the cameras advanced, Ophelia seemed to be ready; even towards the end of the ceremony when she must have been tired, even when she had been eating. The mere thought of it exhausted Nnenna, but Ophelia never tired. Perhaps, mused Nnenna, Ophelia did exercises to strengthen her smiling muscles. Hugh, slightly less wealthy than when he proposed but every bit as resentful, only frowned handsomely at the camera.

'Do I *have* to sit at the children's table?' said Nnenna afterwards, as they filed into the monastery's gardens.

'Sweetheart, we were given a seating plan in advance. With clear instructions to commit it to memory. I don't think they'll budge, now. They'll have planned it out like a game of chess.'

'But I want to sit with *you*, Mum. And I'll be seventeen, soon.' Joanie smiled, despite herself, at this juxtaposition. 'And I don't even *like* children.'

Joanie resisted the urge to point out that Nnenna was still a child herself, but then Nnenna was not like other children. She was simply *better*, as objectively as Joanie could possibly see it. Besides, Joanie forgot so often that Nnenna was not an adult.

'Well, maybe just sit with the kids for the meal and then sneak over to my table for dessert. Hopefully,' she said, as she saw two ushers greeting guests and guiding them unsmilingly to their places, 'the bride and groom will be too busy to care by then.'

'All right,' sighed Nnenna. 'And who are you sitting with?'

'Oh,' said Joanie. 'An old friend, I think.'

To the left of her seat was an old editor of Ophelia's. To the right, was Jonathan Tucker.

*

'I see. And your father?' said an usher to Nnenna as he seated her, visibly looking around for someone else brown.

'Oh, he won't be able to make it,' said Nnenna, smoothly, easily and finally. Hearing the words leave her mouth once more, she knew that they would sound as though her mother had dictated them to her, asked her to regurgitate them at functions; but she had not. Like everyone whose family is not quite what those on the outside world might expect, Nnenna had had plenty of opportunities to practise and hone her excuses, each time giving a slightly less hesitant narrative. There were times when it felt unfair or like a lot of hard work for someone who would never appreciate it, but most of the time she did not mind; she was getting good at it now.

The facts of Nnenna's life were difficult, but simple: she had never met her father; she did not know exactly why, except that he was not dead, because on the few occasions her mother spoke about him, she did so in the present tense. It pained her mother to be asked about him; she loved her mother and did not like to pain her.

And so Nnenna, almost seventeen, took her seat at the table. She thanked the usher and looked around at her companions for the next hour or so: not even one of them seemed to be over the age of thirteen, and already, most of them were industriously embedding butter into their waistcoats and dresses. Nnenna resigned herself to an evening of having to summon some non-existent maternal instinct until she could get away: an hour of listening to inane, endless and literally pointless stories about grandparents; an hour of trying to keep her dress and the children's food separate.

Someone tapped her on the shoulder.

'Yes?' she said. She found herself addressing a white boy of about twelve, with greasy hair and a greasier smile. Undeterred by the knob of butter on his collar, he was perhaps embold-ened by what looked ominously like contraband red wine in his glass. He cleared his throat and slowly looked her up and down, approvingly.

'Hey, babe.'

It is not difficult to make conversation with strangers at a wedding breakfast but, Joanie found, it *is* often difficult to make good conversation. This is due partly to the nature of the event, which necessarily involves giving over at least 40 per cent of your time to people who have nothing interesting to say beyond the intensely boring minutiae of their lives, but an awful lot to say about those minutiae ('Oh! Why yes, I would like to see more photos of your new home gym. How ... *darling!*'). Sadly, Joanie's friendships with many of her Cambridge classmates had become strained not long before graduation. Also sadly, guests at wedding breakfasts are usually seated in circles so that, even if you are sitting next to someone you want to talk to, the home-gymmers of the world tend to muscle their way into the conversation.

Cornered by a man who was in the throes of divulging to her the vast depths of the knowledge he had acquired twenty years ago from his Latin GCSE, Joanie cast a longing look over her shoulder at Jonathan: he was being similarly detained by a couple who were taking advantage of the strides made in technology by showing him what looked like eighteen physical photo albums' worth of photographs in the happily condensed form of a mobile phone's image gallery.

Then again, a part of Joanie was glad that she was trapped; being free to talk to Jonathan Tucker meant confronting what a terrible friend she'd been to him. She'd barely kept in touch at all since graduation, and she knew he'd needed her. Her more than most. His church friends had melted away when he'd got out of hospital. But things had got so scary, so quickly. She'd been too ashamed to speak to him for years afterwards.

'I suppose you'll know "Caecilius est in horto", won't you?'

said Max, a (presumably single) television producer. Joanie wasn't sure, but he seemed to be hoping that a woman who'd studied Classics at Cambridge might be delighted by the Latin equivalent of 'the cat sat on the mat'.

'Err, yes,' said Joanie. 'Rings a bell. I mean, I did my undergraduate dissertation on—'

'I *loved* my Latin GCSE. Such a rich subject, isn't it? And so *diverse*.'

'Yes, absolutely. At university, we studied a lot of different—'

'*Everyone* should study Classics. I have *so* many happy school memories. We had the most marvellous teacher, easily my favourite; had the most *exciting* lessons. Mr ... Mr ... Mr ...'

As Max laboured to recall the name of his beloved school teacher, Joanie took the opportunity to take a swig from her glass of wine.

'Quick,' Jonathan said to her, in an urgent whisper.

'What?'

'Just look like you're saying something to me.'

'... I *am* saying something to you.'

'Something important.'

'Why?'

'Because if I have to look at another holiday photo, I'll ask the bride to cut *me* instead of the cake.'

'Ah.'

'You as well?'

'The charming gentleman to my left has spent the last two courses bringing me up to scratch on Latin grammar.'

Despite her thirty-eight years, Joanie still found the boldness of people's stupidity surprising – men patronising her at social events, people making casually racist remarks about her daughter in public, people referring incessantly to refugees as 'immigrants'. Even though she knew full well that it happened every day, she somehow always forgot that it could happen (and did happen) to *her*. It was a bit like realising that the creature you used to think was hiding under your bed at night – the one you'd told yourself was imaginary – was real, all along. And that he spoke rudimentary Latin.'

'Ah,' said Jonathan.

'Yes. I think I might be able to construct whole sentences by the time they clear away dessert. Good thing I spent three years at university preparing for this dinner, or I'd be stumped.'

'Didn't you get a first in the end?'

Joanie smiled. 'In the end, yes.'

'And what are you doing these days?'

'I write crosswords, mostly. I do the odd bit of journalism to make ends meet, but I've never been able to find anything steady, unfortunately. What about you?'

'Financial auditor.'

'Oh. How ... *darling.*'

Jonathan cut his eyes at Joanie playfully and then looked over at their neighbours; they were fully occupied with their new victims. Max appeared to be busy informing an A&E doctor about his A* in GCSE Biology.

'Joanie, I—'

'Jonathan, I want you to know ... I'm so sorry I never kept in touch.'

Jonathan didn't say anything. For a moment, Joanie looked down at her hands in silence; she'd only blurted it out because a part of her had hoped that Max would interrupt her too quickly for Jonathan to reply. How many times had they found themselves in the same room at weddings, birthdays, anniversary parties? How many times had she wished that she was courageous enough to confront what she had done to him, and apologise? How many more times would she hide from what she had done?

Maybe one more, at least in part. She was sorry, and she wanted Jonathan to know that she was sorry. But she couldn't bear to know what he must think of her.

Eventually, Jonathan said, 'I know why you didn't. I understand.'

Joanie looked at him sharply and nodded. That was Jonathan for you. A less honest person might have said, 'It's okay.' But of course, it wasn't okay. What she had done to him could never be okay.

'I'm so sorry, Jonathan. For everything. Everything.'

Jonathan said, 'Joanie . . .' But then he fell silent. He didn't look as though he was thinking of something to say. He just wanted her to stop. Sometimes, Joanie thought, people can hurt you so badly that the apology is almost as bad as the act itself.

'Okay,' she nodded. She realised suddenly that she was crying and dried her eyes.

'Don't cry, Joanie,' said Jonathan, putting his hand on her knee. He always was such a warm person. How could he comfort *her* now? After everything?

He gave her a mischievous smile. 'Dry your eyes. We're at a wedding.'

She laughed.

'And,' he said, as he saw Juliet and Cressida approaching, 'we're in *marvellous* company.'

'So, what do you think?'

Nnenna had to take a moment. Jason (she didn't catch his surname, but she suspected there were a few of them, connected by one or two hyphens and several centuries of careful inbreeding) had just spent the past few minutes outlining the vast fortune at his family's disposal. True, he had at first experienced that deep and gnawing discomfort with which enormously wealthy people discuss their enormous wealth. But he had soldiered on and, with the help of a glass of 'peeno greedge', he was soon drunkenly laying out his inheritance like a baboon showing off its arse at the zoo. Tantalisingly (and yet persistently), he had given Nnenna to believe that he was fully prepared to whisk her away to any one of at least four castles at a moment's notice – so great, he explained, was her beauty.

Nnenna had never been to a castle before, and so she might have been tempted, were it not for the fact that she had a boyfriend, some sense, and a great deal of shock at the way in which Jason expressed the beauty he perceived her to have.

'I mean,' he said, breathlessly, 'there's just something *about* you. I just find you randomly beautiful.'

'Err. Thank you?' said Nnenna. She wondered again why she was old enough to be put through the gauntlet of Jason's amorous advances, but not yet old enough to drink wine, gallons of wine. She had the urge to tell him that she was significantly older than him and that he had bitten off more than he could chew, but she found herself speechless at the sight of his twelve-year-old mouth engulfing a slice of cake that was at least half the size of his head. Most of it ended up smeared around his mouth, as when a child might put on lipstick for the first time.

'I mean, I don't get it,' he said. Utterly uninhibited by the fact that his face was barely visible beneath layers of buttercream icing, he reached for Nnenna's cake. She was too horrified to stop him. Instead she silently stood up and backed away.

At what was, in theory, the grown-ups' table . . .

'I hate weddings,' said Juliet.

'Me too,' opined Cressida. They had descended upon Joanie and Jonathan suddenly, blithely disobeying Ophelia's strict injunction to keep to the seating plan, and interrupting what had looked like it might become a kind of reconciliation between Joanie and Jonathan. At first, Joanie had tried to encourage them to think more optimistically, but she found herself awash in a sea of negative thinking. Somehow, Cressida and Juliet had a way of turning even the most promising love story into a tragedy.

'I reckon it'll all end in tears,' said Juliet.

'I give them a month,' said Cressida. She had spilled some wine on her sleeve and was dabbing at it distractedly with a napkin. 'I mean, they come from completely different worlds. That sort of thing never really lasts.'

'I don't know,' said Jonathan, hopefully. 'They do have slightly different outlooks, I suppose, but I'd hardly say they were from different worlds. Don't they both own horses?'

'And you never know,' said Joanie. 'It could work out. Sometimes, people—'

'No,' said Cressida, 'they don't. To be honest, I'm a little surprised she's even getting married in the first place. She used to be so exciting, and marriage is so—'

'*Boring*,' said Juliet. 'It's a boring wedding, with a boring groom thrown in for good bore. The whole wedding thing is so predictable. And all our friends are doing it, you know. This is the third wedding I've been to this year. Doesn't anybody want any, you know ... *danger*, any more?' Joanie watched, askance, as Juliet played expertly with her steak knife.

'Exactly,' chimed Cressida. 'When did we all get like this? What happened to the kind of guys we used to date when we were younger?'

'Mmm,' said Juliet, dreamily. 'We had some good times at uni. Especially you, Joanie.'

'Me?'

'Yeah, what happened to that guy you were dating? Boris?'

'Maurice.'

'The Christian?' said Cressida, unimpressed. 'No thanks. And what's up with that name?'

'Well, actually he—'

'No, he wasn't boring,' explained Juliet. 'Granted, he was a bit of a Bible-basher and everything, but ... well, he was black, wasn't he? So didn't he have a—'

'Oh, who cares?' said Cressida, wearily. 'When you get right down to it, one man's much the same as another.'

'Well, I only hope Ophelia knows what she's getting herself into with all this— *Hi*, Ophelia! You look *great!*'

Meanwhile, the A&E doctor had been released from Max's scintillating mini-lecture on the benefits of red wine when enjoyed in moderation (and in his hotel room) and turned to Jonathan. After the ordeal of Max, she was more than relieved: there was a hungry look in her eye and she talked, sometimes, at great length, as though breathing fresh air for the first time after a long internment.

'Hello! And how are you? Sorry, who are you, I should say. Gosh, that's not the way to do it, is it! My name's Aparna Mukherjee.'

'Nice to meet you, Aparna. I'm Jonathan Tucker.'

'Oh,' said Aparna.

'What's wrong?'

'Nothing, it's just that name sounds familiar,' she said.

'Mine?' said Jonathan. 'Have we met?'

'No . . . I think you knew my friend, Alastair.'

'What?'

Joanie, on the other hand, was becoming increasingly frustrated. She wanted to have a conversation with Jonathan, she wanted to get up the courage to talk about what had happened to him on that night, fifteen years ago in Cambridge . . . but she found herself returning, over and over, to the small talk that sticks to weddings the way plaque sticks to teeth.

She was trying to steer the conversation towards it, gently, both for her sake and his, so that it wouldn't be too much of a shock. She wasn't sure exactly which topic of conversation would allow her to segue neatly into years-old trauma, but she knew it wasn't what they were talking about now.

And then there was Max. Every time Joanie thought she was getting closer, Max joined in the conversation with some wearisome diatribe on Latin verbs. Every time Joanie thought she was nearly ready to say what she had been wanting to say to Jonathan for years, she found herself politely indulging this entitled stranger's remarks about the weather in Rome. But she was thirty-eight. And she was tired of being polite.

'I mean, I can't say I know Alastair all that well,' said Dr Mukherjee, 'To be honest, he's not so much my friend as my contractor.'

'Oh.'

'Yes, he did my kitchen.'

'Right. But he mentioned me? After all this time?'

'Well, he was in there for quite a while. Structural issues, you know. Don't get me started.'

'Sounds complicated.'

'It was. Gave us plenty of time to chat, though! And as soon as we realised we both knew Cambridge, we got to talking about our younger days ... Do you keep in touch? It *is* Jonathan, isn't it? I do hope I'm not thinking of someone else. I think the two of you were friends at one point, weren't you? You were in that church group.'

'Yes, a long time ago.'

'In fact, I think I remember getting one of the postcards from someone. Never got his name, but he seemed rather intense.'

'That'll be Joel.'

'Ah, I see. Well, Alastair always said that group could be a bit ... difficult, sometimes.'

'Did he?' said Jonathan, trying to sound airy and unconcerned. 'I suppose we were quite a collection of characters. We must have made strange bedfellows.'

'Well!' laughed Dr Mukherjee. 'It's funny you should say that.'

'What do you mean?'

'I, er ... I don't like to gossip, but he used to talk about the hypocrisy of the group.'

'Hypocrisy?'

'Not you, of course; this Joel person. Apparently Joel had some ... issues ... to work through at the time. Alastair said that he and Joel had a bit of a fling. Is that right? I think I'm thinking of the right person. Joel? I suppose there were a few of you in that group. I'm terrible with names. Anyway, the fling didn't last long.'

'Oh? What happened between Alastair and m— er, Joel?'

'I can't remember, now. Alastair always said this Joel chap was a bit, you know, dysfunctional. Bit of a messed-up guy, really. About his sexuality. I think Alastair was well rid, from the sound of things.'

'Er. Yes. Good.'

'Still, we've all had rubbish exes, haven't we? We laugh about it sometimes, so it can't be that bad, I suppose.'

'No, you're right. It's good to laugh,' said Jonathan, after a moment. His throat was very dry.

'But you never know where life's going to lead you, they say. Alastair met his partner not long after he split up with Joel. They've been together ever since, as a matter of fact.'

'How wonderful,' said Jonathan quietly. He tried to smile.

'Yes, yes. Actually, Alastair and I met our partners in the same week, so we share an anniversary, almost. Life's funny, isn't it? So funny. Yes. And what about you? Are you seeing anyone?'

Taking a deep breath and doing some quick mental arithmetic about the number of mutual friends she and Max were likely to have, Joanie turned to him and spoke, calmly and evenly, into the middle of his invective about the many advantages of the toga. She drank a little more.

'Max,' she said.

She paused for a second, waiting for him to stop speaking.

'I actually already understand Latin. I have a degree in Classics. Now, I don't mean to be rude but I'm trying to talk to my friend.' She gestured towards Jonathan.

For half a moment, she wondered if Max might enter into a loud and involved argument about the merits of her reaction, but he did not. He barely even registered that Joanie had spoken. Instead he looked past her at the black man sitting next to her and, for a moment, his eyes widened as if in realisation. Addressing Jonathan (and ignoring Joanie), he said, 'Sorry, mate. Didn't mean to interrupt!' And then he winked at Jonathan and stalked off jauntily, in search of another glass of Prosecco, an extra slice of wedding cake and a more willing ear.

When she turned back to Jonathan, he was smiling his warm smile. It was the first genuine thing either of them had said for the past hour.

'I'm sorry,' she said. 'I'm sorry. You went through such a hard time when we were at Cambridge. And I knew it. I was there. I saw what happened to you. And we'd become friends, and I didn't do anything to help you. Before ... before ...'

'Before I tried to hang myself.' He said the words with no expression, as though he were reading something from a note that someone else had left for him.

Joanie swallowed. 'Before you tried to do that, yes. I feel terrible, Jonathan. I want you to know that, because I want you to know I care about you, very much. I feel terrible and I've *felt* terrible. For years. I really have. I'd hate for you to think that ... that you don't matter to me.'

Jonathan took a deep breath and looked away as though searching for someone. He had imagined this scenario many times, and was never sure he would have the correct response. 'I can't pretend I ever ... got over the memory of it, Joanie.

That kind of thing stays with you forever. But I've come a long way, since then. I'm okay. You don't have to worry about me.'

He paused. He'd forgotten the listening way that Joanie Maloney had. She could listen so hard that you forgot she was there, forgot she wasn't your own self. It was a kind of self-abnegation that made him feel curiously sad for her, because he was pretty sure that no one but the terribly lonely could achieve it. He glanced at her quickly, searchingly, as though to check that he had not told her too much, had not burdened her.

'You know,' he said, 'I'm glad we're meeting now.'

'I am, too. Funny that we're meeting today.'

'Yes. Maurice's birthday.'

They sat quietly for a moment, listening to the silent echoes of the name.

'Yes. I don't suppose . . . ?'

'No. Maurice is somewhere far away. Still.'

'I see.'

'Can you tell me why?'

'Muuuuuum, can I please sit with you?' came Nnenna's voice. Joanie wiped a tear from her eye that she hadn't noticed was there and turned to face her daughter – who noticed that she and her friend had been talking about Grown-Up Things; worse, Grown-Up Things that Made Mum Cry. It must be very bad. Nnenna froze unconsciously but recovered herself quickly.

'Are you okay? What's happened?'

'I'm fine, Nnenna; we were talking about some old memories, that's all. This is Jonathan – we were at university together. Jonathan, this is my daughter, Nnenna.'

'Nnenna,' said Jonathan, a smile breaking across his face. Nnenna saw him search her face for signs of her father's features, and he found them: the serious, slightly severe eyes; the quick and broad smile.

Nonsensically, Nnenna found herself searching the face of this man, who was surely an old friend of her father's, for signs of him: some line on his face or twinkle in his eye that bespoke some memory he had shared with Maurice, some private joke, some clue to the man she had not yet met. She found nothing.

Joanie, perhaps sensing this, put an arm around her daughter's waist: Nnenna was tall, these days, and Joanie had to stretch her arm a little to reach. She said, 'What's going on at your table?'

'I wish I knew.'

'Sweetheart,' said Joanie. She did feel sorry for Nnenna, sitting with the children, and she would have liked to have her nearby, but if she didn't talk to Jonathan properly now it might be another year before she got the chance again. 'Sweetheart, would you give us a few minutes?'

'Why?' said Nnenna.

Jonathan made as if to say he didn't mind, but Joanie cut him off. 'If you must know, I'd like to ... run some ideas past Jonathan.'

'What ideas?'

'About your birthday party.'

'Oh.'

'Um. Yes.'

'Really?'

Joanie paused. She tried to never lie to Nnenna. 'Could you give us a few minutes?'

Nnenna made some wordless plaintive noises and then ambled away, vaguely wondering how inappropriate it would be for her to assume the identity of another guest and sit at a different table altogether.

'She's great,' said Jonathan.

'She is.'

'How old is she now? Sixteen?'

'Yes, nearly seventeen. I love her so much.'

'Of course. She's lucky to have you.'

Joanie smiled a thank you.

'I wish I still had family around.'

'You don't have anyone?'

'Not a one. Parents both died years ago.'

'And you never had any siblings, did you?'

'Nope. Just me.'

'You must have loads of friends, though? You've been living in London since we graduated. You must know plenty of people, there.'

'You'd think so, wouldn't you?' said Jonathan, wistfully. 'But actually, London's not the place for a guy like me. I'm not that outgoing; I'm not that brave. The *bigness* of the place intimidates me. I've lived there all this time and I've never really adapted to it. It's why I'm moving here.'

'Here?'

'Well, not *here* to this ruined monastery. The repair work alone would be murder.'

'But where else will you find all this natural light?'

'I mean ... ' He cast his hands around in an estate agent's gesture of display.

'But seriously, you're moving?'

'Yep. To Manchester. In a couple of weeks.'

'What prompted you?'

'I'm tired of London. Most of the friends I did have, have begun to move out to start families; it doesn't feel like there's much left for me there, any more. Every neighbourhood seems to get more gentrified, more expensive; it's starting to feel like a different city from when I moved there after university.'

'A lot of people I know have said that. None of this lot, that is,' she said, taking in the wedding guests around them. 'Together, they probably own most of East London.'

'Still, it's a relief to know that the prices are so reasonable.'

'Exactly.'

'So, when a job came up in the Manchester office, I asked to be transferred. Sure, I'll miss sunshine and the comfort of an effective public transport system, but I have been here a couple of times for work and things, and it feels like a nice place. Friendlier than London, too. And you always made Manchester sound so great. So I thought . . . why not?'

'Have you got any friends here? People to help you settle in?'

'Two or three, yes. They've all got kids now, but I see them every so often. I'll be okay.'

Joanie looked at him again for a moment. It was hard to tell when he needed you. 'Well, I'm probably not the person to help you shift furniture, but if you'd like to hang out some-time . . . let me know?'

'That would be really nice,' said Jonathan. He smiled a gen-erous smile. 'And don't worry about the moving: I've hired a removal company. I found a nice little flat in the city centre, too, so you should come round sometime when you're free. It's a beautiful space. In London I'd be sharing it with eight flatmates and eating cold pasta every night.'

'Do you mean that?'

'Well, maybe not *every* night. I'd probably have the odd beans-on-toast . . . '

'No, I mean about us spending more time together. Don't say it to be polite, Jonathan. I'd like to, but I don't want you to feel obligated, so—'

'And I don't. It'd be nice to see an old friend again. You can help me get used to the city.'

'This is such good news, Jonathan,' said Joanie. 'Honestly. I think you'll like it here. The people are so much friendlier.'

'Nina, you shouldn't be attractive. But you *are*,' he confirmed, reassuringly. 'It's so weird.'

'Right.' Nnenna wasn't sure what 'attractiveness' really meant. She knew what it was supposed to mean, obviously, but she felt more and more that beauty was a very slippery concept. Unfortunately for her, it seemed to have slipped in between the soup course and the main.

'I'm not normally attracted to girls like you, but I am tonight. Look at you. Must be something about the light!'

'Or maybe it's just past your bedtime.'

At this, Jason raised a quizzical eyebrow and leered forward. 'You remind me of my mother, you know.'

'Well . . . isn't that sweet?' said Nnenna. 'You must remind me to tell her that.'

'Tell my mum?'

'Oh, yes. Tall? Pale skin, dark hair, dark green dress?'

He frowned through three layers of wedding cake. 'How did you know?'

'She's coming over now. Can't say I see *much* of a resemblance. But then, maybe it's just the way that scowl warps her face.'

Jason's mother, her fascinator quivering with rage at the sight of her inebriated pre-teen son, reached the kiddie table just in time for her to see her darling boy raise another quizzical eyebrow . . . leer forward again . . . and gift Nnenna's best dress with his semi-digested meal.

'Are you seeing anyone, Joanie?' Jonathan asked. 'I noticed you don't have a plus one.'

'No. Nothing to report on that front. I'm beginning to think that a crossword compiler in her very late thirties isn't so much of a catch.'

'Don't be daft, Joanie. You're wonderful. Bloody smart, too. Those crosswords are far more interesting than any reports I do for the firm.'

She waved this away. 'And you? Are you seeing anyone?'

'Nope. Can't say I am.'

'It's hard, isn't it? Dating. I don't think about it the way I used to. It doesn't feel like fun any more.'

'Not at all?'

'Well, I've been on a few dates, here and there. A few mishaps, a few missed connections. But after a while I got so tired of it: with Nnenna, I don't have so much time any more. You know, to meet losers.'

'So what's my excuse?'

Joanie put a hand on his shoulder and squeezed. It felt audacious, the way kindness sometimes can, when extended to someone who's been starved of it. She thought that he might flinch, but he didn't. He placed his hand on hers. It was so light, there. What was he afraid of?

A warm breeze blew through the orchard now, shaking the blossoms as though harvesting their petals for fruit, which fell to the ground and peppered the dark grass. Glasses tinkled as waiting staff refilled drinks. For the first time, Joanie noticed the string quartet that had been performing in the background. They were playing some arrangement of a pop song, but it wasn't one that she knew. It occurred to her that Ophelia had been lucky with the weather, even if her husband left something to be desired. She thought it might be time to leave.

As if on cue, Nnenna walked towards her again, a plaintive expression on her face and a stream of pale yellow vomit on the bottom of her dress. 'Mum,' she said sternly, not needing to finish the sentence.

'I think it's time to go,' said Joanie, to Jonathan. Jonathan, smiling the knowing, generous smile of the childless, released her.

'Bye, Jonathan. Take care of yourself.'

'Bye, Joanie.'

'You have my number.'

'Yes. I meant it, you know. About meeting up, sometime.'

Joanie smiled, unsure but hopeful. She put an arm around Nnenna's shoulders and they smiled as they walked out into the early evening.

Chapter 2

[...] for the former things have
passed away.

Revelations 21:4

Being black can be hard sometimes, and it can be harder if you're a woman. Harder still, if you have an active imagination-slash-undiagnosed anxiety disorder and a high proportion of white people in your life. If the actual racism doesn't get you, the worrying will: not merely what *did* happen, but what *might* happen. Because who knows what people are thinking? Maybe that retail assistant is only having a bad day; maybe she wasn't having a bad day until you came along. Maybe that security guard follows lots of people round the shop; maybe he reads *Twelve Years a Slave* every night and salivates like a hungry Alsatian.

The thing is, after you get enough wary glances on public transport, after enough people cross the street to avoid you, after you've heard how attractive you are 'for a black girl' enough times, you start to wonder about all the things people might be saying before they say them.

So it was that as Parents' Evening approached, Nnenna began to dream up potential scenarios involving all the less generous things her white teachers might be saying about her behind her back. Here's one:

'I hate Parents' Evenings,' says Mr Perry, tiredly. He is a History teacher, so Nnenna imagines him alphabetising the VHS videos he keeps in his classroom for no reason. As he does this, Mr Black (her French teacher) keeps him company, also for no reason.

'Charles,' says Mr Black, 'you hate everything.'

'I've been teaching all my adult life, James; I'm entitled to hate everything. I haven't been touched by a woman since my mother gave me my annual hug last year. Also, I sweat a lot and I shouldn't wear grey shirts to work.'

'That is true,' concedes Mr Black, as he bites into a nectarine. 'But Parents' Evening . . . '

'Why? I quite like meeting the parents. It's so revealing! Have you noticed that the smelly children always have smelly parents?'

'Yes! Also, the stupid children have stupid parents. Isn't that fascinating?'

'It is! I am fascinated by that fact! The world is such an interesting place.'

'Indeed. And how many students will you see, this evening?'

'I have about fifteen in my Year Twelve class.'

'Do you teach Nina?'

'Eh? Nnenna, you mean? Yes, great student. In fact, tonight, when I meet her mother, I'm going to suggest—'

'You've heard about her dad, though, haven't you?'

'No, why?'

'She's never met him. Something murky went on in the family, years ago. Sounds awful.'

'Oh *dear*,' says James, absently, as he stares at his phone, scrolling through ugly-second-hand-jumpers.com. 'How ghastly.'

'Yes, it's lucky that Nnenna's turned out the way she has. Imagine what her home life must be like.'

'Yes. So *unbalanced*. What's the mother like? Harpy?'

'Never met her, myself, but I've heard she's a crossword compiler.'

'Never.'

'Yep.'

'You can actually do that for a *living?*'

'Apparently. By all accounts she's pretty sharp. Obviously never made very much of it, though. Perhaps that's why Nnenna did so well in her GCSEs last year, and won all those school prizes – maybe the mum's pushy. Trying to compensate for something in herself by pushing Nnenna.'

'Well, she wouldn't be the first ... Oh, how *awful*. I almost wish you hadn't told me that, James.'

'Mmmm. Terrible shame. I mean I understand that absentee fathers are sadly all too common. You know, in the black community. All that rap music ... '

'Oh? Her father's black?'

'Yes, she's half and half. You know.'

'Ah! So, her mother's ... '

'Yes, white.'

'Gosh. Black people are so *interesting.*'

'Aren't they?'

'Nnenna, I'm not touching him with a ten-foot bargepole.'

'How about five-foot?'

'Nope. Next.'

'We're running out of men, Mum. We've only got three left, and the women aren't any better this year.'

'Don't care,' said Joanie. 'I have standards and I'm sticking to them.'

This was their pre-Parents' Evening ritual. Three years ago, Joanie had made the mistake of remarking that she found Nnenna's Art teacher mildly attractive in his overalls. Her slight reservation was completely ignored, as her teenage progeny latched on to the idea and went wild. Suddenly, Joanie was to be escorted around the school with the utmost care, lest she lose all sense of restraint and be found cavorting with Mr Miller in the supply cupboard after hours. Joanie found herself laughingly but mercilessly accused of using Parents' Evening to cruise for educated bachelors on the sly.

Now, before the first appointment every year, they ran through the list of Nnenna's teachers with a fine toothcomb – male and female, to make things equitable – and they clinically but spiritedly assessed the pros and cons of a potential date with each. Joanie did wonder if there was something not entirely proper about allowing herself to have this kind of frank conversation with her daughter, but she still felt somehow responsible for Jason vomiting on Nnenna at the wedding a few weeks ago.

And Joanie had noticed Nnenna getting anxious about Parents' Evening. She felt the nervousness was utterly unfounded, since all Nnenna's teachers liked her, but nevertheless, became more and more pronounced as each Parents' Evening approached. Joanie could not say exactly what was wrong, but she had found that their playful ritual seemed to calm Nnenna down, somehow. In a way, it was like getting ready to give an important speech and picturing your audience naked. One more time, she got to watch her daughter's fears melt into a wry smile.

'Okay, well ... how about Mr Maclean?'

'Didn't he teach you last year, as well? The sweaty one?'

'Okay – yes – it's unfortunate that he cycles to school in the morning and doesn't shower. But,' said Nnenna, thinking rapidly, 'he wouldn't have *time* to shower because he's so *dedicated* to his *work*.'

'Good grief,' said Joanie, pursing her lips. 'I think I'm entitled to be a little pickier than that.'

Nnenna drew a firm line through the name of another potential mate.

'Well, if you *are* going to be picky, we'll have to dig into our reserves. May I present Mr Coyne?'

'You may *not*. He's married.'

'Divorced. I heard him talking to another teacher about his ex-wife.'

'Nnenna!'

'Sounded like an amicable split – you could definitely get in there.'

'Mmm ... okay. I'm listening.'

'He's tall.'

'Mmhmm, how old?'

'I'd say about fortyish?'

'Facial hair?'

'Minimal.'

'Good, this is good. Body odour?'

'Negligible. I'd say he smells nice, actually. Cedarwood.'

'I've always liked that smell. Why's he in the reserves?' (Nnenna always kept one or two names up her sleeve in case, like tonight, none of the rest passed muster.) 'What does he teach, again?'

'Physics ... '

Joanie felt as though she had been led into a trap. She frowned her disapproval. 'Next, please.'

'Miss Stevens.'

'What does she teach?'

'Maths. But don't let that put you off.'

'Do you like her?'

'She's nice. She knows *everything*.'

'How old?'

'I'd say late twenties?'

'Mmm, bit young for me, I think. What would we talk about?'

'I don't know, she does seem interesting. And outdoorsy – maybe she could take you on a hike somewhere.'

'Well, now you're just trying to get rid of me, Nnenna. Who's next? Anyone else left?'

'Okay ... umm ... Mr Black?'

'Who?'

'Mr Black. He's my French teacher.'

'And?'

'Well, he's a bit older than you.'

'Sweetheart, pickings are slim, tonight. I'm not going in looking for a bargain. Is he nice, at least?'

But Nnenna said nothing.

Joanie walked through the gates of Nnenna's school and felt a kind of chill roll down her spine: something about this place always made her feel like an impostor. The vaulted ceilings and ubiquitous oak panelling made her feel underdressed; the huddles of parents, talking warmly amongst themselves as they waited for appointments, made her feel like she was back at Cambridge again in the 1990s, trying to make friends with the students who'd known each other since high school. She resented herself for it, but she still wanted to belong, at least a bit. Just once. She wondered if she would always want this. She shook her head as though to clear her thoughts and went with Nnenna to the appointments, fully aware that Nnenna was guiding her from one to the other and leaving French till the end. It was her strongest subject and her French teachers had always loved her; no doubt she was leaving the best for last.

'I think,' said Mr Black, almost as soon as Joanie sat down, 'that Nnenna should apply to the Sorbonne.' He was smiling away as though he hadn't just told Joanie the most devastating, ridiculous, outrageous ...

'Why?'

Mr Black blinked at the question as if she were stupid. He kept staring at her as though she were some fascinating species of iguana he had seen in the zoo. It happened, sometimes:

people, when they found out that Joanie had had a child with a black man – and that, worse still, she *wasn't still with him* – looked curiously at her, surprised that she was in fact an articulate human being in full command of her senses, trying to understand what madness had consumed her seventeen years ago . . .

But all that seemed like nothing in comparison to this . . . this insult.

For his part, Mr Black considered repeating himself, in case she hadn't heard him properly. Or – perhaps she simply hadn't heard of the Sorbonne? There was always the odd one . . .

'Well, to say nothing of spending a few years in Paris, the Sorbonne is one of the most respected universities in the world. The quality of their teaching and learning is absolutely—'

'I know what the Sorbonne is,' said Joanie.

Next to her, at the table, Nnenna looked at her in awe. She had never seen her mother so angry. It was as though Mr Black had told her mother that she had a freak or a failure for a daughter. Wasn't this good news? Mr Black was so excited . . .

'I know what it is. What I don't understand is why you want to send my daughter there. She's only sixteen.'

Nnenna felt her cheeks fill with blood. 'I'm nearly seventeen, Mum. God, what's wrong with you? This is good news!'

Mr Black, caught in the midst of a family drama, looked anxiously from mother to daughter as though hoping to find some kind of consensus as to what he should say next. 'Errr. Obviously, Nnenna wouldn't be matriculating for another year or two . . . but, Ms Maloney, this really is the time to start thinking about her application; making sure she's done her research, got plenty of extracurricular activities and so on. The exams, of course, will take care of themselves with a student like Nnenna . . .'

He paused for another moment, to see if this had improved his position with Joanie at all. It hadn't.

'By all means, take some time to think about it, but not too long – these places are extremely competitive, so we'd want to start thinking about the application as soon as possible. Here, I've printed off a few things that you might find useful to read.' When Joanie did not acknowledge the leaflets, Nnenna took them in her hand, wanting to read them but unable to focus on the words. It was as though she was seeing French for the first time. And the leaflets seemed oddly heavy, somehow.

'And I assure you,' continued Mr Black, sounding nervously cheerful, 'you needn't worry about how Nnenna will get on in Paris. She's the best student I've ever taught, very mature indeed, as you'll know. She's perfectly well equipped to handle anything university could throw at her. Most students, of course, I wouldn't recommend ... But Nnenna has an unusual gift. All her teachers think so. And after an education like that, her career prospects would be—'

'She's just a child,' said Joanie, not looking at Nnenna's shocked, humiliated expression, unable to bring herself to look at Mr Black. 'She's just a child. How could you do that to her?'

In the car, Joanie was silent, but it was a difficult kind of silence to ignore, like a wasp that has flown into a room and cannot leave. Nnenna looked over at her from time to time, totally confused. Her mother wore an expression that looked like rage, like a mad, burning rage – but why? It didn't make any sense. She had never acted so strangely before. Had something else happened?

Joanie drove through the darkness, her hands gripping the wheel so that her skin stretched and her knuckles went white, her mind playing the evening back again. Something had been torn away from her when she was least expecting it. She could feel the anger building up in her mind, each wave adding to it like layers of hard sediment.

But, just on the other side of rage, Joanie could feel her heart breaking. There was someone in the world who thought that Nnenna was nearly old enough to live by herself – more than that, to live by herself in another country! He hadn't even hesitated to suggest it. He'd smiled his way through the entire evening as though he were delivering a generous gift. As the memory of his words replayed, over and over, in Joanie's mind, she wondered – if Mr Black could think of Nnenna this way, who else had? Did the whole world see her this way? Had everybody else but her realised that Nnenna was an adult, now?

The thought pressed on her mind like an accusation and she felt guilty; stupid, even. It made her want to clam up, it brewed resentment in her. But more than this, it grieved her. It wasn't as though she had never known that Nnenna would grow up and leave home; it was more that, somehow, she had always imagined that this process would be a gradual one, a gentle thing, like falling asleep or feeling an anaesthetic wear off. Somehow, in the hazy blur of her mind's eye, she had imagined that the whole thing would be altogether kinder, fairer. Perhaps it might even be faintly signposted, somehow, like a long road on a night-time drive. Shouldn't there have been events along the way that she was supposed to look out for? Little rebellions? Claims of independence? Shouldn't they have at least fallen out about something by now? Or had this been happening all along without her noticing?

No, there had been nothing. She was sure there had been nothing. All this time, Nnenna had been quietly growing up in secret, but leaving no obvious trace, no trail of breadcrumbs. And now Joanie felt as though she had fallen asleep in a car that Nnenna was driving down a road at night at two hundred miles an hour.

Even as a tiny child, Nnenna had had an anxious disposition about the world in general. She needed to be held much more often than other children, she was never happy to play by herself, didn't want to learn to ride a bike.

Around the age of four, she got into the habit of asking about what she would do if she ever got lost. At first, Joanie thought that she had taken some fairy tale or other to heart. Little Red Riding Hood, maybe. She decided to switch to bedtime stories with less geographical confusion involved.

But Nnenna wasn't like other children. Other children were direct in their suffering: the other children that lived on the street, for example, cried more, complained more. And Nnenna did these things some of the time, but increasingly, she would only look up at her, stare silently at her mother's face, as if waiting for some sort of cue. Sometimes she would get out of bed in the middle of the night and silently climb into bed with Joanie or, more often, she would sit on the end and wait to be acknowledged, waiting to be asked about what she could not say aloud.

'What's wrong, sweetheart?'

'What will I do if . . . '

'Yes?'

'What will I do if I can't find my way home?' she'd said, one evening as Joanie tucked her into bed. It was winter and the days were short; darkness had descended for the night, to make the world wide and unknowable and complicated to Joanie's daughter.

'Sweetheart, I'll always be with you! You know you mustn't wander off by yourself, don't you?'

'Yes, Mummy.'

'So, you'll be fine.'

'But what do I do if I can't find my way back home?'

Joanie looked deeply into her daughter's eyes, sensing the unspoken in the repeated question. In her daughter's terrified mind, something was tormenting her. A darkness had descended in her mind: it was a darkness full of murky caverns and under-the-bed spaces where monsters of all descriptions hid, and she was far too young to know her way around this frightening world, far too young to ask what would happen if the unspeakable happened; what would happen if her mother ever left her. She could only say the same words again, and hope that this time her mother would understand without her having to speak the truth, the hurtful, dangerous truth.

'Come here, sweetheart, my own sweet heart.' She drew Nnenna close to her. She was so small – but every inch of her, Joanie could feel, was panic and fear. So young, to be so afraid! 'I'll always be with you. Look at me. I'll *always* be with you. You never, ever have to worry about that. Okay? I'll never leave you. I promise.'

But Nnenna still shivered. Sometimes, the anxious have a way of walling off their anxiety beyond touch, beyond reassurance.

'I know, let's look out of the window.'

'Mummy, at what?'

It was only a small window and the light pollution from the city obscured much, but Joanie could make out enough. A few stars making up broken constellations, like an incomplete text. No matter that Nnenna could not comprehend North or South; no matter that she would never be out of her mother's sight and would never need this. Even the dimmest, loneliest light would do.

'Can you see those four stars, there?'

'Where?'

'Just here, where my fingers are. Look,' she said, taking Nnenna's hand in hers. 'See?'

Nnenna nodded, solemnly.

'That's a group of stars called Ursa Minor,' said Joanie, pointing to Orion's belt and Venus.

'Oosa Mina,' said Nnenna, confidently.

'That's right, Ursa Minor,' said Joanie. 'Now, can you see

the brightest star, right there? That's the North Star. As long as you can find that, you'll always be able to find your way home. Okay? And I'll be right there with you to help you find it. Always, Nnenna.'

In the car, Joanie felt tears well up behind her eyes. She gripped the wheel harder, to distract herself, make herself angry enough not to cry in front of her daughter. But again and again, she thought of that night. Only a few short years ago, Nnenna had been too terrified of abandonment to leave her side; now, it seemed, she wanted to get on a plane. And if she could get on a plane to Paris, where else might she go? Joanie had given up her life to raise Nnenna: if she still wasn't enough by now, when would she be?

Joanie slowed down the car and turned into a side street.

'Where are we going?' asked Nnenna.

'Let's go and get some food.'

'I thought we were eating at home?'

'We're both too tired to cook, and I don't want another take-away. You've got that free period tomorrow morning, anyway. Let's just go to a cheap restaurant. We'll be quick.'

Nnenna hesitated, unsure about this new direction her mother was taking. Wasn't she angry any more?

'Which one?'

'Let's go to Cucina.'

Chapter 3

[...] the one who doubts is like a wave
of the sea that is driven and tossed
by the wind.

James 1:6

Cucina was not the restaurant that Nnenna would
have chosen.

They both loved the food (Joanie had spent a summer in
Italy while a university student), but Nnenna found the staff
somewhat aloof. They always seated the two of them in the
corner at the back, the waiters always hovered uncomfortably
close by and the food, although delicious, was always whisked
away the moment they were finished. Because Nnenna had
never been there without her mother, she wasn't able to be
sure if it was because she was black, or because the waiters
were a bunch of jerks in a more general sense; but in her more
anxious moments, she felt sure it was the former. Had Joanie
had more presence of mind – had she not been distracted by
Mr Black's news – she might have remembered this.

'Table for two?' said the hostess when they arrived. She
barely looked up from her desk.

'Please,' said Joanie.

'Come with me.'

It was about 9 p.m. by now. The restaurant was nearly empty, and there were only a few people still eating as the hostess wound her way between empty tables, to seat Joanie and Nnenna at their usual table, near the back.

Once again, Nnenna found herself wondering why this was, since there were plenty of other tables to choose from. But she could never ask. So, as the hostess trotted off to find a waiter, she worried. She imagined.

Nnenna saw the hostess signal a waiter and then return to her station, where a waitress was waiting. They had a brief conversation, which Nnenna imagined as follows:

'That black girl's here again,' says the hostess.

'Eurgh. Again? Did someone put fried chicken on the menu and not tell me?'

'I thought when we put the *Open* sign on the door, the *unless you're brown* bit was implied?'

'What can I say? People see what they want to see.'

'True.'

'What's with her hair, anyway?'

The hostess shrugged. 'It's not our job to judge them.'

'No.'

'But let's judge them anyway.'

'Yes!'

'I think they're probably poor. And stupid. Especially the daughter, who has brown skin.'

'One hundred per cent. And what about the dad?'

'What dad?'

'*Exactly*. Obviously, he's black and therefore a gangster.'

'You think?'

'Well, he's black and he's not here. What other logical explanation can there be?'

'I certainly can't think of one. And I've met two whole black people!'

'Looks like they're ready to order.'

'Poor Tim.'

'Yes. Still, at least he gets to spit in their food.'

'Thank you,' said Joanie, as the waiter brought over their food. He nodded curtly and left. Nnenna was certain she saw him wipe his mouth.

'I mean, how do *you* feel about it?' Joanie asked. 'He never stopped to ask you about it, did he? You wouldn't want it, would you? Studying abroad? For three years. Would you?'

Joanie didn't know quite what she was doing. She liked Mr Black; she liked most of Nnenna's teachers, but Mr Black especially. He'd been Nnenna's teacher last year, too, and he had always seemed gentle, and smart, and fair; he was one of those teachers who didn't seem bothered by the fact that one of his students was more intelligent than he was. He'd always looked out for Nnenna, always mentioned little opportunities and things she might be interested in. Why was she trying to turn things round on him, now?

As for Nnenna, she knew that there was no right answer to this question, but she also knew that she couldn't *not* answer it. She didn't want to hurt her mother's feelings, but the truth was the truth; and it didn't seem fair to deny the truth about what she wanted. She felt so divided; as much as she resented her mother – as bewildering as her reaction had been this evening – she felt sympathy for her, too. To be close to someone in so much distress for you is to be distressed yourself.

But wasn't there something deeply iniquitous about her mother's apprehension? Shouldn't this be for Nnenna to decide? Hadn't she earned it? Hadn't she worked hard for this? In fact, Mr Black had mentioned the Sorbonne to her a week ago, after class one afternoon. She hadn't known what to say. Actually, she had stood with her mouth open for a few moments, while he'd smiled and told her he would mention it on Parents' Evening. She'd saved Mr Black's appointment for the end and told herself that she had done this as a good surprise, a treat that would make her mother happy and proud. But she knew now that she had been afraid, too.

So, was it her fault? Should she have told the truth straight away? Joanie always seemed to avoid having difficult conversations; every time Nnenna brought up the subject of her father, her mother became tight-lipped and changed the subject or, worse, she pretended she hadn't heard. There was a kind of weakness to her mother: a weakness that was hard to love, sometimes, but it was a weakness nonetheless, and something in that frailty called out to Nnenna for comfort, and for help. Maybe it would ease the situation if she told the truth now – the kind part of the truth.

'Well, it wouldn't be for three years all at a time,' she said. Her voice was too sweet, too cheerful.

'Honestly, Nnenna, I don't get it,' said Joanie, her voice suddenly cross. 'What do you need to study abroad for?'

Nnenna was lost for words. Need? Of course she didn't *need* to study abroad. When you put it like that, applying to the Sorbonne sounded ridiculous; extravagant; pretentious. Maybe her mother was right. Why, really, was she doing this?

Her mother's voice burst in on her guilty reverie. 'What about Danny?' she said.

'Danny?' Nnenna was startled. What did her boyfriend have to do with any of this?

'Well ... I mean, what would happen to the two of you if you lived abroad? He's never going to study in France, is he?'

'I ... I don't know,' said Nnenna, confused. 'I hadn't thought about it.'

Joanie looked at her daughter for a long moment, and Nnenna had the realisation that, in fact, her mother was being completely unreasonable. She didn't want to comfort her, now. She didn't want to be kind.

Need? Why did she have to *need* to go to Paris? Why

couldn't she just ... go? Why did she have to justify herself? And why was Danny suddenly relevant to any of this? Why was her mother suddenly *on her boyfriend's side*?

Looking at her mother as she chewed her food, Nnenna saw something strange beginning to happen: the woman she loved most in the world, the woman she had always felt safe with, the woman who, only a few hours ago, she had teased and joked with, was turning into someone else. Before her very eyes, Joanie morphed and mutated into someone else entirely – some*thing* else entirely – a monster, a gargoyle, an ogre bent on ruining her life. Her eyes were not bright, now, but lurid; her nose was not merely pronounced but hooked. And she was always chewing, chewing, chewing ...

Nnenna was overwhelmed, not only by the completeness of this transformation but by the feeling of revulsion it occasioned in her. Whatever this beast was, however it got here, Nnenna knew she had to defeat it, and defeat it utterly. She had to take a blade and plunge it into the beast's dark heart, and step over its thrashing corpse to get to freedom.

'You're completely overreacting,' said Nnenna. 'Even if I got in, I wouldn't go for almost two years.'

Absently, Joanie waved away Nnenna's words. She said nothing, and only laughed bitterly as though Nnenna had said something incredibly naive.

'You don't know what you're talking about. I've been your age, Nnenna. You'll be eighteen before you know it,' said Joanie, almost flatly. 'Besides, I went to university early, you know. It happens.'

'You say that like it's a bad thing.'

'And you *will* get in. You have to assume you will.' Nnenna was taken aback by this out-of-place compliment, and she was starting to think that she might have been too harsh, when her mother scoffed and said, 'Mr *Black* certainly seemed to think so.'

'*What?*'

'Everything all right with the food?' said their waiter, previously unnoticed. Nnenna wondered how long he had been standing there.

'Yes, it's all lovely, thanks,' Joanie said, and the man walked away. Her train of thought was lost for a moment, and the whole thing seemed stupid again. Maybe Nnenna was right? Maybe she was overreacting? She was about to suggest this to her daughter, when she looked up and saw Nnenna's face; she hadn't seen it properly in the car because it had been too dark. But now that she could see Nnenna's face in the candlelight of the restaurant, she saw something strange happening. Her face began to transform: the boldness in it, which she loved, became impertinence; the determination, ingratitude. And the features in her daughter's face which she normally tried to pretend weren't there – Maurice's eyes, Maurice's chin, the way Maurice's mouth crumpled at a frown – were now impossible to ignore.

She hated this. Nnenna was the person she loved most in the world, but in this moment, there was a part of her that was difficult to love: the part that belonged to Maurice. Everything in Nnenna's face tonight made Nnenna seem entirely independent. Up until now, Joanie had thought of sixteen as being worlds away from adulthood. And it was still far away – Joanie found it hard even to call herself 'grown up' – but not as far away as she had thought. Nnenna was more than old enough to fly unaccompanied, now, and once she'd travelled to Paris, what was there to stop her travelling further?

Her daughter's voice burst in on her.

'What's that supposed to mean?' Nnenna was tensely whispering. Her mother's lazy dismissiveness only infuriated her more. She wanted to fight with her mother; she wanted to punish her. The need was like bloodthirst. 'Mr Black was telling the truth.'

Joanie shook her head again: she was older, wiser; nothing

that Nnenna could say could possibly make a difference. 'I think it's a little naive of you to go running off to Paris because one of your teachers mentioned it.'

'What are you even talking about? I'm not fucking *running* anywhere, I'm—'

'*Don't* you swear at me, Nnenna Maloney! I am your mother,' Joanie snarled. But it made no difference; they were having two different conversations now.

'I'm not *fucking running* anywhere. All I want to do,' said Nnenna, her voice tremulously quiet, 'is live my life.' For half a second, she waited, to take a breath, to consider whether or not to say what she wanted to say next. 'All I want to do is *make* something of my life, instead of *wasting* it. Instead of getting knocked up by some random guy and left to raise a child—'

She was interrupted by the sound of a side-plate smashing as Joanie hurled it to the floor.

For a moment they both stood in silence, catching their breath, surprised to find themselves panting. Joanie had never slapped Nnenna but this felt worse than slapping. Still unable to speak, they looked at the shards of china on the floor. *Is that what she wants to do to me?* they both thought. *Is that what she's trying to do to* me?

Hurried footsteps. A waiter, hovering again, a few steps away from the table this time, as though there were a poisonous animal by the centrepiece.

'Everything . . . all right?'

Nnenna looked to Joanie to explain, but she sat in silence, her eyes lowered, her arms folded as though she had given up.

'Yes,' said Nnenna, quickly. 'We're fine, thanks. I dropped a plate, that's all. Please could you bring another one?'

'Of course,' said the man, and he went off to fetch a dustpan and brush. He turned away before Nnenna could see his expression, but she guessed it. He knew what sort of family they were.

*

In Jonathan's flat, the phone rang. It was the only sound, echo-ing through the room. It was sparsely decorated; a few prints in small frames hung on the walls, mounted next to each other in pairs. He'd thought, at first, that he wanted to preserve lots of white space; then he realised that the pairs of small frames had the appearance of piggy eyes squinting at him like an unimpressed head teacher.

He'd been cooped up inside all day, unable to think of anything to do. When the phone rang, he let it echo for a few moments, enjoying the way the flat was filled with a sound he had not made himself.

'Hello? Oh, hi! Bronagh! How are you? Yeah? Oh, I bet. You must be absolutely exhausted. Everyone always says that having kids is so full on. I couldn't do it myself. I mean, I've tried, but the science just wasn't in my corner on that one. Mmm. Yeah. How old is Thomas now? Seven! Wow, it seems like yesterday that he was born ... Oh no, you're kidding! I thought this babysitter was pretty reliable? I guess not ... Well ... No, no, absolutely. I mean, I could drive to yours? It's not far. No, honestly, I don't mind! I'm dying to see you, that's all. It's been ages and I've got so much to ... Oh. Are you sure? It won't be a late one ... No, you're right. I understand. I under-stand. Yes. Yes. You and Harry should get an early night ... Yes. Yes. We'll meet up again before you know it. No, don't worry! Don't be daft! Yes, okay. You sleep well. Bye. Bye! Bye.'

Chapter 4

I slept, but my heart was awake.

Song of Solomon 5:2

The next day, on his lunch break, Jonathan found an empty meeting room, closed the door and took out his phone. After a lot of procrastination, he had gone to see a doctor to talk about his depression. The appointment had not been successful: he couldn't bring himself to admit that he had once tried to kill himself, and evidently the doctor could not bring himself to believe that someone who looked like Jonathan and sounded like Jonathan could have any serious problems. Jonathan felt an odd mixture of pride at this, and frustration that even though he had tried, his problems had not been addressed.

Still, the trip to the surgery was not a complete waste . . .

'Hello,' said his voice into the phone. It always sounded extra posh on the phone, even to him. 'Hellew thar, I'd like to meek an appointment with the practice narse.'

'Did the doctor ask you to book a blood test? Can I have your surname and date of birth, please?'

Oh no.

This was not the receptionist he was expecting. This one sounded . . . efficient. He sounded confident. He sounded like he knew what he was doing. Jonathan had banked on speaking to the flustered newbie he'd spoken to on his last visit to the surgery, not this revved-up detective with a thousand questions.

This would not be as easy as he had hoped. He felt a snow-flake of panic touch him.

'Er ... no. Not a blood test,' he managed to say.

'So – what did you want to see the nurse for?' His tone was almost-but-not-quite rude. Jonathan knew he was running out of time; realistically, he was only a few moments of dilly-dallying away from a curt remark and the flat rebuff of the dialling tone. This man wanted answers. But Jonathan's mind was getting cloudy with panic and he knew that he wasn't up to this. This kind of thing was meant for more experienced men; suave men. The kind of man who could boast confidence and charisma and (he suspected) the type of man who had never tried to kill himself.

Jonathan knew he ought to go home and forget all about his dizzying eye contact with the hunky nurse. But he had tried to forget, and it hadn't worked.

'I have a bit of a ... ' he racked his brains for a suitable ail-ment to pretend he had. What could he say? It had to strike the right balance: something innocuous enough to merit a visit to the practice nurse, but urgent enough to warrant an appoint-ment in the next day or so. Something like ... Something like ...

'... a sore heart.'

Hearing this, the receptionist audibly stopped shifting papers about on his desk for a short, important moment. Jonathan could hear the man's frown through the phone.

'You have a sore heart,' said the receptionist, both patron-ising and wary at the same time, as though he were speaking to a precocious child that had picked up a kitchen knife and was waving it about. 'And ... you're asking to see the prac-tice nurse?'

'No, that's not quite what I—'

'Sir. If you've got a sore heart, you should be ringing 999.'
Jonathan wasn't sure if the man was concerned for his health,
suspicious of his story, or baffled at the stupidity of a grown
man who, even in the throes of a heart attack, was capable of
wasting NHS time.

'Mmm?' said Jonathan, frantically trying to think. He
sounded distracted but hurried, as if he were waking up from
a vivid dream. It was rapidly becoming clear that his credibil-
ity was slipping away faster than a loosely tied hospital gown.
Perhaps, he thought optimistically, the receptionist might think
he was drunk, hang up the phone and put him out of his misery.

But he didn't. Instead, the receptionist waited calmly for an
explanation which, in fairness, he deserved.

'Mmm,' said Jonathan, his voice still sounding strange.
'No ... No, not a sore heart, that's not what I said. You must
have misheard me. I said I've got a sore, er ... a sore arm.'

The receptionist sighed heavily into the phone. Again,
Jonathan could not detect if it was relief or frustration, but
he had the dim and bizarre sense that a more professional
receptionist would have taken a sympathetic tone, even with
a fictional ailment of uncertain nature.

'Right, well. You'll need an appointment with a doctor,
then. I think Dr Fuller had a cancellation earlier this morning,
let me check ... Yes, she did. She can see you at four p.m. on
Thursday – will that do?'

She? thought Jonathan. No, that certainly will *not* do.

But maybe if he got an appointment with Dr Fuller, he could
find a way to see Nurse Barker while he was in the building ... ?

'You know what?' Jonathan said, his voice taking on an
incongruously bright tone, and making him sound a little maniacal – a little *more* maniacal. 'That sounds great,' he chimed,
as though he were signing up for a spa appointment or hearing
about the specials at a restaurant.

'Right, I'll book you in,' said the receptionist, becoming

brighter and less impatient now that things were proceeding as he would expect. 'The practice nurse mostly does vaccinations, blood tests, routine care, you see. The doctors do the consultations.'

'Absolutely, yes,' said Jonathan, not really listening. He was too relieved at the notion that he might – accidentally – walk into Nurse Barker's office on his way out of the practice and find him unoccupied, perhaps removing his latex gloves with a tiny, professional flourish ... Perhaps he would see his head turn to face his as the door opened, his startled, startling blue eyes wide, wider ...

'What time did you say the appointment was? I'll just check my diary.'

'It's four p.m. on Thursday.' Bloody man, thought Jonathan, does he have to say everything at breakneck speed? The other receptionist, the slow one, might have given Jonathan more time to think. This one gave him nothing, checked everything, followed procedure, asked too many questions and left him no space to hide, no time to wait and make sure that this was the right thing he was doing, after all. And the problem with thinking on the tips of your toes was that, at any moment, you could stumble, overbalance and fall flat on your face.

Jonathan held his diary up to the handset and flicked noisily through it for effect. 'Ah yes! I think I am free on Thursday. Put me down for an appointment with Dr Fuller. That sounds great.'

If the receptionist thought Jonathan sounded unusually happy to see the laziest, most emotionless member of their medical staff; if Jonathan sounded as though he were having a different conversation from the one the receptionist was having; if he sounded as if he were organising a seaweed wrap rather than a doctor's appointment, then he obviously had more important things to do than mention it.

'Ah!' cried Jonathan. 'I think – what a coincidence – I

think it's Nurse Barker's birthday on Thursday. According to my diary. He's a friend, you see. Yes. Er – we'll be going out for drinks later – just like last year – but – er – will he be in? For me to wish him a Happy Birthday? On Thursday? Do you know?'

'Nurse Barker's no longer working here,' said the receptionist, flatly ignoring all four of Jonathan's questions which, he realised, had been squawked at the pitch of a field mouse on helium. 'Can I take your name, sir?' His voice began to take on a testier tone again, as Jonathan wandered off the beaten track.

He hung up. Almost before he knew what he was doing, he'd put the phone down, leaving his arm sore from being on the phone so long; and his heart.

After a moment, he picked up his phone again: Joanie was calling.

'Jonathan! Hi, how are you doing? I'm not disturbing you, am I?'

'No, no. I'm working from home today, sitting at the computer, doing a bit of . . . self-admin.'

'How's Manchester treating you so far?'

'It won't treat me at all,' muttered Jonathan. 'Won't even give me an appointment.'

'What was that? Couldn't hear you.'

'Nothing, sorry. I was reading out something from the screen . . . '

'Are you getting out? Have you made friends?'

'Well not yet, Miss Maloney, but maybe at break time, I'll—'

'Very funny. I'm actually calling to ask a favour, but I think it might help you, too.'

'Oh?'

'I've got this work dinner for the newspaper tonight and everybody's bringing someone – they're all married at the office, or with someone. I hate networking and I'm only going so I can talk to my boss about my writing, but he's a bit nosy about my private life and I can't talk to him about my work if he's trying to fix me up with some friend. Would you go with me? I hate to ask, but I think it could really make a difference ... What do you think? Will you go?'

'I don't know, Joanie. I won't know anyone. And I'm not massively keen on pretending to be straight for a night,' said Jonathan, wearily. He had accompanied single white women friends to parties a few times in his early twenties and he knew exactly how the evening would go: nosy, unhappily married journalists with barely concealed suspicions of prostitution would ask provokingly intruding questions about where Joanie had met this young black man, what kind of things she did with this young black man, whether he knew any other young black men who were looking ...

'I can't see myself having a *great* time,' he said.

'They're nice people, Jonathan. And it won't be a long evening. Just long enough to talk to my editor about what I want to write for the newspaper, and then I'll make our excuses and you and I can go back to my house and catch up. I promise.'

'Well ... '

'I'll love you forever?'

'All right. But only because I have absolutely no other plans and nobody else to spend time with. And I'm a truly selfless person.'

Nnenna was lucky enough to live within walking distance of her school. Sometimes, she fell in with a friend on the way, but today, walking home, she didn't want to. She wanted to be alone so that she could think freely for the first time about Paris. Later she would send breathless, excited messages to her best friend Stephanie (Nnenna had told her as soon as Mr Black had first suggested the idea, of course, but she needed to be

updated). But for now, she wanted to indulge herself, to wrap herself up warm in the thought of being young and in Paris ...
Paris.

Her imaginings of it were vague (she had only been once before; her mother's salary being unable to extend to holidays each year) but passionate. It did not even occur to her to imagine that she wouldn't love every moment. Paris! Her mind saw a kaleidoscope of images of herself: riding around the city on a bicycle; sporting a beret; flirting in advanced French with attractive young French men; flirting in advanced French with attractive young French men while wearing a beret; leisurely attending a couple of morning lectures before meeting her sophisticated friends for red wine at midday ...

It would be perfect. In her mind, going to university in Paris would whisk away everything in her life that was mundane or awkward or incomplete, and turn it into something sleek and extraordinary. If – *if* – she decided to come back to England after graduation she could explain to new friends, at sleek and extraordinary dinner parties, that she had studied at the Sorbonne; and that this was where she had learned the secret of how to stay enviably thin while dining exclusively on pastries and cheese; and that this was where she'd met her husband. Alphonse? Edouard? Philippe? She could decide the details later. Alexandre? Antoine? Jean-Baptiste?

Danny?

She realised only now that absolutely nowhere in her imaginings was her boyfriend of one year. Until her mother brought him up, she hadn't even thought about him.

She felt a pang of guilt and tried to imagine him in Paris with her; but her life with Danny flashed before her eyes, and she didn't like it. Dashing Parisian men shrugged disappointedly because Danny was the boyfriend they'd always hoped she would not have, and they walked resignedly away. Danny wouldn't drink red wine with her because it was too feminine and holding those delicate glasses made him feel 'vulnerable', so he'd neck lager instead and make fun of the names on the bottles she'd collect on her windowsills. He would never be able to go to lectures with her because he wasn't sure that he wanted to go to university at all – resented the assumption that he would – wanted to be a footballer. Could he try out for French teams? Of course, but he wouldn't want to live in France with her; he hated languages, couldn't get his head around them.

There was no way. No way he would live with her in Paris; no way he could be happy if he did. She could try and help him have some fun – take him to see films with her, with subtitles in English – but he'd never appreciate it. He'd pretend not to care, but he'd be resentful of her. He'd be so busy pretending that he wouldn't, couldn't for a moment enjoy Paris the way she would. He could never live there; he could never really *live* there.

A moment ago, Nnenna hadn't fully realised she was going anywhere at all. Now, she seemed to be hurtling away from everyone and everything she knew.

She got home and went up to her room, but as soon as she sat down on her bed, the phone rang. She ignored it, deep in her own thoughts. It rang again. She ignored it again, preferring to sit somewhere between sadness and sulking. She felt a bit guilty for making her mother get it, but then none of Nnenna's friends used the landline.

'Nnenna?' Joanie's voice sailed through from her room.

'Yeah?'

'It's your Aunty Mary. She wants to speak to you.'

'What's she calling about?'

'How should I know? Pick up the phone!'

Nnenna got up and walked to the small desk in her room, where the telephone was. 'Hello?'

'Nnenna! How are you?'

'Hi, Aunty Mary! I'm fine, thank you. How are you? Sorry? I can't ... Sorry, Aunty Mary, could you say that again? Hello? Hello? I think this is a bad line. Are you calling from your mobile?'

1992

'Hello? Hello? I think this is a bad line, Aunty.'

'Maurice,' said Joanie from the sofa, 'why don't you put the phone down and then try again?'

'Hello? Hello?'

'Maurice?'

Joanie was at Maurice's flat for the evening; the plan had been to make dinner and then go out to the cinema, but Maurice's phone had rung almost as soon as she arrived, so when she realised it was his family calling, she sat and waited for the phone call to end.

Joanie did not know anybody in Nigeria, so she had never experienced first-hand the joys of a phone call to Nigeria from the UK: the crackly static; both people shouting so loud that what little of the conversation could be heard between them was heard for miles around; the three-second delay that made it sound like even your most exciting news was greeted with stony silence; the moments of *actual* silence that dogged each conversation like a slow, irregular pulse.

Naively, she thought that these problems could be solved by simply hanging up the phone and trying again. Maurice closed his eyes and shook his head to signal that this was definitely not the case.

'Aunty, what did Dad tell you? Aunty, please! Slow down!'

The static began to clear and her voice became audible, even to Joanie. She watched his face change, as trouble registered from the other end of the line. She mouthed the words, 'What's wrong?' But he only closed his eyes again and shook his head.

'Aunty ... You know I have to decide this for myself. I can't keep it up if ... Yes. Yes, I know. No, I'm not. No, that's not fair. I just .... Aunty, please, don't get so ... Joanie? Joanie – could you just give me a second, I just need to ... Yeah, thanks. Close the door? Thanks.'

On the other side of the door, Joanie stood in stunned silence as the phone call continued. She tried to listen, but Maurice was speaking rapid Igbo with only a few English words scattered amongst it, and she could not understand what he was saying. He was angry and scared, and it was nearly forty-five minutes before the phone call ended and Maurice emerged, his face drawn and anger sitting in his eyes like a dark cloud.

'Maurice? I ... What's wrong? Is there anything I can do?'

He laughed bitterly, closed his eyes and shook his head.

2009

The foyer of the Grand Northern Hotel was about as intimidating a structure as Manchester boasts. Awash with gold filigree inlay and polished marble, it was a Victorian architect's wet dream. Its every stone, every tile, sang sweet songs of prosperity in the Industrial Revolution. It was precisely the kind of place where you could imagine men in top hats and women in bustles. It was the kind of place where, a couple of hundred years ago, a gentleman might have come to have his moustache twirled professionally before that all-important meeting with the candlestick-maker. Or, if you were Jonathan, it was the kind of place that made you wish you'd worn smarter shoes.

'The invitation said "smart casual",' he said woefully to

Joanie, whose hair was carefully arranged in ringlets, her patent leather shoes shining in the lobby's evening light, her green silk jumpsuit perfectly complementing her bracelet and earrings. He had seen fit to pair chinos and trainers with a floral-print shirt whose top button was dangling perilously from its place. He was going to get it sewn on firmly the minute he found the time ...

'Well, I suppose that can be a bit of a confusing instruction,' she said. She had wanted to sound forgiving but she came off a bit like a nursing-home orderly who'd just seen an elderly patient wet the bed. 'And I'm sure nobody will notice – they're all nice enough people.'

'Nice enough? You said they were nice, before. Now they're nice *enough*?'

'Oh relax, nobody cares. And you look great. People will probably just be surprised I managed to scrape together a date for the evening. And thank you again for doing this, by the way,' she said, laying a hand on his arm. 'I do appreciate it. It sounds so silly saying this in the twenty-first century but I know this editor and, believe it or not, the conversation will be much easier if he thinks I'm not single.'

'Won't he want to know who I am?'

'We can cross that bridge when we come to it.'

'But—'

'Marco! Hi!'

Joanie took her hand from Jonathan's arm and embraced a man in a crisp white shirt, brown brogues and a dark blue suit that looked carefully tailored. From a couple of feet away, Jonathan could smell his cologne, mixing rapidly with the smell of his own nervous perspiration.

'*Great* to see you, Joanie,' said Marco enthusiastically. 'And,' he said, his eyes sliding over to Jonathan with a naked curiosity that made him sweat even harder, 'who's this? Is this the elusive father of your offspring?'

'Ah – no. This is Jonathan.'

'Hello, Jonathan!' said Marco approvingly, slowly pronouncing every syllable of his name as though it were the model of an exciting new car.

'Nice to meet you,' said Jonathan.

'*Very* nice to meet *you*,' beamed Marco.

'And Cal?' said Joanie, by way of a distraction. 'Is he inside already?'

'Oh,' said Marco, rolling his eyes, 'no, he can't make it.'

'Oh. I'm sorry. He's not sick, I hope?'

'No, no, just bad timing – he's got another dinner. A birthday.'

'A friend's?'

'His,' said Marco, airily. 'I'm bringing a friend to take his place at the dinner table.'

'Oh.'

'Anyway, I'm off to spend a penny. Shall I see you inside?'

'See you inside,' said Joanie. 'And, actually, I'd love to talk to you about my—'

But he had already made his way across the foyer to the toilet, leaving behind a cloud of expensive cologne. Jonathan's face asked the question which Joanie answered with,

'Sorry. I promise we'll be done by nine.'

In the bar, Joanie bought Jonathan a drink to apologise.

'I'm so sorry, I didn't realise he'd be like that.'

'Isn't he normally?'

Joanie's brow furrowed in concentration. 'I suppose he is. I must be used to it by now. I've been working there so long, I almost don't notice any more. If it makes you feel any better, he's more or less the same with me.'

'You know what he's thinking, don't you?'

'What do you mean?'

'First Maurice, now me? I think he thinks you have a thing for black men.'

'Oh God, you're right. I never thought about that.'

'Well, obviously after Maurice left, you must have had a black hole in your life, literally. So you went out and got a replacement for Maurice.'

'Like the pet hamster I got for Nnenna when the old one died. I'm so sorry. I'll try to keep you away from him. I'll still have to try and talk to him about my work, but I'll make sure he steers clear. And then this evening will be you and—'

Jonathan smelled Marco before he saw him. 'There you are!' he crooned, a pint of beer in his hand. Behind him stood a taller man, also white, with dark, sharp features. He said nothing, but held a Bloody Mary lightly in his hands. He looked carefully at Joanie, almost uncomfortably closely, as though he were going to sketch her.

'This is Silas,' said Marco. 'The friend I mentioned. Silas, this is my colleague, Joanie, and her ... guest, Jonathan.'

'So nice to meet you,' said Joanie.

'Have you come far for this evening?' asked Jonathan.

'No,' said Silas. Joanie and Jonathan waited a moment for him to elaborate. Eventually, he didn't.

'He works here, actually,' said Marco. 'He's the head chef.'

'Gosh,' said Jonathan. 'Busy night for you, then! You'll be shuttling back and forth between the table and the kitchen!'

Silas smiled sadly at Jonathan as though the bad joke he had told was a dead rat that had fallen out of his mouth and onto the floor between them.

Marco laughed awkwardly. 'Shall we go through to the restaurant? I think they're ready for us, now.'

Joanie walked over with Marco, leaving Silas and Jonathan to walk behind them. Either by habit or by design, Silas walked very slowly, making Jonathan feel like a primary school teacher on a walk with a six-year-old.

'So what's on the menu?' he asked, trying to keep his voice bright. He had little desire to talk to this surly man, but the alternative (being talked to by Marco) was even less appealing.

Silas shrugged. 'I imagine they put ... words ... on the menu.'

'Doesn't sound very filling!' said Jonathan, regretting his joke as soon as he said it. He glanced over at Silas and saw that he had regretted it sooner. He looked over at Joanie, who had taken her seat by Marco, a few seats down the table. She was busily trying to tell him about her idea for an article on single-parenthood in a mixed-race family; Marco was busily inspecting the menu.

The starters and mains came and went, and conversation bubbled and simmered along the table. For a long time, Silas said nothing, and Jonathan's neighbour on his other side was deep in conversation with her wife, next to her. Jonathan wondered again why he had bothered to come in the first place, but then contemplated the alternative: another evening spent at home, alone, no friends, only the television for company. At first, he had thought he was hibernating, recovering from the stress of moving home and moving cities, allowing himself to unwind at the end of each busy day at work. But increasingly, hibernation felt more like hiding and the thought of going out and making friends only got harder the longer he left it. The idea of joining a club ... What if people didn't like him? What if—

'Your shoes,' said Silas, suddenly. He was wiping his expressionless mouth and staring down at Jonathan's feet underneath the table.

'Thanks,' said Jonathan, nervously.

'For what?'

'Sorry. Never mind.'

'You don't seem very comfortable,' said Silas.

'What do you mean?'

'You've hardly said anything all evening. And the things you have said have been a little ... awkward.'

'Are you always so complimentary to strangers?'

'I try to be myself,' Silas said. He gave Jonathan a long, meaningful look that Jonathan didn't quite know how to answer.

'I feel as though you're trying to tell me something,' he said, eventually.

Silas leaned to the side as a waiter placed his dessert on the table in front of him. Not waiting for Jonathan's food to arrive, he took up his knife and fork and started eating. Unhurriedly, as though he could simply set down his conversation with Jonathan, and then pick it back up again when he was ready to do so. Slowly, he chewed a few mouthfuls before he spoke and while he did, Jonathan took in his appearance for the first time. He was handsome. Much more so than Marco, who was striking at first but unremarkable upon a second glance. Looking at Silas now, Jonathan wondered if there was something he had overlooked when they'd met earlier on. If, perhaps, there was something more, waiting under his cool exterior, if only the right person could uncover it.

His dessert arrived and he started on it thoughtfully.

'I'm sure it's fine, what you're doing,' said Silas. 'I suppose I was just a little surprised to see a gay man pretending to be straight, at this point in history. Although I'm told it's quite common among black men.'

Jonathan was too stunned to respond to this and had almost made up his mind not to speak to Silas again, when Silas got up to use the toilet. As he did so, he laid a hand on Jonathan's shoulder. It was partly to support his weight as he stood but also, surely, partly ... affection? It was electrifying, and for several moments afterwards, the spot where Silas's hand had been seemed to pulse of its own accord, as though Silas had left life, a living thing where he had touched him. And a thought flowered in Jonathan's mind: that, even in the deep warrens of his loneliness, someone had seen him, even if only a part of him.

He waited patiently for Silas to come back.

*

In the lobby after the dinner, Joanie apologised and apologised.

'I'm so sorry to do this, Jonathan – you don't hate me, do you? I only wish the dinner hadn't gone on so long – we would have had more time, but now I've got to catch my bus or I'll be late.'

'Don't worry about it. Honestly.' He was still holding a napkin from the dinner, as though it were some kind of precious souvenir from a much more enjoyable experience. 'You're not driving?'

'I took the bus. I had a feeling I might need a couple of drinks to get through the evening. Look, I feel terrible, but I'll make it up to you. We'll hang out, properly. I promise. I'm not neglecting you.'

'I know,' Jonathan said. 'Don't worry, it's fine. Did you get to talk to Marco about your article?'

'I did, but I don't think he took it in. He seemed pretty determined to talk about almost anything else. I don't think he takes me very seriously at all.' Her face fell. 'And I don't know how to *be* any more serious than I am. What do I do? What do I change?'

'It's not you. Believe me, I've been through similar stuff at work, and it's not you. And maybe he'll come around, you never know. Things change.'

'Oh, I don't know. I was really hoping he would think my idea was worthwhile. I was counting on it, to be honest. I've been wanting to write more long-form articles for ages now, and God knows this crossword work doesn't pay much, even with the other things I do to supplement it. And Nnenna's going off to university soon, and I want to be able to support her, and I want her to be able to look up to me and be proud of me, not feel like she's left silly old mum behind doing crosswords.'

'Joanie,' said Jonathan, putting an arm around her shoulder. 'Come on now. I'm sure Nnenna's proud of you, whatever job you're doing. And your time will come. I'm sure you'll find something. You're so smart. It's only a matter of time, I promise you.'

'Thank you, Jonathan. You're a very kind man, d'you know that?' She sniffled. Both of them had the vague sense that this lobby wasn't the kind of place you were supposed to cry in. 'Oh God, I really must go and catch my bus. I'll text you, okay? We'll hang out.'

'Okay. I'll see you soon. And keep your chin up.'

'Thank you!'

She ran a few steps towards the door and then turned towards him. 'I almost forgot – was Silas okay? He didn't look very friendly, did he? Was he as bad as he seemed?'

'Oh. Ahh ... yeah,' Jonathan laughed quietly. He played with his napkin. 'He gave me his number.'

Chapter 5

1992

Kissing Maurice was not like kissing any of the other boys
Joanie had met. It wasn't just that the others were absolutely
terrible kissers and Maurice wasn't (although that was true).
Cliff pecked at her with small, quick, darting kisses, like a
pigeon picking at breadcrumbs; her lips were sore afterwards.
Smelly Roderick had actually transferred plaque from his
mouth to hers. Maurice, on the other hand, kissed her as
though he were kissing another person who wanted to be
kissed, and who was kissing him back; his kisses were long and
slow and generous.

But it was more than that. She had never experienced a desire
like this, even as a teenager. It was like nothing she'd ever wanted
before: even when she wasn't kissing him, she thought about it
all the time. But somehow she could never reproduce the actual
experience of it in her mind in any detail. It was as though
something in her refused to contemplate an experience so pure
in abstract; as though she could not allow herself to enjoy it in
any diminished way because that might cheapen the real thing.

At their most specific, her fantasies of Maurice revolved around what she knew about him, what she could remember from that afternoon, after they had left the café to find another, less crowded one: his kindness; the smile that never seemed to leave his face; his eyes that seemed so dark but, when she looked closely enough, were a soft brown. His soft hands that seemed strong, and his large shoulders. The smell of soap on his skin.

And yet at first, she had almost regretted agreeing to go on a date with him at all: once she got home and the spell of him wore off, she worried that he was too serious, too severe. He was a Christian – a Christian! And he was the worst kind – an evangelical. Were those men in the café really his friends? Would they have to be her friends? Would they ever be able to relax around one another if he knew that she would never be a Christian?

Her Cambridge friends buzzed with polite middle-class excitement at the idea of her going on a date with a man whose skin was *brown*. They weighed up the idea of making jokes about Joanie being unable to get back on her bicycle after a date with a black man, and prudently decided it was better to drop more general hints about the protuberance of a phallus into her otherwise unphallic life. Ophelia left cucumbers in her cupboards; Cressida threw phallic vegetables at her door in the early evenings and ran away, giggling.

But when she got to the restaurant on King's Parade that night; when she was with him ... She realised suddenly why people so carefully avoid those they know they might regret falling in love with, those whose faith or family prohibited a lover of the same gender or a different faith. It was because there's no stopping it, once it starts. Right or wrong, practicable or wholly impossible ... She did not and could not care.

They ate their meal as though under some strange kind of hypnosis, all talk one moment, silent in wonder the next. He offered to pay for the meal but she, forcing herself to forget her yawning overdraft, refused. He took her for ice-cream afterwards, and then they sat on the wall outside King's College, and they talked, and they kissed. Kissing him, because it was real, was even better than she had imagined.

'You're a very nice man,' she said, because it was all that she could think of to say afterwards, and she wanted to break the silence that had started as intimate and was growing into something she could not name. But he only laughed and said,

'Are you surprised?'

'Well, when I met your friends ...'

'Yes, they're odd. But they're good people, I think. Jonathan's confused. But most people are.'

'You think?'

'Yes. Sometimes we know about it at the time, and sometimes we don't realise until much later. Jonathan doesn't know.'

'Have you ever been confused?'

He laughed his large laugh again. 'Not like that, no.'

'But about other things?'

'Absolutely.'

'Like what?'

'Living here, in England. I still am, sometimes.'

'Why? You seem to be doing pretty well for yourself, Maurice.'

He laughed again, but this time it was quiet, and almost rueful. 'I seem like a lot of things, I think. You know, Maurice isn't even my name.'

Joanie stared at him. 'But everyone calls you Maurice. It's what you told me to call you.'

'I know, but it's not my name. Not my first name, anyway. It's my middle name. When I moved to England, I decided to use my English name. I think I thought it would help me fit in better.'

'And did it?'

Maurice shook his head. 'The opposite. Most of the time, it only makes people stare at me even more, as though I have no right to an English name, as though I must have stolen it from someone. As though, somewhere in Cambridge there's a confused old white man walking around wondering why he's called *Chinedu* now.'

'Chinedu . . . ' said Joanie, as though trying it out on him.

He smiled at her wryly. 'You can ask, you know.'

'What does it mean?'

'What does *your* name mean?'

'I asked you first! And I . . . don't know. Nobody's ever asked me that before, and I never asked, myself. I suppose I always assumed I was named after Joan of Arc, but saying it out loud, it seems silly.'

'Why silly?'

'Because I'm nothing like her. I think my mum wants me to be like her, though.'

'You're not all that different. I'd say you're pretty determined. I heard what happened with your uni supervisor, you know. I'm impressed you're still here.'

'Well, thank you,' said Joanie. She smiled. 'But to be honest . . . most of the time I feel like I'm hanging on by my fingertips, here. And my mum . . . she doesn't only want me to be brave, she wants me to be the bravest. Not just clever but the cleverest.'

'And what do you want?'

Joanie let her legs swing back and forth. She shook her head and shrugged. 'If I ever figure it out, I'll let you know. I want to know what your name means, though. I did ask first.'

'Ah, you've got me. Chinedu means "God leads". Although where God is leading me . . . I do not know.'

Joanie was silent for a moment, before she asked, 'Do you think Jonathan will be okay?'

'I do. I had a friend like him, once, who was confused like him. Or rather, afraid.'

'What happened to him?'

'He struggled for some years while we were growing up. Nowadays, he's happy, though. He's living the Nigerian dream, in fact.'

'And what's the Nigerian dream?'

'He's a medical doctor. Married to a woman.'

'And is he happy?'

'I haven't seen him in a long time. I pray he is, but ... '

'I don't think that's Jonathan's dream. I think Jonathan wants—'

'Alastair.'

'Yes.'

'Or I think perhaps Jonathan wants a kind of peace. And I think he thinks he'll only find it with Alastair.'

'And do you think they'll get together?'

Maurice sighed. 'They're already as together as they'll ever be.'

'And how together is that?'

'Well, Jonathan is in love, and he believes Alastair is. Alastair, however, is very much in love with someone else, who loves him back.'

'Oh ... Oh?'

'Yes. Alastair doesn't help things, I'm afraid; he's one of those people who wants everyone to love him, so he'll never tell Jonathan he's not got a chance. And the sad thing is, I think Jonathan probably knows this already. But he doesn't want to admit it to himself.'

Joanie looked at Maurice for a long moment; he was looking out onto the street, where people walked slowly past King's College as the sun set on the beautiful little town.

'Is Jonathan a very close friend?'

'Hmm? No, not really.'

'You seem to know a lot about him. How he's feeling.'

'I suppose I understand some things about him, in a way. I thought ... ' He paused for a moment, as though sharing something so intimate could not be done fluently, but reverently, and with hesitation. 'I used to think that coming to study here, to Cambridge, would give me something I wanted. Knowledge, maybe; certainty about the world.'

'About God?'

Maurice nodded slowly; she could tell from his face that he was unsure how she knew to ask that. 'I think I used to think that somehow, if I left my home and came somewhere so different, I might find him here. That I might find him in the difference.'

'Do you think he's real?'

Maurice laughed a slightly bitter laugh. 'You make him sound like an imaginary friend. You make him sound silly, like I made him up as a child.'

'Isn't that what you're afraid of?'

Maurice looked at her sharply, then nodded and looked away.

If someone were to ask her to identify a particular part of Maurice's character, a specific *thing* that she had fallen in love with, she would have been unable to do so. It was his large ears that she loved, every bit as much as his big laugh; his gait, just as much as his heart. It occurred to her that if, for some reason, she had to give up any part of him, she would be unable to surrender even the smallest thing. She knew, then, that loves like theirs were formed in just as complicated a manner as they were torn suddenly apart.

2009

Maurice's love for her cast long shadows into her life, even now. The heat of him had gone cold on her in their seventeen years apart, as other things in her life had cooled and gone hard. For the most part, she thought of her life as mundane, ordinary: good enough, just about.

A few days after Parents' Evening, Joanie went into her bedroom and noticed that yet another troop of moths had arrived to nibble through all the clothes she could not afford to replace, and torment her with their dizzyingly evasive circles of flight. Cedar never seemed to deter them.

She killed them quickly and without hesitation, and then she remembered that the guilt always comes afterwards, not before. She imagined the inner lives of the moths that she had not crushed between wads of tissue paper. Did they miss their recently dead friends? Had she been eating into the family of one lone remaining moth? A child-moth? Would it now be an orphan, forced to survive without its parents and wander through the world alone? She paused for a moment to consider this properly. Did moths mate for life? Why did she never see two parent moths with a baby moth? Were their young made to be independent as soon as they were born?

She squashed another one between thumb and forefinger,

forgoing the nicety of tissues, in order to catch this one before it fled. She went to the bathroom to wash off its corpse – would its family smell the dead body?

When she came back to her room, Nnenna was there, sitting on her bed, waiting.

'There's a coffee stain on your duvet cover, Mum,' she said.

Joanie cocked her head at Nnenna and considered her words carefully before replying. Ten years ago, her daughter might have sat in silence, staring at her feet, or even cried; now she criticised. Nnenna, a teenager, was somehow more inept at communicating than when she had been a toddler. Years ago, she might have simply given her mother a hug; now she gave her unsolicited advice about the laundry.

Joanie cocked her head the other way, her gaze still intent. Motherhood was a funny thing. She'd only spilled the coffee there this morning while getting dressed. If anybody else – a friend, say – had walked into her bedroom and, without apology or introduction, pointed out that she needed to change the bedspread, she would have made an excuse or a joke, perhaps changed the subject. And yet because Nnenna was Nnenna – because they had lived together for sixteen years; because Nnenna was under her care, because she loved her child – she took a deep breath and said, calmly,

'Well, my dear, it's a funny thing – I was *just* about to change the cover when my beloved child trudged in and started running her mouth off, as per usual.' And she thought about how odd love is; how strangely it treats us, how sometimes it makes us reserve even slight impatience for those we love the most.

Nnenna smiled, but vaguely, as though she was remembering a joke that someone had told her years ago.

'I'm not even seventeen yet, Mum,' she said quietly. She put an arm around her mother; it was easy, now. Joanie had changed again; her mother was back. She had missed her.

'I know, sweetheart.'

'And I know it's all a bit sudden. But it is supposed to be good news.'

'I know. I know.'

What did that mean? Had Joanie given permission? Was she angry again? Nnenna searched her mother's face, but she saw nothing. She was so, so tired.

'Anyway, what about your birthday? Not long, now. Have you thought more about what you want?'

'I think I'd like a new dress.'

'Ahhhh. Which dress? Have you found one?'

Nnenna shook her head and smoothed down the fabric of the duvet cover. She obviously wanted to go to bed now, but she wasn't going.

'What's up?' said Joanie, but she knew. She knew that there was something that Nnenna wanted to say but could not. And she knew that if she were a kinder person, a stronger person, she would let her say it, let her ask. But she was not stronger, or kinder, or braver. She would start no revolution tonight; she could free no captive soul. She was not Joan; she was only Joanie.

She hoped that, maybe, Nnenna would see that she cared; that even this disappointment was her best effort, the most that she could do.

In her mind, Nnenna considered the possibilities: yes, she knew that she could never ask her mother why she had never met her father, or why her parents broke up, or where her father was now. She was old enough to recognise that she and her mother had a kind of unspoken understanding which meant that Nnenna could ask her mother about *something* (it hardly mattered what) and they would both know that Nnenna wanted to ask about Something Else. It was like an elaborate, futile game of charades, in which both of them already knew the answers but still carried on making ridiculous gestures at each other.

Nnenna quickly examined each of the things that might possibly be concerning her at the moment and filtered out those which would not meet with her mother's approval. She had learned that this was a delicate process with high stakes: succeed, and she could remind her mother that the question of what had happened to her father was still, always, on her mind; if she were to fail, her mother would race off in the wrong direction, forcing them both to have an uncomfortable and unnecessary conversation about personal hygiene, peer pressure, drugs or – the worst of the worst – sex. Once, Nnenna had come into her mother's room and made a passing joke about how Joanie always bulk-bought tampons, filling her cupboards with them in inordinate quantities, as though some sort of natural disaster were imminent in which sanitary products would be the first casualty. The next thing Nnenna knew, she was being cross-examined like a key witness in a murder trial – when was the last time she'd had her period? Were she and Dan having sex? Did she feel nauseous? (Yes.) What, currently, was the size of her chest, *as measured in centimetres and grams*?

Et cetera, et cetera. Nnenna knew that she could not say what she wanted to say. It was too enormous. But she had to say *something*, or she would explode. And what would be so wrong about talking about this? She knew her mother didn't want her to go, and she also knew that her mother wasn't entirely sold on Danny. Telling her that she was afraid that he would never go with her to a university in another country might make them both feel better.

So, when her mother asked, 'Is it Dan?' she took a deep breath, and said,

'Yes. Sort of. Yes.'

'You're joking.'

'I'm not joking.'

'Wow. I mean I guess I shouldn't be that surprised, we've known him long enough. But seriously? *Your* mum?'

Nnenna shrugged. 'My mum. If I'd thought to make a recording of her forbidding me to have sex with my boyfriend, I'd be playing it back to you now.'

Joanie was strict about some things – manners, homework, takeaways on the first Sunday of every month – but this was totally unlike her. For one thing, Joanie had never told Nnenna to break up with Danny; in fact, she still seemed bizarrely keen on him. She just definitely didn't want Nnenna to have his children. Ever. She'd been quite clear on that point, actually.

Nnenna saw Steph the next day at school and told her straight away. Talking to her friend felt self-indulgent, sometimes; she felt like a burden. But she did it anyway, because it felt good to be able to say certain things out loud.

'Well . . . did she write it down?' said Steph.

'Did she write what down?'

'The forbidding?'

'Jesus, no. Of course not. It wasn't a board meeting, Steph.'

'Well, I wouldn't put it past your mum. Last week you told me she used the words "vaginal discharge".'

'Okay, right, yeah, I take your point. But no, she didn't write anything down.'

'Well then, I say you're good to go. Get those boots a-knockin', girl.'

'What?'

'Come on. I'm not saying you have to marry him, but don't tell me you don't want to do it twice as much, now you know you're not allowed to.'

'I . . . might do. I don't know. I don't know. Is that how it works?'

'Yes. Don't act coy.'

'I'm not acting coy. I'm just not sure if I want to.'

'You haven't *thought* about it?'

'Well obviously I've *thought* about it, but ... It's such a big thing, you know? What if everything's different afterwards?'

Steph laughed. 'Of *course* everything's different afterwards! Colours are brighter, the air smells sweeter ... '

'Yeah and I won't be able to sit down for two days. You know it hurts.'

'Only the first time. After that, you and Dan will be doing it all over the shop.'

'Nobody says "doing it" any more. And we're not going to be having sex all over anywhere.'

'You say that, but you're seeing him on Saturday?'

'Yep.'

'You think you might deflower him then?'

'I ... I don't know. I'm not sure I want to. I'm not sure I want to, yet. And I'm a bit grossed out by "deflower". Do you talk about everyone's sex lives like this? Or just mine?'

'Everyone's,' she said with relish. Nnenna looked at her for a long moment, and then Steph said, 'My mum's not like yours. Sex is a bit of a non-topic in our family. I'm not even sure my parents ever *had* sex – I don't think they're allowed to. I think someone forbade them. I'm pretty sure my dad stole me from a maternity ward one day when nobody was looking. Come on – you've met him.'

'Mmm. Fair enough.'

'And with you and Dan ... I guess it just feels like the two of you don't have to deal with any of that.'

'Are you ... jealous?'

Stephanie didn't say anything for a moment. 'Sometimes. A bit.'

'You don't need to be.'

'I am excited for you, you know. Danny ... I dunno. But I am, for you. So, if I'm being gross, I guess I'm just excited for you. But not sexually.'

'Glad to hear it.'

'Well then, I look forward to hearing a very brief and vague outline of what happens next.'

'I'll keep you posted.'

'So, what else did your mum say?'

'She said that she knew we loved each other and—'

'How did she know that?'

'I told her. You know what she's like, normally. Most of the time, I can just tell her stuff. Is that ... weird?'

'Yes.'

There was a look on Steph's face that Nnenna couldn't read, before Steph shook her head and said, 'You just ... God, you don't know you're born. I can't talk to my mum about *anything*. If I even said anything that *rhymes* with "sex" she'd start showing me brochures for nunneries.'

'Do nunneries have brochures?'

'Nnenna.'

'And what are you saying that rhymes with "sex"?'

'Nnenna.'

'Pecs?'

'Stop it.'

'Annex?'

'All right.'

'Quebec's?'

'*Nnenna.*'

'Sorry.'

'I just ... I just wish I could talk to my mum about the big things.'

'Me too.'

Why, Nnenna wondered, did everything have to be this way? Shouldn't there be some things, like family, that just *worked*? Why did everything have to be near misses and making do, even with the people you loved and relied on the most? Everybody was always somehow incomplete, and it was like some sort of inheritance that you passed on, like some disease, everyone's mistakes impacting everyone else.

'Still not asked about your dad, eh?' (Steph made the concerned, slightly apologetic face of someone who cares deeply but is ultimately powerless to help.)

'I can't seem to get the words out. I don't know what's wrong with me.' Talking to Steph about it still seemed wrong, as though there were an ongoing investigation and some terrible secret might yet come to light. 'Sometimes I just wish she'd tell me about him.'

'Like where he is now, you mean?'

'Maybe. Is that too much to ask? I wish she'd tell me *something*. Even something small, like his mum's name, or how they met, or the town he comes from. She never tells me anything. And then I feel so dumb for even asking.'

'You're not dumb. But ... '

'But what?'

'What if it's something awful, and that's why she doesn't want to tell you?'

'What if it is? I think I'm old enough to handle it, now. Whatever it is, isn't it better for me to know?'

'Well,' said Steph, cheerfully putting her arm around Nnenna's neck. 'Until we're proven wrong, let's just stick to our working theory.'

'Billionaire scientist stuck on a desert island.'

'*Mad* billionaire scientist stuck on a desert island. And I wonder what *he'd* think of your boyfriend?'

'Hi, Silas, how are you? It's Jonathan. Jonathan Tucker. The guy from the dinner ... yeah, yeah, exactly. The black one. No, er ... that's not me. I'm from Edinburgh. I mean, I've spent the last few years living in – yep, sure, I'll take my shoes off.

'I'm not late, am I? Oh, great! Congratulations. So glad you're ... Absolutely! You *should* have some people over, you should celebrate! No, I wouldn't expect to be invited. It's your party, and the two of us are only ... I've got things to do this evening, anyway. Got some friends coming over for a ...

'Hey, that smells lovely. What are you making? Is it ... What, right here? Okay, just let me take off my ... Damn, they're stuck. Stupid skinny fit. Could you give me a hand? No, absolutely, you're busy with. That. Sorry. Yes, you're right, I shouldn't talk so much. Spoils the mood, doesn't it? I think I'm a bit nervous. I should stop yammering on, shouldn't I? All this talking, it spoils the mood, doesn't it? I've got to admit, I'm nervous! I already said that, didn't I? Do you ever get nervous?

'What, like this? With my leg ... here? Sure, whatever. It'll be a bit painful, but I think I can manage ... Yep. Got it. We can start, now, if you—

'Ow. Ow. Ow. Ow. Ow. Ouch! Sorry. Yep. Could we

just ... ? For a second? Just need to catch my breath for a bit. Yeah, sorry. I know, I know – "Stop talking, Jonathan!"

'Oh, okay. Yeah, that's fine. We can try the ... Oh, gosh, that's new. Feels a bit ... No, it's fine, you go ahead. Yeah, it's fine. Actually, that feels kind of ... Yep. Gosh, I didn't realise I could do that ... I mean, this is like *yoga*. Could we try just ... yep, okay. Ready. Do you want to mmmf mmmf mmm mmmm aaaaf. Hmmmm ormmmmm aaamm aaaaf. Mmmmmmmmmmf!

'Oh, already? Right, then I'll just see to myself. No? Do you have to? Right now? Okay, that's fine. No, don't apologise, you're in a hurry. I'll be out of your way as soon as I find my – here they are! Under the footstool – and I'll be going. Yep, I remember the way out. Thanks. Bye.'

Chapter 6

Do we not have a right to eat and drink?

1 Corinthians 9:4

'Are you okay?'

'Yeah, I'm fine. How are you doing?' asked Nnenna. Her voice sounded awkward and formal, as though she were checking how Dan was getting on with memorising a vocab table, instead of wetly kissing her bra.

Being only sixteen, Nnenna knew only a limited amount about this sort of thing, but she was starting to get the sense that there was something not quite right about this whole set-up. Dan's technique, for one thing, was a little unorthodox. His tongue was completely rigid but his head moved back and forth from one breast to the other, as if he were watching a tennis match, or keeping a close watch on two wily criminals.

In the back of her mind, she couldn't help but think that ten minutes of clumsy fumbling around in the dark was not the stuff of great love stories. Did Mr Darcy schedule Elizabeth in for sex between a trip to the cinema and a family dinner? Did Mr Rochester have onion breath? Did Cleopatra get cramp in her left leg, two minutes in?

This wasn't anything like Austen, or the Brontës, or Shakespeare. It wasn't anything. And then there was the fact that they were in the adult magazine section of Steph's parents' shop, a small room separated by a beaded curtain ('Don't worry! I work here, remember? He leaves his spare keys around sometimes. He won't find out.'). Whoever heard of romance blossoming in a place like that? Surely, true love could never flourish in a place that was heavy with the twin smells of disinfectant and guilty masturbation. Nnenna had read her literature and she was up on her films, and she had a strong sense that this was not how love was generally supposed to happen, even in postmodern novels. Even in French cinema.

Danny was still mumbling contentedly into Nnenna's left boob when she was struck by the thought that, actually … she didn't want to have sex. She didn't want to, right now. Not like this.

To an adult, this kind of thought often comes in peace, like a neighbour calling for tea. To a teenager like Nnenna, it was like a neighbour calling for tea and then defecating in her kitchen.

She tried to suppress the thought, but it wouldn't go away. The small but persistent voice in the back of her mind saying, not that she never wanted to have sex, but that she didn't want to *at that time*. She might want to have sex tomorrow, or in a week …

'Mmmm,' said Dan, obliviously, into her belly button.

… And a week seemed so reasonable, so little to ask.

But it also seemed like an interminably long time. If she didn't *do* it, then she wouldn't have *done* it. And if she didn't do it now, then who knows? She might go on *not doing it* forever. When she closed her eyes and looked into the future, she saw years and years and years of *not doing it*: she saw virginity rolling over the horizon like dry ice in a bad play, covering everything, the way dust covers things that have not been touched for years. She shuddered.

She imagined the burden of her virginity following her through life like a clingy friend with a weird, unsightly ailment that had to be explained at parties.

'Oh – that? She's had that rash for ages. Don't worry, it's not contagious.'

'Oh – that? There's no antiperspirant that works for it. It's best to open a window and stand near the flowers.'

'Oh – me? I'm waiting for the right time.'

She imagined the nods of patient understanding, the respectful tilt of the head that people reserve for virtuous choices that they have no interest in making.

And, after all, she had been living with Virginity for sixteen long years – almost seventeen, now – and she knew that it was not always a genial inmate. It had been fine at first – she hadn't even noticed it – and sure, most of the time it was minding its own business, but at times like this it rattled the cage until her head hurt.

At times like this, Nnenna didn't want to simply lose her virginity: she wanted to *evict* it. It was impossible to live with it any longer. Nnenna had served her time with good behaviour and now she wanted to get out and get on with her life. She was on course for a *very* timely release, but at the last minute, Virginity clung to her and wouldn't let her go.

A week? She had to shake it off before it was too late. And aside from all this was the very real awareness that having sex with Dan would really, really annoy her mother. More than that, it would mean that Joanie's interdiction had no power over her; this was more than sex, it was a prison break. It was liberation.

Her mind was made up. She opened her eyes, took her boyfriend's head in her hands and kissed him firmly on the mouth.

When she came up for air, Danny was grinning. 'I like it when you take control,' he said. 'It really turns me on.' Evidently it did, as Nnenna felt something about the shape and size of a four-colour biro harden against her thigh; but all the same it was sort of an annoying thing to say, somehow, and she wanted to shut him up before he said anything else that made her think too hard. Thinking was not part of her escape plan. In fact, she had a feeling it might earn her another twelve months inside.

So, she kissed him again, more firmly this time, and felt him wrap his arms around her. It was as though he'd been waiting for some signal from her to begin in earnest.

The booth was lined with shelves and there wasn't much space, but he sat her on top of a box of VHS tapes that Steph's dad had been meaning to shift, and she took off her bra with a flourish. Dangling it in the air for a moment, she grinned, then laid it down on the shelf by her side and turned back to him.

He stared at her chest for a moment.

'What's wrong?' asked Nnenna.

'Nothing . . .'

'What? What is it?'

'Nothing. It's – nothing.'

Was this what breasts were supposed to look like? Dan thought. *Was there something . . . wrong . . . with this pair?* He blinked a couple of times, struck by their looseness, the way they slumped downwards, rather than pointing nobly towards the sky. These breasts seemed a bit . . . defeatist.

Despite his reservations, Dan had the dim sense that knowledge of the real nature of a woman's body was something to be proud of – however disappointing the body might ultimately turn out to be. Maybe he had judged them too hastily – maybe real breasts were an acquired taste, like classical music, or olives. Maybe these were the kind of breasts only appreciated by people *in the know*: he imagined himself hosting all-male dinner parties in a smoking jacket and holding forth with knowledge and authority on a cracking pair he had picked up at the cutest little bistro on the outskirts of the city.

He buried his face in her, surprised by how soft and warm she was.

He squeezed her more and more tightly, and began to peel

off her leggings. More slowly this time, he kissed her neck while he took off her knickers. He told her to leave her bangles on. He told her to lie flat on her back while he removed his clothes and took a condom out of his back pocket, where it had been sitting conspicuously for the past two days. Lying on top of her but not quite on her, he began.

He was finished after only a few moments but he was short of breath. Nnenna felt eerily calm, as though she had been watching the entire thing from above. Later that day, she would realise that she had expected to feel more ... involved.

'I love you,' said Dan, and then: 'We should probably get dressed.'

Nnenna quickly pulled on her knickers and bra, her black leggings and her white T-shirt. Dan wasn't watching her, he was busy looking for his socks, but all the same – she tried not to look as though anything out of the ordinary had happened, as though she did things like this all the time.

By the time Nnenna emerged from Steph's father's shop, she felt like a new woman. She felt extraordinary. She felt power-ful. She felt sore, but confident in her new identity. Fifteen minutes ago, there were things she could never have compre-hended – now, the world had opened itself up to her like ... like a *virgin*.

Love was a beautiful secret and only she and Dan under-stood it. Nnenna's friends wouldn't get it: they were too young. Being in love at sixteen, *really* in love, was like bringing an exotic pet to school; her friends poked and prodded at it and wondered (aloud) what it did when it thought nobody was looking. Lacking her experience, they had already observed her budding relationship with wariness and envy ('Do you think you'll be together forever?' 'Is it true you're going to get married?' 'How big is he?' 'Does Nnenna make animal noises when she's enjoying it?').

Nnenna looked both ways twice on Warwick Street (not because there was any traffic at the time but because there was an opportunity to whip her newly straightened hair attractively from side to side), crossed to Oldham Street and walked up to Piccadilly Gardens, where there were no gardens but she could catch a tram for the thirty-minute journey home. She smiled up at the sky and felt a kind of oneness with the bigness of it, how it comprehended everything.

As she passed the kora players in Piccadilly Gardens and the people dancing with them, her phone vibrated.

Nen, where have you been? Are you coming home ASAP pls to explain yourself? Lol, mum

Nnenna stopped dead. She usually got a smug sense of satisfaction from her mother's misguided use of 'lol' to mean 'lots of love', but this time she was too full of rage. She had been *summoned*. And what kind of question was that, anyway? *Are you coming home to explain yourself?* She tried to call back, but there was no answer – her summons was abrupt and it was final.

Determined to have the last word, she decided to ignore the message and take a quick detour around the trendy boutiques of Manchester's gentrified Northern Quarter. She could always say she'd missed her bus by accident; but she wasn't going to be ordered around.

Going back the way she'd come, she wandered for a few minutes. It was a beautiful day at the very end of summer, and she had nowhere to be. Anything might have happened.

She might never have seen it.

She might have gone her whole life without it if she'd never known.

She could have missed her turning or changed her mind – got on the tram and gone home to the quiet, leafy suburb where her mother was waiting, but suddenly there it was: in the window of a tiny shop tucked away between a gaming store and an Oxfam.

This dress – a midi, reaching down to the mannequin's knees – was made for her: it was tight, made of a thin velvet the colour of strawberry ice-cream, and it looked lightweight enough to be just-about comfortable. Mid-thigh downwards, the velvety fabric gave way to a thin, almost transparent material which she couldn't name, but which suited her exactly. She smiled at it as though she were greeting a long-lost friend, and the clear, playful sound of the kora echoed through the city.

'Hi, Joanie. Yes, I'm still sleeping with him. I'm just walking to his house, now, actually. Joanie, let it go. Let it go! I wish I'd never told you I was seeing him today.

'Stop taking everything so seriously! Oh, *very* clever. Yes, I do take myself seriously enough. You know, I think you think that I'm in some sort of awful relationship with him. Like he's taking advantage of me, or something. Well, he's not. We're not in a relationship, so there's no advantage to take. There's no anything. I . . . we don't . . . It's not like that. We're not going out or anything. Silas is not my boyfriend, and I don't need one. I've had boyfriends before and they were fine, as deceitful, intimacy-shy, selfish and emotionally stunted boyfriends go. But I just want something casual, now. Something easy.

'Listen, I'm at his door now, so . . . He's a great catch, Joanie. And besides, he's always so busy preparing for his dinner parties. He's got people to cater for, Joanie; important people. Television execs, journalists, important people from the food industry that would really help his career. No wonder he doesn't have all that much time for me. And if I'm never invited to those dinners, well, I can understand it. I'm not important enough, not like that. And besides, I have a job of my own, too, you know. Being a financial auditor takes up a lot of my time. Yes, it does. *Yes, it does!* Look, I'm at his door now so I've got to go. No, I can't wait until he gets to the door. Because I need to concentrate. On the knocking! It's complicated and if I get it wrong, he'll be annoyed, right from the start. So I'm going. I'll see you for dinner next week. I'm hanging up. I'm hanging up! Yes, I am. Goodbye. Bye. Bye. Bye! Bye.

'Silas! Hi. You look ... What? No, I'm not Toby. Why? Who's Toby? I'm Jonathan. Jonathan Tucker? Four slow knocks and two quick ones? Oh! Four quick and two slow. Sorry. You know, this might be easier if you gave me your phone number, and then we could ... What, really? Why? No, no, it's fine, it's fine. We can ... Okay. Thanks, I'll just take off my shoes, shall I?

'You know, it might be more comfortable if we just used your bedroom. I don't mind if it's untidy, but you see my back gets a little sore with these hard surfaces, is all. And there was a lot of parmesan after the last time. Oh. Really? You're sure? It really wouldn't take much longer ... Okay. No, it's fine. Let's just. Okay. Right. Yeah, we can —

'Ow. Ow. Ow. Ow. Ow. Ow. Ow. Ow. *Ow*. I think I've found your cheese grater. Yeah, here you go. Wait, where should it be? Here? Right. Oh. Sorry ... *Here*. Sorry. Sorry! It's dark. Can't we turn on the ... Oh. Yeah. Yeah. No lights. Sorry.'

Chapter 7

[...] love covers over all offences.

Proverbs 10:12

When Joanie came back from the office that evening, something was different. At first, she couldn't think what it was, but then she realised – it was a smell. Not new, exactly, but unusual. Her bedroom smelled strange, but familiar, somehow. It was a nice smell – a sort of floral smell, but chemical like ... *fresh laundry*.

She froze, as though sensing a foreign presence in her room.

After a moment or two, she collected herself enough to try and ascertain the source of the new fragrance. It was coming from somewhere in particular. And the coffee stain was gone.

The bedsheets? Had someone washed the bedsheets?

'Nnenna?'

'Yes, Mum?'

'Have you ... did you wash the sheets?'

Nnenna appeared at the bedroom door, laundry basket in hand. She shrugged. 'Your beloved child had some spare time, after she stopped running her mouth.'

Joanie looked at Nnenna for a moment and then hugged her and gave her a kiss. 'What on earth possessed you to do my laundry?'

'I was doing mine. It wasn't any trouble.'

'Are you sure . . . ? Nothing, never mind.'

'What?'

'Are you sure nothing's wrong?'

'Mum!'

'All right! Never mind. I only . . . Are you sure?'

'I'm going to my room.'

'Come here, you silly mare.'

She hugged Nnenna again, this time for a few moments. 'Thank you,' she said, softly. 'Will you want dropping off tomorrow at work?'

'No, I'll be all right to walk. Thanks.'

'Will you want picking up? It'll be dark.'

'Um. Please. Thanks, Mum.'

'You're welcome, love.'

The fast-food restaurant where Nnenna worked wasn't always a pleasant place to be, so in her mind she thought of it as a kind of role-playing game: the restaurant ordered ingredients that only distantly resembled food, and the customers ate and pretended it tasted kind of like chicken.

When you thought about it, it was like a kind of magic.

Nnenna herself was still only sixteen, however, so the owners of the ambiguously named Chicken Co-op fast-food outlet – a middle-aged couple whom Nnenna thought were much too kind to sell what she thought of as low dosages of poison – wouldn't let her use the machines with hot oil except under supervision. Mostly she took orders from customers, checked the stockroom and daydreamed.

'What's wrong with you?' says Philip, morbidly. In Nnenna's mind, he is wiping his forehead impatiently while staring at his wife, Amy. Amy is leaning over the grill, her head bowed.

'Don't talk to me, Phil,' says his wife. 'The first delivery from that new supplier came in a minute ago and . . . I've seen things.'

'We've been running this place for twenty years,' says Phil. 'We've both seen things.'

'No, Phil. I mean I've *seen things*. I'm not talking about that time we saw that rat standing upright in the queue for orders. I'm talking about the kind of things you can't unsee.'

'What—'

'I've seen things you wouldn't put in a sausage.'

'But—'

'I've seen things you wouldn't put in a Louis Theroux documentary.'

'I—'

'I've seen things you wouldn't put in a down-on-his-luck celebrity.'

'Stop it, Amy! We've been through this, every time we've changed suppliers. Unless the meat starts talking directly to us, we don't ask questions. Remember our pact?'

'Oh God, Phil.'

'Get a hold of yourself and wipe down the counter, will you? I need to pop round the corner for a bit.'

'Er . . .'

'Hello? Nnenna? Anybody in there?'

'Sorry,' said Nnenna, returning to reality. 'Yeah, of course.'

'Right,' said Phil, looking at her strangely. 'You okay?'

'Yeah, I'm fine. Just . . . miles away. I'll wipe down the counter, don't worry.'

'Right,' said Phil again, sounding unconvinced. 'I'll be five minutes.'

There weren't many customers today: busy periods and quiet periods were predictable sometimes (football matches, weekend evenings, for example) and at other times, people seemed to come and go randomly. Tonight, there was only one old man, gingerly inspecting his dinner before shrugging and digging into it with a hungry abandon that made Nnenna blush and look away.

Her mind wandered. It was nearly the end of her shift.

Deep in Nnenna's heart was ... her mother, yes, but also a certain duo-tone midi dress that reached down to her knees.

Oh, it was more than a dress! It was the way to somewhere new. Its sleeves were underground railways; its structured bust pointed onwards and upwards.

She had already begun to build a future on it. At first, she was only trying to justify the idea of spending the money she'd saved up from her job at Chicken Co-op. But on the way home Nnenna had thought about it more and more. By the time she realised she had unthinkingly forgiven her mother for sending a text which had, at the time, rankled deep in her soul, she knew she was serious about it.

And so she should be – it was a serious dress. She hadn't tried it on (there hadn't been time) but already she knew: there were things she could *achieve*, wearing it. Great things.

It was at precisely the right point between smart and casual, allowing her to articulate herself as sexy, fun, easy-going; but also, quietly no-nonsense. Whatever it was to be a woman after nearly seventeen long years of being a girl, a new, shapely silhouette might express it succinctly and with punch. This dress would strip her of all childish things and furnish her with a new sleek, pared-down self. This dress would usher in the dawn of a new era.

And high time. Already, these last years before university felt *wrong*: like being called the wrong name, or being held back a year in school. Nnenna knew she couldn't fast-forward time; but could she pass up the opportunity for a preview?

As Joanie waited in the freezing cold car for Nnenna to come out of the takeaway, she replayed in her mind bits of her early relationship with Maurice. Was she foolish? It had never been a joke to her, however wild it seemed now, for her to have had a child at twenty-one. But the way things had turned out ...

She felt judged by her circumstances. She felt that her hopes, if not her entire self, had been made a joke of.

Joanie shook her head as if to clear her mind of a silly thought. She saw a figure walk quickly out of the takeaway and look around. Yes, it was Nnenna. Joanie flashed her headlights and waved out of the window, and Nnenna trotted across the road.

Nnenna had her music in her ears at full volume. It was The Smiths, and she congratulated herself once again on the aptness of the music. She had appropriated the *Meat Is Murder* album as the soundtrack to her life ('This Charming Man' was catchier but her mother had said she liked it) and she told herself, although not in so many words, that it was made for her.

She listened to it on repeat. Sometimes, when she was walking alone, she pretended she was in a gritty low-budget movie about her life, and that the music was underscoring her every move while an invisible audience watched, awestruck by her beauty and her sheer significance, although these things were worn so lightly, so carelessly, that you probably wouldn't notice them if someone hadn't made a film about her and underscored it with The Smiths.

Joanie quickly wound up the window and commanded her face to betray no reaction to the smell. Nnenna had worked at the takeaway part-time for most of the summer, and Joanie was starting to get good at pretending. She held her facial expression fast and tried to busy herself with minutiae about the car, to give the impression that she had other things on her mind. Before, air-fresheners used to hang in thick, accusatory bunches on the rear-view mirror while Joanie made tiny, explosive comments about the smell and suggested that Nnenna's personal hygiene might be partly to blame.

Joanie tried to ignore it, now. Even as autumn was rolling

in, even when, as now, it was very cold, she wound down her windows as far as they would go (which varied according to the car's mood) until she saw Nnenna coming out of the building. She wound up the windows when Nnenna arrived because not to do so would hurt Nnenna's feelings; but she convinced herself that the smell wasn't as bad if she'd given the car a good airing first.

For her part, Nnenna only plonked herself down on the back seat of the car and said 'thanks' (with her earphones still in). For picking her up – Joanie was never, ever late – and for not wanting to hurt her feelings, which were always out in the open. Nnenna knew why the car was cold.

Love can be such a tiny thing. Neither of them even noticed it as they sat silently in the car, smelling of unholy meats and vowing to have a wash, a really good scrub, at home.

Chapter 8

Your cheeks are like halves of a pomegranate
behind your veil.

Song of Solomon 6:7

1992

Having handed Joanie the love poem he'd written, Maurice
waited precisely one minute before asking, 'Do you like it?'

Joanie – who did not like it but was beginning to love
Maurice – only smiled and pretended to still be making her
way through the sonnet. 'I'm a slow reader,' she said, reading it
absently for the third time while trying to understand what could
have caused such odd behaviour. Was this a reaction to some
discussion they'd had? She hated to think that she might have
inadvertently said something to suggest that this was the sort of
thing she was into. Joanie did not disapprove of love poetry in
principle – what people did behind closed doors was their own
business – but the thought of being caught up in that scene herself . . . well, it made her feel deeply uncomfortable. Dirty, even.
She breathed an inward sigh of relief that Maurice had had the
sense to present this poem to her in private, in his flat, so that
nobody else would see. She didn't want to get a reputation for
being the kind of person who liked men to write poems for her.

But maybe she had been too hasty. Yes, he was an engineer

with a poor sense of scansion, but perhaps this was normal in Nigeria? For all she knew, this might be part of some time-honoured courting tradition, and here she was, looking down her nose at it.

Her momentary guilt, however, was appeased when, upon the fourth reading, she remembered that he had rhymed 'affection' with 'convection'; that the poem involved a thinly veiled reference to a steam train going through a tunnel; that the opening lines posed the mysterious question, 'What happens to a rod of copper getting hotter?'

'You hate it,' said Maurice, desultorily.

'I don't. Of course I don't.'

'It was an experiment.'

'I think it went well ... mostly.'

'I've embarrassed you.'

'No. You haven't. I'm ... '

'What?'

'You've caught me off guard, here.'

'With the poem?'

'I suppose. It seems a bit ... Well, why did you never tell me how you felt?'

'I did. In lines twelve to fourteen.'

'Yes, but why didn't you tell me, you know ... in a sentence? Out loud?'

Maurice was quiet for a moment. 'I suppose I was afraid of how you might react.'

Joanie looked hard at him. His head was bowed and the look on his face was one of defeat and resignation. Why did he have to make out like being together was so complicated? To her it was simple. That was one of the things she liked about being with him, because she could be herself and not feel self-conscious. But now, with this poem ... It felt as though they were embarking on some grand endeavour, something epic and huge, huger than the two of them.

But weren't they? When she was with Maurice, she felt happy and warm and understood; but sometimes when she was alone and she thought about the two of them, the whole thing seemed like an experiment, like a poem with odd rhymes and images that didn't quite fit. When would she ever meet his family, that lived in Nigeria? He talked about them all the time but clammed up whenever she asked him questions – it was the strangest thing. And she knew her mother would never approve: they had never discussed the pros and cons of Joanie becoming romantically involved with a Nigerian engineering graduate with a close connection to God, but Joanie knew instinctively that this did not fit her mother's ideas of the way Joanie should be spending her time at Cambridge, or the type of man she should be spending time with.

She knew all about the type of man her mother had in mind: casually wealthy, tall, athletic, with perfectly blow-dried hair, academically brilliant, preferably a rower but a rugby player would do; and, of course, white. But she'd met those men. She'd studied alongside them. She'd dated them. She hated them, and their coiffed arrogance, their easy assumptions about the world. The thing about Maurice that excited and terrified her in equal measure was that he understood perfectly how strange and non-sensical the world could be and wanted to make it better, but at the same time he had a sense of humour about it. He could still make her laugh, even though he knew the things that upset her most. So why did he have to make this all so serious?

But she did love him. There was that, after all.

'I love you, too,' said Joanie. Maurice looked at her.

'I love you,' he said. 'I honestly do.'

She kissed him.

'And this poem,' she said, smiling gently. 'It's beautiful. Why don't you give me a chance to read it properly? To appreciate it. Let me take it back to college with me tonight to think about it by myself.'

No such luck. As soon as she arrived back on her corridor, her friends were waiting to hear the news of her latest date with Maurice. She tried to underplay the whole thing, to put them off the scent. But her vague descriptions and off-hand manner only made her friends question her even more closely, and before long they had pulled her into Ophelia's room, dragged it out of her that a poem had been written, and read the offending text aloud.

'Yuck,' said Ophelia, when they finished. 'A sonnet!'

'Surely not?' said Cressida, breathless with indignation.

'Eurgh,' said Juliet. 'I'm so glad nobody's ever written a poem for *me*. I'd kill myself!'

'I think you might be being a little dramatic,' said Joanie.

'No! Me too,' said Ophelia. 'I hate that sort of thing. Drives me *mad*.'

'Sonnets are the worst,' said Juliet.

'Poetry in general is a Pretty Bad Thing,' said Cressida. 'It's so overwrought. It always puts me right off – men who are poets. The minute I find out they write poetry, I think, Next!'

'You're being ridiculous. You've met Maurice. You like Maurice! What's changed?'

'Well, he writes poems now,' said Juliet.

'One. One poem! This is a one-time thing. You're making far too much of this.'

'Or maybe he's the one making too much of things,' said Juliet.

'Absolutely,' chimed in Ophelia.

'He may have only written one sonnet—'

'That we know about,' chimed in Ophelia.

'Precisely – but he's written that sonnet for *you*. And it's so grand! It means he thinks of you in . . . I don't know, a certain way, or something,' said Juliet. 'He worships you. He'd do anything for you. He'd die for you, even.'

'*If* you read lines four to five literally,' chimed in Ophelia.

'I'm not seeing the downside,' said Joanie.

'So you feel the same way about him?'

'Yes!'

'Are you sure?' said Ophelia flatly.

'Yes. I love him. I've told you that already.'

'But he's talking about more than love,' said Juliet. 'He's talking about spending the whole of your lives together. He's talking about you and him against the world – didn't you read the second quatrain?'

'I think that's beautiful,' said Joanie, hurt. 'He's a good guy, and he feels strongly about me. I would have expected you all to be more supportive, frankly.'

'Well, yes, he's a good guy and he seems nice,' said Cressida. 'But what do you actually know about him? How long have you even been going out?'

'What more is there to know?' said Joanie. 'You can't spend the rest of your life waiting until you find out absolutely everything about someone. After a certain amount of time, you either love someone or you don't. And I do. I love him.'

Her friends looked at her sceptically and said nothing.

'Why are you being so weird about this?' said Joanie, angry now. 'We've all spent a lot of time dating guys that don't even compare to Maurice, all those selfish, thoughtless, immature guys. And now I've actually met one who cares about me, who genuinely cares about me, and all you want to do is pour cold water over it? God! *I wonder why.*'

'Don't be stupid,' said Juliet, laughing. 'You can't seriously think we're jealous. You don't think we could find better men than *Maurice*?'

'She does!' said Ophelia. 'She thinks we want her little chocolate poet all for ourselves!'

'*Chocolate*? You can't be serious. This is a joke. *You* are a joke!'

'Let's all calm down,' said Cressida. She took a deep breath and considered her next words carefully. 'I just think ... we could all do better. All of us, Joanie.'

Joanie fought back tears but could not fight hard enough, and she ran out of the room before they fell, one after the other, from her disbelieving eyes.

2009

At first, it had been difficult to find him – Jonathan had thought he might never succeed.

First, he'd tried Facebook. He had never had an account before and he realised with some chagrin that one had to open one before beginning the process he had heard Nnenna refer to as 'Facebook stalking'. Still a neophyte in the world of social media, Jonathan was fresh enough to allow the word 'Facebook' to soften his discomfort about what was still, essentially, stalking. This was different from standing outside someone's window at night. This wasn't the same, surely, as going through someone's bins? Still, he felt as though his hands were dirty.

But he couldn't stop himself. He watched images cascade down his screen as his curiosity got the better of him. Silas had made himself as unknowable as it was possible to be: all the doors in his house were shut and whenever Jonathan went to his house (it was never the other way around) Silas barely spoke. Jonathan had never seen any of his friends, never met him outside his home, never heard him mention anything he was interested in. All Jonathan knew about him was that he liked food and sex (preferably at the same time). Food and sex and ... nothing else. Everybody liked that. Woodland animals liked that. Jonathan had realised with no small degree of alarm that he couldn't think of anything that differentiated Silas from the mice he had glimpsed in his building.

He had work to do.

He created a profile under an assumed name and an anonymous email address (one never knew when one's personal information would be made public, these days), left the profile picture blank and began his search.

It took twenty minutes to find his profile. There were a great number of Garfields on Facebook and it occurred to him in a panicky moment that he might not be the only one online with a false name. Maybe he would not know Sila's profile if he saw it. Maybe he had something to hide.

He found the filter function and narrowed his search results down to men who lived in the Manchester area. It occurred to him that someone, somewhere, was coolly observing him as he scrutinised the search results. He half died at the thought that his baldly horny search criteria were being collated by some spotty adolescent at Facebook HQ, or worse, some tepid civil servant at GCHQ. He shivered in fear that he, in the nakedness of online browsing data, was being laughed at over a water filter before being filed away with other desperate middle-aged men, men who were busily sifting through the male populace with the most toothless of combs, the most starkly desperate criteria ('male + local'). But he carried on.

It was some time before he realised that he could cross-reference his Facebook search results with what he found by googling Silas – a few photos, something about a marathon ...

Yes. *Yes.*

Silas William Garfield. There he was, the full disclosure of him. All three names of him, each one truer than the last, the middle one like a gift, like fresh water, his smile totally unsuspecting in his profile picture, his privacy settings bliss-fully loose.

And it was as simple as that. Silas was his, now. He, or a part of him at least, was Jonathan's.

So, what did he know about Silas now? Jonathan flicked through Silas's photos, his status updates, his life events ... In one photo, Silas wore running gear and a medal, and posed with his arm around the shoulders of an older man – his father? a new friend? – at some sort of finish line. Other people milled around. So, Silas was an athlete. He looked tired; proud, too, but he had a funny look on his face, as though he couldn't quite believe what he'd done. Was this his first run? His run-ning jersey was partly obscured, but Jonathan could make out the word 'cancer': had Silas lost someone to cancer? Was that why his mother wasn't in the photo? Perhaps she had been the one to take the photo. Or – had Silas overcome cancer himself? Jonathan moved on, clicked past photos of Silas in various different scenarios, in formal dress before a dinner, in a dinosaur onesie at a fancy-dress party, a couple of photos of him wearing drag ...

There were photos of his food, of course. Curries, soups, noodle dishes, salads, each with a pithy caption (some story about how and where he came across the recipe) and several hashtags, each one carefully treading the line between blank-faced irony and naked self-promotion. It was pure varnish, Jonathan knew. And he could see through it – but he was spell-bound. Here, right in front of him, was Silas's entire life, like he'd never seen it before. Many of the photographs had been taken in rooms in Silas's house that Jonathan had never seen.

Further back on the timeline there was a photo of Silas at a Pride parade, standing next to a muscular white man wearing bright yellow underwear and sandals. It was a sunny day. They both grinned big grins.

Jonathan felt a pang of impotent jealousy, and shame: he

could stare at these photos all he liked, but he'd never be any more a part of Silas's life for it. In fact, it would only make things worse, because now he knew the things that Silas did, the things – good things, charitable things – that Silas didn't want to do with him. And he could never do those things: he could never be someone who shrewdly used hashtags, who looked good dressed as an eighteenth-century duchess wearing crudely applied rouge. He would never run marathons, or smile insouciantly alongside trendy friends in Pride parades. And he'd never be white. Unlike every single one of the friends Silas posed with, Jonathan would never, ever be white. He'd always be something foreign to Silas, something exotic and odd, to be kept in the kitchen with the herbs and spices.

So what good was he, then?

He shut down his computer and went to bed.

Chapter 9

Then he took the fat and the fat tail and
all the fat that was on the entrails and the
long lobe of the liver and the two kidneys
with their fat and the right thigh, [...]
and presented them as a wave offering
before the LORD.

Leviticus 8:25, 27

The next day, at school, Nnenna sat down and waited for her friends to arrive at her table. She checked the time – she was early. That was good. It gave her time to consider what she would have to face over the next hour.

Her heart always beat a little faster at this time of day. Later in her life, she would realise that this was not a normal reaction to lunchtime.

'Hi, Nnenna,' said a girl in a pleated skirt which swished gracefully as it descended into its seat, opposite Nnenna. Hannah Goldstein placed her lunch tray on the table.

'They're mushy peas,' said Nnenna, with an edge of forced conviction in her voice.

'Are you sure?'

Nnenna looked at Hannah as if to signal the futility of the question. The South Manchester Academy had many great qualities but when it came to the lunch menu, there were very few things of which one could *ever* be sure. Despite its excellent academic record and impeccable reputation, the dining hall at SMA was a wild, lawless landscape in which almost anything could happen between the hours of one and two p.m. However, over the past five years, Nnenna had learned that there were, in fact, two things of which you could be reasonably certain:

1. Trust No One and Nothing.
2. The Peas Will Always Be Mushy.

Nnenna had seen many things on her tray over the years – most of which could be identified without an autopsy – but never once had she come across solid peas. And yet the mushy peas provided weren't mushy in the traditional sense – not the vivid green, life-giving mushy peas you get from a fish and chip shop. No, these looked like normal peas that had been stepped on. Downtrodden. Defeated. If you thought about it, they were not so much 'mushed' as '*smushed*'. Crushed. As though the kitchen staff had had high hopes for them to come out whole but somehow *life* got in the way.

'Where's Stephanie?'

'She texted me, she's coming in a second.'

The three of them had met early on in their time at the school and got on straight away, but they had not always been as close as they were now. They had been more or less thrown together in mutual horror and fear at the speed with which some compromising photos of some girls in their year had begun to circulate around the phones of the boys (it was rarely the other way around). The advent of mobile technology was accompanied by a new age of fear in which a moment's weakness could trigger years of regret. Clara Templeton's left buttock had been snapped three years ago and it was still a staple of instant messaging. It had been turned into GIFs, into memes and (this being a school full of mostly affluent children), lately into a core element of one sixth-former's Friday night stand-up routine. Rumour had it that one of the more artistically minded Year 9 boys was turning it into a surrealist collage.

For Nnenna, Hannah and Stephanie the daily ritual, performed on their corner table tucked away from the worst excesses of the dining hall, was a kind of sanctuary. While their contemporaries sent anonymous body parts back and forth along a virtual highway, Nnenna, Hannah and Stephanie shared more enlightened lunch hours, using their phones to peruse the musings of bloggers, vloggers and columnists around the world while they investigated the less inspiring offerings on their plates. Stephanie had once or twice confessed to Nnenna that she thought the whole thing was becoming a bit 'wanky', and it was true that Hannah tended to use unnecessarily long words. But that, as Nnenna reminded her, was only because her parents had been forcing her to use word-of-the-day calendars since she was out of nappies. Nnenna liked their lunchtime meetings. It was like the best bits about talking to her mum.

'Oh – hey, Steph,' said Hannah.

'I don't even want to ask ... ' said Nnenna, as Stephanie plonked down today's plate of miscellaneous semi-edible goo. Her main course continued to move about on the plate long after it had been set down. It was, Steph observed, like jelly – except that jelly would have wobbled. This ... looked like it was *brooding*.

'I wish I'd had your smarts,' said Steph. 'I *did* ask.' She was still reeling. As he served her, the man behind the counter had let slip that what she was getting was the 'Chicken Surprise' (as opposed to the vegetarian option, cryptically named only 'Surprise'). When she had asked what the surprise was, he had said, in a grim voice that spoke of deep trauma and unthinkable horrors,

'Everything except the chicken. Sometimes ... the chicken.'

In truth, Steph always brought a sandwich from home just

in case, so almost preferred the pleasure of recounting these stories to the pleasure of having food that fulfilled her statutory rights. She recalled for her friends the shock with which she had watched the man scoop out something he referred to cryptically as 'mashed ...' (he had furtively mumbled the all-important second word); how she had watched it slop desultorily onto her plate; how she had watched him give her a second scoop; and how the second scoop, from the same container, had been a *different colour from the first*.

'It's gross,' she said, and they laughed as they ate. 'One of these days, somebody's going to complain.'

The truth was, as they all knew, nobody would complain. At least not to anybody who would do anything.

'So, what delayed you?' asked Hannah.

'Mr Black,' said Steph. 'He wanted to talk about my French homework.'

'Oh!' said Hannah, sounding genuinely pleased. 'You do French homework, now?'

Steph rolled her eyes. French was not her strength: she preferred the clean, generous beauty of Physics. It enchanted her to think that, if you worked hard enough, you could find an equation for anything in the world: not merely the speed of light but the direction in which it would travel from one surface to another. Not merely sound but its nature and quality, its habits and preferences. Physics, for Steph, was like retuning her ears so that they could hear things they'd never heard before; like understanding the language in which the world spoke. It was, sometimes, like being able to speak back.

French, on the other hand, was a lot like listening to someone – specifically Mr Black – bore on for an hour about something she had no interest in. French, as they all knew, was Nnenna's subject: Steph merely subjected herself to it. After choosing Physics, Maths and History, she had considered Religious Studies for her optional fourth A level. In fact, it had been the memory of their last family holiday (and their first in years), taken after their school reports were in, that had made the decision for her. Steph's top grade in French was at the forefront of her mother's mind: she was always asking Steph to show off, to show how well she'd done, use what she'd learned. It had been annoying at the time – Steph had made one or two sour remarks, in English, about how much translators get paid in real life – but it was so hard to resist her mother's pride, hugging her and beaming at her accomplishments. For Steph, only fifteen, pleasing her mother was like a drug.

Unfortunately, this year Steph seemed to be having an allergic reaction. French bored her now, frustrated her: as tiring as it had been speaking French all the time on holiday, Steph had learned more in that short week than she had in several lessons at school, because she was immersed in the language. After that, it didn't make sense to study it in school: she wanted to travel and learn the language first hand. Learning it in a classroom seemed sterile, now, and pointless. She'd only ever done well in it because she'd worked so hard. It didn't come naturally to her, like it seemed to for Nnenna. Nnenna had won prizes in French ever since she started at the school; now the only thing Steph got from Mr Black (as she told her friends over lunch), was a tired sigh.

Mr Black had held Steph back after the lesson to suggest that she either buck up her ideas or consider dropping the subject. He outlined, with a painful gentleness, that there was no shame in only doing three A levels. Even at a school like theirs.

'He is right, though,' said Hannah.

'No, he's not,' said Steph. 'And he knows it. Hardly anyone here's doing three A levels. And I wouldn't want to stand out, now, would I?'

Nnenna rubbed her back in sympathy. She looked glumly down at her food. It seemed like everything was a battle, today.

*

'Danny, mate. You're punching above your weight, there.'

Danny's other friends, having eaten the same lunch as Nnenna, Hannah and Steph, were too stunned to speak. Instead they communicated their agreement through a series of mmms, nods and one belch that was so thick it was almost visible.

Sam, the only boy left with powers of speech after the ordeal of the 'chicken surprise', had made the remark, but everybody had been thinking it. They picked out the remains of their food from between their teeth and silently wondered what they were.

Most people are not in a position to realise the complexity of human beauty. Maybe it's advertising; maybe it's because, somehow, we never quite grow out of our teenage minds, but most people seem to be under a desperate illusion. Most people seem to think that 'beauty' – especially for people who aren't men – is a thing you *have*. The same way roses *have* a smell or responsible people *have* savings accounts.

Nnenna, partly by virtue of not being white, knew better: perhaps more than most people, she was sometimes beautiful, and sometimes less so, depending on who was observing her at the time. Arguably (and beauty is always arguable), she fell somewhat short of the standards of beauty in the country where she had grown up, and so she knew better than to think beauty was something you could ever truly have or hold: no matter how you look, you can be beautiful to one person and utterly invisible to another. Being 'beautiful', Nnenna knew, is of little use in the painful moments, in the days, in the long hours, when you are ugly.

When it came to Nnenna's boyfriend and his friends, however, she was in much more hospitable company. While this could be gratifying for Nnenna, Danny was in a less fortunate position. For one thing, he was only about the same height as Nnenna; he had a scruffy, wispy beard whose only justification was that it covered more of his face. He scored badly in exams, and in football these days he rarely scored at all. Yes, he was a nice enough person but ... by rights, he should have been single. If there were any justice in the world, he would have been inventing a girlfriend for attention – someone he'd met on the internet, maybe. Someone who went to another school, someone nobody else had ever met. Someone who'd turn out to be a middle-aged man from Croydon who went by an Old Norse nickname on weekends.

So why was he dating *Nnenna Maloney*?

Turning to Sam, Dan bridled. He scoured the blackest depths of his heart for a retort that would silence this doubt, once and for all.

'Shut up,' he pronounced.

'Oooh! Have I touched a nerve?'

'If you have,' said Dan, regrouping, 'it'll be the first living thing you've touched for six months. How *is* celibate life treating you?'

'Easy, boys,' said Amit. 'No need to fight.' Amit was a friend of theirs who wisely brought in crustless sandwiches from home. The three of them made up the school's debating team, and as such enjoyed a friendly but occasionally vicious rivalry in many areas of life besides public speaking. Amit tacitly agreed that Dan was punching well above his weight; however, he had long since decided that, if Nnenna didn't have the sense to date *him*, then she wasn't worth bothering with. Besides, he was getting tired of Sam and Dan's antics disrupting his serene completion of the morning's Sudoku.

Sam scowled and stabbed his fork into a piece of unidentified, unidentifiable meat. Why should Dan have all the luck? Wasn't Sam more handsome? Wasn't he a full inch taller? Hadn't he *just* achieved Grade 8 Distinction on the harp?

'I'm *sorry*, Amit,' he said, his voice so sarcastic as to sound almost peaceable. 'I'm only concerned for Dan's health. He must be getting very dizzy watching Nnenna run circles around him.'

'Sam,' said Amit, a warning note in his voice. He spoke the way a weary parent speaks to their warring children at breakfast-time: sternly, but not taking his eyes off his newspaper. He was warning them more out of habit than out of the belief that warning them would actually make the blindest bit of difference. 'Here, why don't you read some of my newspaper? *I'm* reading; *Daniel* is reading—'

'Yes,' said Sam. 'I can *see* he's reading. His lips are moving.' He'd said it slightly louder than he'd meant to. The boys at the next table along heard him and tittered.

'*Sam*,' said Amit again.

'Sam,' said Dan, finally. 'What's eating you?'

Amit finally lowered his paper, in full recognition of this low blow. They all knew what Dan meant by this: it was a reference to the time – now well publicised – when Sam had received oral sex from a girl in the year below who had been under the impression that all men liked to be *nibbled*. Sam had borne it with admirable patience at first, but Ella Garrett, with the best will in the world, had only made her technique more pronounced when Sam did nothing to indicate that he had noticed it. When she walked away, she had walked away with a great weight of shame, a not inconsiderable amount of skin between her teeth, and an injunction to avoid the sex advice of glossy magazines. Sam, sorely disappointed (and sore), had barely been able to walk away at all.

'That,' said Amit, unhelpfully, 'was below the belt.' It wasn't the most diplomatic thing he might have said; but then teenagers have a strange idea of diplomacy and besides, he was still finishing his Sudoku.

Still, there was something in the viciousness of Dan's remark that Amit could actually get on board with. Dan definitely wasn't the sharpest pencil in the box, but every so often, he did come out with something that made Amit look at him differently and made Amit feel less like a grandparent and more like a peer. And, at these times, it seemed like things might be possible that hadn't seemed possible before. There was, after all, something endearing about the way Danny flicked his hair out of his eyes, about the way he pouted when he was sad, or angry.

Fed up, Danny folded his chair, stood up, and with a parting missive about biting off more than one could chew, stalked off to find a football.

And Amit watched him walk away. He watched, and he began to wonder.

'Zut alors!'

Later that day, during a free period, Nnenna was watching French daytime television on one of the school library computers. Nnenna couldn't understand absolutely everything that was going on, and there were a few gaps she had to fill in by guesswork and the occasional flick through a French–English dictionary, but she could parse most of it. She allowed a smile of self-satisfaction to creep across her face.

It was fortunate that Nnenna had an aptitude for learning languages, because she loved it more than almost anything. Language was – maybe not life itself – but, to her, speaking it and understanding it was close. You had to be able to peel its fingers back to see what was going on. She had loved Physics for the same reason: unusually, perhaps, she had found it comforting that so many things in the world could be explained in clean, measured equations. Music perplexed her entirely – she had inherited the famed Maloney tone-deafness – but no energy spent on understanding French and Physics felt wasted.

Cheesy French gameshows from the 1980s (or, as her mother called it, 'Soft Porn with Subtitles') were her guilty pleasure. On the screen, a wasp-waisted young woman with perky breasts and a white top that had become more and more see-through with each water-related challenge, had been tasked with trying to slide her way across a broad metal cylinder and ring the bell at the other end. Meanwhile, her team mates yelled words of encouragement, criticism or self-centred exasperation, according to their moods.

'*Continuez, Chloë, continuez!*'

'*Oui, oui!*'

'*Vite!*'

You had to feel sorry for the young woman, Nnenna thought. It wasn't Chloë's fault that she kept slipping off the cylinder, over and over again. And she was obviously trying her best – she had thoughtfully agreed to wear what seemed to be the uniform for women (a tight vest and short shorts) to make herself more aerodynamic; and she had, on the advice of her teammates, tactically manoeuvred herself so that one breast lay on either side of the cylinder, to spread her weight equally and help keep her balance.

Nnenna's eyes flicked to her left and right and, guiltily, she looked behind her to see if she was drawing any attention to herself by what she was watching. She wasn't.

It's a kind of unofficial rule that, if a library enforces a code of silence, the computer area offers a kind of refuge. In theory, this was because students often worked collaboratively using a single computer and needed to discuss their ideas. In practice, Nnenna listened to the boys and girls at the computers next to her, chatting noisily away, throwing in details about their lives in the anxious, over-eager manner conceived of by everyone under the age of twenty-one as being 'casual'. They raised the pitch of their voices at the end of each sentence so that their conversations, sounding like a series of questions, took on an evasive, dance-like quality. Someone listening to them without understanding might have likened them to very polite disagreements between two double agents firing rhetorical questions at each other, neither one of them willing to own up to the truth.

Occasionally, she might overhear a student say an African-Americanism: a quote from a TV show in a 'blaccent', say, or a certain swivel of the head. As Nnenna was the nearest black person, she was the unwilling recipient of occasional guilty, uncertain glances thrown her way.

To most of the students at the majority-white South Manchester Academy, most products of popular black cultures were seen as a kind of performance, something that you put on. What was not easy and natural for the white and middle-class could not possibly be easy and natural for others.

Still, Nnenna could tell they felt it was wrong for them to appropriate another culture to make themselves seem less square, because they acted as though they were each being watched – Gemma Richards flashed an apologetic smile every five seconds. Even when she wasn't actively paying attention to any of them, they looked uncomfortable, as if they were being observed by a ring of black gangsters with gold teeth and a sharp eye for social criticism.

Nnenna wanted to say something: she felt as though a more morally upright version of herself might march over there and not take Gemma's guilty looks for an answer. But ... then what? If she confronted them, they'd only ignore her, or get defensive. And she'd have even fewer friends than she did already. She wanted to pretend she hadn't heard it. Did that make her a ... bad black person? She didn't want to be a bad black person.

She stared at her video.

'What are you watching?' said Dan, suddenly sitting down next to her.

Nnenna told him the name of the show in a completely authentic French accent, before she could stop herself. She tried to fudge it by making a sarcastic gesture, pursing her fingers together and kissing them like a chef. Dan raised an eyebrow and said,

'Sexy! Do it again. That thing with your lips.'

Nnenna, so uncomfortable with large groups, loved that she could talk to Dan naturally, saying almost the first thing that came into her head. Sometimes she thought of their conversations as a kind of updated version of the tête-à-têtes Jane Austen's heroines had with their love interests that confirmed their compatibility. Except that Austen's heroines never went at it on a pile of smutty videotapes.

This was the first time they had spoken since having sex. As such, Nnenna thought, this was the conversation that would determine the meaning of their first time – which had somehow become so rarefied, so holy in Nnenna's mind that she was beginning to worry about it now. Had sex proven their love for one another? Or would he lose interest now he'd got what he wanted?

'Sorry,' she said, tucking her hands in her pockets. 'One-time only. Like a going-out-of-business-sale kinda thing. Once it's gone, it's gone.'

'Seriously?' said Dan. He lowered his voice to a whisper and smiled. 'Because I'm pretty sure we're in business, now. Like, officially.'

Nnenna felt like she should carry on talking to him, but she didn't want to. Not if he was going to talk to her like this, like some moustachioed cad in a 1920s murder mystery. She liked talking to Dan, and telling silly jokes with him, but not *now*. This wasn't how it was supposed to go.

She had mentally planned this discussion with great precision, scripting the breathless professions of love, the hand-holding and long moments of silent eye-contact – but instead, here she was being ambushed by Dan and his innuendo while she half watched Chloë, twenty-seven, from Bordeaux, slither across another phallic 'obstacle'. Nnenna tried to concentrate, tried to keep her wits about her as she navigated this daunting new conversational terrain. She could see the prize at the end – but somehow, she couldn't quite stay on course. Maybe it was because the memory of Dan's phallic obstacle kept rearing its head, but she found herself completely avoiding everything she knew she needed to say, and saying a whole load of things that would make Lizzy Bennet blush to her roots.

'*We?* I'm not talking about us, babe. I've got my own operation.'

'A bit on the side?'

'Yeah, nice little earner. Drives the boys *wild*.'

'Going into the porn business, are you?'

'I don't trust cameras. I'm more into the face-to-face.'

'Like the mafia?'

'Babe, when I'm done with them, *all* the boys are sopranos.'

'Gotta get with the times, Nen. We're going digital.'

Nnenna flexed her fingers. '"Digital" is my middle name.'

I can't believe what's coming out of my mouth, she thought.

Dan's talk of digital recording made her feel queasy – she was fighting the urge to ask Dan if Steph's dad's shop was fitted with CCTV. She was having premonitions of adult films in Mr Asquith's store with her face on top-shelf DVD cases and the words 'Going Digital' in large lurid italics. But before she could muster the courage, Dan said,

'Why do you watch game-shows in French?' – even though he knew the answer.

'What? Oh. It helps me learn new words, I guess,' said Nnenna. 'And it's more fun than reading a book.'

'You've already read all the books, though, haven't you?'

Nnenna rolled her eyes. She could do this kind of back-and-forth with Dan on autopilot now. (They had fallen into a pattern of make-believing she was a university lecturer in French Literature masquerading as a sixth-former, and that he was holding her back in her search for herself, for truth and for the perfect all-butter croissant.)

'I thought you didn't have any free periods today?'

'Lesson got cancelled,' said Dan. 'Mr Grove didn't turn up on time so we've got a free period. Think he's ill again, lazy bastard. Thought I'd come and distract you, but it looks like you're already doing that for me.'

She smiled but couldn't think of anything to say. After a short silence, Dan said, 'Not taking notes?'

Nnenna smiled almost apologetically, as though he had caught her out in something. She didn't know why.

He said, 'So what's happening now?'

Nnenna put the large, worn and slightly sticky school headphones back on and listened for a moment before explaining. 'Well, Chloë – this woman here, in the white top – she was meant to complete a different challenge, earlier on ... and she lost, so she's being removed from the game and given a penalty – look, they're taking her off to a cage – not sure why they do that, to be honest. And because they've finished the first phase – oh!' Nnenna laughed. 'Okay ... So, they need a certain number of keys, right? To go on to the next stage. But they don't have enough so they need to sort of "sacrifice" someone in their team instead.'

'What happens to them?'

'They get locked away and the game's over for them.'

'A lot of people getting locked away in this game. What happens to them after they get locked away?'

'Dunno.'

'Seems harsh.'

'Yeah, it's pretty rough, but it's funny watching them argue over who has to go. And I *bet* ... Well, it's hard to understand them when they're all speaking at the same time, but basically this guy says he's happy to sacrifice himself and his friend's not having it and she wants that guy over there to get locked up because he's been making these stupid jokes all the way through ... ' She did not notice Dan pulling a strange face as she more or less fluently translated rapidly spoken French.

'Oh *Nen!*' He kissed her on the cheek. 'You take it so seriously! It's only soft porn! How can you not know?' He stood up, laughing. She *did* know. And he knew it.

'Where are you going?'

'Back to Amit and Sam. Sam wants to organise this night-out thing.'

'Can you wait? Like, twenty minutes? I've got to finish some homework, but then I can go with you.'

'Sorry, Nen. Got to go.'

'But I've hardly seen you since the weekend.'

They were so different. He would never watch her silly shows with her. But he loved to watch her speak.

Even Stephanie said Nnenna could be too intense, sometimes. And she certainly took herself more seriously than her friends: she would never skip classes with Dan, and when she had seen him doing his homework in the morning before registration, she had seemed, for a moment, genuinely hurt.

But Dan knew she wasn't just 'intense'. She didn't walk around looking miserable for the sake of it, like the emo kids; and she wasn't like the other Physics kids who spent every lunchtime playing Warhammer and smelling meaty. She was passionate, but she wasn't fake: she was happy when she was happy, and sad when she was sad. And whereas Stephanie mostly ignored the parts of Nnenna she couldn't understand, Dan was fascinated by them. He loved to watch her while she spoke and thought, as though she were far away. In these moments, his vague feelings of inferiority somehow became a kind of avuncular, distanced pride, and he realised that even when he resented her or was jealous of her, he still loved her. So, he didn't completely understand why it was that he said,

'I think you can probably chill out a bit with the French, you know.'

'What?'

'Aww, you're gonna get offended now, aren't you? I only meant ... don't you ever want to learn *your* language?'

It took Nnenna a couple of moments to realise what he meant: he meant her father's language. Igbo, the language she had hardly ever heard spoken, and which Dan had never heard of until she'd mentioned it to him one day. And by the time she realised what he meant, by the time her eyes widened in horror, Dan was mortified. He knew it was a stupid thing to say, but he didn't know what *kind* of stupid; he didn't know how deeply he'd hurt Nnenna, how far his words had gone. He suspected, of course, that he had said something deeply hurtful about Nnenna's relationship with her father, something she had never properly discussed with him; and he saw for a moment the nakedness of his jealousy of Nnenna's academic success, and inwardly he shrank from the ugliness of it. But he did not see, perhaps, that now there was a great chasm between the two of them. He knew that things would always be different now, but he did not know what that would mean. So he didn't know what to say next.

He didn't say anything. Amit poked his head round the library door and called Dan's name. Dan laughed awkwardly, kissed Nnenna on the cheek and was gone in a few moments. Nnenna stared at the screen, unable to move.

'*Merde!*' said the computer.

People sighed angrily, in French.

Chapter 10

My soul yearns for you in the night; my spirit
within me earnestly seeks you.

Isaiah 26:9

When Nnenna got home after school that day, the house was
silent. She stood in the hallway for a moment before shutting
the door, listening for the telltale signs that her mother was in
the house, quietly working in her room: the sound of her softly
typing away on the computer's keyboard, or checking a word
in one of her reference books. After a moment, she heard her
mother's finger slam down on the Return key. Nnenna closed
the door softly and smiled.

Their home, a small terraced house in South Manchester,
was tidy in every room except Nnenna's, which was a pigsty,
both from her mother's point of view and in objective, scien-
tific terms. It was the fourth place that Joanie and Nnenna
had lived together: they'd moved around Manchester every
three or four years when the landlord they were renting from
had decided to sell the house, or when the rent went up too
much, or when the mould became too bad. And although
they had reason to believe that they wouldn't have to move
again for a while (Nnenna thought their current landlord, a
Thom Pickering, had taken a shine to her mum), it was always
a possibility, and Nnenna hated it. She tried not to hate it, and

she knew that her mother was not to blame – she knew that her mother could not afford to buy a house in the school's catchment area – but while Joanie habitually tidied every space that she used, Nnenna, almost consciously, kept her room in a mess because some small part of her mind thought that, if they ever did have to move, an untidy room would take just a little longer to pack away.

Nnenna reached the door of her mother's bedroom and stood quietly again, listening and watching: her mother worked at her desk with her back to the door. Joanie's room was small, but perfectly organised: shelves, plastic storage boxes, desk tidies and compartments multiplied in every space so that there was room for everything, and almost nothing in the room was in sight. Joanie always said that mess made it hard to think.

Nnenna wanted to talk to her mum, to tell her what Dan had said and try to work out how it made her feel – she never felt comfortable telling Steph or Hannah when Dan upset her – but as much as she wanted to talk, she also wanted to watch her mum work. She'd always loved it. When she had been little, the house they lived in was too noisy to work in and Joanie had taken Nnenna to the Central Library. Nnenna would sit on the floor next to the desk where her mother worked away in the vast, circular Wolfson reading room, awed into silence by its seriousness, its high ceilings and the way even the smallest noise would echo. She was only a year or two old at the time, too young to be able to read; but while her mother worked away, Nnenna pored over newspaper articles she could not understand, copying out letters of the alphabet when she felt particularly industrious, and at other times adorning the newspapers with colourful, if not always relevant, illustrations. Part of her missed that, even now: her mother sitting at a table so high up it seemed far away, and Nnenna trying to crack the code of language bit by bit.

'Hello, love,' said her mother, without turning around. 'How was your day?'

'It was all right, thanks. We had a Physics test today.'

'How did it go?' said her mother's head, still bowed down in deep concentration.

'It was fine, I think. We'll get our marks back tomorrow. How was your day?'

'Not too bad, love,' she said, distantly. 'Not too bad.'

Nnenna paused for a second. 'Mum?'

'Yes?'

'Did you and ... did you have lots in common? With ... '

Joanie raised her head and turned round in her chair. She looked at Nnenna for a long moment.

'With your father?'

'Yeah. With him.'

Joanie thought before she spoke, unsure whether to answer the question that had been asked, or to try to understand the motivation behind it. It was hard to know what to do for the best.

It seemed the right thing to be honest, at least; but if she started to answer questions now, there was only one place it could end.

And yet, Nnenna had asked. And she seemed so desperately sad, staring down at the floor, her bag half off her shoulders. She looked exhausted. And she'd barely even been able to finish her sentence.

'No, we didn't, to tell the truth. Not really.'

'Oh,' said Nnenna, sadly.

'At least, not in any obvious way. I mean, we'd been to the same university, but he was a few years older than me.'

'*Was?*'

'Is. Yes.'

Nnenna's eyes widened with an unspoken question, but Joanie avoided her gaze and continued, saying only what she could bear to say. 'We were very different people on the surface: I liked arts, and he liked science; I was hesitant in some ways and he usually seemed fairly confident and sure of himself. I grew up in England and he, as you know, was – is – Nigerian. He was a Christian when I met him, but I didn't believe in God at all. I tried to understand it but I thought the whole *religion* thing was ... well, I thought it was silly. All those people beating themselves up for not being born perfect, always looking to a future that might never arrive. It just made me sad.'

'So then ... why did you get together?'

'Because we fell in love.' Joanie was quiet for a moment, as if to mark the fact that she had spoken such heavy words for the first time in years and years. She frowned. 'So that helped.'

Joanie glanced at Nnenna, as if to say, 'Are you sure you want to ask about this?' But Nnenna only inclined her head, waiting.

'And you know, the surface is only that – the surface. Once you got past those things, we were actually very similar. We both felt quite lost, I think.'

'Lost?'

'Something happens to you in your twenties, sometimes. You realise things; or you think differently about what you thought before. I think we'd both got to the age where a lot of the things we'd always believed in didn't seem to make as much sense any more.'

'Like what?'

'For him – for your father – it was God. And this country, I think. For me, it was university itself. I'd always thought I wanted to go and study because I loved Classics – and I did love it. But I think what I began to realise was that I'd gone to Cambridge mostly to please my mum. I think I thought that something about me wasn't quite good enough, wasn't quite right. I think I felt that if I could just achieve that one great thing, I'd compensate for it, somehow.'

'And did you? Compensate?'

'No,' she said, eventually. 'And it took me a long time to realise that I had nothing to compensate for, that I was wasting my time. It seems strange to think I'd never realised it before, it seems so clear now. But that's the benefit of age, I suppose.

'And your father, well ... I think he wondered what he was doing in England at all, for the same reasons. He'd wanted to make his family proud and stay close to his culture while he was living here; to stick to his roots, he called it. But in the end, he found he'd changed. I think when he started to have doubts about God, he felt a lot of shame about it: religion was very important to his family, I think, and they had expectations of him. But you can't choose these things, and Maurice was seeing parts of the world he'd never seen before, never thought of.'

'Like what?' said Nnenna, seriously. 'Like ... Cambridge?'

Joanie laughed. 'Maybe. You find surprises everywhere, I suppose. But more ... love. I think it was love. I think that, for both of us, love became very complicated very quickly. We loved each other, of course – you know that' (this had been one of the few things Joanie had shared with Nnenna) '– and I think that sometimes, when you love someone, when you really start to get to know them, it forces you to get to know yourself. And sometimes that's hard. It was hard for both of us, I think.'

'Mum, you're crying.'

'Am I? Gosh, I'm sorry. I didn't even reali—'

'I'm sorry. I shouldn't have asked.'

'Don't be ... I mean, don't worry, I – gosh I feel so—'

Joanie turned round again and took a tissue from a box on her desk.

'Nnenna, you're so full of questions today! I think that's more than enough, for now. I haven't even thought about dinner,' she said, vaguely. Her voice sounded as if it were far away. 'Is it my turn to cook? Yes, I think so ... Come on, let's ... You go and put your school things away in your room and have a wash, and ... and I'll ... I'll go downstairs and see what's on the menu for tonight. That's enough questions.'

Nnenna nodded quickly as her mother swept past her out of the room, still far away, still speaking in a language that she could only partly understand.

1993

Joanie woke up slowly; she had the feeling of drifting upwards through layers of sleep, towards the sunlight that streamed in through the paper-thin curtains in Maurice's flat. His bed was much more comfortable than hers, she had found. It was firmer and, being a graduate rather than a student, he lived in a quieter part of town.

It was January 1993, and Joanie had just come back to Cambridge after Christmas. It was cold here, but bare: there was no snow (it hardly ever snowed there properly, on the flatlands of East Anglia) and hardly any students. Joanie had returned to college ten days early. Ostensibly, she was here to get a head start on her work for the term, but in reality, she was here to see Maurice, whom she hadn't dared to bring home. She'd told herself that this was because they'd not been seeing each other long enough, but she feared her mother's reaction. Ironically, if she had been braver – if she'd been closer to her mother's expectations – she would not have cared. And there would have been another terrible row. And they would have both said awful, hateful things, and she wouldn't have been able to think properly for days, or get any studying done . . .

'Morning,' said Maurice, rolling over and sleepily laying an arm over Joanie's chest. She was grateful for the way he did not insist on cuddling at night (a romantic notion which she did not believe to have any practical value); less grateful for the quiet but potent farts he passed while he slept. She discreetly opened the window shortly before bedtime.

'Good morning,' she said. She smiled at him and quickly searched his face for signs of resentment, of anger that she had not wanted to bring him home with her: it had been almost five weeks, after all.

But he didn't seem to be annoyed. Or at least, he didn't seem to want to show it: he turned his head away abruptly but with a smile, and got up to open the curtains.

'You might as well have left them closed, you know,' said Joanie. 'You'd let just as much light in.'

'Ah, but I wouldn't be able to see the beautiful day outside. Look at that . . . Cambridge is so beautiful in the sunshine.'

And he was right: a bright, cold day had started outside. They heard the whisper of bicycle chains rotating as people began to go about their mornings.

'Are you hungry?' he said.

'Mmm. Yeah, a bit.' She'd gone straight to his house from the train station last night, and they'd gone straight to his bed. They'd both forgotten to eat until now.

'Pancakes?'

Joanie laughed. Given the right tools, Maurice was a fine cook; but his kitchen, like the rest of his house, was a stupendous mess. 'And where are you going to find those? Underneath the rice cooker, perhaps? Hidden behind a pile of dirty plates?'

'Oh, it's not so bad.'

'*Not so bad*? Yesterday, I thought I saw last week's spaghetti move. How can you live like that?'

Maurice shrugged and smiled complacently. Joanie shook her head in silent amazement. Everywhere she went, there was mess: old engineering journals, dirty dishes, clothes that had been flung to the floor where he'd taken them off . . . How was it that someone like Maurice could be so chaotic in his home? In his mind, in the way that he thought, he was methodical, even at his most confused he tried to think logically, not emotionally. And more – having known Maurice for a couple of months now, Joanie saw the way Maurice was treated in Cambridge. Shopkeepers keeping a beady eye on him at all times, even following him, un-self-consciously, around their shops; drunken students in white tie singing reggae songs at him and touching his hair when they saw him in the streets at night. Even some of the people at his church treated him with a wary fascination – one of them had charitably assumed that he'd got into Cambridge as a result of some sort of positive discrimination scheme for black people. *Yes, how wonderful that you're here . . .*

Joanie expected someone whom the city had treated so coldly to be different. Before seeing his flat for the first time, she had imagined that every piece of his life – including his home life – would be carefully regimented; ordered, like bricks in a strong outer wall. But this was not the case: he lived in a state of constant chaos, and appeared to be happy with it.

But Joanie, who had grown up under her mother's rule, was not and could not be. She got out of bed, grabbed Maurice's arm and marched him to the kitchen.

'My God,' she said. A more demanding woman would have walked away when she saw the state of his flat for the first time, she thought. Even an only *slightly* more demanding woman would have sat down and made him tidy up until the flat looked hospitable enough for a guest. But she did neither: part of her felt somewhat guilty. Unlike her, Maurice had been a virgin before they'd met, and now he wasn't. She felt an unaccountable sort of grief for what he had lost: not so much his virginity but the belief that it was a thing worth keeping, something prized by the Lord. Although he would never say this, Joanie felt as though Maurice, by sleeping with her, had been unfaithful to God, and she was plagued by insecurities about this, even though his relationship with the Almighty was clearly on the rocks already. It had the bizarre effect of making her want to be maternal towards him in a desperately old-fashioned sense: she wanted to help tidy his home and keep it clean, as though Maurice's God would look more kindly on this destroyer of one traditional value if she took stewardship of something else; as though scraping the mould off his cutlery would compensate for having deflowered him right before the Christmas holidays.

'I'll wash, you dry,' she said, grimly.

'And what if I want to wash?'

'Then you're out of luck. There's not enough room on the drying rack for all this washing up, so you'll have to put some things away in cupboards and I don't know where anything goes.' She took the dirty dishes out of the sink and (after quickly washing the sink itself) filled it with hot water that could just about be considered soapy – she was at a loss to understand how someone who washed his plates so sparingly could be nearly out of washing-up liquid.

'Don't you rinse the plates?' said Maurice, a look of half-confusion, half-fear spreading across his face as Joanie deposited the first plate onto the drying rack, dripping with suds.

'Of course not.'

Maurice's frown deepened. 'At home, we rinse plates.'

'But in Cambridge, you don't wash them?'

'Joanie!' he half laughed, half gasped.

'What? What's the big deal?'

'They could still be dirty.'

'The parlous state of your kitchen sink notwithstanding, I can vouch for the fact that the plate I have set before your gaping mouth is, in fact, clean.' She relented slightly. 'Honestly. It's fine – hot soapy water and a good scrub is all they need. Now, come on: dry.'

Soon, they had a rhythm going. While Maurice dried plates to make room on the rack, Joanie found a CD player (splattered with pasta sauce) and a Sam Cooke CD inside.

'I love Sam Cooke,' she said.

'I never used to, myself. His music was always my cousin's favourite, not mine. But for some reason, I love it now.'

'What's your favourite song?'

'"Just For You",' he said, without hesitation. Joanie consulted the reverse of the CD case and selected the song. The percussion struck up and Sam Cooke's smooth, agile voice began to ring out.

She returned to the sink to find that she had been usurped. 'And what is the meaning of this?' she said, one eyebrow raised.

'A change is as good as a rest, Joanie Maloney,' he said, throwing the tea towel in her face. She threw it back, and soon they were chasing each other round the kitchen, dodging unpacked boxes, flicking each other with tea towels and howling with laughter.

Maurice, as though alight with a new idea, suddenly dashed back to the sink where he took a handful of dishwater and flicked it at Joanie – who froze where she stood, panting, the smile melting from her face. He'd meant something innocent, only the start of a water fight, but Joanie could only think of the time, nine years ago, when another man, in another city, had stormed into the kitchen in a blind rage and thrown a pot of near-boiling water at another woman, who had sat in her chair, almost too stunned to scream.

2009

It was only leftovers. Joanie breathed a sigh of relief – she knew there was no way she'd be able to cook, now.

Joanie so rarely spoke about Maurice – Nnenna so rarely asked – that when she did, it was like throwing up: afterwards she felt slightly better within herself, but could not shake a sense of disgust. Nor could she shake the feeling that she had been unwell for some time without realising it.

What could have moved Nnenna to ask about Maurice, now? Joanie had not missed the fact that Nnenna could not say his name. Why was that? Was that because of her?

Joanie opened the microwave and put two chicken breasts and some mashed potato inside. On the stove, she set a pan of frozen peas and a steamer full of broccoli. She did not feel hungry.

'Nnenna! Love, dinner's ready now.' No reply.

'Nnenna?'

Still hearing no response, Joanie walked upstairs and poked her head round the door of Nnenna's bedroom. 'Nnenna?'

It took her a moment to make sense of what she saw. Nnenna was not exactly a tidy child by nature, but Joanie wasn't used to seeing her bedroom in this state: it was like seeing a familiar text in a foreign language – it took time to translate. There were books everywhere, and pages and pages of notes strewn around Nnenna like dead leaves from a tree. Nnenna's laptop, an aged thing that Joanie had bought second hand three years ago, was on the floor, its ventilator fans whirring away discontentedly on the carpet. It must have been at least eight years old. Joanie could always hear it wheezing away when she was working in her room next door; it sounded like it was praying for death. It was barely worth using, except for typing up essays. What was Nnenna doing with it now?

'Dinner's ready,' said Joanie, softly, distractedly; but there must have been a note of panic in her voice as she spoke, since it was only now that Nnenna responded. Joanie saw her tuck one book in particular – a large black volume whose spine she did not have time to read – away under a pile of notes. What was she hiding?

'I'm here,' said Nnenna's voice. Joanie had never seen any of these books before. Had she gone to the bookshop after school? Joanie scanned the titles quickly: *Igbo for Beginners*, an Igbo–English dictionary ... Joanie could not imagine that the local bookshop would have those readily in stock: they would have had to order them in. Nnenna must have been thinking about this for some time, then.

And then something else she had never come across – from outside the room she had heard Nnenna speaking – something she couldn't quite make out – yet familiar enough to draw her, creeping, to the door – and Nnenna had stopped when Joanie called for her. Nnenna wasn't secretive, sometimes she didn't even take the phone out of the room when Danny called. Joanie knew, rationally, that there must be some things that Nnenna did not tell her, but she had always felt reasonably confident that Nnenna would share anything important with her, even if she took some time to do it; even if she could only get the words out by wandering into her mother's bedroom and sitting, silently, on the bed, waiting.

So why was she hiding this?

'Dinner's ready,' Joanie said, her eyes on the mess.

'Okay,' said Nnenna, her eyes on her books.

'What are you doing, love?' Joanie asked. The gentleness in her voice was too much – it was too deliberate. Her words had the air of trying to avoid upsetting Nnenna, which, naturally, only set her on edge.

Nnenna frowned slightly and said, 'I'm learning.' When her mother didn't say anything, when the self-righteousness of the expression hung in the air for a little too long and became uncomfortable, she said, 'I'm working. Thanks, Mum. For dinner. I'll be down in a minute.'

'Okay. But . . . '

'But . . . what?'

'Nothing. I only . . . Is everything . . . okay?'

'Yes!' Nnenna burst out, from nowhere. 'God. I'm fine. I . . . I want to finish this. It's not a big deal.'

Joanie stuttered an incoherent reply.

Nnenna was confused, too. They'd never even had a real fight, not like the ones her friends had with their parents. And she and Joanie weren't exactly fighting now, but it was as close as they'd ever come, which made it feel all the worse, all the more obvious. Danny said that sometimes it seemed more like they were sisters than mother and daughter.

'But . . . why now?' said Joanie. There was something in her voice that was like a red flag to a bull – the vulnerability in it was all too . . . much. It was unearned. Greedy.

'I'm only . . . I don't only want to learn French. There are other important things.'

'But did something happen? Did somebody say something?'

Nnenna threw down her pen. 'No! *No!* Jesus—' Nnenna shook her head in frustration, as though what she was about to say was the obvious answer to an unspoken question. 'Can you leave me alone?'

Then, 'I'm sorry, Mum. I'll be down when I've finished this bit but– can you leave me alone? Please. I won't be long.'

'Okay. Okay. But— you can't do it like this. I'm sorry, not – here, like this. It's too messy – look, I mean, it's all over ... everywhere.'

'What?'

'Please don't make such a mess, that's all. Can you try and be tidier?'

'Fine. Okay.'

'Okay. I ... I've ... Dinner's ready. I'll see you downstairs in a bit, okay? Okay ... Okay.'

She walked out of the room, lightheaded, her stomach churning, all thoughts of food far away.

PART II

PART II

Chapter 11

Even in laughter the heart may ache, and
the end of joy may be grief.

Proverbs 14:13

The following Saturday, passers-by in the art gallery smiled on
as a woman and her – daughter? Niece? Friend? It was unclear
from the difference in skin tones – sat down and quenched
their thirst for artistic nourishment by drinking in some aus-
tere portraits of the aristocrats of yesteryear. They inclined
their heads worshipfully to the left and studied hard the works
before them. Regular patrons might have recognised the two:
the woman in her late thirties, the girl in her mid-teens, looking intensely at a portrait of a lady who was gaily smelling a
posy presented to her by a man wearing black tie and a beatific
smile. If those passers-by observed that this painting did not
seem to please the girl as much as the woman, they might
smilingly put this down to the difference in ages; the girl might
well grow to share her elder's appreciation of art, in time.

'Come on, Nnenna,' said Joanie. 'I can't do this by myself.'

Nnenna frowned, but said nothing.

'Shall I get you started?'

'No, Mum.'

'Don't you want to? We always do this. It's no fun if you
don't join in. Come on, you'll like it once we get started.'

Nnenna sighed; she didn't want to refuse outright – that would mean having to explain why she didn't want to engage in their time-honoured game of simulating interviews between a prospective employer and a subject in a painting. But to play the game as always seemed wrong somehow. Things weren't the same as always, now. Things had changed.

But Joanie nudged her, and the idea of not playing the game seemed suddenly larger than itself: to Nnenna's teenage mind, everything symbolised something else; everything pointed towards some larger significance. Not playing the game – or at least, not playing the game without talking about it properly, which she was not prepared to do – seemed to gesture towards loneliness, towards a more permanent separation from her mother than she was ready for. She was angry with Joanie for not telling her more about her father, and for always making her ask about him instead of offering to talk, and for Joanie's inexplicable, quiet but apparent disapproval of her study of the Igbo language; but she was still her mother, and non-participation was too much, too serious.

Joanie nudged her again.

'All right! Fine. I'll play. But you start.'

Joanie scanned the frames on the wall for an inspiring piece for a moment, before settling on one to the right of her.

'Good morning, good morning. Thank you for sending us your application, Ms … Err, I'm sorry, how do I pronounce your name? I don't believe we've had the pleasure of many applications from your part of the world, Ms …'

'Jane Smith.'

'Juh-ane Suh-mith?'

'Precisely, sir.'

'I see, I see. Goodness me, how terrifically *exotic*.'

'Thank you, sir.'

'Might I ask from which part of the world you hail?'

'Shrewsbury.'

'Oh, delightful. Delightful!'

'No, not really.'

'Well, how exciting to have someone of your ... *background* in our midst. We're terribly bland, here, you see. And what with us being an all-male establishment ... '

'Yes, I read the ad*vert*isement carefully: PaleCorp has long held a certain ... aspirational gleam for me.'

'As for so many young women around the world.'

'My appreciation for your brand runs deep. Of course, I would rather be judged on the basis of my skills.'

'Ah! Indeed. Now, I see that first and foremost amongst your skills is ... er ... '

'Stroking my hair.'

'... Indeed.'

'Stroking my *brown* hair.'

'Oh, of course! How did that escape my notice?'

'I can't imagine. As a matter of principle, I stroke my brown hair conspicuously whereso'er I go. Observe.'

'Marvellous! Marvellous. We here at PaleCorp like a woman with that kind of ambition ... Goodness me, brown hair! You'd make something of a contrast here, you know.'

'Is that so?'

'Absolutely. We here at PaleCorp tend to have more, well, pale hair.'

'I see.'

'We are, however, trying to diversify, as you will have seen from our outreach programme for women blighted with hair of the darker hue.'

'Yes. Quite daring, I thought, in today's world.'

'Well, I hate to say it, Ms Smith, but we have faced some backlash for this outreach work from our more ... *traditional* shareholders.'

'Oh, dear me.'

'Very sad, very sad. But then, you know what people say

about women whose hair is *brown* – or even, ahem, black – as opposed to *blonde* ...'

'Irredeemable whores.'

'Precisely, precisely. Heavens, we seem to have got somewhat off the beaten track, Ms Smith. Why don't we discuss some of your most recent work? I see you have a slight gap in your employment history ...'

'Two hundred years, yes.'

'The reason being ...?'

'I was being held in a private collection in Surrey.'

'How *ghastly*. How on earth did you keep yourself occupied during that time?'

'Listening to men, mostly.'

'How enterprising!'

'Yes, one likes to keep one's most marketable skills as sharp as one can.'

'And that will pay handsome dividends, Ms Smith. I must say, you are a very impressive candidate. What would you say is your greatest ambition?'

'Heavens, what a question. I think that would be ... to sit down. I've been standing at this mirror for centuries, now, brushing my hair and holding my powder puff just so.'

'Naturally. And what would you say is your point of greatest weakness?'

'My wrists.'

'Excellent, excellent ... Ah! I see time is getting ahead of us. Shall we discuss your hobbies?'

'Oh, I try to keep myself busy, you know: looking downcast, evading direct sunlight, slowly dying of consumption. That sort of thing.'

'How very enterprising, Ms Smith.'

'I do my best, sir.'

'Well, I believe I've heard everything I need to hear ... When can you start?'

'I expect my darling husband to recognise my right to independent means imminently – any century, now.'

'Splendid, splendid. Well, I shall look forward to welcoming you aboard!'

A passer-by, if they stopped to look, might have seen a woman and her friend, perhaps, laughing, cautiously hugging, and enjoying art a little too much. They might have seen a mother trying to make amends; they might have seen a daughter trying to forgive.

'Danny? Danny! Time to get up!'

'Okay, Mum.'

'*Up*, Danny! As in, *not lying down*, capisce?'

'Yes!'

'Don't you waste the whole morning in bed – I mean it. There's a whole world outside of those bedsheets you've never washed.'

'Okay, okay! Five minutes!'

Danny, who had been wide awake for an hour, looked back at his computer, where Amit was sending him photo after photo of his completed crossword puzzles, and Sam was sending him a video of him practising the harp.

Why was he friends with these people?

They'd been sending messages, videos and photos back and forth all morning, sometimes separately, sometimes in a group chat.

Dan, said a photo of a camel riding two skateboards through a busy street. It was Amit's account. **Wag1. Hows the [bored-face emoji] with Nnenna goin?**

By way of reply, Dan sent a picture of a black man looking confused.

Sam: [a photo of a black woman looking impatient] You n Nnenna. uve not spoken since you [eggplant emoji]ed her in the shop have you

Danny: I told you not to talk about that its private

(Danny hated using the word 'private' to talk about this. It made the whole thing sound so sophomoric and vulnerable. The only reason he'd said anything in the first place was because it was impossible not to.)

Amit: Chill, chiiiiill. Weve not been tellin any1

Sam: Yeah its just uz girlz [GIF image from the 'Summer Nights' number in the 1978 smash hit musical film, *Grease*. (The context of the image was lost on other the two boys, but the sentiment was clear.)]

Danny: weve just not had time to talk much

Amit: [image of black woman rolling her eyes and swivelling her neck] mmm yeh rite mate

Sam: was she very disappointed

Danny: wiv wat

Sam: wiv YOU

Amit: [image of cocktail sausage]

Danny: shut. up.

Sam: oooh touched a nerve have we???

Danny: at least ive touched somethin other than a harp in my entire life. come on sam. u make it 2 easy.

Amit: [image of black basketball player scoring a slam dunk]

Amit: [image of black baseball player hitting it out of the park]

Amit: [image of black heavyweight champion celebrating victory in the ring]

Danny: anyway were chillin. we dont hav to b obv about everythin like u do

Danny: [typing . . .]

Sam: speakin of boxin . . .

Amit: drumroll please . . . .

Danny: i am not punchin. fuck off

Sam: [image of black woman rolling her eyes]

Danny: your just jealous cos your still a virgin

Sam: [typing . . .]

Amit: tru. U r.

Sam: [typing . . .]

Danny: a virgin who plays the fuckin harp at 9am on a saturday

Sam: [typing . . .]

Danny: NINE EH EMMMMMMM

Sam: [typing . . .]

Danny: i mean honestly who does that. do you want to die alone wiv no friends

Sam: shut up tiny dick

Amit: [image of black woman looking shocked and offended]

Sam: well if u n nnenna break up theres plenty of others whod like 2 take ur place danny

Danny: were not breaking up

Danny: others like who?

Amit: [image of fifty homeless people queueing for soup; all of them are black]

Danny: neither of you is going out with nnenna ever

Sam: never said we were

Amit: never said we wanted to. u don't know.

Danny: what?

Danny: shes my girlfriend n u r both ugly

Amit: we're not ugly

Amit: okay maybe sam is ugly

Sam: what? fuck u

Danny: fuck u both

Amit: wait were just jokin

Danny: im gettin cornflakes

Amit: Danny?

Danny: [offline]

And Danny, offline, stared for a moment at the profile pictures of his friends in the group chat: Sam, his face half-hidden behind a large beanie hat, only a huge grin visible; Amit, the subject of an obviously staged photograph taken during piano practice. Not for the first time, Danny wondered why he was even friends with these boys in the first place: they were so different. All Danny wanted to do was get through school without too much trouble, but the other two seemed to want to *wallow* in it like some weird bathtime activity with sudoku and harp recitals. The two of them seemed like they were built for school, while he ... He didn't know what he was for.

They had seemed to have more in common when they were younger, but now Danny wondered if their age had only masked their differences. When they first met years ago, Amit hadn't even been able to pronounce 'Shostakovich' on the first attempt. Now, all he talked about was classical music. And Maths, and university, and debating.

Never girls though. Was that weird? You couldn't shut Sam up about girls, but Amit just rolled his eyes. Which would be fine, except Amit didn't talk about boys, either. He never really talked about anyone. And Danny had to admit there was something quite nice about this, but he couldn't say why. Maybe it was just nice to know that Amit wasn't interested in pursuing Nnenna. Considered alongside most of the boys in his year, that would put him in the minority.

And Amit was a good friend. Sam could be a bit selfish sometimes, but not Amit. Amit let Danny finish his sudoku, leaving the last space blank for him to write in the 1, the 9, the 7. It had become a funny ritual of theirs lately, Amit figuring out the answers but leaving enough space for Danny to feel as though, despite his shortcomings, there might be some sort of space for him after all.

*

Later that day, Joanie left Nnenna at home and took the tram into the cramped offices of the *Manchester Post*. She didn't need to be there in person and she preferred to work at home or in a café, since there wasn't much desk space in the office, but she'd been trying to be more of a presence in the office, lately.

Sadly, Marco Guterres, the Features Editor, had noticed her presence, and was peering over the top of her cubicle again. Out of earshot, she called him 'the Periscope' because he barely cleared the top of the separating wall and because his nose – wide, round, assertive – had a more than slightly investigatory air.

'Morning, Joan,' he said, brightly, letting his chin rest on his hands which, in turn, were folded on the top of the dividing wall. Joanie knew without looking that he had achieved this height by kneeling on his desk, where he kept a cushion specifically for the purpose. Marco was a short, spindly man in his late twenties who looked to Joanie like he was largely made of spaghetti. Joanie, who usually felt like the product of one over-rich carbonara sauce after another, actually felt an odd kind of kinship with him. He was not a terrible person; it was more that she didn't know anyone else who could possibly be more annoying.

'How are we today, Joan? Still living life in the feast lane?'

Joanie forced herself not to visibly acknowledge either his remark or her largely feta-cheese-based lunch, which was packed in a blue plastic food storage box that sat on top of a pile of old clippings. It had been hard to find opaque Tupperware in a colour she liked, but listening to Marco itemise her meal would be harder. After Marco had 'accidentally' opened her lunchbox instead of his own last Thursday ('I should have known – the weight difference') Joanie had taken to keeping her meal in a blue box, taking it out of the fridge shortly before lunch, and keeping it discreetly on her desk.

When she replied to Marco, she tried to keep her voice neutral. Breezy.

'I'm fine, thanks, Marco. How are you? Good weekend?'

'Oh, you know. This and that.'

'Anything exciting?' Joanie didn't particularly care what Marco did with his spare time, but she had noticed that Marco was one of those people who often used a conversation about other people's lives as a springboard for talking about his own. Fortunately for Joanie, once Marco had jumped off the springboard and into the deep end, he rarely resurfaced.

And Joanie didn't want him to. Although her primary work concern was still her weekly crossword, she was starting to get up the courage to ask for the journalistic work she had wanted for years and, *technically*, this meant that Marco would be her line manager at the just-right-of-centre newspaper. And *technically*, this meant she had to be nice to him.

Which was no mean feat, particularly on a Saturday afternoon. Joanie had only been working for the *Post* for about sixth months, but with staggeringly easy self-assurance, Marco had gradually given himself permission to critique Joanie, her lifestyle, and her measurements. Although she had never invited his opinion on anything other than her spelling, punctuation and grammar, Marco allowed his pointed proboscis to sniff its way around Joanie's entire life, bit by bit, while Joanie either clenched her teeth and strove to ignore him or made pointed sotto voce remarks about his nose. Today, for some reason, even his own life couldn't distract him from hers.

Normally, he was liable to discuss any combination of her diet, wardrobe, hair conditioner and her parents' decision to forgo orthodontia – but always, his periscope was ultimately trained on one thing.

'Your love life, sweetheart. How's it going?'

'Fine, thanks, Marco.'

'Any dates yet?'

'No, Marco. Nothing to report, I'm afraid.'

'Mmm,' he said; quietly, in a way Joanie observed was much

like her dentist when she forgot to brush her teeth before a check-up. 'So, there's been nothing since Simon? Or that gay chap you brought along to the dinner?'

Joanie's blood froze. 'Gay?'

'Silas told me, sweetheart. Commiserations.'

'We weren't really—'

'So there's not been anybody since then? No . . . signs of life?'

The fact was, Marco knew very well that there had been nothing since Simon. Marco also knew very well that Joanie had recently dated a string of over-emotional men-children who were unequal to a relationship that spanned more than a fortnight. Marco knew extremely well that, since Simon (the cellist who had dumped her six months ago), there had been almost no 'signs of life' at all; that her romantic life resembled an A&E ward after a major road accident, in which a series of semi-anaesthetised victims briefly appeared, cried and promptly gave up the ghost.

Simon.

Joanie shuddered at the thought. Simon the Amoeba, the 'non-event', as Marco had called him – although in the end he had dragged on for eight months like a maiden aunt in a regency drama, stubbornly refusing to die.

'I'm a lover, not a fighter', Simon's online dating profile had said.

'I'm a lover, not a fighter,' he had said, whenever they were having an argument and it became increasingly clear that his position (on finances, on politics or indeed on the couch) was untenable.

'I'm a lover, not a fighter,' he said, when it became blindingly obvious to both of them that a serious discussion about their relationship was both necessary and, in all likelihood, would be extremely uncomfortable.

And the truth was, he wasn't a fighter.

The whole truth was that he was also not much of a bather,

a flusher of toilets or a thinker-through of things. That he was no great cleaner of bathrooms, wiper of mouth or brusher of teeth. And that Joanie didn't want or need another child.

All of which might have been tolerable, except that he wasn't much of a lover either. If there were any justice in the world, his abilities in this regard would have balanced out his numerous deficiencies, but he kissed Joanie like a baby Labrador (enthusiastically but with only the haziest of ideas where her mouth was) and made love like one, too – panting heavily from behind her and letting his tongue loll out.

'Why did you go out with him in the first place?' said Marco now, determined to get to the bottom of what he believed to be a sign of the root cause of Joanie's problems.

'I don't know,' said Joanie.

'Why didn't you at least dump him before he dumped you?'

It was a question she had asked herself countless times.

One fine day, Simon had called Joanie to say that he'd decided it was time, finally, to start taking himself more seriously.

'What do you mean, *taking yourself more seriously?*' Joanie asked.

Taking himself more seriously involved, he said, training up to teach music in a secondary school, finally getting his car fixed and, apparently, taking a new lover. Angela. Joanie had slammed the phone down so hard she broke the end-call button and for a week afterwards she had to finish phonecalls melodramatically by unplugging the receiver at the wall.

She never spoke to him again after that, but she saw him once or twice, from afar, at the supermarket, at the bank. His clothes were clean and ironed, his shirt starched, his hair combed and his breath undetectable at twenty paces. Finally, it seemed, all her hints and subtle gestures had paid off. All the same it did seem unfair that another woman entirely was the one to reap the benefits. True, he had eventually turned his life around; but

Joanie was furious that, when he did turn 180 degrees, he had found himself face to face with Angela, a dentist from North Yorkshire who, in Joanie's imagination, spoke three languages, took yoga and had never had a cavity in her life.

Fortunately, Marco was a comfort in these difficult times.

'Look,' he said, adopting the Tough Love voice of a stern coach, as though Joanie's attention had wandered aimlessly away from the full-time job of her ailing love life, to the piddling matter of her full-time job. 'Look. You're okay. You're probably just in recovery. He was your first real boyfriend in a few years, wasn't he? So, it's a big step. And Simon was . . . fine. He was fine. A bit boring, a bit grubby, but basically safe. Like a minibus.'

'A minibus?'

'He gets you from A to B and he's not dangerous when he gets behind the wheel. It's not as though he's going to plough into some secretary that's out on her lunch break.'

'No. She was a dentist.'

'Exactly,' said Marco, evidently unwilling to let this metaphor go. 'And he's not the one for you. Your true love still awaits. Simon was nothing but a placeholder, keeping you warm until you met someone better. He was an album filler. He was breadsticks. Prawn crackers. He was . . . ' Marco searched his mind for an apposite image, '. . . he was daytime television. You see, you'd been watching *Cash in the Attic* for six months. And okay, it probably feels like a depressing waste of time now, but you wait until *Downton Abbey* starts after the break. Then you'll have forgotten all about him.'

Marco beamed at her as though no woman could conceive of any higher pleasure in life than finding herself engaged to a fictional character in a nostalgic upstairs-downstairs drama. He was probably casting Joanie in some antiquated role now: mentally dressing her in a flapper's dress, giving her a mildly confrontational haircut and wishing she was two pounds lighter.

Marco's rhetoric left Joanie too overwhelmed to speak.

Simon, it seemed, was a mode of transport, cheap food and entertainment, too. She'd only wanted a boyfriend.

Not that she would have said much anyway: Joanie so rarely did say anything. The courage that had found her when she was talking to a stranger at Ophelia's wedding, deserted her everywhere else. A braver woman, perhaps, might have objected to Marco's grandstanding, or made a witty retort, but Joanie only left silence. Acres of it – whole fields full of the stuff, like great big verdant pastures. Perfect for the cow-brained Marcos and Simons of the world to come and graze in, farting like billy-o and leaving their shit everywhere. Their unsolicited advice and their toenail clippings.

But why didn't she say anything? It was a good question, Joanie thought.

It wasn't as though she didn't have the courage to stand up to someone like Simon, or Marco, or the man at Ophelia's wedding. She was capable of speaking her mind more often than she did – she was almost certain she had it in her. But she didn't know where it went when she needed it. People aren't like lunchboxes that you can see straight through. And what's inside doesn't always come out when you turn them upside down.

So, she had stayed quiet while Simon made a mess of things; she stayed quiet while she drove over to Simon's flat to drop the last of his things in a box outside his front door. And while Marco asked impertinent questions about her lunch and poked around her personal life.

'Don't worry, Joanie,' he said. 'You'll find someone. Maybe not right away, but it'll happen for you. You'll get married again.'

Joanie, once again, said nothing.

Again?

'*Bonjour!*'

'*Bonjour, Monsieur Black,*' chorused the class.

'*Asseyez-vous, s'il vous plaît.*'

Nnenna, Danny and Steph took their usual seats next to each other – Nnenna in between her boyfriend and her best friend – and got out their books; Nnenna quickly, Steph and Danny rather more slowly. Nnenna had never thought about the seating arrangement until now, but she hadn't spoken to Danny properly for weeks; not since they had slept together.

It wasn't that he was avoiding her, exactly, but he had started acting very strangely. His texts – even though they were almost always monosyllabic – seemed to take a very long time to send, now. And he was always doing homework when Nnenna asked if she could call him. Part of her was glad that he was taking school more seriously – maybe he'd changed his mind about university? Maybe he'd join her in Paris one day? – but a much larger part of her wanted him to return her messages within seventy-two hours or less.

She hadn't spoken to Steph about it yet, but this was only through her own dexterity in avoiding the conversation:

'So, have you and Danny had sex ye—'

'Whoa! Is that Beyoncé?'

and she could tell it was coming. She'd been dreading this French class, and here she was, sitting between them.

The class was small – around fifteen students – but Mr Black's room was just big enough (and his hearing was just poor enough) for Steph to be able to say, undetected,

'Oy. Have you and Dan broken up or something?'

'... What?'

'Well, have you?'

'Jesus, Steph. I don't want to talk about this now.'

'Well, something's wrong.'

'What are you talking about?'

'You two; you and Dan. Something's up, and how come you haven't come round?'

'I've been busy. I told you, I'm learning Igbo.'

'How long does that take?'

Nnenna frowned and pretended to concentrate. The lesson was a topic she already knew, so she doodled and translated short quotations from her diary into French.

'Nnenna?' asked Steph.

'Stephanie!' called Mr Black. *'Tais-toi!'*

'Sorry, sir.'

'Pardon?'

'Je suis desolée, Monsieur Black.'

'Bien. Tournez-vous à page soixante-trois . . .'

'Oy,' said Dan. 'What's up?'

Nnenna looked at him, puzzled. He'd never asked her this before. *What's up?* Was he asking for some sort of update? That seemed unfair, given that he'd spent the last few days communicating in grunts and shrugs. She wasn't sure if she'd expected them to be closer, now that they'd slept together. She didn't know what she'd expected, but she hadn't expected this . . . This weird awkwardness, this silence that persisted even when they were speaking.

'I . . . I . . .' said Nnenna. 'Nothing. You?'

'Nothing much. Was just wondering how you were getting on with your Igbo.'

'What?'

'Your Igbo. Amit told me he saw you in the library with your books yesterday.'

Nnenna frowned. This sort of leak was inevitable, she supposed, but she'd have preferred Dan not to know that his remark had had any effect on her.

'It's fine. I got some books and I'm learning. It's fine.'

'Just books?'

'What? Yes.'

'Is that enough?'

'What do you mean?' And why did he care?

'I only meant . . . don't you need to speak the language? Err . . . *oui, Monsieur Black. On dirait . . .*' He read unthinkingly from Nnenna's notebook: *"Si réellement j'ai péché, Seul j'en suis responsable."*"*

'Err ... Daniel, are you sure you're on the right page? "And even if it be true that I have erred, my error remains with myself"? Doesn't sound like the Marseillaise to me ...'

'Errr ...' Daniel looked confusedly at Nnenna.

'Allons enfants de la Patrie, le jour de gloire est arrivé,' said Nnenna, quickly.

'Très bien. Alors ...'

'What just happened?' hissed Dan. 'Did I— did you get an answer wrong, in French?'

'Shut up, Dan,' whispered Steph. 'Nnenna, was the sex bad? Is that it?'

'What?'

'Well, was it?'

'How did you even know we had sex? I haven't told anyone.'

'Amit told me. Look – don't get angry. Even if Dan never said it out loud, it's obvious. He's been so cocky.'

'Okay, okay. Yes. We have, but I honestly don't want to talk about it right now.'

'Why not? You don't tell me anything any more. It's not my fault you and Dan are fighting.'

'I'm not—' Nnenna sighed. 'Can't we talk later? Dan's right here.'

'Nnenna?' said Dan, urgently. 'Did you – *ah, oui, Monsieur. Cela signifie, "Il a éloigné de moi mes frères, Et mes amis se sont détournés de moi."*'**

'"He has put my brothers far from me, and those who knew me are wholly estranged from me?" Dan? Are you sure you're with us? Why don't you have another look at the English version and then—'

* Job 19:4
** Job 19:13

'*Ils viennent jusque dans vos bras, egorger vos fils, vos compagnes.*' said Nnenna.

'*Très bien, Nnenna, très bien.* Beautiful. *Bon, on continue . . .*'

'What are you writing, Nnenna?' said Dan. 'Are you ahead of everyone else again?'

'It's—'

'Shut *up*, Dan!' whispered Steph. 'And no, Nnenna, we can't talk about it later. You've been avoiding me.'

'No I haven't,' said Nnenna. 'And me and Dan haven't actually talked that much since we did it, anyway, and that's fine. I just haven't . . . seen him very much since.'

'What?'

'So Nnenna,' interrupted Dan. 'I was thinking . . .'

Nnenna turned to Danny, eager to hear what he might have to say about their ailing relationship. Was it a renewal of his feelings, perhaps? An undertaking to change his ways? He was reaching into his bag . . .

'And I got you this.'

Nnenna glanced down, looked askance at it: for it was not a written apology, not tickets to a concert or even jewellery . . . It was a flyer.

'The Nigerian Centre?' she said slowly.

'Yeah, it's this place in the city centre. It's, like . . . a community centre. But for, you know . . . Nigerians.'

'Yeah. I got that.'

'Come on, Nen. I know it seems random but I went past it at the weekend and I thought about you. I just want to try to . . . *Ah – oui, Monsieur Black . . . Cela signifie, "Mes pensées me poussent donc à répondre, à cause de cette impatience en moi."*'

'Honestly, Dan . . . "Therefore my thoughts answer me, because of my haste within me"*? What are you doing? It's page 94. Can you show me your—'

* Job 20:2

Nnenna discreetly tapped an earlier page in her notebook.

'*Marchons, marchons, Qu'un sang impur abreuve nos sillons*,' said Dan.

'I think we're getting there, finally,' said Mr Black, archly. '*Au suivant . . .*'

'Thanks.'

'No problem.'

'Look, with this flyer thing—'

'It's fine.'

'I'm only trying to help you! Jesus. Would you look at it?'

'Fine, okay. I'll look.'

'Hey!' whispered Steph. 'What's that? What did Danny—'

'Yes, Mr Black,' said Dan. 'I'll get it right this time.' He glanced at Nnenna's book again, not seeing that she had turned back to her doodles. '*Or voilà le Béhémoth, à qui j'ai donné la vie comme à toi; il mange de l'herbe comme le bœuf.*'*

Mr Black's face was a picture of bewilderment. '"Behold, Behemoth, which I made as I made you; he eats grass like the beef*"?'

'"Like an ox,"' corrected Nnenna.

Mr Black looked from Dan to Nnenna sharply. 'Dan . . . Shall we have a chat about this after the lesson?'

'Yes, sir,' said Dan, shooting a resentful glance at Nnenna. She returned a weak smile.

'*Tremblez, tyrans! et vous, perfides, l'opprobe de tous les partis, tremblez!*' said Stephanie, confidently.

'*Très bien, Stephanie, très bien. Alors . . .*'

The bell rang, and Mr Black gave them their homework assignments and dismissed them. Dan nodded compliantly while Mr Black gently suggested that he do his own work in future, before he pelted off to talk to Amit about the debating

* Job 40:15

club. Nnenna and Steph were left alone to talk. Standing up, Steph saw the flyer on Nnenna's desk.

'What's that?' said Steph.

Nnenna handed it over.

'From Dan?'

'Yeah, why? What's that look for?'

'Nothing, I was going to say ... I'm impressed. Well, surprised, anyway.'

'Why?'

'Well,' Steph said. 'Dan's not normally so thoughtful, is he?'

'I think he probably feels guilty.'

'About what?'

Nnenna blushed, still too ashamed to share it with anyone. 'Oh, nothing. Something stupid he said. Anyway, the flyer's nice.'

'Yeah, I guess ... ' said Stephanie.

Nnenna stopped putting her books away and stared at her friend. 'What? What is it? You've been weird about Dan all day. What's the problem?'

'Come on, Nnenna.'

'What?'

'Don't act all surprised. You know I don't like him.'

'Come on. I know he's not your favourite person, but don't make it bigger than it is.'

'Don't you make it seem like it's nothing when you know it's not! He just spent the entire lesson reading out answers from your book, Nnenna. You know he's not good enough for you.'

'What does that even mean?'

'It means he likes you—'

'Loves me.'

'—but he doesn't appreciate you. Not the *great* things about you – not *you*. He can't. Because he doesn't even see you. He doesn't like how smart you are because he's not smart. He doesn't get that it's great that you're thoughtful because he's usually not that thoughtful. And yes, okay, he's done something thoughtful for you today. But how often does he do that? How many times have you been annoyed with him because he's forgotten your birthday, or because he's asked you what you're doing for Father's Day? How many times?' Stephanie heaved her heavy canvas bag over her shoulder. 'And now!'

'What?'

'You said yourself that ever since you had sex, he's been weird. Don't tell me that's not a bad sign. And it's not like he doesn't have the time, since he's spending all that time with Amit, getting ready for their stupid debating competition. Come on, Nen. You must have thought about this. Haven't you?'

'Wait – slow down! Steph, where is this coming from? How long have you been thinking about this?'

'Look,' said Steph, trying to make her voice gentler. 'I'm not going to tell you what to do, and I'm sorry if this comes as a shock. I honestly thought we were both thinking the same thing, so it didn't seem worth bringing up before. But when you got all excited over such a tiny thing ... Come on, Nen. You know I'm right. I mean, how long can this last?'

Chapter 12

Put no trust in a neighbour; have no
confidence in a friend; guard the doors of your
mouth from her who lies in your arms ....

Micah 7:5

The following week, by the time Jonathan left Silas's house
and started to make his way over to Joanie's, he was a mess –
physically and emotionally. He was an emotional mess because
he felt unduly shut out of Silas's life. He was a physical mess
because he was covered in food.

'Good grief,' said Joanie when she saw him. She put the
kettle on and they both sat down at the small, round kitchen
table where Nnenna had been doing her homework a few minutes before. Nnenna was pleased that her mother still socialised
with one friend from university who had not been named after
a tragic literary heroine, but she saw an opportunity for an
extended online conversation with her own friend. She found
that this was easier when her mother was too busy to wax lyrical about the slow, painful death of face-to-face interaction.

'I can't say I'm happy to see you like this,' Joanie said to
him as she took two mugs from the kitchen cabinet, 'but I am
happy to see you.'

'Me too,' said Jonathan. He wiped the last of the butter from
his Adam's apple. His voice sounded absent.

'No,' said Joanie, 'I mean it.'

The agitation in her voice turned him to face her. 'What do you mean?'

She had played this apology in her head countless times, but she struggled to form words, now. 'I mean ... I know that, at the wedding, I promised that we'd stay friends. And this is the first time we've met since then, and it's been months, and I don't want you to think that I said that out of guilt, because—'

'It's fine, Joanie,' Jonathan said.

'Do you mean "it's fine because I don't blame you" or "it's fine because I don't want to talk about it any more"?'

'Yes.'

'Jonathan ...'

'Honestly, Joanie, it's okay. Just – help me, would you?'

'Well, that I can do. I think.'

'It's not as bad as it looks,' Jonathan replied. 'I've been worse.'

Joanie looked at him for a moment, her eyes wide with shock. Did he mean what she thought he meant? Of course he did. And of course, now was the time for courage, for finding the right words, and for listening.

But she quailed. She had no courage. She could not bear to listen and the only words she could say were,

'Yes, it does look bad.'

'It's fine, Joanie.'

'How did you even get dried *parsley* down your *neck*?'

'What?' Jonathan, who hadn't noticed this seasoning of his flesh, tried to bend his arm behind himself so that he could dust it away. But he couldn't reach and only ended up looking silly, as though he were inexpertly performing some sort of coquettish dance with herbs. Joanie felt a kind of guilty gratitude for the distraction; she got up and took a tea towel to his neck.

'This is ridiculous,' she said, firmly. 'You look like he was getting ready to put you in the oven and then got distracted.'

'Well ...'

'Well ... what?'

'Well ... he did get distracted.'

'Jesus, Jonathan. Heaven forbid he would take the time to offer you some food before he shags the life out of you in his pantry.'

'Scullery.'

'What's a scullery?'

'I'm not sure. I didn't get the best view of the room.'

Joanie rolled her eyes. 'If he were a proper gentleman—'

'And if anybody still *used* the word "gentleman" since they invented steam trains—'

'—he'd *cook* something for you instead of rolling you around in a bunch of ingredients like a chicken he'd picked up in Waitrose. I don't like him.'

'I know.'

'Well?'

'But he doesn't owe me anything. Just because we're ... doesn't mean he has to be ...'

'Nice?'

'A *gentleman*. Whatever that means. He's not my boyfriend. We haven't promised each other anything.'

'You never even spoke about where you stand?'

Jonathan shrugged. 'What's to talk about? He's made things pretty clear.'

Joanie frowned at this and sat down again; it somewhat took the wind out of her indignant sails. Her friendship with Jonathan was still new, and she wasn't sure how to talk to him. For want of a better idea, she had instinctively taken on a protective role towards him, and it made sense in her head. But it felt awkward, as though she were always one step away from who she was supposed to be for him. Joanie didn't mother anyone except her daughter, and even Nnenna didn't often need to be spoken to like this.

'Well, I still don't like him. Even if you're not dating, that doesn't mean he can't treat you with a bit of respect.'

'I honestly don't think of it like that. I'm happy with things, Joanie. I don't think of things the way you do.'

'And even if your relationship only consists of sex, that's still a relationship, you know.'

'Joanie ...' But he couldn't finish. He had nothing to say.

Joanie looked at him, seeing him for the first time, perhaps, in years. He was just a little boy. He didn't know anything. 'People give food to strangers, Jonathan. People give food to beggars on the street. You're telling me he couldn't offer you a sandwich? A slice of ham? A grape?'

'I just—'

'It's like he's feeding you piecemeal, giving you a meal one crumb at a time.'

Without moving from his seat, barely changing his body language, Jonathan exploded quietly. His whole body became so tense that Joanie instinctively backed away. When he spoke, his voice was so angry and so sad.

'Love isn't food, Joanie! And if it was, I can't ... I don't ...' He sighed. The kettle had boiled long ago. 'Can we change the subject?'

Joanie nodded silently. She didn't know Jonathan. She didn't know anything about him, what he was thinking, or hoping for. She concentrated on wiping her hands, already clean and dry, with a tea towel. She waited for Jonathan to bring up something new. She watched him. She watched his sadness like a ticking thing.

'Shall I make the tea?' he said quietly.

'No, I'll do it. I know where everything is.'

'Okay.' Joanie shuffled to the counter, picked out two teabags, added milk, checked: sugar? Sweeteners? Upstairs, Nnenna giggled in her room at what her friend was saying on the other side of town.

'Is that the Peak District?'

Joanie strained the tea and brought it over to where Jonathan was standing, by the bricked-up fireplace. Above it, on the mantelpiece, was a framed photo of her with Nnenna, standing in a stream, smiling at the camera. Behind them was a ravine, bordered by walls of rock with faces so flat and smooth they might have been chopped apart by grand design.

'Yes,' said Joanie, handing Jonathan the mug. 'Nnenna and I went there for her sixteenth birthday.'

'Where is it?'

'It's a stream in a ravine called Grindsbrook.'

'It looks beautiful.'

'Yes, it was. We had a lovely walk around the valley and then we went to a pub for food at the end. I sorted out a cake for her. I bought it at a supermarket, before you ask. Candles and everything.'

'It sounds like you had a great time.'

'We did.' Joanie took the frame from the mantelpiece and stared into it, smiling, as though it were speaking words of kindness to her. 'It feels like such a long time ago, now. Right now, it's hard to imagine Nnenna going on a walk with me for four or five hours and both of us coming back alive.'

For a moment, Joanie hesitated. Was this what you did with a depressed person? Did you tell him your problems? But she didn't know what else to do. The problems were there; the sadness was there. And so was his. So the thing to do was to share it.

'Teenagers go through phases,' he said, gently. 'You'll be right as rain before you know it. And at least you try: my parents never did anything like that with me. If I hadn't spent so much time in church, we'd never have done anything together. And compared to the church we went to, Grindsbrook seems like ... well, it seems like it'd be a breath of fresh air.'

'Do you know the Peaks?'

Jonathan shook his head. 'Never been.'

Joanie turned to him, her eyes slowly widening in shock. 'What? You've never been to the Peak District? Jonathan, how long have you lived in Manchester, now?'

'I'm pretty rubbish at reading maps,' he shrugged. 'If I went by myself I'd probably get lost and have to be airlifted off the side of a hill.'

'But I could go with you!'

'You could?'

'Yes! I can read maps fine. I'll go with you one weekend when Nnenna's staying with a friend. It'll be so good for you, Jonathan. Honestly. It's so big, out there. And it's not far, either. You hop on a train and you're there before you know it, and out there in so much space, all your problems will seem so small.'

'That would be great, if you wouldn't mind. It sounds like exactly what I need.'

'I'm lucky, I suppose: it's like a part of my heritage. I've been going to the Peaks since I was very young. My Aunty Mary used to take me along with her whenever she knew I needed to get out of the house.'

'She sounds like a godsend.'

'She was. She always seemed to know when things were bad.'

'Is that her?' Jonathan pointed to another frame, this one older, the photograph showing a younger Joanie in her graduation gown, Aunty Mary's arm around her shoulder.

'Where are your parents?'

'They didn't want to come. I was showing by that point. Can you imagine?' Joanie shook her head as if in disbelief. 'Pregnant at graduation. Unmarried, the black father nowhere to be seen. These things aren't supposed to happen to people who go to Cambridge. Or vice versa, I suppose.'

'Where was Maurice? Where was I?'

'He was in Nigeria with his family by then. And you were at

a different college, so you must have graduated on a different day. It was only me and Aunty Mary.'

'That must have been hard for you?'

'I often wonder what on earth I would have done without her, you know. I wonder where Nnenna and I would be.'

'You'd have found your way, somehow. You're pretty brilliant, you know. Both of you.'

Joanie shrugged, replaced the frame. 'I'm lucky,' she said, simply.

'How is Nnenna, anyway?' said Jonathan.

Joanie blinked away an early tear, glad of a change of subject. 'She's fine. She's starting to learn Igbo.'

'Oh, Maurice's language? How wonderful! Was it hard to find a tutor?'

'I didn't. She's teaching herself.'

Jonathan said nothing, his face a question.

'She went out and ... got a load of books on it.' Sometimes, Joanie could almost feel Nnenna wanting to ask for a tutor.

'It sounds quite sudden. What's brought this on?'

'I wish I knew. One day she's acting normal, the next ...'

'I think this *is* normal, Joanie. I mean, it's not my business to say, but ...'

'But what?'

'Well, I was going to say that I was surprised that she'd never showed this kind of curiosity before. I was lucky – my parents couldn't afford to take me to Jamaica more than once, but they told me about it all the time, made sure I knew how to make the food ... I always *knew*. But Nnenna doesn't know. And to be sixteen and not know ... I mean, I know something terrible happened—'

'Who knows what's going on in her head,' said Joanie evasively. 'She's not like I was when I was her age.'

She said nothing for a moment, unsure how to say what she had to say next.

'I've read her diary.'

Jonathan's eyes widened. He half whispered, half guffawed. 'You did what?'

'I'm not normally like this,' said Joanie. She glanced at the kitchen door, then walked over to close it. She paced around the room. Her next words, things she'd told herself many times, came out in a rush. 'I don't want her to think I don't trust her – because I do trust her. I think she's wonderful, Jonathan, honestly. And I don't normally go around invading her privacy – that's not the kind of mum I am. But I think that sometimes, you have to do certain things that might seem wrong to an outsider, when you're—'

'Curious?' said Jonathan quietly.

'What? No, it's not like that.'

Jonathan scoffed, more openly disapproving of her, now. 'Come on, Joanie. Don't tell me you weren't curious. Most people would be. It's not even the curiosity that's the problem. That's natural.'

Was it? Whatever it was, she hadn't been able to resist it. And she'd had the chance to – she'd had the opportunity to back out before it was too late. She'd seen Nnenna try to hide a black book in her room that day, sliding it underneath a pile of notes. So, she'd gone into Nnenna's room the next day while she was out at school and found the book, hidden underneath her daughter's pillowcase.

It was a Bible. Nothing more, nothing less.

But what did this mean? Was Nnenna converting to Christianity, now, too? Why? Why now? How long had this been going on? It occurred to Joanie, briefly, happily, that this might mean that Nnenna was less likely to be having sex with Danny; but her relief was to be short-lived.

Flicking through the Bible, Joanie saw that it had been annotated in various places, and that certain verses were underlined. But they were not the kinds of things one would expect, not the oft-quoted verses that might be popular with the newly converted. Not the sort of soundbites that Maurice would have wanted, for example. They were odd verses, things Joanie didn't recognise. Many of them from the more obscure books, books that Joanie had forgotten existed. And when Joanie looked closer at the margins, there were no notes on the meanings of the verses, only numbers: *4/11, 15/7, 21/3.* Were they dates?

Joanie put the Bible back under the pillow, careful to leave it exactly where she had found it. Now she looked around the room again, but she was not sure what for. She only knew, now, that she was looking for something that she did not want to find. She knew that, whatever it was, it was some permanent change, some shift that might poison her relationship with her daughter forever; but she looked, and she looked, unable to stop herself.

After a few minutes of slow searching – replacing everything carefully when she moved it – digging through her bags, rifling through her drawers, she found it. Behind the books on Nnenna's bookshelf. Her diary.

Except, it wasn't a diary. Under each date was, not a description of what Nnenna had done that day and her feelings about it, but a Biblical quotation. It was like some sort of code: each quotation referred to a sentiment, or an event, but did not describe Nnenna's feelings about it. It was like looking at a footprint in mud, outlined roughly by hand: it imitated, but did not reflect, anything individual, anything personal. There were no feelings; only hints. She could not hear Nnenna's voice in the words, only God's. She remembered it. It was a voiceless voice, booming, and grand, and inaudible. Like God, Nnenna was everywhere, and nowhere to be seen. Wherever she was, Joanie realised, she was terribly lonely.

'She's a very clever girl,' said Jonathan, awed.

'What do you mean?'

Jonathan shifted uncomfortably in his seat.

'Please,' said Joanie. 'Tell me what you mean. It's okay.'

'I hate this, I honestly hate this, Joanie,' he said. 'We haven't seen each other in such a long time, and this wasn't how I imagined us reconnecting after all these years – me showing up with food all over me. And you . . . '

'Jonathan. It's okay. You can say it.'

'I think . . . I think Nnenna must have known for a while that you might read whatever it is she wanted to write down.'

'You're saying . . . It means she doesn't trust me.'

Jonathan said nothing, but his face was consoling, as if to comfort Joanie for the realisation that was to come a few moments later.

'She's been writing this diary for a while. The entries go back months. It means . . . it means she's not trusted me for a long time. Maybe never.'

'Well,' he said, 'diaries are pretty personal. Trusting people with your private thoughts is hard, you know. Sometimes . . . sometimes it's even easier to trust the wrong person than trust someone who's close to you, someone who can actually hurt you. I think maybe I should— Joanie? Are you listening? What are you— Oh God, Joanie! Come here.'

Jonathan put an arm around her while she cried. She wiped his neck and picked leftovers out of his hair. Their skin smelled of salt and bitter herbs.

The woman stared at Nnenna, and at the money in her hands. 'You sure you want to pay in cash?'

Nnenna tried to keep her voice as steady as possible: 'Yes.' She was familiar with the stereotypes of Nigerians carrying around wads of cash, but the reality of walking through the centre of Manchester with over two hundred pounds in her bag felt dangerous and weird.

'It's a lot of money, this Igbo language course.'

'One hundred and eighty pounds, I know.'

'Plus the money for the books.'

'That's okay. I've got it here.' Nnenna took the money out of her pocket; she wanted to get it off her hands as soon as possible – she'd spent the last hour worried that someone would rob her, that someone would *sense* the money on her and rob her – but when she took out the cash, she realised she'd probably seemed too keen to get rid of it. The woman eyed the banknotes as if they were a snake.

'You know . . . normally we take card payments for this course. On the website. Can't you get your mum or dad to do it for you?'

'No, I . . . Mum said to do it like this. She gave me the money because . . . her card's not working.'

The woman's frown deepened. 'You're not a very good liar, are you?'

'I suppose this would be a bad time for me to try and lie, wouldn't it?'

'It would,' she said, her face beginning to relax into a smile.

Nnenna took a moment, as she sometimes did, to notice the receptionist's appearance and make-up. Nnenna wasn't sure if the woman was half white too, but her skin seemed to be of a similar colour. She wore a lipstick that was somewhere between red and deep purple, and there was a navy-blue scarf in her hair, which was wavy but not curly. She wore a crisp white blouse and a black pencil skirt. Everything was simple, conservative even; but chic.

Nnenna felt an urge to try to be the woman's friend, even though the receptionist – her name-tag said 'Ijeoma' – was probably seven years older than her, which seemed like an enormity. Even though she'd been lying to the woman through her teeth only a minute ago. Nnenna hated lying; the more you lied, the more you had to lie and in the end, the administrative burden of it was just too great. She was a bad liar every bit as much out of pragmatism as out of ethics.

'Okay, well, this is unusual, but since you've got the money we might as well take it from you ... Let me go and check with my boss ... '

While the receptionist was gone, Nnenna took a moment to look around the foyer of the Nigeria Centre. It was a new building, all gleaming chrome and plastic, hints of white and green everywhere. The ceilings were high, and on each wall was a portrait of a Nigerian man or woman of distinction: experts in medicine, military leaders, ambassadors, writers ... Nnenna realised with some sadness that she hardly recognised any of them. Each one could be a household name, for all she knew. None of them had ever been spoken of in her household.

It was a building that looked small from the outside, but the city centre plot of land must have cost a fortune to buy. It can't have been more than four or five years old, she thought. And she was surprised: in her mind, in films, on television, almost everything about Africa was ancient, was crumbling, was poverty.

Her mother didn't know she was here. She'd said she was going to go home and make a start on her homework – which she still hadn't begun – and instead she'd gone over to the Nigeria Centre with all the money she'd saved from her job at Chicken Co-op.

The receptionist was back.

'Okay, so the course leader says it's fine, but we need to take all the usual details we'd take for payment anyway: full name, address, telephone number, email, date of birth. If that's all right with you, you can fill out this form and we'll get you signed up.'

Nnenna filled out the form as quickly as she could, checking her watch every few minutes; the bus wouldn't take long, but she didn't want to risk getting home after her mum, and having to explain ...

'So, errr ... ' Ijeoma peered over the counter at the registration form. 'Nnenna, is it?'

'Yes.'

'Obviously, as we're in November now, you've missed the first term's classes; but I'm sure you'll be able to catch up soon enough, if you work on it at home. What made you want to learn Igbo when you've not learned it before?'

'I just . . . I just think it's time.'

'Oh, that's great! That's great. I mean, I can't imagine not speaking,' she said, using 'speaking' as a shorthand for 'speaking Igbo' in a way that Nnenna had never heard before. 'But most of the kids who learn, well, their parents pay for it as part of their education. It's a lot of money for someone your age. You didn't want to get your parents to give you the money and spend your savings on something else?'

Yes, there was something else. Nnenna's hand froze as she finished filling in the last box on the registration form. How would she pay for her dress now?

Chapter 13

[...] so that we may no longer be children,
tossed to and fro by the waves and carried
about by every wind of doctrine, by human
cunning, by craftiness in deceitful schemes.

Ephesians 4:14

Generally speaking, Joanie liked shopping. Strangely, she had less money for it now than she'd had as a university under-graduate, but she liked doing it when she could. She liked the exercise of judgement, of choice; the augmentation of a small but well-tended collection. She was an astute shopper, and sensible. If someone were to examine all her life's receipts, pore over each of her purchases one by one, they would find very little amiss, very few anomalies. One's spending, she believed, represented oneself; and as she had gone through life, she had augmented and adjusted herself accordingly.

She had dressed up and down with the seasons of her life, and although she firmly believed herself to be in what was no more than the late summer – and, with the right scarf accompaniment, an Indian summer at that – she had to admit that some changes had taken place. But those changes had all been for the better. The most satisfying element of the shopping experience was knowing that she knew what she liked; and knowing that what she liked now was a sleek, streamlined evolution of what she used to like ten, fifteen, twenty years ago.

Still, through all the years she had hung on to a core contingent of essentials upon which she always relied in some iteration or other: plain, versatile blouses; shoes which were equally suited for office and eveningwear; jeans that were hard to come by but whose fit justified the search; the occasional, small impulse-buy. It was, at heart, her taste that she most enjoyed: the communion with her exact and final sense of what was right.

Nnenna, she had come to realise, did not experience the same degree of joy and communing with her mother's taste. They had tried shopping trips before; and Joanie had tried to be forbearing . . . but the inexorable and urgent truth was that she, Joanie, the parent, was deeply, deeply correct. Always. It was, truly, a burden. It would have kept her awake at night, if it weren't so blindingly self-obvious.

She tried to be kind about how and why she was always right – Nnenna had taken to referring to Joanie as a benevolent dictator – but nothing she needed to say ever seemed to be kind enough. Joanie was not like Nnenna: although Nnenna was sensitive, easy to hurt, it was difficult to go over the hurt with her, to get her to admit that her feelings had been hurt at all. The damage, once done, was glossed over, stored away, smiled away.

Gradually, joint trips to high street stores had slowed to a trickle. Nnenna made polite but transparent excuses: she invented extra French homework; feigned tiredness and timely foot injuries. At the same time, however, discreet brown cardboard boxes began to arrive in the post like spies in foreign territory, slowly invading their home from the arcane and insouciant world of 'online'. In muted agony, Joanie could only watch as their once-private club – only big enough for two – expanded to welcome thousands of members she had never met. ASOS. Debenhams. Topshop. Arseholes.

Joanie could never see the clothes first, so she could not offer opinions. She quickly realised that this was the point. Reduced to the role of spectator, she saw the new fashions elbow their way into her house: 'jeggings'; 'distressed' jeans that made her want to weep for her daughter's bare knees; baggy jumpers that seemed like rejects from the wardrobe of a mid-1990s TV presenter . . . And these were Nnenna's choices. Joanie was genuinely happy to see Nnenna bloom and start to discover a sense of her own style, but . . . but . . .

The problem was, sometimes it was so easy to forget how far apart they were in age. Nnenna, so mature and calm for someone so young – usually – so often seemed older, less fragile than she was. Less new. Joanie was liable to forget that Nnenna was not, in fact, a middle-aged woman inexplicably trapped in the body of a teenaged girl. That Nnenna was still, in many ways, a child.

Joanie often thought that Nnenna's youth was nowhere more evident than in her fashion sense. If you looked at the things she wore – and Joanie often did, askance – something was almost always a bit . . . off. There was always some adventurous impulse gone awry. The faux antique brooch coupled with a crop top; the red socks worn without occasion or justification; the ornamental fan that went (they had both discovered) with absolutely nothing else she owned, and sat resentfully in her wardrobe, emanating regret but silently demanding she buy the trousers to match.

The leg-warmers that she hated as soon as she saw them. The baggy, flared jeans that made her feel like a groupie on *Top of the Pops 2*. She persisted in wearing them, but kept looking down at herself when she did, as though her jeans held some kind of secret, like elephantiasis or a nappy.

Joanie held, as always, a small hope in her heart that Nnenna was creeping towards a small sartorial maturity but ultimately, she was relieved that Nnenna was not too old for her yet. That, even if she didn't want her guidance, she still needed it.

*

Nnenna was sick of shopping with her mum, and they only did it twice a year.

Certainly, she believed, there must be some parent–child duos for whom the act of shopping for clothes is a bloodless, painless, even enjoyable affair – like giving birth while on an epidural, or those people in circuses who walk on hot coals.

Nnenna had never witnessed such domestic bliss first hand, so she could not say for certain that it existed; nor could she know exactly what it looked like. She could, however, paint a very precise picture of what it did *not* look like.

It did not look like Joanie Maloney marching her towards the scarf section (*'just try one'*), and insisting she sample at least five itchy, heavy items that aged her by fifty years. It did not consist of being told that everything – literally everything – that she liked was too bright, too busy, too short, too tight or too attention-seeking. Nor did it consist of whispered arguments in the queue for the till. Successful parent–child shopping experiences did not, surely, involve loud, resentful reminders that Joanie had dressed Nnenna for the first eleven years of her life, or that she also used to choose Nnenna's friends, before she got so big and clever with garish colours and her – her . . . *Snoods*.

Nnenna was sure Stephanie never had to go through any of this with her mum. She was sure that Stephanie's mum never criticised her daughter for wanting to show off her bum or wear red. Yes, there were some benefits to her mother coming along: she had more money, for one thing. And yes, it was nice not being followed around by security guards: being with a white person tended to make them relax. But, as they reached the shopping centre, Nnenna felt a heavy, sinking feeling in her chest. There was no way this would end well.

'What do you think of this, Nnenna?'

Her mother held up a heavy grey dress that looked to

Nnenna like a repurposed funeral shroud. It had a pattern on it that appeared as though someone had tried to recreate the effect of fabric being forgotten in a dusty chest for years, before it was pressed into service as a cleaning rag.

'It looks great!' Nnenna heard herself say, brightly, with an additional, 'I love the colour!' She smiled at her mother, took the dress and placed it in their shopping basket, trying not to shiver as it became the first in a shortlist of dresses that she would walk away with. *What was she doing?*

But a force stronger than Nnenna, stronger than common sense, was at play: guilt.

She had lied to her mother. That morning, when Joanie had asked her if she was still happy to pay for the dress (Nnenna's birthday present would come separately and was still a surprise), she'd lied and said that she was. It felt awful.

But maybe it was because she was out of practice. In fact, she'd never actually lied to her mother before. Stephanie did it all the time, and she said it was like riding a bike: at first you were wobbly and it could be a bit painful, but once you got the hang of it, it could take you to places you'd never been able to get to, before. For Stephanie, lying to her parents – albeit about relatively small things – was verging on being a hobby. It felt natural, now, she said.

But to Nnenna, it felt bad, even though she felt entitled to pay for Igbo lessons. Her mother had never actually said that she couldn't learn the language, or explore her heritage, or try to find some common ground with her father. But only because she'd never had to say the words. Nnenna knew that Joanie would prefer for Nnenna to leave the whole thing alone, and the fact that this seemed totally irrational sort of made it feel okay to go behind Joanie's back – but only sort of. It wasn't only that she felt that she ought to tell her mother the truth: it was that she wanted to. She was learning something exciting and real and beautiful and useful; but she had to keep it private, and that felt terrible.

And the worst thing was, she knew her mother would never lie to *her*.

'I think that one looks nice, too,' said Joanie, looking at what appeared to be approximately twelve pieces of lurid green tissue paper stitched together and placed on a hanger. Ruinously expensive nevertheless, it was the kind of thing that Joanie always suspected her daughter picked out purely to wind her up.

Nnenna smiled gratefully and put the dress in the basket while her mother cringed inwardly. *What was she doing?*

The word came to her almost immediately: overcompensating.

She had read her daughter's diary. *Her daughter's diary.* It was as though she had read *Betrayal for Dummies* for inspiration and got bored after the first chapter. It wasn't even creative betrayal, the kind of thing that might happen in some screwball comedy or comic opera. It was just hurtful.

The guilt of the act followed her wherever she went, and it put a cloud on everything she did. No matter how hard she tried to ignore it, there was a voice in her mind that told her she was the thing she had always dreaded she would become: a Bad Mother. She had become her worst nightmare; the lowest of the low. She might as well give Nnenna condoms with holes poked in them, or replace Nnenna's evening meals with cigarettes.

And what had Nnenna ever done wrong? She'd been the perfect child, from the day she was born: hard-working, decent, kind, patient – but above all, she was honest. Joanie always knew where Nnenna was and what she was doing. She never had to worry about how Nnenna was spending her time. And how did Joanie repay her? By stabbing her in the back. She deserved all her guilt, and much worse.

But the thing Joanie had learned about guilt, was that it was surprisingly easy to live with. Guilt could be cruel, saddening and inordinate; but it was not unbearable, never unbearable.

'And, you know, I'm not so sure you look good in scarves.'

'No, Mum, I think maybe I should give them a chance. How about these? I'm sure I'd get used to the itching. Look at this one on me—'

'But they're too big for you. You were right all along, they make you look much older than you are.'

'So? They're aspirational! I'll grow into them.'

'No, Nnenna, they're ... they're not right for you. Let's have a look at some of those leather trousers you mentioned.'

'Are you serious?'

'Yes! I've changed my mind: they don't make you look like a vampire from the nineties.'

'No, Mum, they do and I ... respect your judgement.' Uttering the words was like throwing up and then eating the vomit with a spoon.

'Well, that's nice of you, but this isn't about me—'

'I think I was too quick to judge those cardigans ...'

Joanie watched her daughter dutifully indicating a shop across the court where two women in their early sixties were gesticulating emphatically at a little grey knitted number on sale at half price in the window.

'You know, Nnenna. I've realised something.'

Nnenna froze, scarf number seven in hand.

'You have?'

'Yes.'

'Oh.'

'And I don't think it's fair—'

'Mum, don't.'

'No, honestly. It's not fair—'

'It's not as bad as you think, Mum—'

'—that you should be buying this dress with your own money.'

'What?'

'Your birthday's so close now, and you're doing so well in

school and everything, and you've been under so much stress lately . . . I think you deserve a reward.'

Nnenna felt the words 'I can't let you do that' bubbling up inside her, but her inability to back up the words with money made it hard to speak. 'I . . . Mum, I . . . Errr . . . It's . . .'

'No, I've decided. And that's that. You choose something you want – any dress, as long as it's reasonable – and it'll be my treat.'

'Oh, Mum. Thank you, Mum, really. I—'

Joanie gave Nnenna a kiss on the forehead. 'You're welcome.'

Nnenna looked up at her mum: she couldn't say how grateful she felt. It shouldn't have meant so much – it was only money, only a dress – but she was being so kind . . .

'Nnenna? Why are you crying?'

'Nothing, it's nothing.'

'No, what's wrong?'

'Nothing, I'm only tired, I think. I've had all this home-work to do and . . . ' She didn't want to say she'd been up late researching the Sorbonne. 'And it's all got on top of me.'

Joanie frowned, sensing the incompleteness of the truth but unsure where it was exactly. 'Are you sure you're okay? Do you want to go home?'

'No, I'm fine, I'm fine. Let's go. There's a dress I . . . I really want.'

'Well, why didn't you say so? Where is it?'

'It's in another shop, it's a few streets away . . . But I don't think you'll like it.'

'I . . . ' Joanie hesitated. 'Come on – dry your eyes. Let's go and have a look at it.'

'Are you sure?' Nnenna sniffed.

'Your choice. My treat.'

'Here it is,' said Nnenna. She walked out of the dressing room and waited, uneasily. 'I mean I'd wear it with different shoes. Those grey ones, maybe.'

Joanie held her breath and said nothing, looking closely at the velvet midi dress: pink, close-fitting and lightweight. Then she nodded.

'It's perfect.'

Nnenna looked at her mum quickly, unsure if she meant it. She'd been acting so strangely, today.

'For you,' said Joanie, 'not for me. It suits you.' And it did. The colour of it was youthful, but not infantile. It made Nnenna look mature; confident. Adult.

'You think so?'

'Absolutely. The colour's right for you, and the fit. I like it a lot.'

'Are you sure?'

Joanie nodded. But she didn't smile. And she looked so sad.

'And you're sure you don't mind paying for it? It feels so—'

'Shush. Give us a twirl.'

Chapter 14

He will wipe away every tear from their eyes,
and death shall be no more, neither shall there
be mourning, nor crying, nor pain any more ...

Revelation 21:4

1993

'You know,' said Maurice, 'from everything you say, your mother sounds a lot like my father.'

Joanie scoffed. 'Seriously?' She couldn't imagine anybody being quite like her mother, but now she had the mental image of a female version of Maurice, thirty years older, and giving him a lecture on the types of skirts to avoid. 'How so?'

Maurice laughed and shook his head at her, smiling. They were in a bar in the centre of Cambridge; Maurice didn't drink, so they ordered alcohol-free cocktails in expensive-looking glasses. Earlier that day, Joanie had finished an essay on Roman law, and Maurice was taking a few days off work; he'd only been at his engineering firm for a few weeks, but he needed some time away from them all, he said. He couldn't afford to go abroad on holiday – he sent so much money home each month – so he'd decided to stay in Cambridge and spend time with Joanie, who was always happy to take a break from her essays, from the library, from the university.

Maurice and Joanie were an official couple now; Joanie's Cambridge friends had officially decided not to speak to her. Meeting each other's parents seemed like too much of an enormity, somehow, so it was enough for them to tacitly accept that an interracial couple having virgin cocktails attracted a certain amount of attention. Instead, they only talked about their parents. It felt just safe enough.

'You're really something, you know that?' said Maurice, still laughing. 'You think you're the only one with tricky parents?'

'I don't! I only meant I find it hard to imagine anyone like my mother.'

'She wants you to be the best you can be.'

'And then some.'

'That's my dad,' he said, with some finality in his voice. Joanie, sensing a serious conversation, shifted in her chair to angle her body towards him more.

'Like, how?'

Maurice gave a deep sigh.

'It's not any one particular thing; it's . . . everything, it's the way he talks to me, the things he wants me to do.'

'Like being in Cambridge?'

'He always told me that black people have to work twice as hard as white people to be half as successful. Don't look so horrified!'

'I can't help it, I'm . . . I'm trying to do the maths of it.'

'Take your time.'

'I'm sorry, I suppose I'm a bit shocked.'

'You've never heard that before?'

'No. My God – Maurice, that's *awful*. Twice as hard, for half as much? Is it true, do you think?'

'Absolutely.'

'*Twice* as hard for *half* as much?'

'Absolutely.'

'My God.'

'Yep.'

Joanie thought for a moment.

'Do you talk to your dad about it much? About your life in England?'

'I don't talk to my dad much about anything. We're so different. Whenever I call, we only end up arguing.'

'How so?'

'Well . . . he tells me I'm a disappointment, and then I say I'm glad I'm thousands of miles away from him, and he—'

'No, I meant, how are you different?'

'Oh. Well. God, where do I start? We come from different worlds, and we've pretty much stayed there.'

'But why does he think you're a disappointment?'

'I don't pray any more.'

'What? Yes, you do. You go to church, still. And what about the postcard group?'

'We're still having creative difficulties. And I go to church, but I don't pray at home. I only go to church because I hate lying to my dad, and if I told him I don't go to church any more, he'd be so sad. I couldn't do that to him.'

'Surely he'd understand if you told him you were having doubts about God?'

Maurice laughed so hard that Joanie had to pause to think about what she'd just said. Perhaps it was true that she was being slightly delusional. Sometimes the unfairness of her mother's own expectations made her feel as though she was the only exception to the rule that parents must always be kind and understanding. But she hated the way Maurice did that – the way he spoke about the few things in his life he was unhappy with. He simply presented them, impatiently, as brute facts, as though they were self-evident. It made her feel stupid.

'My father,' said Maurice, 'doesn't have doubts about God. Sometimes I wonder if it's truly God he believes in, or if it's more that he needs somewhere to put his unshakeable faith. I think he's a little lost.'

'What do you mean?'

'My father came to the UK a few years before I was born; he'd hoped to make a career here.'

'And didn't he?'

'He had a good degree from one of the best universities in Nigeria, so he should have – he should have been accepted anywhere. But society in those days was even more racist than it is now. He had a terrible time: he was rejected everywhere he turned, nobody would give him the kind of jobs he should have been able to walk into. So eventually he went home, found a job – not the perfect job, but still. He got married and he settled there.'

'My God, that's terrible. To come all that way, only to go back again.'

'I can't think of a single person I know who's gone back like that. It's hard for everyone who comes here – everyone, Joanie. Sometimes it takes people years to get anywhere. But my father ... He thought England would be ... well, not *fair* to him, but not so unremittingly cruel. He came here full of hope, and the country broke him.'

'Is that what he said to you?'

'No. Never. He acts as though he always knew it would be difficult, as though he never wanted to come here. But my mother tells me differently.'

'And you think she's right?'

'When it comes to this, I'd believe her over him.'

'So, she understands what he went through, at least?'

Maurice laughed again, but sadly this time; angrily. 'She understands him very well. She always says my father's the cleverest man she's ever met.'

'Sounds familiar,' said Joanie.

'But he's impatient. He was a young man when he first came

to England, and the thought of him wasting away his youth while he slaved away at some second-rate job ... He couldn't stand the idea.'

'Then—'

'Then, what? White people like that get jobs all the time. This country is full of them. Here, they call it ambition. In my father, it was arrogance.'

'I ... only meant to ask what happened next, Maurice.'

Maurice took a breath, gave a wan apologetic smile. 'He'd have got any job he wanted if he'd been willing to work twice as hard for it as any white applicant. But my mother says he wasn't. This country's happy to have us if we follow your rules – if we're on our best behaviour. But that's so hard to keep up all the time! And what then? What happens when we get tired, or angry, or frustrated? People just shake their heads and tell themselves that's what *all* black people are like. And then ... '

Joanie looked at him, saw his face turn harder than she had ever seen it. And sadder.

'You know, I learned English faster than anyone I knew?'

'I thought everyone learned it in school in Nigeria?'

'Yes, but I was different. I needed to learn to speak as much English as I could, as soon as I could. One day, when I was tiny, my mother told me about my father's time in England and ... I don't know, I had to know about it. I read every scrap of English I could get my hands on. I begged my teachers to give me extra help. I would save up and buy books, films, anything. I was fluent by the time I was ten. But I love Nigeria. I've always loved it more than anywhere. There's nowhere in the world like it, Joanie. It's home.'

Joanie stayed quiet. She wanted to speak but was too scared to ask the question. She knew the answer.

'I miss Nigeria,' he said. 'Sometimes ... I want to go back.'

'Oh,' said Joanie. Maurice ignored the sadness in her voice because he did not know what to do with it.

'And my dad is angry with me because he knows I could make it here if I wanted to. But sometimes ... I'm not sure I want to.'

The two of them sat in a silence that grew and grew, enveloping them both. Maurice took a cube of ice from his drink and played with it, his brow furrowed in a concentration that seemed not to match what he was doing. Outside, students tripped along to their college bars, to their rooms, to formal halls.

'I grew up ... differently,' said Joanie.

'Better?' said Maurice, sensing the import of what she was about to say. 'Or worse?'

And what would she say in response? What truths could she tell, without exploding the way he saw her? She knew, by now, that if she told the truth, he could never look at her the same way. At best, he'd ignore it completely, pretend she'd never said anything. At worst, he would look at her more kindly, and with pity.

'I know,' said Maurice. 'I know it's hard. But you can trust me. If you want to.'

And could she? Trust him? Could she trust him with what she'd carried since childhood?

The first time she remembered it happening, they'd just moved house – they wanted to be nearer to Joanie's grandmother, who was getting older – and so she'd had to move school. Joanie was so sad at first, but she was excited, too. She was only eight years old.

That first time, the first time that she remembered clearly – God only knows how many times it had happened before she was old enough to remember, she'd some hazy memories of it happening before, when she must have been tiny – that first time that she remembered, it was the night before her first day in her new school. Joanie was in her room, she couldn't remember what she was doing; and then it started. She never knew what set him off, what maddened him. He could be completely calm one moment, enraged the next.

It was a banging noise she heard downstairs, like a door closing. And then his voice as he ran up the stairs; he was so fast. He was a heavy man, and he'd been drinking, but still he was fast. There never was a chance to get away.

She'd curled up in a ball in the corner of her room, her hands up in front of her face, but he was just hitting, over and over, just ... tearing at her hands, trying to force them away, trying to get to her face. It was mad. He was mad. He was so mad—

'Joanie—' Maurice's voice was softer than she remembered ever hearing it before.

'I didn't know what to do. I didn't know what to do. I didn't know ...'

He pulled her into a hug, and they rocked backwards and forwards on their tall stools, the ice in their tall drinks slowly melting and dribbling down the sides of their glasses while she cried, and cried.

Later that day, Joanie walked out to the phone box at the end of her college's road. From memory, she dialled the number. As the phone rang, she thought about hanging up and walking back to her room, to her friends. But she couldn't. She had to tell someone, to make this feeling real and solid. Like anyone in love, she had the bizarre feeling that if she didn't tell someone how she was feeling, the feeling would die away, and she would die with it.

And she knew who to tell.

'Hi, Aunty Mary, it's Joan. How are you? Oh good! Good. Yeah, I'm really well, thanks. Uni? It's all right, I guess. Not got a clue what I'll do when I graduate, but I can't wait. I'll figure it out. Actually, I've got some news for you in the meantime. Yeah. Yeah, it's good news. I've met someone.'

*

2009

'I mean, it was great that she offered to go with me. To the Peak District. I love the countryside, you know? I've not been much, but I just love it. I think it'd be good for me to get out, get away from the city, forget everything that's ... It'd be exactly what I need. I should just go, shouldn't I? Find a walking group or something. Maybe I should do that, instead. Stop waiting. Stop putting it off.

'But you and me, we're okay, aren't we? I mean, I know we're not together or anything – and don't get me wrong, I'm not asking to be – but I think we've got a good thing, right? It's relaxed. It's easy. Easier than Joanie, I think.

'I do like spending time with her, but ... People say that your family is the family you choose, don't they? I used to like that idea, but now I'm not so sure. What happens if they don't choose you back? What happens if they can't choose you back because they're too busy? With family of their own? And I can't blame her for that, but ... I don't know. Sometimes you want someone you can depend on. Sometimes you want someone whose reactions you know you can predict. No surprises. There's a lot to be said for having no surprises, you know what I mean? Silas?

'Silas? Are you awake?'

Chapter 15

2010

Joanie

Blessed are the peacemakers, for they shall
be called sons of God.

Matthew 5:3

When Joanie pulled up in her car in front of Chicken Co-op,
there was no sign of Nnenna. She tried to spot her through
the shop window, but she couldn't. This was good: it meant
she wasn't late to pick Nnenna up from work – in fact she
was there a little over ten minutes before the end of Nnenna's
shift – and it also meant that she could get on with some writing. She reached into her bag and took out a dark blue notepad
and a biro.

She didn't normally like to write in shorthand (the small
number of romantic notions she held did not include a biro) but
bringing her old laptop with her would have been impractical,
today; by the time it had finished firing up, Nnenna would
arrive and it would be time to shut it down again. Besides, she
was writing something that she didn't necessarily want Nnenna
to see. At least, not yet.

Joanie opened her notebook and took a moment to appreciate the blank page: there was something beautiful about it; how pristine it was, in the moments before she wrote. There was also something exciting, perhaps because she knew it would not stay blank for long; perhaps because she knew she had the power to fill it with things. She'd been thinking about this article for some time, unable to put the thoughts into words (or rather, into tolerable words, words that she didn't hate) and suddenly, for some reason, her thoughts had very recently crystallised. She picked up her pen and began to write:

Being a parent is strange. Especially being the parent of a teenager. You wake up one morning and you find that all the joy you used to share with your child – every silly joke, every secret smile, every tiny reference that used to make you both laugh for reasons nobody else could understand – has packed up and left. And then you realise that maybe these things haven't disappeared, that maybe your child is not, in fact, a humourless lump; it's just that, maybe their sense of humour, their smiles and their laughter, are not for you any more. They used to be only for you, and now they're for other people, instead of you: your child has friends.

And that's fine. But, try as you might, you find yourself missing those things. You miss sharing small pleasures with your child in the way that you used to. In this way, being a parent is like being a wolf: you hunt. You hunt for the things that you miss. You dart back and forth between your child's life and your own, and you don't find anything.

So, you go back. And you go back, always looking for something; you usually don't find it. You retreat instead, perhaps with a quiet little whimper. But you go back, and you go back, and you go back. And occasionally, when you do find something – when you get the scent of the thing you've been looking for, even the barest hint – you pursue it. You chase it down and, when you find it, you're so excited that you grip it between your teeth and you shake it and shake it and shake it until all the life goes out of it, and it hangs from your mouth, dripping with blood, its eyes frozen open in fear.

And then you wonder what happened.

'Hmm,' she thought. 'Maybe that idea's a bit aggressive.' Writing, especially the kind of observational writing that she was going for, so often looked different on paper, from how it sounded in her head. She tried again:

Being a parent is strange, even for those of us who are relatively close in age to our children. No matter how much you try, you end up feeling far away.

She took out her phone and sent Nnenna a quick text to let her know that she was waiting and then found she had a notification: someone on Facebook had sent her a message, some funny little video that she could watch at home, using the WiFi instead of her precious little mobile data; it would make sense to watch the first few seconds now so that she could say she'd enjoyed it, but Joanie couldn't concentrate on such a thing now, with her head still full of ideas (good and bad) for her article. She had to get this thing published.

She felt a pang of guilt. She'd been reading Nnenna's diary again. Somehow the fact that she knew Nnenna didn't trust her only made her want to know more, as though she had nothing left to lose. And, worse, under Nnenna's bed she'd found yet more research about the Sorbonne. She'd hoped Nnenna had forgotten about that by now. She hadn't. Nnenna was going to leave, at some point. Part of Joanie knew that she was only delaying the inevitable, or rather, ignoring the inevitable, which did nothing whatsoever to delay it. But she could do nothing else. And the piecemeal, drip-feed of progress towards the day when Nnenna might move to another country only made things worse; it was like slow torture. It would almost be easier if Nnenna left tomorrow morning. It was as though Destiny, instead of making a date with Joanie, had decided to drop a series of pointed, passive-aggressive hints about how Joanie never called, never wrote.

She tried to distract herself by scrolling through Facebook, but it was always the adverts that got her attention most of all. Always slightly mistrusting of social media, she'd long since withheld information about her gender, age and profession, so the internet took lucky guesses as to what she might be interested in clicking on and paying for. This time Facebook offered a heady cocktail of mail-order brides, cheap razors and (for good measure) some slimming underwear that looked like it had cut off circulation to the model's thighs. In moments like these, Joanie pictured the internet as a monolithic creature that was trying to build a picture of her using incomplete data, and she wondered what that picture looked like. At the moment, it was unmarried, fat and battling body hair that was wildly out of control.

She had decided not to reflect on the accuracy of this summation when she heard a tap at her window. It was Nnenna.

Jonathan

Jonathan tried his best to flick the last few broccoli florets off himself as he walked down the street. They seemed to have a habit of getting everywhere, and they lingered stubbornly in his hair, no matter how much he brushed it after seeing Silas.

There was something painfully ironic about the fact that he'd enjoyed a very close intimacy with Silas's egregiously well-stocked pantry (if not with Silas) for seventeen minutes and yet was now forced to buy fast food that was even greasier than he felt after an assignation with Silas; but this was the routine he'd got himself into. He saw up-close all the ingredients for Silas's next elaborate dinner, but before every dinner took place he was cast out, exhausted, covered in the contents of Silas's chopping board and absolutely starving. Sometimes he went straight home, but he was hungrier tonight, and Chicken Co-op was only round the corner, beckoning with its neon lighting and easy sustenance. Time spent with Silas could leave him physically and emotionally exhausted; he didn't have the energy to cook and he needed food, fast; and besides, Nnenna worked there sometimes and it was nice to see her. She'd inherited her mother's gift for recognising familiar faces, but hadn't known where she had known him from; the first time he walked in, she'd only stared at him intensely, knowing the face but not the name.

She looked so much like her mother. Much more so than she resembled Maurice; the clarity of it brought to mind details Jonathan thought he'd forgotten long ago. Nnenna's height, she'd got from Maurice, and the shape of her nose; but most of the rest was Joanie, especially the eyes, which were as dark as Maurice's but had Joanie's occasional squint, and the same quiet, patient intensity. That stare had gone right through him; she'd smiled when she realised, but all the same Jonathan thought of the night, eighteen years before, when Joanie had stared at him in a similar way – as though she recognised him but somehow did not know him – and the memory had made Jonathan shiver.

And yet he'd gone back, again and again. Perhaps it was the resemblance alone; there was something magical about the fact that Joanie Maloney, indifferent student turned mother turned star classicist, now had a brilliant, beautiful child. She'd been a curious woman as long as he'd known her: uniquely bright, warm, though a bit afraid in a way that sometimes obscured it. It seemed somehow miraculous that someone could be replicated, even in part, even only the visible parts. But there she was, much younger but (from what he could see, and from everything Joanie had told him) all the same, exactly like her mother: brilliant, warm, afraid.

Or maybe it was the fact that Joanie had saved his life, years ago. He'd tried to hang himself one night when he felt as though nobody would truly mourn his absence, and she'd happened by his room. To this day, he didn't know why she'd been there at that time, with Maurice waiting outside, unable to come in once he'd heard Joanie's scream. Nor did Jonathan know why he'd left the front door unlocked; perhaps because he hadn't expected that anyone would come along. Perhaps because, in the end, he had hoped that someone would.

His semi-regular trips to Chicken Co-op had come to feel like keeping watch over Nnenna, which in turn felt like a kind of recompense to Joanie. It felt good to do something good for Joanie; or for anyone. Although he did not miss the Church, he did miss the feeling of being needed and valued – if only by a bunch of prudes and weirdos – for the good he could do. Once, he'd felt like he could hear God's call in everything he saw and heard in the world; once, it had seemed like everything he touched, God had touched. Now, everything felt silent, unresonant, lonely.

And, as much as he protested to Joanie, seeing Silas only made him feel lonelier. Was it too much to ask, that he be allowed to eat with Silas once in a while? Would it be so hard to give him a seat at the table? Sometimes he even felt like confiding in Nnenna, although he never did.

But today, when he went in, she wasn't there. He'd asked the old couple who worked there what had happened to Nnenna, but they hardly seemed to know.

'She stopped turning up one day,' said the man. He didn't have a name tag. 'Very odd.'

'Is that Nnenna?' said his wife, overhearing. The man nodded while he counted more change into the till. 'Very strange. She was great. Always on time, very hard-working, always polite. Always stayed until everything was done. I don't think she ever missed a day's work until she quit.'

'Quit?' said Jonathan. It was quiet in the shop – Jonathan had never come in this late before – and there were no customers in. He watched the man slice the buns and put them in the toaster and then put the meat on the grill.

'Not sure you can call it "quitting",' said the man. There was a sour note in his voice. 'Honestly, she just stopped coming in.' He quickly flipped the meat over on the grill and readied a box for the burger.

His wife *mmmm*ed agreement. 'One week she was here, the next we didn't hear from her. Didn't answer the phone when we tried calling. And it was so busy that night! United were playing City at Old Trafford – tons of people in – we could have used an extra hand, then.'

Her husband, still irritated by the memory, took up the baton of the story. 'And then, the next day, she rang in and said she was sick. Wouldn't explain, wouldn't tell us what was going on.'

'She only said she was sorry, and that she didn't expect to be paid for any work she'd not done. And she said thanks; although what she was thanking us for, I don't know. Almost sounded like someone had taken her hostage.'

'We never normally take on kids her age,' said the man, placing Jonathan's burger in the bun and piling on the extra salad that Jonathan liked. He squeezed tomato ketchup on top. 'But her references were so good. And when we gave her a trial, she was great. No idea if she plans on coming back, but I can't say if there'll be a job for her if she's off much longer.'

'You don't think she's sick?'

'Who knows,' said the man, in a voice that suggested he knew very well. 'Here you go – chips with that? Right. And would you like a drink?'

Jonathan took one out of the fridge in front of the counter.

'That's eight pounds exactly, please,' said the woman.

'So, are you her . . . ?' The man started to ask the question but floundered in the ethnic disparity between the two of them. He fished his mind for something appropriate. '. . . Cousin?'

'Family friend,' Jonathan smiled. He handed over a ten-pound note, took his change and his food and left the shop. He could see Joanie's car, a blue saloon parked in a small street off the main road. He could make out Joanie's head, bowed and focused on something, he couldn't see what. He had just started to walk over to her to say 'hello', when something collided with him at great speed, knocking his food out of his hands. It was Nnenna.

Nnenna

'Oh God, Uncle Jonathan!'

'Nnenna! I ...'

'I'm so sorry, I was running and I wasn't looking where I was going. Here, let me try and pick those up.'

They both looked for a moment at the mess of the food on the floor. It had fallen directly into a rather grainy-looking puddle of vomit.

'Well,' said Jonathan, 'if it wasn't bad for my health before ...'

'Oh God, I'm so sorry. I'll get you another one – I'll go in and get you another one, I'll be right back,' said Nnenna, immediately moving towards Chicken Co-op. And then she seemed to think better of the idea and stood still, as if frozen on the spot.

'Don't worry, Nnenna. It's fine, I'll get it. I'll pick up what I can without touching the ...'

Nnenna watched, aghast, as Jonathan gingerly fished out a bit of bread and some chips from the puddle of vomit and placed them in the nearby bin.

'Are you seriously going to do that?'

'Well, I don't want to touch the vomit, obviously, but ... You know, it's God's green earth and all that.'

'Jonathan, we're in Manchester city centre – I don't think there's anything green round here.'

'Or anything godly, actually.' He fished out one last chip, placed it in the bin and inspected his hands, which were in fact clean, aside from a bit of ketchup.

'I didn't realise you were religious.'

'I'm not. Or not in any real way. And I didn't realise you were lying to your mum.'

'I'm not ... Okay, I am. But ... it's complicated.'

Jonathan looked across the street, where Joanie was still in the car, still deep in concentration.

'Well, I don't want to keep your mum waiting, but ... Why don't you come with me and we'll get some chips from the place two doors down? And then you can tell me what's going on.'

Nnenna looked over at her mum's car.

'I know things aren't perfect, right now. Maybe I can help?' said Jonathan. 'I know a thing or two about lying. It can get pretty complicated pretty soon.'

'Well ... okay,' said Nnenna, sadly. She sent her mum a text (*Nearly ready! Sorry!*) and walked with Jonathan to the chip shop, where he got a meat and potato pie and some chips. They sat in the shop's window seat as Jonathan ate and listened, and Nnenna looked askance at his soggy chips.

'I don't know how you can do that,' she said.

'Do what? Put vinegar on them?'

Nnenna nodded, too distressed to speak.

'You mean ... you don't?'

Nnenna nodded proudly.

'You'd never know I was the southerner and you were the northerner, would you?' he laughed. 'So go on, tell me.'

So she did.

'... And then it turned out that the Igbo lessons were on the same night as my shift at Chicken Co-op.'

'Couldn't you ask them to change your shifts?'

Nnenna shook her head. 'What if they'd said no? It'd look

pretty bad, my calling in sick after I'd asked to have my shifts moved. And I couldn't not go to the lessons, because I'd already paid for them and I want to learn Igbo so much, Uncle Jonathan. I feel like such an idiot not understanding any of it. I feel like people are just waiting to tell me I'm some sort of bad black person, or that I'm not really black.'

'Which people? Your mum? I don't think she'd say that.'

'It's not her. It's not one person, Uncle Jonathan. It's this feeling I have, all the time.'

'I know what you mean. I've been told that, myself.'

'You? Why? What haven't you done?'

He laughed. 'Believe me, Nnenna, there's almost nothing I haven't done to fit in. But the reality is, there's nothing you can do that will make you any more or less black than you already are. You don't have to earn it.'

'Do you really think that's true?' She sounded so hopeful. It broke his heart to hear her uncertainty.

'I do,' he said, firmly. 'I think it's wonderful that you're learning Igbo, and I think it's fantastic that you're a principled and determined person. But you don't have to work to be a black person. That's not what you get out of this.'

Nnenna thought about this for a moment. 'It's really hard, Uncle Jonathan, it's not like French. But I love learning it. Do you know what I mean?'

'I can imagine. But why didn't you tell your mum?'

Nnenna sighed a deep sigh. 'She wouldn't understand.'

'About your wanting to learn Igbo?'

'I can't explain it, but every time I say anything to do with my dad, she starts acting so *weird*. It's as though something happened, or he was a terrible person. We almost never talk about him, and I don't want to upset her but sometimes I feel . . . lost.'

Jonathan looked at Nnenna seriously and tried to summon as much gravitas as he could with vinegar on his hands. 'Your dad was not a terrible person. He was . . . complicated.'

'But – did something happen?'

'Nnenna, I—'

'Please? You knew them, didn't you? You were all at Cambridge together. Something must have happened.'

'A lot of things happened to all of us, Nnenna. It was a difficult time for everyone, then. Every one of us was going through something.'

Nnenna nodded gravely, and looked a little uncomfortable.

'What is it?' he asked.

'It's just that, after the wedding, my mum told me—'

'She told you what?'

'Nothing, really. She never does. But she said that you weren't very well, at university. She said you might have been hurt very badly.'

'Oh.'

'What does she mean by that? You don't look hurt. Or weak. You look fine.'

Jonathan looked at her sharply for a moment, as though she had suggested something new and somehow challenging. 'I . . . Thank you. I can't talk about it much . . . But thank you. I'm not sure you're right, though.'

He went quiet, and it was a while before Nnenna asked, 'Was it something to do with my dad? Was he unwell, too?'

'It's not like that, Nnenna. For one thing, Maurice wasn't at Cambridge with us, exactly; he was a few years older than your mum, so he'd already got his degree from the university by the time they met.'

'So how did they meet? And why did they break up?'

'Nnenna, I think that's something you need to talk about with your mum. I'm sure that if you asked her – if you explained what it is you want to know – she'd tell you. She's not a monster, you know.'

'I know. I know that,' said Nnenna, frowning. 'I love my mum. I think she's amazing. I'm so grateful for her, every day.

I keep worrying about what I'd do if something happened to her ...'

'Nothing's going to happen to her. You worry too much.'

'I know. But it's because I need her, and there's nobody else. I know it's not been easy for her, doing everything by herself. But there's so much I want to talk to her about, aside from my dad.' She thought about Danny, and how things had been with them since they'd slept together. She had so many questions, now, and it seemed like she had more every day. Like, was it wrong to have sex with someone if the sex made you realise that you didn't love them? Did that make you a bad person? Sometimes, she wasn't even sure if Danny had ever loved her, in the first place.

'God! I hate lying to my mum. I hate it. It makes me feel so ... so lonely.'

'Then why don't you talk to her?'

'I can't!'

'What do you mean?'

'I can't explain it. It's like there's a spell on us and neither of us can ask for the truth, not the whole of it.'

'Come on, now.'

'I know it sounds silly, but I mean it. And then ... sometimes I'm not sure I want to know. Whatever it is, I'm nearly seventeen, now, Uncle Jonathan. And she's never told me. It must be something bad. It's something terrible, isn't it?'

'Nnenna, it's ... complicated.'

'So, you *do* know. You know what happened. But you won't tell me.'

'I'm sorry. Honestly, if I could—'

'It's fine. And I should go now, anyway. My mum's waiting. She'll be cold in that car.'

'Nnenna. Ask. You should know.'

Nnenna shook her head. 'Please, please stop. I'm sorry – I can't cry.'

'It's okay,' he put an arm around her shoulders.

'No. I mean if I get back to the car and I'm crying . . . Mum will know something's wrong, and she'll want to ask me all about it and I can't talk about everything yet. I'm sorry, I have to go. Please don't tell my mum about this, please – you won't, will you?'

'Nnenna, maybe if I told her . . . '

'Please.'

'I suppose she doesn't absolutely have to know. So, okay. I won't. But *you* should, Nnenna. I think you have to.'

She only shook her head as she pushed the door open into the cold night air, tears in her eyes, after all. 'I'm trying,' she said. 'I try. All the time.'

PART III

PART III

Chapter 16

[...] by the open statement of the truth
we would commend ourselves to everyone's
conscience in the sight of God.

2 Corinthians 4:2

2010

In a secluded corner of the school library, Amit revised and revised his speech for the final round of the debating competition. It had to be perfect.

At first, he had used his lunchtimes to write, but increasingly he had found himself needing to use that time to coach the other members of the team. Slowly, coaching had turned into outright teaching, as it became more and more obvious that his teammates were no match for their rivals in the nationwide tournament, and that their teacher, Mr Black, lacked the killer instinct required for victory in a debating competition. Instead of telling Danny and Sam outright that their arguments were shaky, their facts unchecked and their delivery uninspired, he kept trying to ... *encourage* them. It was revolting, and Amit was not at all sure it would do them any good.

Their opponent in the final round of the tournament was a highly selective boarding school from the south-east, boasting a clutch of QCs among their alumni. The students were rumoured to dress up in *actual togas* to practise their rhetoric on Wednesday evenings after school, at meetings where hummus and red wine were provided. On the school budget.

Mr Black's nurturing approach would certainly explain why he had given Dan the crucial, central role of Second Speaker. Nobody had questioned it at the time and, to the untrained eye, it had seemed an innocuous move: in the rules of their tournament, the First Speaker was given the least amount of time to speak, while Amit himself, the third speaker, was given much more time. The first speaker (Sam: bright but inexperienced) merely introduced the team's perspective on the given topic; the second speaker (Danny: a bit pedestrian but a solid performer who smelled like honey and sunshine) was given a few minutes to deliver a persuasive speech; while the third speaker (Amit: charming, witty, irresistibly persuasive and a very snappy dresser into the bargain) rounded off the competition by providing a rebuttal. In theory, it should all have worked . . .

'Amit!'

'Dan. Hi – one second, I'm working on this . . . '

. . . And it did work – but barely, and only because of Amit. Danny, being the main speaker, naturally got all the praise; but Amit was the engine of the team, and they all knew it. As the third speaker, he had to think on his feet – something he knew that neither of the others could do as well as him. In fact, if Dan could have thought for himself at all, he wouldn't have needed to submit his speeches to Amit for approval and revision in advance.

Amit had thought about quitting the team, given that he already had more work than was sustainable. But then again, he could not imagine not being on the debating team, for one simple reason: as far as Amit was concerned, being a member of the debating team was the single most sexually attractive thing you could do. The fact that the other students in his year had so far proved immune to his charms was immaterial: plenty of artists are under-appreciated in their own time.

Besides, it might well be that the magic of debating – the floral bow ties, rife with sexual undertones; the formal modes of address, so clearly expressive of prowess in the bedroom – was simply taking its time to build up. No investment worth bothering about could be expected to mature overnight. And when it did, Amit had no doubt in his mind that the third speaker of the debating team would be first in line to collect the dividends.

Or, as it seemed, the second. Or perhaps the third.

'Sorry, Amit, I'm kind of in a rush.'

Amit looked up from his work and stared impatiently at Danny. It was a curious experience, looking at Danny, because Amit could never help trying to see him through Nnenna's eyes. Amit had never been in love but had his own, very specific ideas of what love was. Amit's ideas seemed worlds away from Daniel. Where were Dan's love poems? Where was his lute? Amit gave them a month.

And yet, there *was* something about Dan himself. With those full lips, that perfect skin ... maybe he didn't need a lute, after all.

'What is it, Dan?'

'What's this about a night out you're organising?'

Amit rolled his eyes. 'Look: for the last time, I don't organise nights out. You can give me your name and I'll see if I can get you in, but I'm not promising anything.' Amit's cousin, Imran, was a bouncer at Aura, an exclusive city-centre club which sold overpriced drinks to under-18s with laughable fake IDs. Imran, upon receipt of a small fee, did his best not to laugh.

'Well, if you're not organising anything, could you?'

'Why?'

'Nnenna's birthday.'

Amit frowned. 'It's her seventeenth ... and you're taking her clubbing in town? Why not just vomit on her now and save yourself the taxi fare?'

'Come on, Amit. It'll be good. It'll be a surprise. I think she'll like it.'

Amit remained unconvinced, but decided that anything which could hasten the demise of a relationship whose only apparent purpose was to testify to the cosmic unfairness of life, was good news.

'Fine,' he said, picking up his phone and typing. 'I'll see what I can do.'

'Cheers, mate.' Dan got up to leave. 'Did you like my speech, by the way?'

'Hmm?' Amit swiftly covered his work with a copy of that day's newspaper, obscuring a copy of Dan's speech which was recovering from deep-tissue surgery. 'Yes – yes, it's great. I had to make a couple of adjustments; but I think it's safe to say that things are looking up.'

'A night out?' said Stephanie, talking on the phone as she walked home from school.

'Yeah, that's what I heard,' said Nnenna, on the other end of the line. 'I've heard Danny's arranging it and it's meant to be a surprise. Go on: I'm right, aren't I?'

'I won't lie to you,' said Steph, matter-of-factly. 'An evening of elegant dancing and fine wine is on the cards for the night you turn seventeen.'

'Oh.'

'Well, try not to sound *too* excited.'

'Sorry. I've got so much on my plate right now. I don't have the brainspace to think about going out clubbing with a bunch of people.'

'You don't have to think about it: Danny's actually getting off his bum to sort it out for you. Not sure what sort of magic you did to make that happen, but it's a pretty big deal as far as I can tell ... In fact, I can see him now.'

'Where are you?'

'I'm on our street; looks like he's forgotten his keys again. I'll have to go.'

'Okay, speak to you tomorrow.'

'Right, bye.'

Stephanie walked the few steps to her front gate. The houses on her street were huddled close together like cold children. On the street, kids played games of hide and seek, shrieking and running, riding bikes, drawing in chalk on the pavements. Alone, Dan was standing in front of his own front door, holding himself eerily still. She was about to call out to him when he heard her approach and put his finger to his lips. She mouthed, 'What's going on?' and he motioned to her door, which was open just a crack. Inside, they could hear her parents talking. Concerned by the unusualness of the situation (normally, Danny didn't even care this much about conversations he was actually a part of) she leaned in and listened, too.

'... I'm not doing it, John,' said her mum. 'I'm not doing it. We'll find a way.'

'We've tried, Lisa,' came her dad's voice. He was pacing around, the way he did when he was trying to get his wife to agree with him, as though he might get round her more easily if he was physically in motion at the time. 'We've *been* trying for months, and it's not working.'

'What are they talking about?' Steph whispered.

'Moving,' said Dan, quickly. 'I think they're saying you have to move.'

Steph reddened.

'And why the fuck were you standing there and listening to my parents arguing?'

'Couldn't help it. Anyway, I think I heard something about the shop. Something's happened.'

'What? When?'

'Shh! Listen.'

'... Well, you don't have to shout,' said Lisa. 'I'm only saying I don't want it interfering with Steph's school work.'

'I don't either! But I don't think we have much of a choice.'

'Steph,' hissed Danny. 'What are you doing? Don't you think you should let them have it out and just—'

But it was too late: she had already pushed the door fully open and marched into the living room, where her dad stopped pacing suddenly and her mum sat with her head in her hands.

'What's going on?' said Steph. 'What's this about moving?'

'Jesus, Steph,' said John. 'It's rude to eavesdrop. You never get the whole story when you eavesdrop.'

'Okay, so give us the full story now, then,' said Steph, impatiently.

'Stephanie,' said Lisa. 'Watch it; you're being rude.'

'Sorry. But I heard you arguing and ... What's going on?'

Silently, Danny slipped away to his house next door.

'Are we going to move to a new house?'

Her mum heaved a deep sigh. 'Nothing's decided, yet. We're only talking.'

'But you're thinking about it?' said Steph.

'Yes,' said John. He sounded resigned; tired. 'We might as well say: we've had an attack at the shop recently, and ever since then, business has been—'

'An attack?' said Steph. 'What attack? When was this?'

John and Lisa looked sadly towards the centre of the room, where a brick lay on the coffee table. Stephanie stepped forward to pick it up, and held it in her hands. As though from a distance, she heard herself ask why they hadn't given it to the police.

'We didn't want to make things worse,' explained her mum. 'We thought if people saw police coming in and out of the shop, it would scare them off.'

'It's scary anyway!' said Steph, almost shouting.

'Calm down, Stephanie,' said John, his own voice shaky.

Steph turned the brick over and over in her hands: it felt somehow hyperreal, every bump and raised edge of its texture calling for her attention. She wondered if this was because of the way it must have arrived in the shop: despite the familiar, clearly malicious intent behind it, it felt somehow alien, as if it had arrived from another planet. Perhaps it was because a brick is the kind of thing one sees every day but never touches. Perhaps because it was a way to avoid paying attention to the conversation at hand.

'Is this why we have to move?' said Stephanie. 'Because someone smashed up the shop? It was probably just some kid from around here, being stupid.'

'Even so, it's a little more complicated than that, love,' said her mum gently. She took the brick out of Stephanie's hands and set it down on the table. 'We . . . we're not sure we can afford to live here, any more. It's expensive to live near your school, you know that. But when we moved here, the shop was doing well and we could afford it, if we scrimped and saved. But lately, the shop's not been making enough money.'

'So where are we moving to?'

'We haven't decided yet,' said her mum.

'Like we say,' said John, 'nothing's been decided. We have been looking for places nearby, but . . . '

For a moment, nobody said anything.

'But they're too expensive, aren't they?' said Steph. Her parents nodded. 'Would I have to move school? Are they kicking me out?' she said quietly.

'No,' said Lisa, firmly. 'We've checked with the school, and because you were in the catchment area when you started, they have to continue to take you until you leave.'

'But we might be a long way from school,' said John. 'The places we can afford, at the moment . . . It might take you a long time to get there. And you wouldn't be so near to your friends any more.'

'But nothing's settled?' said Steph.

'Nothing's settled.'

Stephanie walked rather than ran out of the room and up the stairs to her bedroom. She needed to sit down somewhere, away from everyone.

After a few moments, she heard her dad walk up the stairs and knock gently before coming into her room, not waiting for an answer. She wasn't sure if he was going to tell her off – often angry himself, he got frustrated with anger in others – but he only sat down on the bed in silence for a few minutes.

Soon, Stephanie realised that he must simply be unsure of what to say. There was nothing more that any of them could do – he'd said it himself. It was just a question of money that they didn't have. So what could he say?

'I know you won't believe me when I say this,' she said, eventually, 'but it's not as terrible as you'd think. Us having to move.'

'Nothing's decided, yet, Stephanie.'

'I know. I'm only saying ... At the end of the day, it's hard.'

'What's hard? You're doing well, aren't you?'

'God, Dad!' Stephanie virtually exploded. She hadn't known she was this angry before. 'It's not all about grades. Do you have any idea how hard it is to go to a school like that, and not fit in? To be different in any way, even a small one, never mind us being ...'

'Being what?'

'Being poor!'

'We're not poor, Stephanie. We—'

'Oh, I know, I know, we've got ... you know, food on the table. But almost nobody else at that school even has to *think* about that stuff, none of it. They all ...' She searched for the words to express herself. 'They all *go on holiday all the time*.'

'We go on holiday!'

'They go skiing. People keep going to places I've never even heard of. I'm always the odd one out in that school and sometimes it's exhausting. The amount of effort I put into – into knowing what Saint Tropez is, or into . . . '

'I thought . . . We always thought you were doing okay. Oh, Stephanie – don't cry,' he said quietly.

'I'm not getting kicked out. And nobody's beating me up. But sometimes I hate it, anyway. People assume all sorts of things about me – stupid, fucking *stupid* things – before they've even met me. And they tell their friends. And then they tell their friends.'

'It'll get easier.'

'I kept thinking it would, and it has, I guess. But I'm just . . . I'm always so afraid to screw up because, if I do, I'll be the poor girl that screwed up. But I screw up all the time, Dad; everybody screws up sometimes.'

'What about your friends from outside school?'

'They're okay. But I hardly have time to see my friends any more, because I spend all my time doing school things! Homework, and music and athletics . . . All I have is school, now. I don't *have* anything else. God! Why do you think Nnenna's one of my only friends? Because she is one of the only people who doesn't . . . doesn't judge me. Everybody else . . . everybody else . . . '

John couldn't hear the rest of what Stephanie said, because she was crying too hard. He put his arm around her shoulders and told her, 'We only wanted what was best. You know that, don't you? We wanted you to have the best education we could find you. I'm sorry it's been so hard for you. I wish you'd told me sooner, Steph. But you've only got a couple of years left there; less than that, since you're halfway through the year, eh? We'll make it all right. We'll make it all right, love.'

'But what does that even mean?'

John hugged her a little tighter, and he thought and thought and thought . . . what did it mean?

*

'Hi, Silas. Yes, I know, I forgot the knocks. Listen, I – no, get off my leg, I'm not doing that, today. Just stop. Stop. I came here to tell you . . . I'm done.

'Yeah, I know you don't care. You never cared. And that's fine, I guess. I mean, I can't make you care. And it was my choice. But – no, wait. Listen. I'm not here to blame you. I need to say . . . Do you know what my friend's daughter said to me, yesterday? Her mother'd told her that I'd had some struggles with mental health. *Had*. She thinks it's all in the past. She's only sixteen, she doesn't know. She thinks I'm fine, now. She doesn't know what I've been doing to myself, with you. She thinks I just got over it and everything was fine because it's been such a long time. Because I'm not still trying to hang myself. Because I'm not taking a bottle full of pills, or . . . she thinks I'm fine because I didn't actually die.

'But I've *been* dying, Silas. What would it have cost you to give me your phone number? What would it have cost you to look me in the eyes? I'm trapped inside a mind that wants to die, that can't stand to be touched with warmth, or fed. And how perfect for me that I met you, when all you wanted was someone to starve.

'You know what? I'm angry, but actually I didn't come here to have a go at you. I know it's not about blame. I'd like to thank the teenage girl responsible, if anything. Maybe I'll tell her one day, when she's older. I reckon she'll have enough on her plate, for now.

'Well. Goodbye, Silas.

'No, no. I'll shut the door.

'Should I send the next one in?'

Chapter 17

So also you have sorrow now, but I will see
you again, and your hearts will rejoice, and no
one will take your joy from you.

John 16:22

'... Right. I see.' Joanie's voice quivered; she wasn't sure why.
'I mean ... thank you for letting me know. Gosh, I ... Was
she in any pain? Are you sure? Well, I'm glad for that, at least.
Okay. When's the ...? Oh. Oh. I would have thought we ...
Okay. Gosh, I don't even know what to ... Of course. Yes, I
understand. Thank you for letting me know.'

She put the phone down, breathed in and out a few times,
feeling suddenly very distant from the room she was in. For
a few moments, she didn't even hear Nnenna at her door.
She was almost shouting by the time she'd jolted Joanie from
her reverie.

'Mum!' she said.

'Sorry, Nnenna. Sorry.'

'What's happened? Who was that, on the phone?'

'It was ... Well, it was my cousin, Theo.'

'And what did he say? Mum, you're scaring me now.'

'It's Aunty Mary. She died last night. She had a stroke.'

'Oh my God.'

'The doctor said she probably felt no pain.'

'Oh.'

'She was eighty-seven years old, Nnenna, she had a good life. And she loved you very much, you know. Come here, it's all right.'

Aunty Mary was Joanie's aunt. Perfectly well until her last day, she had always had a particular soft spot for Joanie – more so than for her own stepson, Theo, whom she had never liked. Aunt Mary was firmly independent and spent much of her time by herself. Her husband had passed thirty years ago, and since then she had spent most of her time writing music, or with her friends from her choir. She had always seemed a little ambivalent about her family. But she spent every Christmas with Joanie and Nnenna, and had done since Nnenna was born.

Joanie suspected that Mary had done this out of pity, not wanting her to be alone; although she never said as much out loud, and never even mentioned Maurice's name in her hearing. Still, it was nice to have her there: Joanie remembered her from childhood as being brisk, but kind, and one of the few adults in her life who seemed to think that children deserved to be treated with dignity and affection. For Joanie as a young mother, she had been an invaluable help, providing Joanie with a home, support, encouragement and advice. For Joanie as an adult, she was an eccentric but comforting presence, bringing small but beautiful gifts, each year: a new song she had written, a story about someone interesting she had met.

For Nnenna, Aunty Mary's visits were a gift. She was fascinating, kind and clever: it was Aunty Mary that had first taught a five-year-old Nnenna to speak French, when she came back, full of excitement, from a trip to Paris. Every Christmas, she insisted that they ignore the usual films being screened on television and brought along offerings of her own, or poems, or stories or music, all by black women. Zora Neale Hurston; Jackie Kay; Sarah Vaughan; Aretha Franklin; Zadie Smith; Ella Fitzgerald; Maya Angelou. In Aunty Mary's presence,

Nnenna was no mystery child but the beloved scion of a long line of dedicated, passionate, intelligent artists who had striven and made their way through hard work, expression and deep thought. And Nnenna loved Aunty Mary's finds, and the beautiful Christmas cards she gave, each with a quotation by Audre Lorde inside; the love and care which inspired them, and the stories she had to tell about each one. Like the conversation she'd had with the sales assistant after he'd tripped over her walking stick; like the tribute concert she had attended with an old colleague who had waited years and years to ask her out on a date.

One evening, when Nnenna was fifteen, Aunty Mary had taken her to the theatre, to see a black poet perform. Nnenna had read up about her beforehand, and she liked her work: she couldn't wait to see what it would be like live. She was surprised when Aunty Mary arrived at her door with a friend ('Christina heard about it and she was dying to come! She *loves* black writers, too. You don't mind? I think you two'll really get along!').

And Nnenna didn't mind at first. But a few minutes into the performance, she became aware – dimly, at first, and then painfully – of Christina's face turning towards her after every poem was recited. Christina leaning over at her; Christina beaming at her; Christina *nudging* her. Nnenna was never allowed to simply enjoy these things with her mother and great-aunt; instead, as soon as the first words were read aloud, Nnenna could feel this white stranger's eyes on her, watching carefully for her reaction, for the thoughts on which she had no right to intrude.

Are you enjoying it, yet? she pressed, in Nnenna's mind. *Are you enjoying it? Are you enjoying it? Are you enjoying it?*

Because if you're not, you know, you're not really *black.*

'And if I am? Enjoying it?' Nnenna thought.

Mmmmmm ... I'll let you know.

Nnenna felt like a work of art on display, while observers scrutinised her and checked for signs of authenticity. And as much as she loved her aunty for thinking of her, for wanting to curate her experience of the world, she could never be comfortable while Christina attempted to disturb her deepest, most personal enjoyment of the thing before it was even finished. Her anxiety, she felt, was hers only because she could not see how to share it but her joy, her crystalline, private joy, was hers alone that evening.

'When's the funeral?' Nnenna said to her mother now, 'I think she'd like us to say something. Wouldn't she? Or read something. One of the poems she gave me, maybe.'

'That would be lovely, Nnenna, but ...' Joanie shook her head, sadly.

'But what?'

'Theo doesn't want us to come to the funeral. He was always a bit sore about his stepmum spending Christmas with us, instead of him. He seemed to take a lot of pleasure in informing me that his stepmum had left us hardly anything in her will – as if that's the kind of thing I'd be interested in, after everything she'd done for me. For us.'

'But ... can he do that? I mean, if we're family, can he really stop us going to the funeral?'

'I don't know. But I'd rather not fight with him about this. I hate it, I do, because she was like a mum to me. But I know Theo, and he won't give in. And if we try to fight it, he'll make the whole thing into one big ugly mess. I don't think Aunty Mary would have wanted a fight. We'll have to find another way to pay our respects. At home, maybe.'

Nnenna, unfamiliar with the unkindnesses of adult life, sat silently on her mother's bed, her brows furrowed in thought. With her Aunty Mary gone, she would have to find her own wisdom, now; her own art and music, her own words. She wasn't sure she was able.

Finally, she said, 'How can people be so petty? How can people be so ... low?'

Joanie sighed and said, 'Never underestimate people's ability to disappoint you.' She regretted the words as soon as she heard them; but they were true. So, when Nnenna looked at her – confused, on the verge of tears – she said, to soften it, 'But never stop expecting people to be good.'

'Do you think they deserve it?'

'I think ... I think that, much of the time, they try.'

Out of breath, Jonathan took a seat on an outcrop, looking over the valley. He still wasn't completely convinced that Manchester was the right city for him, but he could say this for it: it was easy enough to escape. Forty-five minutes on the train and he was out on Mam Tor, a hill in the middle of beautiful countryside. Light and shade chased one another over the land in front of him, as clouds and sunshine alternated above. The valley was broad but as he looked at it, it seemed small somehow, as though he might reach out a hand and lay it down on the valley, encompassing everything in sight.

He had come out here on impulse. Months ago, he had signed up to a meet-up group that went on regular walks to the countryside, but never been: the prospect of finding himself in the midst of another version of the Bible study group (repressed men with martyr complexes) was enough to make him forswear human company for good.

But the idea of escape had caught him. After leaving Silas's house, he had spent all day in his flat. Exhausted but unable to sleep, he had lain on his bed, replaying the moment over and over in his mind. Had it been a mistake? Had he let Silas go too soon? Perhaps, if he had only held out a while longer ...

He looked out from the top of the hill. There was nobody here; it was too early in the morning for most walkers, and the weather, though clement, was not yet warm. Still, it was a beautiful day. He took a bottle of water out from his bag and sipped, considering where to go for lunch in a couple of hours.

Unbidden, a Biblical verse came to him, from the book of Job:

Where is the way where light dwelleth?

The search had been so long, and so tiring. For much of it, he had been ardently looking in the wrong places: the wrong friends, the wrong men. Had he found it, now? Was he there? Surely, it was too soon to tell, too soon to know what would become of him. The darkness of his past might still rise up and overcome him again, perhaps. He had contacted a counsellor and the idea of talking about his problems terrified him; at the back of his mind there lurked the fear that no amount of talking would solve his problems, and that he was, at heart, unreachable.

But it was good to be scared, now, for the right reasons. It felt almost bracing, like removing an old bandage and feeling the breeze on his skin. What next? What might his life be like? Where might he find light, if he tried? He still wasn't sure how to read the map.

Turning to the land in front of him, he took off his hat and let his ears sting in the wind. It was good. He opened his mouth to speak, and let his words of freedom echo through the hills and valleys.

Chapter 18

For false Christs and false prophets will arise
and perform great signs and wonders, so as
to lead astray, if possible, even the elect.

Matthew 24:24

1993

Even before hindsight, everything about that night had felt somehow heightened. At the time, Joanie only thought it was because it was one of her 'good' nights with Maurice. They were fighting more and more now, and it was a relief to be getting on well.

Except that they didn't fight, exactly. When she fought with her mother . . . *that* was fighting. Loud, angry arguments that they both lost; shouting matches that left her shaking and in tears.

With Maurice, it was different. They didn't shout, because they knew it wouldn't get them anywhere. And shouting, Joanie knew, had a way of making people say things – true things – that they wish they hadn't said.

And yet, more and more, these days, they disagreed over Big Things – family, religion, ethics – things too big to avoid, but so big that they were both terrified to approach them. Sometimes they tiptoed as though towards a precipice, and then withdrew at the last minute, both agreeing to calm down and talk about it later. But they were never really calm enough, any more, so nothing was ever talked about. Nothing was ever resolved; nothing was ever right.

The smallest things seemed to set them arguing. Sometimes Joanie wondered if she should end it. What had seemed at first like a mad adventure into the unknown, now seemed mad. They were different in so many ways that the whole thing seemed like an impossible quest. But she felt so alone, with her mother not speaking to her, her father long dead, her friends ignoring her. Even if she should have given Maurice up, she didn't have the strength.

She tightened her grip on his hand as they walked through the gardens of her college in the late afternoon light. Blossom petals carpeted the ground. She felt the roughness of his skin: it dehydrated quickly and unless he moisturised a few times a day, it cracked and bled. His hands were bony, too, and tonight the strength of them surprised her; they seemed more fragile, somehow, when his skin was dry.

'You didn't moisturise?'

As soon as she said it, she regretted it and almost winced.

But Maurice only raised an eyebrow, smiled and shook his head. 'Forgot. Besides, it's cold. Skin dries out faster when it's cold.'

'Sorry.'

'For what?'

'I didn't mean to sound like I was criticising you.'

'You didn't. God, Joanie, did you think I'd . . . ? I'm not a monster.'

'I didn't mean that.'

They unclasped hands and took deep breaths, as if sucking in the words they did not want to say. But then Maurice said,

'I'm sorry, Joanie. I didn't mean to upset you. I love you.'

'I love you too. But, Maurice . . .'

'I know. It's been awful lately.'

'Why?'

'It's nothing.'

'It's not nothing. We're so different, now. *You're* so different. And, Maurice ... it hasn't even been that long since we met, but sometimes I look at you and I barely recognise you.'

'What does that mean?'

'You're angry.'

'Hold on. I've never, *ever*—'

'It's nothing you've done! It's nothing you've said!' She was shouting now. She was the failing girl, shouting at her black boyfriend. But it felt oddly sweet, as though she had been saving it specially. And she had. The words came easily to her because she'd rehearsed them in her head. 'All the time, Maurice. There's so much that you don't like, so much that you don't trust.'

'I trust you. I love you.'

'But you don't like me. Not any more. You're so angry, Maurice. At everything. Even me. And I don't know why.' She cried quietly. She felt as though she had flayed her own flesh: as though the wind was blowing coldly on everything inside of her, muscle, bone, guts.

Maurice was quiet for a moment. He did not put his arm around her.

'We're not supposed to say it.'

'Say what?'

'We're not supposed to say we hate it here. Immigrants; Nigerians. We're not supposed to say that we hate it here.'

'What are you talking about? Maurice, every time you're on the phone with your family, you barely talk about anything else. You love talking about how much you don't like it here. It's like some big in-joke to you all.'

'It's not that simple. I can make jokes on the phone, laugh about the British, about British weather; even about the racism.

But in my family, we don't admit weakness like that. I've never heard my parents talk about giving up on anything. Ever.'

'Maurice, they must have. At some point, they must have. Everyone finds some things hard. And you said your dad—'

'But we're not supposed to *talk* about it. And even if I wanted to, I wouldn't know how, not properly. Not openly. I can't put the words together. I can't even tell what I'm feeling, sometimes, because it's buried so deeply. Can you believe that? I can feel something and have no idea what it is.'

She looked at him through tears. Everything was a mess, such a mess. 'Do you think that's why you're angry?'

He nodded, his head cast down. 'There's so much I don't know how to say, Joanie.'

'Like what?'

'Joanie, I don't know how to say it.'

'Try. Please, Maurice. Otherwise . . . '

He looked at her now. 'Joanie, it's okay, it's okay.' He hugged her.

'It's not okay, Maurice. You have to try. If you can't talk about what's wrong . . . we can't go on like this. I feel so lonely. All the time.'

'Me too. And I hate to say it to you, because I love you. But it's true. I feel as though . . . I don't think God's real, I don't think God's *here*. I can't see him here, any more.'

'Well, the truth is, I—'

'What?'

'No, it's stupid. I can't say it, now.'

'Tell me.'

'It's just . . . I never used to believe in God.'

'But you do now?'

'No. No, I don't think so. But how you're talking, now, is how I used to feel. Before . . . I met you.' She looked directly in front of her, at the main building of the college. It must have been at least four hundred years old. It was there long before she arrived and would be standing long after she left. 'It sounds corny, I know. But I used to think we were all just in it for ourselves, and that nothing mattered all that much. And maybe that's still true, maybe there's nobody kind in charge, maybe nobody any good. But when I met you ... I started to think it might be possible.'

'Because of me? You thought there might be a God?'

'I don't know, I couldn't put a name to it. God? Happiness? Optimism? I don't know. The way you believed, the way you *trusted* Him. It made me want to be able to trust something, and it made me think I could. But now, you don't believe any more. And every day, I feel like we're moving in opposite directions, Maurice. It feels like ... like we only passed each other for a moment and now we're getting further and further apart.'

'I'm sorry.'

'It's not your fault. You're not happy. You don't like it here, and you've lost your faith. You didn't choose those things. I can't imagine what that would feel like.'

'I don't know what to do, Joanie. I feel so ... You know what the worst thing is? Usually, when I feel this bad, I talk to God.'

Joanie looked at him hard for a moment, then said, 'Why don't we try that now?'

'Joanie ...'

'The college chapel's starting evensong in a few minutes – we could go?'

'I don't think—'

'We have to do something, Maurice. You can't go on like this.'

'But—'

'Listen. You made me think that it might be possible. God. God! I never believed that the whole world was anything but a hopeless mess. But meeting you ... I can't let you give up on that, now. Not now I've seen even a bit of how it feels to believe in something.'

'But it's not the same, Joanie. It's not the same at the college chapel. I can't go anywhere, it doesn't work like that. It's not home for me, there.'

'So, what, then?'

'My church.'

'St Jude's?' The incredulity made her voice go harsh and crack.

'I have to. I know you don't like it.'

'Maurice, the things they preach . . . they're not good people, there. They're not good Christians – even I can see that. They're not like you.'

'They were the first church I came to in England where it felt like home. I know that you don't—'

'I hate it there, Maurice. Why can't you try somewhere else? There are other churches.'

'It's like . . . It's like family, Joanie. Just because you disagree with them, doesn't mean you ignore them or get rid of them.'

Joanie shook her head. 'You should talk to my mum about family.'

'Come with me, Joanie.'

'I don't want to. And I don't want you to.'

'Please. For me.'

She thought for a long moment. Was this what her life would be like, if she stayed with Maurice? She didn't like it. It felt all wrong. But it was what Maurice wanted; maybe it was what he needed.

'All right. I'll come with you. This time.'

'There you are! The service is starting in a few minutes, you know.' Jonathan had taken to hiding in the vestry before evensong, these days, searching for – what? An answer? An antidote?

'I know, I know. Joel, I'll meet you out there. I need to check over this one last verse.'

'Why? Jonathan, you must know that thing from cover to cover, by now.' 'That thing' was Jonathan's Bible, a gift he'd been given at his confirmation, seven years ago.

'There's always something else, always something I've missed. Maybe the translation ...'

Joel Eberhardt shook his head slowly, pityingly, as Jonathan leafed through his copy of the King James version. Like the bibles belonging to the other members of their group, it was well worn, dog-eared and highlighted on almost every page. Joel had always been struck by Jonathan's approach to the faith; the way he took everything seriously, as though Christ might actually come back to earth tomorrow.

The difference between the two of them was, Jonathan had no confidence in himself. Jonathan seemed to think about the Second Coming the way a teenager thinks about their parents arriving home from a business trip after they've thrown an unauthorised party.

He always acted as though he were in some sort of trouble.

And he wasn't entirely wrong.

On the other hand, Joel knew that plenty of people would be in Big Trouble on the Day of Reckoning. But he also happened to know, with complete certainty, that he wasn't one of them. Jonathan's studious engagement with the Bible – its fury, its demands, its questions, its promises and its doubt – was all very well. But Joel knew in his heart that he was loved by God, and no amount of study or prayer or even repentance would ever come close to that. Joel did know the Bible reasonably well, of course, and he even knew a few of the Greatest Hits by heart. But the scriptural foundations of the Christian faith did not appeal to him. The written word, he believed, ought to make things clearer, more immutable. Instead, God's word, as recorded in the Bible, was forever dependent on context, always open to misreading, mistranslation, misinterpretation ... For Joel, this messed up the whole business. For him, the point of religion was to have something steady to hold onto, something fixed. And the Bible . . . well, it had a slippery quality about it that Joel had never quite taken to. It seemed as though, the closer you looked at it, the less you knew. Better, then, not to look too closely.

'Jonathan,' he said gently. 'What exactly is it that you're hoping to find in there?'

'What do you mean?'

'I mean, what are you hoping you'll find?'

Jonathan only sat and gaped, too flustered to respond. How could he put into words what he was looking for? A loophole? Salvation? Mercy? Pity?

'Look, Jonathan,' said Joel, taking a seat beside Jonathan at the small table. 'I think we both know what went on between you and Alastair. To be perfectly honest, I think everybody in the group knows. No wonder the others haven't been attending as much. Maurice hasn't come to a group meeting for months. You know better than anyone how black people feel about that sort of thing.'

'What's that got to do with . . .'

'Listen, I've got nothing against that lifestyle, Jonathan. But you've got to admit it hasn't been good for you. Or, am I wrong? Are you and Alastair still . . . together?'

'Joel, what are you talking about?'

'Look, do what you want, but don't come crying to God when you mess up your life. What you're doing is wrong, Jonathan. God hates it.'

'No, it's not that simple, there's—'

'What? Have you found some solution in there, Jonathan? Found a handy Bible verse to make everything okay?'

'How can you say that to me? Joel . . . I . . . I'm not . . .'

But Joel only raised his eyebrows, his face a parody of patience. He waited for Jonathan's words to run out.

'Come on, Jonathan. I see you in here every day, now,

scratching around in the dirt for some solution to a problem we both know you can't solve. God doesn't work like that: you can't argue a case in front of him like he's a judge in court, listening to lawyers' arguments, consulting the evidence. This is God, Jonathan. God. Right and wrong. Heaven. Hell. Those things don't change. They don't compromise.'

'What are you saying?'

'Well, there are plenty of people out there who can lie to you, tell you what you want to know. And you're a smart guy: I'm sure you could find something in that thing to twist round and make it seem like everything's okay. But you already know the truth. What you're doing ... *Who you are* is an abomination.' His voice took on an eerily gentle quality, like a nurse talking to a child who has been running too fast and fallen over. 'It's hurting you, Jonathan. It's been hurting you for a long time, I think. And one day, one way or another, it'll kill you.'

His job done, Joel pursed his lips and stood up to take his seat among the gathering congregation. He paused for a moment, unsure whether to switch off the light. He left it on; perhaps Jonathan wouldn't be long.

St Jude's was old. As they left after the service, Joanie thought to herself, grimly, that it was the kind of old building which would have given her nightmares as a child: it was in the gothic style and its light brickwork had been darkened by years of traffic on the tiny, congested Cambridge streets.

During the twenty-minute walk from her college to the church, she and Maurice had held hands but said nothing, each deep in their own thoughts. Joanie could not tell what Maurice was thinking, and didn't want to ask: she was afraid he would say something ... what? Unkind? No. Final?

It was a cold evening. Colder than when they'd walked in the college gardens. She wanted to put her hands in her pockets, but she was afraid to let go of Maurice's hand.

'You've been there before,' Maurice said, pre-emptively, as though Joanie had no right to complain now, as though she'd always known what she was getting herself into.

'Yes, I have,' she said. 'And I hated it then, and I hate it now.'

'Joanie,' he said, trying to force a laugh into his voice. 'Come on—'

'But what I hate more,' she said, 'is how you pretend that you don't hate it. You aren't some naive teenager. You *know*, Maurice. You know what that place is doing to people.'

'They're practising their faith, Joanie. They're trying to find a connection to God.'

'*Stop doing that!*' She stopped walking and balled her fists without realising. Strangers walked past, silently noting an interracial couple arguing in the street. She didn't care.

'Stop doing what?'

'Stop pretending! *Stop* pretending you don't know exactly what's going on in that church. They preach hatred, Maurice. All that stuff about women quietly submitting to their husbands, all that stuff about what men should and shouldn't be ...'

'That is what God wants. This isn't a game to them, Joanie. Not everyone flips casually through a few verses on a rainy afternoon. This is real. This is truth. This is heaven and hell. Those things don't change.'

'Oh, please. It would be one thing if you genuinely thought that. But you don't. You're better than that, Maurice. You don't think like that. For God's sake, I've spent most nights with you for months and months, but we're not married, are we?'

'That's different.'

'No, it's exactly the same. And I hate that you sit through the sermons week after week as if you agree with them. You don't! Doesn't it kill you to hear all that when you know it's not right? Isn't some part of you dying inside when you listen to all that bigotry?'

'I already told you why I go.'

'What, because it reminds you of home? Maurice, don't you think there's something archaic about those churches, if this is how they think?'

Maurice laughed bitterly. 'And why do you think that is, Joanie? Who do you think came to our dark little continent and put that hatred in? Who do you think came in and stripped us of our history? Who do you think slithered into our country and told us that our religions, our traditions were worthless and gave us their own instead?'

'But this isn't about the past, Maurice. We're not living in colonial times, any more.'

'Aren't we? How can you say that after everything I told you?'

'You know what I mean. It doesn't have to be this way. I'm not saying you have to go up to the pulpit and start arguing with the minister. And I know that your family expects certain things—'

'What do you know about my family? What do you know about expectations?'

'—*But you're your own man*, Maurice. And you need to make a choice. You keep associating with this church, and it'll grind down every bit of good in you. It's poison, Maurice, can't you see that? Can't you see what it's doing to you?'

'You know what?' Maurice fixed his face into a snarl, but his voice was cool and decided. 'I've had enough. I'm so sick of you criticising me, judging me like you understand me, like you know me.'

'I love you,' she said, sobbing. She was angry and the words cost her dearly to say out loud, but it was as though Maurice didn't hear them.

'If you can't accept me the way I am, then let's forget this. Let's forget the whole thing. I think we'd both be happier.'

He stalked off into the night. He did not say he loved her too, but she knew he did, just like she knew that he must hate himself for this. But he didn't say it, and it broke her heart.

*

When Joanie woke up, she was in a hospital bed. It took her a moment to remember the details of what she had seen that evening, and what she did remember was not good. Everything was so sad. She hadn't known, somehow, that anyone could be in so much pain, so much torment until tonight. Her bones ached. Was that tiredness? She felt tired.

'You're awake, are you?' a nurse whispered as he smiled over her as he passed her bed. 'You had quite a fall, there: it's lucky my colleague caught you! And don't worry, we're looking after your friend.'

'Yes ...' said Joanie, absently. Her mind was still preoccupied, trying to make sense of what had happened. Still, she found herself taking in her surroundings again: the hospital ward and its attendant clean, plasticky smell that she hated. There was a curtain around her bed with a green and blue wavy pattern on it that she also hated, but the nurse had drawn it slightly when she woke up, and she could see that she was in a women's ward, and that the other beds all seemed to be full. Everyone was asleep. Through a window, a slim moon shone and she had the vague feeling that it must be very late at night. Despite everything, she felt a kind of calm she hadn't felt since she was a child, when it had been socially acceptable to nap at any time of day.

'How are you feeling now?'

The nurse's voice was cheerful; it was soft and sympathetic. All the same, it had purpose and it brought her back to reality. The evening flashed before her eyes again. The fight with Maurice ...

'I'm fine, thank. You?'

And then, she'd gone over to Jonathan's house. He was the only person in the city that she still thought of as a friend, the only person she could still talk to about Maurice ...

'You're on autopilot, I bet. Did you get a good night's sleep, at least? I'm sure you needed it. Can't be easy.'

She'd known something was wrong straight away – Jonathan's front door was ajar and the lights were on, and it was past dark. Jonathan was far too anxious a person to leave his door open, and he always went to bed early. She'd listened at the door but there were no sounds of movement. It had occurred to her that a burglar wouldn't leave the lights on and the curtains open. She'd gone in . . .

'No. No, it's been a difficult night. Thank you for looking after me.'

'Of course, of course. The doctor will be along in a minute. How are your bruises?'

'Bruises?'

That terrible silence, a waiting silence that was coiled like a spring. She'd had no warning of what she was to find . . .

'Oh gosh, yes. You didn't hit your head, thankfully, but when you fainted you banged your legs on a cupboard. You probably don't remember.'

She did remember. She wished she didn't, because it brought the pain back more sharply. She hadn't noticed it before somehow; it was a slow, pulsing kind of ache.

'How's your pillow?'

The simplicity of it had been the first thing she'd noticed. She remembered thinking it was the kind of thing a child could have done without help, and that it should not be so easy for someone to hang themselves. And yet, Jonathan couldn't do it. There he was . . .

'It's all right, thanks. What time is it?'

One end of the necktie in a noose around his neck, the other end tied to the bannister. And Jonathan, standing at the top of the stairs, trying and trying to jump off. He made small but determined movements and his eyes were screwed shut, tears gathering around them. There hadn't even been time to scream, she remembered that. As though the scream was still inside her now. All she could do was run as hard as she could to him . . .

'It's nearly eleven. As I say, the doctor will be along in a minute. I should probably see to the others on the ward, so I'll leave you be. Unless there's anything else you need?'

But he'd heard her coming up the stairs and he recoiled from her as if she were on fire. She'd had to fight him and he was so strong, so strong, like he had a demon inside him. She remembered, too, how much he seemed to want to be left alone to die. She'd had to fight him away so that she could untie the tie from the bannister in time.

'No, I'm fine. Thank you,' she told the nurse. She forgot to ask why the doctor was coming. Maybe she'd fractured something when she fell, or when Jonathan had struggled with her. He was *so strong*. How odd that someone so strong should want to die.

When she'd untied the tie from the bannister, Jonathan had run into his room and locked the door. No matter how much she banged on the door, he wouldn't let her in, so she ran downstairs to his telephone and called first the police – and then Maurice.

'All right. The doctor will be here in a second.'

She couldn't remember what she'd said to him, exactly; or rather, she didn't want to. She'd practically screamed at him as soon as he picked up the phone, screamed about what his church had done, about how he needed to get here and help her before Jonathan tried to hurt himself again while he was in his room.

Maurice was there in two minutes – he mustn't have gone to bed. But when he broke down the door into Jonathan's room, Jonathan was sitting in a corner, crying. He was so *angry* at them. He wouldn't let anyone touch him. Joanie didn't know what to do.

So, she'd screamed at Maurice again. As soon as the ambulance arrived to take Jonathan away, as soon as the police had left, Joanie had screamed things at Maurice that she hadn't known were inside her. Only to her mother had she said such hateful, hurtful things – things calculated to hurt as much as possible, to humiliate and undermine. She'd thought, at the time, how odd it was that she'd spoken to him, in that way, as though he was a part of her family, when they'd broken up only a few hours ago.

But he'd stood there in silence, as though he hadn't heard anything, as though none of it mattered. And that had made Joanie scream louder and louder, say crueller and crueller things so that something, anything would pierce him.

When he punched the wall the first time, she stopped dead. She couldn't move. That look of – not anger, but something wild. Years ago, *he*, of course, had been the one to speak, each word punctuated with a slap, a jab, a thump. *Why—won't—you—stop? Why—won't—you—leave—me—be? Shut—up! Shut—up!*

Maurice punched the wall again and again until his hand bled. And she knew, she could tell then that it was himself that Maurice was really angry with – for his failure, for his weakness – but it didn't matter. Joanie was all fear: there was nothing else inside her in that moment, only the desperate need to run away, run away, run away.

She fled down the street into a phone box, always spinning around, watching behind her in case Maurice had followed her. He hadn't.

Yes, a taxi, please. Addenbrooke's Hospital. As soon as possible. In the phone box at the end of York Street. Right. Okay. Thank you.

'Miss Maloney!' The doctor walked up to the side of her bed, a broad smile on her young face. She closed the curtain briskly. 'I see that a nurse has been to see you? Is there anything else you need?'

'No, I'm fine, thank you.' Her voice sounded croaky. She

took a sip of water from the cup by her bed. 'What's wrong with me? Did I break something? I don't feel—'

'Well, first of all, can I ask when's the last time you ate something?'

'What?'

'Did you have lunch?'

'I . . .'

'Breakfast?'

'I've been . . . A lot of things have happened today. Please tell me what's wrong with me so I can go home.'

'Well, that's probably why you fainted: hunger and stress.'

'And did I break anything? When I fell?'

'I don't think so, but we haven't done any X-rays yet, because . . . Well, actually, I mean . . . obviously . . .' The doctor raised her eyebrows expectantly, waiting for Joanie to get it. Joanie didn't get it. She frowned instead.

'What?' she said.

'Obviously, we can't do X-rays if . . . I mean, were you aware that you're pregnant?'

'What?' Joanie craned her head forward, trying to read the doctor's face for some sign that she was joking, that she was even the slightest bit unsure, that she might have made some sort of mistake. That this was a dream.

'Yes. You're pregnant, Miss Maloney. You didn't know? Well. You're very early on . . .'

Joanie shook her head, mutely. She couldn't move her eyes from the curtains around her bed, couldn't look at the world outside.

'You see, when you fainted, we ran a few tests. Nothing invasive, but we wanted to check some things, and, well . . . I mean, we can go through the results with you if that would be helpful, but I'm sure that can wait if there's anyone you'd like to call, now . . . ?'

Joanie only shook her head. There was no one. Her mother

wouldn't want to hear from her, not with this news. She didn't have any brothers or sisters, any other family she could call on. And Maurice was the last person she wanted to hear from.

'Anyone? There must be someone you'd like to call? I know it's not always the most welcome news, but ... '

Joanie nodded. 'Just one person. I've got one person.'

The doctor's face brightened. 'Of course. I'll fetch a wheelchair and we'll get you to a telephone.'

The phone, inside a consultation room, was an aggressively neutral shade of grey-blue.

'Hello? It's me. Listen, I know you might think I'm stupid and I walked right into this or something but I'm ... ' She took a deep breath. 'I'm pregnant. A minute ago. The doctor told me. I'm at the hospital. And I ... Yes. It's Maurice's. I know it's a lot to take in, but I can't talk to him right now, it's all been so awful, so I need to talk to you. I need you to get here. Please, judge me later and ... Okay. Addenbrooke's, yeah. Please hurry. This place is full of doctors and they want to tell me things and I can't focus on anything right now, and I've had such a horrible, horrible night, Aunty Mary, and I can't be alone. How soon can you get here?'

Chapter 19

[...] the snare is broken and we have escaped.

Psalm 124:7

2010

In his study, Amit put down his pencil and surveyed, not for the first time, his handiwork. Seating plans are difficult, but the memory of the debating competition soothed him, spurred him on.

[Straightens bow tie] And so, despite a very respectable effort on the part of the opposition, I must conclude, not merely that this motion is lacking in any substantial demerits, but that it remains the sole sensible course of action henceforth.

If he got this seating plan right – and he believed that he had, finally – everything would be perfect tonight. He could talk to the people he wanted to talk to, but avoid the people who were boring and yet popular enough to make themselves useful for the social media photos. He could monitor the progress on the whisky, and whisk it away before they drank more than was consistent with the 'few friends' Amit had said he was having round. He could keep Sam from spending too much time with any of the girls, while giving Hannah and Stephanie the opportunity to make their move, should they come to their senses.

He'd hoped to have Nnenna there, but Dan had said she was having a special birthday dinner with her mum at home. Shame.

Yes, there will be detractors. But this great nation [flash of winning smile to the all-white judges] was not founded on self-doubt, nor was it founded on pandering to the lowest common denominator. No, my friends . . .

The truth was, Amit didn't want to go out with Nnenna; if he was honest with himself, he would admit that he didn't even fancy her, particularly. But for some time now, he had been nursing a fantasy. In his heart of hearts, Amit hoped that she, a girl who everybody *else* seemed to find attractive, would one day notice him and, in so doing, make everyone else notice, too. And what was the hold-up on that, anyway? She would, he was sure, enjoy his anecdotes of heroic Sudoku puzzle-solving; she would (somehow – he was still a bit fuzzy on the details) marvel at his sky-high grades in Maths; she would, eventually, come to laugh at his jokes, appreciate his well-oiled hair and his eccentric but tastefully selected bow ties.

And if she didn't . . . Well, if she didn't, the prospect of Danny had begun to glow in his mind like a streetlight just coming on in the evening . . .

No, indeed. For, as William Davy once said, the air of this green and pleasant land is so pure that none who breathe it can be slaves. So, with this in mind, I must request – kindly, but firmly – that the curriculum be amended immediately, to include the compulsory teaching of Britain's imperial history. If we do not learn from the past, it will not merely repeat; it will enslave us, forcing us to act out its behests time after time after time. My language may seem hyperbolic, but the time for mealy-mouthed words has come and gone. My friends, I will no longer submit to the craven servitude of ignorance, and nor, I believe, should you. [applause, applause]

Danny had spoken the words, but they were Amit's. As, now, was the trophy. It amazed him how easily the judges had been impressed by it all. To him, it was rather flowery – the metaphor for slavery didn't, he thought, quite work – but in the right hands (and in the white hands), the speech went off beautifully. As soon as Danny flashed his pre-fabricated devil-may-care bravado and precisely the right dose of nationalism, the opposing team didn't stand a chance.

And yet, what was that look that Danny had given him as he finished his speech? It was something Amit had begun to dream of seeing, but never dared to hope for. It was almost ... Was it ...?

His phone was ringing. It wasn't a number he recognised. Probably one of the caterers.

'Hello?'

'Hi, Amit. Err ... It's Nnenna. How are you?'

'Yeah, I'm all right thanks, how are y—'

'Yeah, that's great. Listen. Do you mind if I come along tonight?'

'Oh. Are you sure?' His surprise, he realised, made him sound unenthusiastic, when he was anything but. 'I mean, it'd be great to see you. I wasn't expecting you, though.'

'Yeah. Do you mind?'

'No, not at all, I just didn't think you'd be able to make it. Dan said you were having dinner with your mum.'

'Yeah, I am. But after that, I mean, I don't think she'll mind.'

'Oh. You're not going to stay with—'

'Listen, if you don't want me there ... '

'No, no, it's fine. Come to mine when you finish dinner – 39 Piershill Street. No need to bring any—'

'Great. Thanks. See you soon.'

She hung up.

Amit sat back in his chair, amazed. So Nnenna would come after all.

He picked up his pencil. He would have to change his seating plan.

*

In her room, Nnenna set her phone down on her bed, and looked at her reflection again. What was wrong?

No matter how good she thought she looked in theory, there was always something wrong, some flaw she couldn't name or find. Sometimes, looking in the mirror was hunting a ghost: was it her chin that made her ugly? Her arms? Her waist? She couldn't see it when she looked; it fled from her gaze. But she knew it was there.

And then, sometimes, like now, the ugliness became contagious and spread to other parts of her life. Her unhappy gaze drifted from the mirror to her room, her small room with only enough room for her bed, her clothes rack, a small bookshelf that her mother had built a few years ago. Her small room in the small house that was the only one her mother could afford to rent in the school's catchment area. Her tiny room where her second-hand books spilled over from the bookshelf onto the floor.

She thought, sometimes, about telling Danny how she felt. More than once, she had thought about telling him about her anxieties, her fear about how the world saw her and where, exactly, she was supposed to fit in. Not for the first time, she picked up her phone, found Danny's number, tried to imagine what she would say.

But she could think of nothing. No scene played in her mind, not even catastrophe, not even the nightmares she was so accustomed to, had slowly come to laugh at and find joy in, after the fact. When she tried to imagine trusting in Danny . . . she couldn't. She wondered if he knew; if, perhaps, he preferred it this way. Sometimes, he seemed to.

She put away her phone. She took one last look at herself in the mirror, then quickly averted her eyes away from what she didn't like, and saw a book, poking out from underneath the bed.

No. Not a book. Her book.

Was it ...? Surely it wasn't ...? She'd put that away. She *always* put her diary away.

> *Hi Joanie,*
> *Thank you for sending me your article – I loved reading it and found your style very readable – there was a wonderful clarity to it, while also being engaging. I think you are a gifted writer, with lots of important things to say and a very good way of saying them. I must say, I'm a bit wary of having children, now!*
> *I'm so sorry, though: we can't afford to take on any more journalists at the moment. I'm so sorry that I can't give you the response you were hoping for. We're barely making any money as it is, with print sales down and advertising rates being what they are ...*

Her first rejection email. Her first rejection. Her first attempt. Joanie knew that she should be resilient, perhaps even print it out and keep it in a ring-binder, to laugh at one day when she was more successful. But how many more of these stretched in front of her?

And what lay at the end? She didn't want to compile crosswords forever. She wanted to be a medium for news, for real-life events. Right now, she felt like an intellectual scratching-post. She had started to receive *fan mail* from her readership. Does a crossword compiler have a 'readership'? She was not sure, and this concerned her. Some of the letters were complaints: this one was too easy, that one was overly Latinate. But these did not bother Joanie so much.

More troubling to her were the friendly ones: the letters from crossword enthusiasts (Joanie reserved the word 'enthusiasts' for people whose lives she believed to be empty) complimenting her. The thinly veiled love letters from long-term 'fans'. From people who had *followed her career.*

Joanie loved her fans, dearly, at least in abstract. But they were not the fans she wanted most. None of her followers saw her for who she was. Not one had noticed that, for the last ten years, each of her crossword puzzles had been spelling out her desperation to stop writing crosswords. Couldn't anyone tell that she'd been going through the motions for years?

Even if they could, none of them could help her. She was fairly confident that no editor of a major broadsheet ever rifled through her sophomoric attempts to amuse the teensy proportion of readers who enjoyed both Merchant Ivory films and anagrams of Chinese tea blends.

No: the people who wrote to her about her crosswords were the very dregs of the world of crossword puzzle enthusiasts. Not the intellectually curious but the pedants. The people who were saddened by her indifference to medieval French, disappointed by her intermittent pop culture references. Joanie used to appreciate their input: when she first started out, it was their letters that encouraged her, told her that someone was listening. But now she was beginning to think that they were the only ones, and it scared her. She was beginning to feel like she had taken on a sort of symbol status: she worried about being recognised in the street and initiated into some sort of secret society with its own handshake. She worried about teenage polymaths googling images of her and masturbating furtively under their bedsheets at night.

Every profession has its downsides. All of this (or almost all of it) would be fine, if compiling crosswords was what she wanted to do, even as a side-job alongside the proof-reading work she did. But it was only ever meant to be a temporary fix, while Nnenna was young and Joanie needed to be able to work from home, and while she tried to decide what she wanted to do with her life. It was never meant to be permanent. Getting over-familiar letters from crossword puzzle enthusiasts in Chipping Norton was like dressing up as a ghost for a Halloween party and then having one person after another tell you that, actually, the bedsheet-over-the-head look was your best yet.

And, come to think of it, what had she done with her life? She'd barely had time to figure out what her dreams were, never mind chase them. There was nothing in her life that was truly hers, nothing she had achieved, nothing she was proud of. Except Nnenna.

But Nnenna was a happy accident.

And one day, she would leave. If not Paris in a year or two, it would be somewhere else, later on. There was nothing keeping her in Manchester, and soon there would be plenty of reasons to leave. Already, Joanie could tell, Nnenna was moving further and further away every day.

There was a knock at her bedroom door.

'I'm going out.'

'What? What are you talking about? Your birthday dinner's nearly . . . '

'What? What's wrong?'

'Nothing's wrong. It's the dress. I think it looks lovely on you.'

'Oh, I . . . Oh. Thanks.' It was a reflex. Nnenna couldn't help it. After all, it was something to have someone who loved her as she was. It was something to have someone who made no bones about the fact that she thought Nnenna was beautiful. It was something that, sometimes, it really did seem like her mother wanted nothing more from her than her happiness. For a moment, she longed to go to Joanie and hug her. But she could not. The transgression had been too great. She hardened her heart.

Nnenna got up, pushed past Joanie and almost ran down the stairs. Her mother's voice called after her as she followed. She could hear her sobbing: Joanie knew that Nnenna knew.

'Nnenna! Where are you going? I've made dinner!'

Nnenna stopped, startled, at the bottom of the stairs. The

lights in the dining room were low, and on the table were two tall, thin white candles. The table was laid with their best plates and cutlery, a new tablecloth in a bright, closely detailed African print. In the centre was a big badge (*17 today!*) and a handwritten menu: homemade bread rolls and butternut squash soup to start; but then there was more. There were things that, for the most part, Nnenna had only seen in photographs, only heard spoken about.

There was groundrice and okra soup as the main course: the groundrice was a fluffy, almost cloud-like doughy sort of thing, dolloped daintily onto their best plates; the okra soup was a gloopy brown mixture, with dried fish and chopped vegetables floating in it. And for dessert, there was *chin-chin* – tiny cubes of hard, sweet, fried dough.

Nnenna frowned. How did her mother know about Nigerian food? Had she made it herself? Surely not. The okra soup alone took hours and hours to make.

'I've been working on the food for weeks while you're at school,' said her mother's voice, behind her, as if to answer her question. 'But I think I've finally got it right. Groundrice isn't easy though; it gets so thick, so quickly. I felt like I should have done some weight training before I tried to stir the pot!'

Nnenna couldn't say anything. She could not take her eyes off the menu. They had given her some Nigerian food during her Saturday Igbo lessons; they called it another part of her education. Some soup, some rice, a bit of fried plantain. Noticing her confusion, they had shown her how to eat the sticky groundrice with one hand so that she kept the other hand clean for holding a glass of water. She hadn't thought that she might ever be able to share any of this with her mother. She wasn't sure how she felt about it.

'Happy birthday, Nnenna,' Joanie said, quietly, as though by speaking too loudly she might break the spell that was somehow keeping Nnenna in the room with her long after she said that she would leave. 'I know we've not been getting along beautifully these past few weeks, but I wanted to do something special for your birthday. I do love you very much.'

Why was she being so disarming, now? Nnenna still wasn't sure she knew what she was going to do: this anger inside her was so unwieldy, so heavy. It made her feel tired. She wished that she could put it down. But she could not.

She walked towards the door.

'Where are you going?' said her mum, sharply, insistently.

'Out.' She put her hand on the doorknob, partly to steady herself, and put her hand in her bag to fish for her keys. She found the front door key and put it in the lock . . .

'Out? Nnenna, you can't go out, I've made you dinner. I've planned a whole evening for your—'

For some reason, it was the incredulity in her voice that enraged Nnenna. She spun round, her eyes narrowed and flashing.

'How can you say that? How can you say that and expect me to sit here with you? You read my diary.'

Joanie stared at her for a moment, now it was out in the open.

'Nnenna, look. I'm sorry. I'm so sorry about that, but you can't walk out. You can't. I'm still your mother, whatever I've done.'

Nnenna shook her head. She hated fighting with her mother. It felt wrong, and everything always came out wrong: whenever she spoke, she hoped that what she said would be the right thing, the perfect thing that would make her mother see, make her understand. But every time it sounded somehow lacking and weak. She took a breath.

'Don't you understand? This is so typical of you. This is everything that's wrong.'

'What on earth are you talking about? Look, come and sit down, and we'll—'

'You!' She was only half aware that she was shouting.

'You're so selfish. I hate it. I hate it, Mum! You want to know everything about me, but whenever I try to ask you something about him ... about *Dad* ... you make some excuse, or you pretend you haven't heard, or even if you do tell me, you make me feel so guilty for asking. And the worst part is, you want to know everything! You want to know everything, but you don't want me to know anything.'

'I'm sorry. I said I'm sorry.' Her mother stood before her, her hands clasped in front of her, as if to say that all she wanted, all she could hope for, was that Nnenna's rage would wash over her, and then end, and they could be close again. But it only made Nnenna angrier. Why did she have to just stand there, instead of saying something, instead of finally telling her the truth? Why couldn't she try? Why couldn't she, for once, just *try*?

'I can apologise to you and I can explain, but—'

'It's too late. Enjoy your food.' She started to walk towards the door, but halted when she heard a glass smash against the wall and saw her mother advancing towards her.

'I swear to God, Nnenna. Don't you dare walk out of that door.'

Nnenna shook her head, choosing her words carefully, hoping again that what she said would get through to her mother, hoping that this time it would be enough, hoping that it would make her stop, hoping that it would make her see. 'Do you have any idea what it's like for me at a school like that? Nobody at that school is anything like me, they haven't got a clue.'

'What? Nnenna, what about Hannah? She's not white. And besides, I already told you, it doesn't matter that you're not white.'

'Well, it does matter that I'm black. And I'm not just talking about the fact that almost nobody else at that school is. It's not only that they're all white. I mean ... they're ... they're all *perfect*.

Perfect house, perfect friends, perfect family. Do you have any idea how many people have asked me why I never mention my dad? And I can't tell them, because then I'd be the girl who doesn't know, who doesn't even *know* why she's never met her dad. Do you know what it's like, every day, to have to pretend? Do you know what it's like to go to a school where everyone assumes that everything's great, that I'm happy at home—'

'You're not happy?'

The question was like a slap in the face. And Nnenna let it hang in the air.

'You've not been happy?' her mother said, her voice a whisper, now. Nnenna knew that she could say something placatory, something calming and fair. She knew that the merciful thing to do would be to say something that was measured, at least. But she could not be merciful, not now.

'You've read my diary. How can you even say that?'

'Nnenna, please, sit down, and we'll talk about this. Can't you see I'm trying? All I've done for the last eighteen years is try.'

'I'm only seventeen.'

'I was pregnant with you for nine months, Nnenna, since you seem to have forgotten. And believe it or not, being a pregnant university student is not an easy thing to do.'

Nnenna was shouting now. 'Oh gee! Thanks, Mum! So, what are you saying? I was a burden to you your entire life, is that it? Do I remind you so much of Dad that you hate me that much?'

'You don't know what you're talking about. Please, sit down. Let me talk to you.'

'I am *not* sitting down. I'm going out.'

Joanie ran to the door and blocked it with her body, her limbs spread across the door frame like some desperate spider. Her words came out as a hiss.

'No, you are *not* going out! You listen to me, you spoilt, silly girl. When I was pregnant with you—'

'Oh, I was *such* a burden,' said Nnenna, bitterly. 'Well, I'm sorry, okay?'

'*When I was pregnant with you*, towards the end I couldn't even do my work – I couldn't do anything! And this was nearly twenty years ago, mind, so every single person in my life was judging me. My own mother, included. And I was one of the first women at my college, and everybody was watching me to see what I'd do, every single person was waiting for me to trip up and fail. So believe it or not, I know *exactly* how it feels to be judged by the people around you.'

'For how long?'

'What are you talking about?'

The rage inside Nnenna was overpowering now. She wanted to throw things, to scream into her mother's face.

'For how long? You said you know what it feels like to be me. Well? For how long? Have you lived with it ever since you were tiny? Is it one of your first memories? Is it with you every time you leave the house? Is it in every shop you walk into, every street you walk down? Is it *in* you, Mum?' She paused for breath. She was panting, now. 'Or is it something you lived with for nine months because you shacked up with some random guy you met on a study break?'

She didn't realise that Joanie had slapped her until a couple of moments after it had happened. Joanie had, sometimes, looked like she wanted to slap her, but it had never happened before. Nnenna's face seemed to reverberate with the force and she staggered to the sofa, unable to speak for several moments.

'Nnenna, I—'

'You think ...' Nnenna was snarling now. 'You think I'm going to *sit down* with *you*? You think I'm going to carry on talking to you about everything except what I want to know? How much longer were you hoping to keep this up? This charade? It's been seventeen years, Mum. Seventeen years! How much longer did you think you could keep me in the dark?'

'What do you want to know, Nnenna? What is it you want from me that I haven't already given you? Because from where I'm standing, there isn't much left to give.'

Nnenna shook her head. She knew her mother knew. She had asked her so many times, quietly, not wanting to ask, not wanting to ask too much of her mother. She had spent so long trying not to strain their relationship, trying to keep the peace by not needing much. But she couldn't help it, she couldn't pretend any longer; the pain was too great. When her mother spoke again, she was so, terribly quiet. She sounded almost calm.

'Nnenna,' she said. 'Don't you dare go out.'

'How can I stay after what you've done?'

'Nnenna Maloney. If you walk out of that door, don't you dare come back.'

'What?'

'You heard. I've spent the best years of my life raising you. I gave up my life for you. I gave up *everything* for you.'

'Sure you did. But you won't give me the one thing I want,' Nnenna screamed into the night.

'You think your dad was some kind of angel, is that it? Never set a foot wrong?'

'You haven't told me anything about him. How should I know?'

'You think,' said Joanie, 'that he's perfect because he hasn't been here. Because he hasn't been raising you. So of course he hasn't made mistakes. Of course he hasn't read your diary, or kept things from you. Because he hasn't done *anything*. I did everything, good and bad. And now you think that knowing all about your father will change your life? Is that what you think?'

'It won't kill me, Mum. I know that.'

'Well then, come inside.'

'I *can't* come inside, Mum. I can't.'

'Go, then. But you'd best hope your dad is somewhere out there waiting to scoop you up, because if you leave . . .'

Nnenna turned around to look at her mother. Maybe this would be the last time.

'. . . if you leave, then don't you come back here. I gave up my life for you. If you walk out on me now, after everything I've done for you . . . Then you're gone. You're not my daughter any more.'

Nnenna took a step forward and looked into the night: there were no streetlights and no moon. Somewhere out there in the world, in the night, there was a man, her father, living and breathing. Where was he? Why didn't he care about her? Why wasn't he here?

'Nnenna. What do you want to know? Please!' Nnenna could hear that her mother was crying now, but she couldn't turn round. It was too late. She could not look her in the eye, and the questions she had, the words she wanted to speak were too heavy, and sank once more to the recesses of her mind, where they would not disturb anyone.

Joanie saw what was about to happen, but could not move, could not stop it.

Nnenna fastened her coat around her. She walked out into the night.

1993

'Yes, Joan. But what are you going to do about it?'

'What?'

'Joan, I'm not here to judge you. You know that.'

'Yes, and I appreciate it. I appreciate you taking me in while I get my head sorted.'

'Well, of course. You're family. But it seems like you've got to make some sort of decision. You're keeping the baby?'

Joanie didn't answer, instead staring down at her mug. She'd left the teabag in too long and it was cold now. The surface of the liquid had congealed against the sides of the cup. Aunty Mary, who lived in a small town outside Cambridge, had answered the phone after three agonising rings when Joanie called. She let her stay the night with almost no explanation. Perhaps she had been expecting something like this, some disaster to come out of the blue. She always seemed to know.

Gently, Aunty Mary sat down next to her at the table. 'I know that it's scary for you, Joan. But I think you could make it work, if you wanted to. If you wanted to keep the baby. I'll do everything I can to help you. Between the two of us, we'll figure it out. And who knows, maybe you'll meet someone, somewhere down the line, and he can be a stepdad.'

Joanie shook her head almost imperceptibly at the word,

but she could not have that discussion now, not today. Instead she sighed, and she found herself having to turn away from her aunt. Mary's optimism was like music played so loudly that it was difficult to focus. The truth was, Joanie didn't know what she wanted to do. She knew that she believed it was her right to get an abortion, if that was what she chose.

But what *did* she choose? Either way seemed miserable. If she kept the baby, she could struggle on and graduate in a few months, or perhaps take some time out from her course and come back the following year. But what then? What would be the course of her life if she had a child at her age? Without her mother's help? Without any real friends? She had hardly even begun to explore for herself what she wanted to do in life, to find her way through life on her own terms. These past two years had been far from perfect in many ways, but at least the mistakes she'd had to contend with were only hers.

But hers was not the only life to consider, now. And what kind of life could she give this child? Though she had never had any kind of plan for her life (except to escape her family forever), it was hard to see where a child could possibly fit in. And the concept of her as a young mother – a young single mother – was not an easy one to stomach.

But then, what was the alternative? A drab student life at university that she didn't care for; back to a coldly respectable life her mother had chosen for her as the best way of escaping their home. She couldn't go back to Maurice. And her mother would never speak to her again, now she knew. But at least Joanie would be free, then to decide, to find her own way.

If she had a child, who would she be? What would her life be? What would be the life of a child, born into a family like hers?

Mary took her hand. Even then, Mary's hands were so fragile, and so small. Suddenly everything in the world seemed as though it might fall apart tomorrow, as though it might shatter upon the slightest wind. What if something ever happened to Aunt Mary? How old was she now?

'You can stay here as long as you like. I know your mother's been hard on you, Joanie. I know your home's not been an easy place to grow up. And I know I can never be your mum. God knows I've made enough mistakes with my own stepson. But I can give you a home. I can give your baby a home. Maybe . . .' Aunty Mary shuffled closer, now. 'Maybe *we* can be a family. A sort of . . . new family.'

Joanie turned back to look at her. She had never, ever, felt happy and safe in her own home as a child. Why? Why had nobody ever offered her protection like this? Or security? Or affection? Did it take a child?

She knew, of course. Deep down, she knew it must be her own fault. Some primal sense told her that she had done something to earn the violence, to tip some sort of scale out of her favour. She had deserved it.

But could it be that, with the arrival of a child, Joan could repair the thing in her that was broken? Could it be that motherhood could restore whatever it was that had been missing as a child, whatever it was that had earned her such pain?

She put her hand on Mary's and smiled at her future, bright and clean and certain.

Chapter 20

Many are the plans in the mind of a man, but
it is the purpose of the LORD that will stand.

Proverbs 19:21

2010

In a crowded restaurant in central Manchester, Jonathan waited by the hostess's desk and looked approvingly at the menu. He wallowed for a moment in the overflow of choices before he thought about trying to make a decision. He was in no hurry: he wasn't urgently hungry and it was good, simply to be there. It was his favourite restaurant, and tonight was a treat. Injera was an Ethiopian restaurant on the ground floor of a converted Victorian mill. It was a popular place, and tonight was no exception: every table was full.

The smells of meats and spices reminded him that he had made the right choice and, as the waitress told him that there might be a fifteen-minute wait, he decided not to mind that there seemed to be a lot of people here tonight, talking loudly over each other as calming music blared in the background. The noise made him anxious, made him feel disoriented. He tried to focus on his menu, taking in the full range of choices and narrowing it down to two or three.

Despite the noise, he breathed a heavy sigh of relief and

satisfaction. This was what he'd wanted: a seat at his own table. Yes, he might have to wait until everything was ready, but that was fine. And yes, he was sad that Silas had never let him in; but there was a kind of irony in the fact that, he remembered, Silas had mentioned this restaurant more than once, and with some envy.

And he didn't mind eating alone. There was something generous to the self in it, in the freedom to look around and indulge his own thoughts. Silas was in them: he'd probably never be sad about Jonathan walking out, and he might never even notice that Jonathan would never come back. Jonathan might never find anyone to love: he hadn't yet, and there was no reason to think that this might change, in such a wide world where people met and then never met again . . .

'Jonathan? What on earth are *you* doing here?'

Jonathan stood on his tiptoes to see over the heads of the customers, straining to see the owner of the voice which had jolted him out of his reverie. He took a second to put a name to it, but it was the nasal whine of boarding-school vowels that confirmed it.

'Cliff? Cliff Harper?'

Amit's house, a near-palatial property in the affluent suburb of Heaton Mersey, was the stuff of estate agents' dreams: his parents, both architects, had bought it decades ago, when its price already rivalled those of the eye-wateringly expensive homes of the princes of industry living nearby. But they had always known that it was not to their discerning, ever-evolving tastes: in the months and years afterwards, they had gutted and remodelled vast swathes of its rooms. Painstakingly, Rahul and Anika Aslam had supervised the knocking down and moving of walls, the installation of a vintage chandelier above the central stairwell, the insulation, the construction of a floating staircase to the top floor, moulded ceilings, double glazing, new windows in the roof for more light in the attic, a balcony in their bedroom and (now that Amit was older) in his, and an imposing new gate at the front of the property with a new intercom system.

It had cost them countless sums of money and time, and there had been many complications along the way, with suppliers, builders, planning permission all going awry at various points. There had been times when they had both thought that their architectural fantasy might never materialise. But one by one, all the new design features fell into place, and although they had no plans to move for quite some time, they had read with some satisfaction the subsequent evaluation of their newly remodelled home at well over two million pounds.

Amit explained all this – at some length – as he gave his guests a guided tour of the house, explaining each design feature in minute detail and pretending not to see the yawning faces of his friends as they nodded distractedly and checked their phones. He suspected (rightly, as it turned out) that they were in fact texting each other about how bored they were, but he didn't care. Anything to stave off the imminent threat of the evening to come.

Dancing. At dinner, someone had suggested that they go out *dancing*. He did not know who it was exactly (he had been trying to talk to Nnenna when the offensive idea was floated out, like a corpse on the Rochdale canal) but the moment he heard the words, he felt the cold hand of fear grasp his heart.

Dancing, he always thought, *should* have been easy for him, in a world that was fair and equitable: his mother, in her youth, had been a superb dancer and had won countless awards. She had tried to help him when he was younger, teaching him herself at first, before enlisting the help of professional dance teachers. Teacher after teacher worked their way unsuccessfully, frustratingly through the basics of one dance tradition after another – tap, ballet, contemporary – before giving up, confused and disappointed, making vague noises about enlisting the help of a chiropractor.

The sad thing was, he had tried. Every time his mother had demonstrated a move, he had put all his effort into copying it exactly, believing that if he tried, he could never go too far wrong. But somehow it always did go very wrong: he had flailed, stamped and stumbled his way through every dance lesson his mother had given or taken him to, until they were both forced to conclude that he was *a hopeless dancer.* He knew it, his family knew it, and if he didn't take decisive pre-emptive action, all his friends would know it too.

Dinner had been enough of a disaster as it was. After he had moved heaven and earth to have Nnenna sitting opposite him on the seating plan, she had yawned her way through all his Sudoku stories (even the one about how he had written to the newspaper editor and helpfully pointed out a mistake; even the one about how he had once seen J.K. Rowling doing Sudoku on a train and helpfully pointed out a mistake), pushed her food around her plate and totally ignored his bow tie. If this night was going to be anything but a total waste, he was going to have to redeem himself, and soon. Crucially, he had to avoid dancing at all costs ...

'So, Amit,' said Dan, swaying slightly, his arm around Nnenna's neck. He'd had rather more of Amit's father's whisky than Amit had planned, blithely ignoring Amit's hints that he should drink something else less expensive. 'What's the plan for the evening?'

'Plan?'

'Come on, Amit,' chimed in Sam. 'You always have a plan. Or are we going to spend the rest of the night walking around your house? I'm sure we could all use the exercise, but ... '

'I thought,' stammered Amit, desperately racking his brain for a distraction, 'it would be nice if we—'

'Come on, your parents are away for the entire weekend,' opined Dan. 'You've got the whole house to yourself and all you seem to want to do is *walk around* in it.' He waved his free arm expansively near a priceless vase. 'I mean, sure, okay, it's a big house.'

'Massive,' chimed in Sam.

'Yeah, it's big,' said Dan. 'Massive. Olympic-sized. Whatever. But what are we actually going to *do* tonight?'

Amit winced. Suddenly his bow tie felt very tight. He adjusted it and, against his better judgement, found himself opening the topic out to the floor.

'I dunno. What would you guys like to do?'

'You're telling me you've been in Manchester all this time, and we're only meeting now? It's our last night here!'

Jonathan struggled to control his facial expression, but felt fairly certain that it told a story of unadulterated horror and fear. He did not trust himself to speak. Cliff was practically bouncing with enthusiasm at the impromptu reunion.

'I've been here on business for two weeks! Consulting on a reorganisation of a hospital's IT system. Normally I'd do this kind of thing remotely, but what with this one's family living here—' he indicated the squat, muscular man smiling silently beside him, '—we thought we'd make a trip of it. He was owed some time off.'

'I see. And you like Ethiopian?'

'*What?* Oh! The food! Yes. Bloody love the stuff. Nice to go au naturel every now and then, isn't it?'

'Err . . . yes,' said Jonathan, awkwardly. 'Gosh. It's been years since I've seen you. And you're here with your friend . . . ?'

'Oh, my goodness – I almost forgot! You remember each other, don't you?'

'I'm terribly sorry, I . . . No . . . Wait . . . Is it . . . ?'

'Yes!' cried Cliff, excitedly.

' . . . Beefy?'

'It's Colin, now, Jonathan,' said the man, evenly. 'Can't believe I still haven't lived down that nickname . . . '

'You must join us for dinner, Jonathan,' said Cliff. His eyes sparkled with an innocent joy that unnerved Jonathan, who only remembered seeing Cliff this happy when he was taking books off the university library shelves, drawing willies in them, and putting them back again.

'No, I couldn't possibly intrude.'

'You must! Can't believe we've been in the same city for two weeks and haven't seen each other.'

'Manchester's fairly big, Cliff,' said Colin, gently.

'Why don't you go and see where the waitress is, Colin?'

'We can wait till she gets here, can't we?'

'No, no – she's busy,' said Cliff. 'Don't wait. See if you can track her down to get a chair and another menu for Jonathan. In fact, make that two menus; I'm suddenly hungry again. I'll convince Jonathan while you're gone, don't worry.'

Colin rolled his eyes good-humouredly and wandered off in search of the wine list.

'*Dynamite* in the sack, that one. Even after fifteen years,' whispered Cliff, conspiratorially.

'Wha—'

'Arse that should be in an art gallery and a dick the size of California.'

'Cliff, are you two . . . are you gay?'

'Absolutely!' said Cliff, as though he were a second-hand car salesman and someone had asked him whether he sold manual-drive vehicles. Jonathan stared at him. The same man was inside there – entitled, insanely confident, untouched by worldly concern. After all this time he was exactly the same; it was just that he liked boys now.

'Fifteen years and counting!' he drawled. 'I can see you're surprised – you should probably close your mouth, you know – but I don't blame you. I mean, *me*! Gay! You'll remember what I was like when we were friends.'

'Err. Yes. Then.'

'I'd never thought about any of the gay stuff at Cambridge, but—'

'Gay stuff?'

'Oh, you know. Bumming. Boyfriends. You know. Tried it?'

'Bumming?'

'Boyfriends! They're *fantastic*. Bloody brilliant. Although I've only had the one, myself. You?'

'Oh, no thank you.'

'No, I mean, haven't you had any?'

'Well ...'

'You don't know what you're missing! Mind you, neither did I of course, until a few years after I graduated, and then I woke up and suddenly I realised ... I can't bloody get enough!'

'Boyfriends?'

'Bumming! Morning, noon and night. I'd do it all day long if I didn't have to work.'

'You have to work?'

'All the time! Internet security, you know. Constant flux, and all that. Takes up so much of my time and energy, these days. And by the way, Beefy – Colin – has the stamina of a long-distance runner.'

'Oh. That's ... yes.'

'You know, like one of those black chaps. What are they called?'

'Jonathan?'

'Ethiopians.'

'Right.'

'Yes! And the musculature on him! Well, they don't call him Beefy for nothing, you know. His legs! His arms!'

'He's back.'

'Yes, mustn't forget his back. Strong, supple ... flexible to the point of absurdity ...'

'No, I mean, he's back.'

'Hello, again,' said Colin.

'Colin! Did you find the waitress?'

'She's on her way. Did you convince Jonathan to stay?'

'I don't know! Jonathan – did I?'

In the split second that it took him to decide, Jonathan looked once more at these two men. They'd been nothing to him at university, just another two mathematicians, another two bullies, another two non-Christians. And now ... Cliff might possibly be the most poshly gay man he'd ever met. It would be like having dinner with the lovechild of the Manchester Pride Parade and BBC Four.

'You know what ... I will. I'll join you.'

Of all the stupid ideas Amit had ever had, this had to be the worst. This was worse than the time he had entered the school poetry competition and tried to wow the judges with a poem *about poetry*, only to drop out when he couldn't find anything that rhymed with 'anapaest'. And this was *far* worse than the time when, bleary-eyed and running late for school, he had mistaken his mother's hairspray for his deodorant and ended up with armpit hair that stuck out for the rest of the day. At least he'd been able to tuck his pubic hair into his vest; this was a mess he might never straighten out.

The six of them (Amit, Dan, Nnenna, Stephanie, Hannah and Sam) were shivering on the train station platform, waiting for the 22:03 to Manchester Piccadilly station. It had been suggested (to riotous applause) that they would go from there to the gay village.

The gay village. And to make things worse, it had been his idea. Two wines in, he'd forgotten all about his careful watch over the whisky bottle and actually joined in the party. And sure, it had been fun for a while, subtly drawing attention to his cummerbund and explaining the etymology of the word. He even got the sense that Hannah was flirting with him.

But then people got bored. The drinks started to run low,

the food ran out and the so-called 'reggae playlist' that someone had put on had shifted very quickly from Bob Marley to
Destiny's Child, as they all realised that they did not, in fact,
know very much reggae. People looked at their phones for
longer and longer periods of time. Dan was getting restless
and started saying things about going home. Amit couldn't let
that happen.

So, in his drunken haze, he had suggested that they go out
to the one place he knew they'd all be up for.

'Where?' Dan had said. 'None of us have ID. Let's—'

'I thought we were meant to go to Aura?' Steph had asked.
'That smelly place with the sticky floors?'

'Yes!' Hannah had slurred, enthusiastically. 'Didn't you say
your cousin could get us in?'

Amit had mournfully shaken his head, and told them about
the text he'd received an hour ago: unfortunately, it had turned
out that this was Imran's night off. He'd be doing push-ups
with his pecs for the next three hours.

'Well, where else are we going to get in without proper ID?'

There was one place.

But if he dared suggest it, it would mean leaving his comfort
zone and venturing deep into the unknown. Here, with his
friends, he felt safe. There was no competition. In his heart
of hearts, he hoped that perhaps he and Danny might end
up sitting next to one another on the couch, gifted a secret
moment together, shoulder to shoulder, and maybe then they
could just ... *see* ...

But if they all went into town, who knew what might happen?

But what if they stayed there, and nothing happened at all?

He had gulped and said the words as brightly as he could.
'What about the gay village?'

'Oh my God!' shrieked Hannah.

'Oh my God,' groaned Sam.

'Sure,' said Steph. 'Why not? We'll probably find somewhere

that'll let us in.' And everyone knew she was right; on a quiet night like this, a few days before payday, the bouncers might not even ask for ID.

But now, standing on the freezing platform as they waited for the train (Steph and Nnenna didn't have the money for a taxi), Amit was replaying the moment over and over in his head, and dreading what might happen next. Not only were they going to go out dancing, they were going to go out dancing with *gays*. It was bad enough that they would be dancing with each other. Bad enough that they had left the confines of his house. Bad enough that they were all intent on dancing with strangers who would feel no compunctions about laughing and staring. But *gays*?

Amit tucked his hands into his armpits for warmth. Silently, he was trying to comfort himself, but he knew it was over for him and Dan, before things had even begun. He had never spent very much time around openly gay men, but he knew what to expect. He was having terrifying visions of a disastrous night out in the presence of countless limp-wristed men, wowing Dan with their astronomically superior dancing ability. Gays watching Amit shuffle inadequately to the latest pop hits. Gays surrounding him, gays making *sotto voce* remarks to one another about his shocking lack of natural rhythm. Gays coolly observing – as they executed a *flawless* paso doble – that Amit stepped as though he was trying to maintain his balance during an earthquake. Gays, gays, gays . . .

Amit hoped that his shivering hid his apprehension. Surely the other boys felt the same way? Sam and Dan were notorious non-dancers, Dan preferring (like most teenage boys) to drink and sulk and talk about how bad the music was – basically, anything that could be done with both feet on the floor and his arms by his sides. Sam, slightly more creative, preferred to leer unsuccessfully at the nearest attractive person, bowing and swaying like an extra from *Thriller*. But neither of them seemed to share Amit's self-consciousness about dancing tonight, and when Amit glanced over at them, they were chatting happily, totally impervious to the nightmare that was to come.

But they didn't have as much to lose as he did. Nobody in the world, he thought, had so much to lose, that night.

'So?'

'So . . . ?'

'What about you, Jonathan? Seeing anyone?'

'Oh. Err . . . ' As he finished off his lamb, Jonathan struggled to put into words the fact that he'd recently spent a lot of time seeing someone who thought he was invisible.

'Cliff,' said Colin. 'Maybe Jonathan's not . . . *allowed* to see anyone.'

'Eh? What?'

'Remember, Cliff? I mean . . . Jonathan, you were pretty religious at Cambridge, weren't you?'

'Oh. Yes, I was. Although, not any more. But . . . I hardly told anyone at Cambridge I was gay. I didn't even know, myself, at first. How did you know?'

Colin coughed politely into his lega tibs.

'So, you're not religious?' said Cliff, eagerly.

'I'm not.'

'And you're not seeing anyone?' He had the nervous energy of a beagle on a hunt. Jonathan half thought he might do a nervous piddle on the floor.

'Well, no, but . . . '

'Cliff . . . ' said Colin, a note of warning in his voice.

'Well, we'll have to find you one!'

'What?' said Jonathan.

'Tonight!' said Cliff.

'No,' said Jonathan.

'Cliff . . . ' said Colin.

'Yes!' said Cliff. 'Now! Ask for the bill.'

'What? I'm not—' said Jonathan.

'Yes!' said Cliff.

'Cliff . . . ' said Colin.

'Off to the gay village we go. We'll have you bummed and boyfriended in no time, just you wait. Gays *love* blacks, you know.'

'I'm not so sure—'

'No! Shan't hear any objections – I'm getting the bill. Where's that waitress?'

Joanie hung up the phone for the last time: Nnenna wasn't answering. Joanie had sent five texts, and received no reply. Where was she? Nnenna had never, ever done anything like this.

But Joanie had. The realisation struck like a chord, and it echoed and echoed. Eighteen years ago, she had walked out of her own mother's house, scared and all alone, her mother calling behind her. She had not wanted Joanie to go – she had grappled with her, slapped her, shouted at her – but Joanie had to get out of the house. Her mother could not countenance the idea of her only daughter being pregnant with a black man's child, could not countenance the idea of an abortion. Her mother – now only a dark figure in her memory – could only rail at her, powerless to make her see, powerless to make her understand.

'How could you do this to me?' she had cried, doubling over with rage as though Joanie had punched her in the stomach. In her fist was a letter from the hospital, taken from Joanie's room. 'This is not what I wanted for you, Joan. This was *never* what I wanted for you. After everything I did for you – after everything I sacrificed to give you a safe home . . . '

For a long moment, Joanie had only been able to shake her head in disbelief. 'This isn't . . . Mum. Please understand. This baby doesn't belong to you. I didn't do this to hurt you. I need to think. I ...'

'After everything I went through, after all these years,' her mother continued as though Joanie had never spoken. 'And you want to go and drop out of university and have a ... a ... a *black baby*. How could you? *How could you?*'

'I never said I'm going to drop out, Mum. I'll find a way.'

'You think you can raise a baby by yourself and still get a degree? From Cambridge? Christ, if that's how stupid you are, you never should have gone in the first place. If I'd known that this was how you were going to end up – if I'd known you were going to completely *fuck up* your life, I'd have torn up your application myself.'

Joanie had run out of the house, pushing past her mother and getting into her car. She had driven to Mary's house just to think about what to do next, just to be, and feel nothing.

And now? Where had Nnenna gone? Joanie sat down in a heap, her legs giving way beneath her as she saw history repeating itself, as she realised that what was happening now was exactly what she had prayed would never happen again.

'I don't like it here ...' said Jonathan, eyeballing the patrons of Extra, a club in the middle of Manchester's gay village where the playlist whizzed from one unfamiliar pop mega-mix to the next and everybody seemed to be ten-to-fifteen years younger than him. Two hen nights seemed to be happening at once.

'Well, *we* love it here,' said Cliff, cheerfully.

'I don't like it here,' said Colin, warily.

'Nonsense!' said Cliff.

'It's too loud!' said Jonathan.

'You're absolutely gorgeous, you are!' said one of the women from one of the hen-dos, to nobody in particular.

'I'm not going to find a boyfriend in *here*,' said Jonathan, as a man strolled past, wearing a T-shirt that said NO FATS, NO FEMMES, NO ASIANS. 'And anyway, I'm not even looking for a boyfriend, right now. This is ridiculous. I'm going home.'

'Don't be so bloody *shy*!' said Cliff, undeterred. 'Let's get some drinks and have a dance. I love this song! Triple vodka coke?'

Cliff took Jonathan's expression of silent horror for an affirmative and ordered accordingly.

'You know,' said Colin, leaning in to shout in Jonathan's ear while Cliff was busy, 'I've been meaning to ask you something.'

'Yeah?'

'You and that bloke you were with for a while ... whatshisname?'

'Alastair.'

'Alexander?'

'I said, *Alastair*!'

'Oh, right! Sorry. It's loud in here. Couldn't hear you. Anyway ... what happened to him? I mean, I'm assuming you're not together any more.'

'No ... no, we're not.'

'What happened?'

'It's a long story.'

'Yeah, I thought he seemed a bit whorey.'

'What? No, I said *long story*. He ... he wasn't a great guy. For me.'

'Oh?'

'Yeah, but to be honest ... I let him get away with a lot of stuff, I know I did. It wasn't a great time in my life, I didn't know what I was doing. Still don't, most of the time.'

'Well, I only wanted to say that, after I came out, I thought back to the gay guys I knew at university.'

'I wasn't gay at university.'

'No, of course you weren't. Anyway, I always thought you deserved better. He seemed like he was all about the chase, with you. You always seemed more genuine than that. Highly strung, maybe. Defensive. A little frosty. But genuine.'

'Oh. Well. Thank you. Thanks. I mean, I think Alastair had his own stuff he was struggling with . . . '

Colin waved a hand dismissively. 'I know Cliff's being a bit aggressive with the boyfriend thing, but he means well. I hope you find a nice guy. Unless you seriously aren't looking for a boyfriend?'

'That's really nice of you, Colin. Thank you. And, to be honest, I don't—'

'Drinks on me!' bellowed Cliff, grinning wide enough to show his wisdom teeth. 'And there was a deal on! Quadruple vodkas half price! Quaddy voddies all round!'

Jonathan resigned himself to the night ahead and sipped, slowly, from his glass.

The enormity of what was about to happen was crushing Joanie. In her mind, it was not merely a possibility; it was almost a certainty, and it was one that she was not ready for. In her mind, Nnenna was already dead, lying in the street, the life slowly draining from her eyes . . .

How could Joanie have done this? To lose a child – to have sent a child out into the night on her own . . . She would never, never forgive herself.

After Nnenna had left, Joanie had stood stock-still for a few minutes before she was able to recollect herself and sit down. She played the argument over and over again in her mind, trying to understand where she had gone wrong. But it was difficult. She couldn't make herself remember the whole thing; some things she could recall so clearly, so painfully, and other things seemed to evade her completely. Why had she said those things? Had she even meant them?

She found that the answer was yes, she had. She *had* been angry with Nnenna all that time. She could see now, only now, that for years she had kept a secret ugliness in her heart, a jealousy of Maurice that she had been afraid to admit even to herself. Because no matter how much she loved Nnenna, no matter how much she gave up for her, no matter how much she fed her and clothed her, encouraged her, praised her, comforted her ... a part of her would always belong to Maurice, to a man who didn't deserve Nnenna. He would never, *never* be able to appreciate what a wonder that child was. And he didn't have the right. Every sacrifice made for that child had been Joanie's. She'd lost her mother, her friends; she'd almost lost her career. Surely, in exchange there could be – there must be – one thing in the world that she could keep, that would be hers alone.

So, yes, she had kept Maurice from Nnenna. She saw it now, so clearly, and the ugliness of it grieved her like the loss of a child. It was as though she had found rotting flesh on her body, or a tumour deep inside her; somewhere so deep and inaccessible she had never seen it until now. Lurking deep inside her heart was something so alien, so horrifying and unfamiliar, that it was not her, it was not any Joan Maloney that she recognised. But it was. It must have been.

Every time Nnenna had tried to ask about her father, she had silenced her, or put her off, or changed the subject, or shamed her. And she had done all this for what? To keep her daughter close?

She stood up, buttoned her coat and went to the front door. She opened it; outside, the night was cold. Was Nnenna with friends? She hadn't said. And the coat that Nnenna was wearing was not warm enough for a night this cold. Was she by herself? Was she alone?

Joanie tried to slow her breathing. She closed the door and called Steph's parents. Danny's parents. Hannah's. Nobody knew where Nnenna was; she wasn't supposed to be with the others, after all. They would call her back, they would try to find out.

She opened the door again and went out into the cold. Perhaps Nnenna had only gone for a walk around the streets nearby? But it was so dark. It wasn't safe for Nnenna after dark by herself. Joanie thought about the kinds of men who might be out there, who might prey on a young black girl who was already distressed and afraid. She shivered.

Too upset to drive, Joanie started walking towards Stephanie's house.

But if Nnenna was there, wouldn't her mother have said so when she picked up the phone? The same was true, surely, for all her friends.

But where else could Joanie go? What could she do? She must do something.

So, she set off. Half-walking, half-running, in any direction, determined that if Nnenna were to be hurt tonight, it would not be while her mother stood still.

Manchester's gay village, a few streets criss-crossing one another in the city centre, seemed like a maze to Dan. It was all so disorienting: the fairy lights, the music blaring from open doors, the bunting . . . He felt like they'd been wandering around in circles for hours.

He only wanted to get inside a club, any club, but Amit was being weird. Every time they found somewhere they liked – every time they found a bouncer who didn't seem to care about the fact that every single one of them was underage and that not even one of them had a credible ID – they would stay for a few minutes and have one drink before Amit decided that they had to go, they had to move on, the music was terrible, the drinks were too expensive, the lights were too bright.

All these excuses were valid in Dan's mind, and ordinarily, he wouldn't have minded this: indecision was an inevitable part of being with any group of people on a night out. But tonight, he wanted to stay put. He wanted to stay in one club, one bar and *sit* for a while. Maybe, he thought, he and Amit could sit together, celebrate the debating win, talk about next year's competition, just talk . . .

Instead, every twenty minutes they all had to finish their drinks and find somewhere new: and on the walk from one club to another, he had to put his arm around Nnenna, to talk to her, to check if she was warm enough, to make some sort of joke to try and make her smile, to shift the mood she seemed to be in, tonight. He didn't want to have to. She hadn't said a word to him about the Nigerian Centre. Or about anything. He'd been trying and trying to keep things going, but everything seemed to be fighting him. Even Nnenna. Even him.

'Amit,' he said. 'Why are you being weird?'

'I'm not being weird,' said Amit. He realised, as he said it, that this was never a convincing thing to say.

'You're being weird.'

'No, I'm not.'

'Yes, you are. Why does it matter so much which club we go to? It's not like any of us are trying to pull tonight. Are we?'

'No . . . ' Amit laughed nervously and nodded, his eyes still scanning the scene. Everywhere they went, there were too many people. His objective, unknown to the others, was to find somewhere that was empty enough that he could be sure that, when dancing did break out among his friends like smallpox in a submarine, there would at least be no witnesses. Where, oh where was a dive bar?

(What Amit had failed to notice, however, was that even though every club was full, every club was full of people who weren't dancing, or who could not dance for more than a moment or two without taking a drink, or a pill, or a drag, without making sure nobody was watching and nobody was making fun. What Amit had failed to notice was that everywhere he went, he was surrounded by people who, like him, were afraid, inexpert, fragile.)

But Dan did not want a dive bar. He wanted somewhere crowded, like the place they were in now, somewhere he could see that Nnenna was still there without having to *see* her. And, perhaps, somewhere he and Amit could be together without being seen.

There Nnenna was now, just out of his direct line of sight, sitting in a corner, on her phone. She had told Stephanie that she was all right, that she only needed a few minutes to check her messages. But Dan could see her crying, even from where he stood across the room.

How was it that he was so tired of being her boyfriend when, for so long, he had put in so little effort, had barely bothered at all? It made no sense. But there it was: it *was* exhausting. Neither of them could have failed to notice that, or failed to notice how he had flagged recently.

He looked around at his friends, who it seemed had finally persuaded Amit to stay as they drank, and drank, and drank. For all the planning that had gone into this night, most of them might as well not have been here, any more.

'What the ffffuck do you think you're doing?'

'What? Leave me alone, Steph.' Her words were slurred and her eyes rolled from one side to the other. 'Why are you so drunk? You're never this bad.'

'Look ... at your *girlfriend*,' she drawled. The alcohol made her put extra emphasis on the words towards the end of her sentences. 'You've fucking *left* her. You *bastard.*'

'What? I'm right here. Why are you being like this?'

'*Bull*sssshhhhhit. You're standing at the *bar*. Probably checking out some other *girl*.'

'There are no other girls in here.'

'So, what's *keeping* you? That *girl* ...' Stephanie paused for a second to suppress a rising feeling in her stomach. 'That girl is my *best friend.* She's fucking *brilliant.* She's the only one at that fucking school who I even *care* about ... And if I have to

move house, I might not get to be her best *friend* any more.'
She started crying. She wasn't really talking to Dan any more.
'And it makes me so *sad* . . .'

'I know. I'm sorry.'

'Look at her. She's *miserable*. She had a massive fight with
her mum. Her mum kicked her out. Did you know that? She
kicked her out of the *house*. She has nowhere to stay tonight.
Did you know that?'

'She told me, Steph.'

'Then what are you *doing*? Go and *be* with her.'

'What about you?'

'I *can't*.'

'Why?'

'Because I have to be *sick*.'

Dan looked over at Nnenna again, now all alone, but he
couldn't move. Besides, he did not have to talk to Nnenna
to know that she was deeply, deeply sorry that she had ever
left her house that evening. He knew that a good boyfriend
would go over to her, comfort her. But he did not. He
could not.

And he did not have to. He knew that he did not have to
tell her it was over. He wouldn't have to do anything. All he
would have to do was sit, and watch, and wait, and know that
she was in pain, and not help.

She would know what it meant. She would understand.

When Jonathan answered his phone after two rings, he could
hear Joanie almost crying with relief on the other end.

'Jonathan. You've got to help me.'

'Joanie, what's wrong?'

'It's Nnenna. She's gone.'

'Where?'

'I don't know! She left. She walked out! She's never done
anything like . . . Jesus, it's so loud on your end – where are you?'

'I'm errr . . . Doesn't matter.'

'Jonathan! Jonathan!' cried Cliff. 'How about this one?' He ushered forward Liam, a rather pale-looking twenty-two-year-old with a master's in philosophy and a sliver of drool down the side of his mouth. 'What do you think, eh? I bet you two'll get along!'

'Mmm sorry,' squirmed Liam. 'I'm not into black guys, to be honest. Just a preference! I'm not, like, a racist . . . You're hot, though.'

'Oh. Errr. Thanks. I'm actually on the phone right now—'

'Is it true that you've all got big—'

'Come with me, Liam,' said Colin, steering Liam away and mouthing an apology to Jonathan.

'Hi, Joanie, I'm back. That's not like Nnenna, running away.'

'I know.'

'Is she at a friend's house? Or with her boyfriend?'

'No, no, I've called. I've called everyone. Apparently, they all went out to a—ehm—ou—or—oh-ing.'

'What?'

'Eh—aw—eh—ou.'

'Joanie, you're breaking up, I can hardly hear you. Let me go outside and I'll see if I can get a better signal. One second. Hang on.'

He pushed past the crowd, past Cliff (still patiently trying to explain to Liam why he was a complete and total idiot), past the hen parties, past a crowd of people who looked about fifteen years old.

The air was cool outside. It was like a different world, somehow. For a moment, he looked around him and took in the scene on the street. Couples kissing and holding hands, couples fighting, friends standing around and smoking, laughing, singing.

He noticed one couple on the street that looked particularly engrossed in each other: one boy was south Asian, the other white. Jonathan didn't know why, but he found himself feeling hopeful as he saw them.

What was it? They weren't kissing. They weren't talking. They were barely touching; only their shoulders kissed as they stood side by side on the street. They were walking slowly, very slowly, away from the village, together.

'Jonathan? Are you there?' Joanie's voice came back to him, alert and tense. 'Are you in town?'

'Yes, I—'

'Steph's parents said they all went into the Gay Village. I'm putting my coat on now, but if you're in town anyway, can you help me find her? Jonathan? Jonathan? Hello?'

'Joanie. I've found her.'

There was a moment's silence on the other end of the line. 'What?'

'I've found her. She's here.'

Everyone else seemed to be wandering off, so they had wandered off too. Without thinking, they had let their feet take them somewhere else, anywhere else, trusting each other's unspoken will.

They were in Albert Square, now. It was only a few minutes away from the bright lights of the gay village but its cobbles and Victorian architecture, the fountains, the statues of statesmen long dead, made it feel like a bubble, like a different world. They could have been standing in a Manchester from two centuries ago; or one. Or today. Or tomorrow.

Amit didn't look at Danny. He looked only straight ahead. He could feel the warmth of Daniel's body through his light jacket; or at least, he thought he could. He could feel something like warmth on him.

It was strange and new, being this close to someone and yet being so still. He wanted neither to move further away from Amit, nor, for the moment, to move closer.

'I know,' said Amit. 'There doesn't seem to be anybody else left.'

And would they go and find them? Would they leave this place, and this peace? It was far too soon to be here like this, and so reckless. Anyone might see. They should probably go.

But would they really have to go?

'I ... don't want to,' said Amit. Being so unused to tenderness, he was uncertain of it. How did it go? What were the steps? Who would take his hands and guide him? Despite everything, he had no plan for this, and he could not script it, could not scheme it.

So he spoke in short sentences and chose his words carefully, so afraid that he might break whatever spell it was that had placed him next to his friend. He didn't want to say the wrong thing and make Danny realise that he didn't want to be here with him, after all.

But Danny turned his head and looked at him, and said, 'I don't want to, either.' There was a sharp intake of breath; Amit wasn't sure whose.

In Danny's face, he saw something like fear, but there was something else there, in both of them, that neither had seen before. They did not know the name for it. There were no rules for it, but it was its own rule, its own space; and outside of that space fled away all cares, all responsibility. As for Danny, he could not deny the pain he had caused Nnenna, and might still cause her; nor could he deny that he had loved her; nor could he deny this, nor could he deny himself. Everything that had led up to this point was still in him, would not compromise, would not hide, and was irreducible.

'It's okay,' said Amit. 'Please, don't worry. I don't know what to do, either. I don't want to upset you or ... I mean ... we can stand here for a minute, can't we?'

Perhaps they could. Perhaps, then, the spell would not be broken. Perhaps, if some mistake were made, there would be – pain, yes, and perhaps even punishment – but no damnation.

As they looked at one another, they felt no fire; only warmth.

'Are you warm enough?' Jonathan asked Nnenna. She shook her head. 'Let's come inside,' he said. 'You do recognise me, don't you? You seem a little ... '

'You're Jonathan,' she said. 'My mum's friend. I recognise you.' Then, seeming to realise how disoriented she seemed, she said, 'I'm okay. I'm ... ' But she didn't know what to say. The instinct to give reassurance was so strong, but it seemed so silly now. She was not okay. She was sitting outside in the cold.

'Let's go inside,' he said. 'Where are your friends?'

He helped her up from the pavement, but when she stood up, she saw that her dress was ruined: without even noticing, she'd been sitting in a puddle of some unknown provenance. After everything, after the trouble it had taken to get the thing, she could never wear it again. What future self would she inhabit now? What was its shape and size?

Together they stumbled to a bar that was warm and empty; exactly what Nnenna wanted. Jonathan bought her a hot cup of tea – the barman gave only the slightest raise of his eyebrows – and found out what had happened: her friends had all gone home to their parents, her boyfriend had disappeared.

'And what happened between you and your mum?' he said. 'If you don't mind me asking.'

'It's complicated,' she said, but it wasn't. It was simple, and ugly, and terrible. The shame of the things she'd said, and heard, was too much for her to talk about. The thought of sharing it with someone so innocent as Jonathan made her cringe and flinch inwardly. She was sure he'd never seen anything as ugly as all that. She blew on her tea to cool it.

'More complicated than suicide?'

Nnenna looked up at him abruptly. He hadn't meant to

say the words, in fact. He was used to dancing around the subject, to finding euphemisms that didn't make people too uncomfortable or, worse, make them look at him with pity. But having said what he had said, he didn't regret it. There was something freeing about allowing oneself to be vulnerable, after all. Sometimes, it made it easier to let other people in.

'I wasn't that much older than you when I tried to kill myself. I don't tell you that to shock you or upset you, Nnenna. But I don't want you to think there's anything you can tell me that'll make me look at you differently. I think you and I are a bit similar, somehow. Not that you'll end up like I was, not at all. But I think ... I think we're both probably afraid to let people see us as we truly are.'

'Because I don't know what that *is*,' Nnenna said. Joanie had – eventually – agreed to let Jonathan stay out with Nnenna for a while, only until she calmed down. But she looked so tired, now.

'What do you mean?' he said.

'Oh, it's ... everything,' she said, wearily. 'I don't know who my dad is. I don't know why he's gone. I don't know where he's gone to. All my life, I've made up stories about him, I've tried to ask about him, but all I've ever got is ... nothing. Nothing. I've never really known ... anything ... about him.'

'Tell me how that feels,' he said, because he could think of nothing better to say.

'It makes me feel ...' she searched for the word. 'Lost. I feel lost. And I can't see how I'm supposed to get *un*-lost unless my mum—'

'Nnenna,' said Jonathan. 'Why don't you ask?'

'I can't!' said Nnenna. 'You don't understand, it's like my mum has this ... control over me. She won't let me. She won't let me. She won't let me ...' Still drunk, she echoed herself a few times into her mug and sipped for a moment before Jonathan said,

'Nnenna. I know your mum's not perfect, believe me. And

I know that it's not always easy. With anyone's parents. But maybe now you're old enough . . . ' He stopped for a moment to rephrase himself. 'What makes you think she has to *let* you?'

Chapter 21

Then the eyes of both were opened, and
they knew that they were naked ...

Genesis 3:7

In the taxi home, Nnenna was silent because Jonathan was silent.

Nnenna was grateful for it. In the single small recess of her mind that was not given over to pain, she knew that this was the end of something. She'd never walked away from her mother before; been so hateful; never run off without saying where she was going. She felt as though she'd broken something, and it scared her because she did not know if what she had broken could ever be fixed, or if she would like what replaced it. It felt, in short, like growing up. She didn't like it. She imagined scenario after scenario, scene after scene with her mother in this vein: Joanie throwing her out, Joanie screaming at her for hours, Joanie slapping her across the face ...

All through the night, Stephanie had watched her check her phone and ignore the phone calls and messages. *Nnenna, please, please come home. Nnenna, I'm so sorry. Nnenna, I'm ready to talk if you want to.*

Dan hadn't said anything. Not when her mother called, or when Nnenna overheard Steph telling Dan what Nnenna already knew. It was over. She felt free. And alone. She didn't know yet if she liked it.

The taxi ride wasn't a long one, and they soon arrived at Nnenna's house. Jonathan gave her a quick, awkward hug before he walked her to the door. 'It'll be all right,' he said, gently. 'It'll all be all right.'

And then Joanie was there, her eyes red with grief and worry.

As Jonathan got back in the taxi and drove away, Nnenna stepped cautiously inside, unsure of what would happen next. She did not know exactly what she had broken, or where the fractures were to be found. But there was Joanie's love for her, still; it was strong and present, always. Joanie drew her into a fierce hug, and they stayed in it for several long moments, both repeating the same words, crying in relief as they heard them echoed back, hoping that they would fix something, anything. There was so much that needed to be repaired.

I'm sorry. I'm so sorry. I'm sorry. I'll never do it again. I'm sorry. I'm sorry.

'Mum, you don't have to do this. Not now.'

'No, I want to. I've waited long enough.'

'Are you sure? Mum, you look so tired. This can wait. I want to know, but it can wait.' She tried to believe the words as she said them, but it was hard.

Not for the first time that night, Nnenna had the strange sensation that she was somehow floating, and that she might fall if she did not do something about it. She had done something she hated to her mother, and she had not been punished for it yet. And what would happen if her mother didn't punish her? Would the world punish her? Would she ever stop punishing herself?

But Joanie was speaking insistently, now, through hiccups and small tears. The delicate reparation of their bond shivered in her watery eyes.

'You've waited a long time. I made you wait. I want to tell you, now.'

So Joanie told her everything. At first, she wasn't sure where to start, so she had to keep going back, back, back to the first time she met Maurice, to that summer in her bedroom in Manchester with a Bible and so many questions and so much anger; back to her first day in Cambridge, to her parents, to how her Aunty Mary took her in and helped her raise Nnenna, to her mother and stepfather. She realised that she had imagined having this conversation thousands of times, but that she had never, could never have prepared for it.

'Do you hate me?' Joanie asked, in a quiet voice, when she had finished.

Nnenna shook her head. Her expression was blank.

'Mum, of course I don't hate you. But I've . . . ' she started to cry. 'I've been struggling with this, Mum. I've been trying so hard to figure out who I am, all this time. And I know you've done so much for me, I know. It's been really hard for you. But I need to learn this about myself.'

'I know.'

'No,' said Nnenna, gently, but firmly. 'You don't. People are different with you. And people are different with me when you're around. They look at me and then they look at you, and sometimes it's like . . . *Oh.* Like some sort of . . . question's been answered. But then when you're not around, when it's only me by myself, sometimes that question doesn't go away. People expect me to have all sorts of answers about what it means to be black, to be mixed race; people assume I'll have answers about where my dad is and why . . . And I couldn't answer those questions because I had no idea who he is, where he is. And Mum—'

'Yeah?'

'You can't be with me all the time. Not all the time. Not forever.'

Joanie nodded and slowly started to cry. 'I understand that. I know that. But it's hard. It's always been the two of us. I suppose, somewhere along the way, I got to thinking of you as a part of me.'

'I am. But not like that.'

'No.' Joanie sniffed. She wiped her eyes and when she looked up again, Nnenna was looking at her with so much compassion.

'And besides,' Nnenna said, 'even if people didn't have those questions, what about me? I want to know about my dad. I want to know what he's *like*, Mum. I have to know.

'And I know it wasn't easy for you. I know you must have been so scared. I want you to know how much I appreciate everything you've done. For me. I mean it.'

Not trusting herself to get words out, Joanie nodded.

'You really were all alone, all that time, weren't you?' Nnenna said.

'I had Aunty Mary, God rest her soul. She took me in until I could get back on my feet, finish my course, find a place to rent.'

'She was like a mum to you, wasn't she? Grandma—'

'No,' said Joanie, her voice quiet but firm. 'She was a lot of wonderful things but she ... I'll never have another mum. Eventually I had to learn to accept that. But I had you. I always had you. And we got on all right, in the end.'

'Yes,' said Nnenna. So, her mother *had* been all alone.

Nnenna stood up and walked over to the window. Despite everything that had happened, despite everyone who'd been hurt, nobody was entirely wrong; there was nobody to own all the blame. It was difficult. She hated it.

She looked out into the night, wanting to hide her tears, as though there had been too many already and there could be room for no more.

'I know it's a lot to grasp,' said Joanie. 'But ... Nnenna, can you start to understand it, now? Can you see why I never told you? I thought ... Nnenna, when you live through what I lived through as a child, it terrifies you. You *never* feel safe, not really. So, you make a sort of promise to yourself that it will never, ever happen to you, do you see? It was the only way I could make sense of it all. And survive. If I'd thought that any man would ever . . . I'd have given up, Nnenna. I would. I wouldn't have survived to eighteen, let alone having you.

'So, when I thought your father might one day do the same to me – when I thought there was even the slightest chance, no matter what he'd been like before, no matter . . . I was terrified. I was out of my mind, Nnenna. I had no choice. I knew I could never see him again. It was as if something took over, and there was nothing, nothing I could have done.'

Joanie realised, finally, that this was true: there was never anything she could have done. She had never told anybody this, before. She felt the first fingertips of her own forgiveness begin to touch her heart.

'Will you take his name?'

'What?'

'Nyemaka. Will you take your father's name?'

Nnenna shook her head. 'Don't ask me that, Mum. Not yet, not now.'

'And will you still go?' she said.

'Go to Paris?'

'Yes, to Paris.'

'Oh, Mum.' Nnenna started to cry again. 'I don't know. This changes so much. But I want to go. I want to try. I have to.'

Joanie nodded, but couldn't look at Nnenna. 'I'll try. I'll try to be okay with it. But please be patient with me, Nnenna. It's not easy to . . . You're the only thing I'm proud of, the only thing I have that isn't stupid or broken or some sort of failure.' Had her own mother felt this way? 'You know, I think maybe the reason I never told you much about Maurice—'

'Yes?'

'Well. This won't make sense to you right now, I suppose. But I think I thought that if I kept you in the dark, I could keep you here with me, somehow. Keep you from going out into the world.'

Nnenna looked at her mother for a long moment, trying to make sense of what she had heard. But the ideas seemed worlds away from anything she would ever know. What was it like to love someone, and to hurt them, and to want to keep them safe at the same time?

'Can I ask you something?' Nnenna said, eventually.

'Anything.'

'Where did my name come from?'

'Your first name? You know it's Igbo.'

'I know, but who picked it? Was it Dad? It must have been Dad.'

Joanie shook her head. 'It was me. He had – has – I don't know – an aunt named Nnenna. He liked her a lot. It seemed fair that you should have a name from his family, and a name from mine.'

'Oh.'

'I wanted to give you something of his. One thing. It seemed right. I'm sorry I couldn't give you more, but I thought you should have something, a small thing. Do you like it?'

'My name?'

'Yes. Do you like it?'

'Of course I do. Mum, I've always liked it. It's mine. But . . . Oh, God, I want to know but I can't ask . . . '

'Ask. You must ask me.'

'Is he a . . . Is he good?' The words sounded childish, silly; but there were no other words for them. 'Do you think he's a good person?'

'I don't even know what that means, any more. But I think— I honestly believe that if he'd known about you . . . '

'Mum, he doesn't even know I exist! My own dad. He might be different now. He could be anyone. You said he was only . . . '

'I wish I had an answer for you, Nnenna. I wish I did. But you must understand: he never knew about you. And as to where he is, or what he's like now . . . I don't know.'

'I understand.'

They sat down again at the table, slowly, exhausted.

'But, Mum – one day, when I'm ready, I'm going to try and find him. I have to try. It doesn't mean you're a bad mum, or that I'm leaving you. It doesn't even mean you made the wrong decision, because I can sort of understand it, a bit. But someday I am going to find him. I have to.'

Joanie gave her a long, hard look. 'I know. Do you still love me?'

'Yes. Do you still love me?'

'Yes, Nnenna,' Joanie said. 'Always.' And she reached in her pocket and pulled out something small and dog-eared. She handed it to Nnenna. 'When you do find him . . . Well. This is something he gave to me a long time ago, when we met. When Jonathan told me you were safe, I knew I had to dig it out. I want you to have it.'

A small, slightly faded souvenir. It had been Nnenna's, all this time.

Epilogue

2012

Nnenna is nineteen, now.

Student life in Paris suits her; she has been here for a little over a year. She spends most of her days in libraries, classrooms and lecture halls but during the evenings, the city is hers: art galleries, walks by the river, cheap bistros. She is becoming adept at cooking Nigerian food. French food still evades her. She and Jonathan trade recipes, sometimes. He says he will visit her soon.

Her mother has been to Paris three times, including the day she moved in. They speak once a week, and now they both try to avoid talking about anything too significant. It's still too soon for that. Her mother is not quite what Nnenna once thought she was, and she has still not decided how she feels about this. One day, they will forgive each other.

In the meantime, she is a young woman in a big, exciting city. The other students like her: she is bright, funny, inquisitive and kind. She shares a small flat with three other students: Alice, Émilie and Brigitte. Brigitte plays loud music every evening, and Nnenna is working up the courage to talk to her about it.

Otherwise, life is good. University, she finds, is much better than school. A lot of people have come from similar backgrounds, but not everyone. She is not the only one, now. And even better, nobody knows her, here. She can reinvent herself utterly. She has decided to tell people about her father, if they ask. She can be brave. She has all the information that her mother had, and she can decide her story for herself. Anyway, things have changed.

Lots of things have changed. She has founded a university society for the appreciation of African food. About twenty students meet every week in her room; everybody brings a dish, everybody eats. She has made friends with a few other students who showed her how to look after her hair, and her hair is braided. She likes it.

Once a week, she speaks to a counsellor about her anxiety. It was her mother's idea, her one condition for letting Nnenna go to Paris. It is difficult, and it feels strange to talk about something so personal. Sometimes it feels self-indulgent. But it is starting to feel good, and she has decided to finish the course of therapy.

And there is other news. She has met a Yoruba boy in the group and they have been dating for a few months. Adebayo's English is almost as good as her French, and he does not mind being less adept than she is. When she told him about her parents, he listened, and he was not afraid.

Adebayo sends her poems in French that he thinks she might like: Baudelaire, Valéry. He is studying history but wants to be an actor. He has not told his parents.

As for Nnenna's studies, she is still doing very well. She thinks she may stay in Paris after graduation, perhaps for further study. Perhaps she will seek work in a publishing house. She is not worried about the future, for now.

One sunny morning, she walks calmly, determinedly to the post office; she comes here often (she prefers the romance of letter-writing to emails), but today she has something important to send, and she has been thinking about it for some time. Her French has become fluent, but somehow the man behind the desk always recognises her as English and, with a flash of a smile, responds in English. They have developed a kind of situational friendship: whenever she comes into the post office to send a letter to Stephanie or her mother, they have a short conversation, provided the queue is not too long. He says he wants to go and visit England one day; generously, he says he even wants to go and see Manchester one day, although she knows he is probably more interested in London. 'Manchester United!' he says excitedly. Nnenna, who does not follow football, nods and hands over her post.

'Oh, my!' says Alexandre, looking at the address. 'It is a long way, yes?'

'Yes,' says Nnenna. She realises she is trembling slightly. Thankfully, the process of posting this particular item is more complicated than usual, and Alexandre is too busy to notice her nervousness.

'It's very old!' he says, gesturing to what she is about to post while he looks up the cost and affixes the correct stamps. The cost pops up on the till's screen and she pays him the money. It is more than she expected, but her mother sent her some extra money this week anyway. It is her birthday.

'Yes,' says Nnenna. 'It's older than me, actually. It's an heirloom.'

'An heirloom ...' He contemplates the word, half-understanding it. 'You are sure you want to send it all this way?' he asks. 'You don't want to keep it?'

She shakes her head and smiles. 'I think it's been long enough.'

It looks familiar, when it arrives.

It is not, as Maurice first believes with a double beat of the heart, from Joanie. The name of the sender is a beautiful one;

one he once thought about giving to a child, should he ever have one. But that was years ago.

The message is brief, direct and urgent, although written in a whimsical hand. Above it, there is a message he once received himself, from God.

He pauses, looks away, looks at it again.

On the back is a picture that he has not seen for years. It reminds him of tense meetings in church halls, of journeys out to cafés on the fringes of Cambridge, of a moment in time with a woman he has not seen for twenty years. The photograph is of King's College, Cambridge. Somehow, the sky above it is still an untrue blue, a single swallow flying across it, dancing, weaving, finding its way home.

Acknowledgements

This book was a difficult joy to write and I'm so grateful to all the people who helped it reach this stage. Some thank yous:

I'd like to thank my big brother, Udobi, for his constant faith in what I can do when I put my mind to it. He helped make the impossible possible.

Claire Malcolm and the New Writing North team, for supporting me with a New Writing North Award and championing this book so tirelessly.

My agent, Cara Lee Simpson, for her advice and input. The Dialogue Team, especially Sharmaine Lovegrove, for such great care and hard work, and for understanding this story and what it needs.

Michael Schmidt, Andrew McMillan, Seán Hewitt, Alice Malin, Marthe Broadhurst: early readers and invaluable friends.

Rosalia and Jane Delfino, Jeff, Sharon and Clare Owens, Owen Patey, Mothusi Turner, Matthew Frost, Emma Palin, Greg Thorpe, Daniel Strange, Thom Andrewes, Sharon Ruston, Jerome de Groot and Maria Stukii for their humour, warmth, patience and excitement. Dr Sinéad Garrigan Mattar for creating such a positive environment at Girton. Chloe Wolff Cousins and Tolu Ajayi for all the brilliant work they do in Manchester and beyond.

Dr Martin Boulton, Dr Paul Thompson, Michael Lowe, Nigel Warrack and all my colleagues at school: for their generosity and understanding.

Bringing a book from manuscript to what you are reading is a team effort.

Dialogue Books would like to thank everyone at Little, Brown who helped to publish *The Private Joys of Nnenna Maloney* in the UK.

Editorial
Sharmaine Lovegrove
Sophia Schoepfer
Thalia Proctor

Contracts
Anniina Vuori

Sales
Andrew Cattanach
Viki Cheung
Ben Goddard
Hermione Ireland
Hannah Methuen

Publicity
Millie Seaward

Marketing
Hillary Tisman
Emily Moran

Design
Helen Bergh
Steve Panton

Production
Narges Nojoumi
Nick Ross
Mike Young

Copy Editor
Anne O'Brien

Proof Reader
Rachel Cross